THE BOY

THE BOY

MARK GYVES

NO EXIT PRESS

First published in the UK in 2026 by No Exit Press,
an imprint of Bedford Square Publishers Ltd,
London, UK

noexit.co.uk
@noexitpress

A CIP catalogue record for this book is available from the British Library.

ISBN
978-1-83501-581-0 (Trade paperback)
978-1-83501-583-4 (eBook)

2 4 6 8 10 9 7 5 3 1

Typeset in 11.4pt Garamond MT Pro
by Avocet Typeset, Bideford, Devon, EX39 2BP
Printed and bound in Great Britain by
CPI Group (UK) Ltd, Croydon CR0 4YY

FSC www.fsc.org
MIX
Paper | Supporting responsible forestry
FSC® C013604

The manufacturer's authorised representative in the EU for product safety is Easy Access System Europe, Mustamäe tee 50, 10621 Tallinn, Estonia
gpsr.requests@easproject.com

For Suzanne: my teammate, my cheerleader,
my umpire, and my heart.

Chapter One

HEADS OR HARPS?

October 1997

AT ITS CREST, IT HUNG a moment there. The men, with bated eyes squinting in the morning sun, searched skyward, then gasped at its dazzling descent, a meteor fading in the fall to land once more in Hegarty's hand.

'Heads it is, fucko. In you go,' Hegarty guffawed, pocketing the coin.

'I'm not doing the talking,' O'Brien protested.

'You lose the toss; you do the talking. You know the rules.'

'I did the last one.'

'I don't give a fuck. I've done hundreds.'

'You should be used to it so.'

'You need the practice.'

'Practice? My bad news technique? On these poor people? It's inhumane.'

'I'm not saying a word, so you better get ready, and sharpish,' Hegarty snapped as he pressed the bell, then stepped back briskly from the door.

'You rotten bollix,' O'Brien hissed, straightening his jacket and cap. Then, waiting a moment and motioning with his chin towards the door, he added, 'I think it's broken. Smart prick – serves you right.'

'What's broken?'

'The doorbell, it doesn't work.' He rolled his eyes. 'Sure look at the state of the place.'

'Well fuckin' knock then, you useless prick.'

'Knock? You knock.'

'You're starting to wind me up now,' Hegarty growled, then stepped forward and knocked out an almost jovial 'rat-a-tat-tat' on the ramshackle door, then retreated, cringing. Three firm non-rhythmic knocks were Garda policy for wooden doors without bells when delivering bad news.

The Boy woke on the second knock, more formal now, a call to order. *Rise ye from your beds peasants and let ye be told of all not well in the world*, it rattled. He listened as his father struggled into his trousers and made his way ungainly to the landing where he stopped, rubbed his eyes, scratched his head uncertainly, then took in the dark figures obscured in the frosted patterned glass, waiting. The Boy continued to listen as Daniel picked his way down the stairs, opened the door and began his muffled exchange. A 'sorry' here, a 'thank you' there, with some 'okay-now's on repeat for a measured finish punctuated by the rattling clang of the closing door.

She was gone. He knew it. In his bones, he knew it. He'd known for some time that she was not long for this world and now, at his bed's end, a once great man reduced to a simmer, confirmed the inevitable.

'Is it Ma?' The Boy asked.

'She's gone, son,' Daniel started, 'the Guards… they said she was already gone when they got to her. There was nothing they could do.' He sat on the bed, looked at the floor and continued. 'I must go to the hospital. I must confirm… identify her… your Mam. I'll ring Fallon and your Nan to collect you shortly… will you be alright here for a bit if I head down there now?'

'I'm grand, go on,' The Boy lied. 'I'll see you down there,' he told him, knowing in his breaking heart that his old man was pub-bound. He pulled the light fleece tight about his neck and retreated to the pretence of sleep as Daniel made his way to the room next door, dressed, then exited the house.

A sigh followed by a whimper escaped The Boy's lips, and he thought about those early days at the big house on Lovers Walk. That high home, with its harbour views to spare and its comings and goings until the goings outnumbered the comings, and all were gone. He sees her now in those dreamy days, standing magnificent by the big bay window in the back room, smoking as the sun raged in its sorry sky and she willed it there aloft. And the people, always so many people. Poets, professors, Doctor Pilkington the eminent extractor. An editor of some national paper, that girl who'd been shortlisted for the prize for that book… what was it called… what was *she* called? He couldn't remember. Freedom fighters on the run. Romantic smugglers of gear and guns. That poor painter fella who, heartbroken, hung himself over that ugly yoke he'd married. Your man off the radio, Ryan… Ryan… Gerry bloody Ryan…! That's the boyo. With your wan who read the news… Anne Doyle. Circling, all of them circling, like moths about his Ma's magnetic flame, each to be burned.

She was beautiful then and Da loved her, he recalled. Loved the bones of her. Every fucking sinew and molecule, he knew them all. It was palpable. He hung on her every word, each utterance prompting some response. A little nod or chuckle, some approving myoclonic return often unnoticed even to himself. Not that he was some lovesick fool. Oh, no! He, too, was a handsome wild bastard. Dangerous, funny and brilliant, with a shock of black hair atop a rogue's ceann. Those piercing blue eyes that could stop a charging rhino dead in its fuckin' tracks. Charm the bastard right down off his huff. Rubbing his tusk now, whispering, *it's all right sure you're grand, don't go wrecking the gaff*, then lilting, *aren't you an awful bollix charging around the place like that ya little fucker.* The rhino in a playful headlock, all bashful and apologetic as they frolic in the grass there, laughing. He, she, all of them – fabled in his mind now, dancing, as the sun set low on their banter and they pushed back the darkness with their faint lights, ever fading.

Chapter Two

DANIEL

DANIEL LEANED AGAINST THE DOOR of the St Leger Arms. 'Locked to fuck', he cursed, then stood back, shielded his eyes to the morning sun and gazed up at the first-floor window. There was light in the back kitchen, though he could detect no movement within. The smell of the pub oozed through the locked door and the hunger in him grew. Walking to the side alley, he put his shoulder to the slip door, hoping. The door gave way, and he stepped cautiously inside, eyeing about the place as he went.

'Tony, are you there?' he called out. 'It's Daniel.'

'We are closed, Dan,' Tony replied, half-joking, from the backyard, barrels rattling.

'Closed, me bollix, I'm serving myself. Come out here when you're done,' Daniel called back as he made his way behind the bar. He started a pint, left it to settle, then drew up a double. 'Fuck it,' he thought, adding a third for good measure.

'One, two, three baby. Doo, doo, doo,' he hummed.

The pint complete, he sat on his stool and made short work of it. The drop followed and momentarily he was back behind the bar, the process on a loop. Imagined punters now, calling for rounds from Daniel the barman.

'Why certainly, my good-lady,' to some woman in her Sunday best.

'But of course, sir, we only serve the finest champagne,' to an old fella, all moustache, monocle, and misery.

'Another? Ya thirsty little bitch,' he joked. 'Sit down and I'll bring it over. And what about himself? Has he not got a throat on him?'

'He can fuck off,' came the reply suggestively.

'None of that malarkey now,' Daniel winked back, all master of the house, but decent.

'No, I'm sorry,' to the fat accountant, 'there'll be no more drink until your current tab is settled in full. Now I hate to be a bastard, but those are the rules, and the rules is the rules as the man says. I only work here.'

'Yes love, what can I get ya?' to a young Mammy. 'Why certainly petal, sit down there and I'll bring it over, some Rolos for the babbie now, perhaps?' And she shot him a menacing blasted glance then turned to her young to reveal her back ablaze, and he called out to her as she bent to the child and he could see that the child too was a raging fiery ball and he screamed to the Mammy to rip off the blanket as the fat accountant, now alight, spun to reveal his melting face that poured down his shoulder where his arm used to be, then he fell to the floor as his legs gave way and the thirsty bitch laughed as she, too, felt the flames and soon the whole pub was engulfed with the flaming souls of troubled Ireland's dead as Daniel's legs failed him too and he fell to the floor and he sobbed like a fool as they climbed o'er the bar to tear shreds from his soul.

'Will you get up, to fuck?' Tony sniggered as he entered the bar, jostling the bottle trolley over the threshold. Daniel jolted from his abstraction, looked at Tony teary-eyed and confused, then stood and gazed about the empty bar.

'Are you alright Daniel?' Tony asked.

Daniel wiped his tears with the heels of his hands.

'Yeah, I'm grand,' he said, looking about the empty bar, uncertain. 'It's Marie. She passed… last night. The Guards called to the house earlier. I'm sorry but…'

'Jaysus Daniel. I thought you were fuckin' about,' Tony said, and he took him by the arm and led him to his seat. ‘Sit down here,’ he said, ‘and I’ll get you a drink,’ then shot behind the bar to fix him a stiff one.

Chapter Three

FALLON

FALLON BOLTED UPRIGHT IN HIS bed and kicked back the sheets, wild-eyed and maniacal. Bawling and gasping for breath, he clutched at his throat, then ripped the sheets to the side, screaming.

'What the fuck, Fal?' Sonya screamed, shocked from sleep. 'What are ya doing, ya crazy wanker…?'

He looked at her, kicked the sheets again, then glanced about the room, confused. 'What?' he said, embarrassed, composing himself, slowly getting a hook on things, her face some tangent to reality.

'Are you alright?' she asked, then reached for him.

He shrugged her off, climbed from the bed and looked for his trousers.

'Fuckin' rats again,' he thought as he picked his T-shirt from the floor and wiped the sweat from his forehead and chest. He'd had the dream again, the rat dream. *What the fuck?* he thought, catching his breath. He picked up his trousers and checked his pager. There was a message from the phone box outside his old man's house. He searched the room, grabbed his phone, and dialled. Three rings later, it picked up.

'Who's this?' some prick enquired.

'It's Fallon here, is my brother about? He paged me.'

'Howya kid? What's the craic? I can't see him. Will I give him a shout?' the prick chimed reverently.

'Sound,' Fallon replied, and waited as the phone box door creaked shut… then silence.

What a fucked-up dream, he thought to himself, trying to remember then trying to shake it off as fast. 'Fucking rats… again?'

He hated rats. In the dream, he wakes in a doorless room, with rotten floorboards and soft damp walls with tiny holes everywhere, nocturnal animals scurrying behind the plasterboard. Then a rat, friendly at first, pokes its head through, and Fallon chases it back and repairs the hole with whatever he can find in the room. And so it goes, rat after rat all through the night, each more menacing than the last, crazed and throwing themselves violently at the walls trying to tear their way into the room over and over in ever decreasing intervals.

A high-powered motorbike rolled past the phone box – he could hear it through the handpiece – throttle down. Then it revved up and moved on.

And he remembered the dream again, where the light flickers and dies and they're in the room with him now, the rats. Some scurry behind his back. Others chance a nip at his toes as the walls, groaning now, implode, followed by a deluge of fat, flopping sounds as they land, then right themselves, sniffing, scratching, seeking him out, Fallon screaming, as the rats in their thousands crawl up his legs and back clawing at his face and eyes, one slipping down his throat as he opens his mouth to bawl—

Fallon jumped as the phone box door creaked in reverse, followed by a familiar voice.

'Fallon? I fuckin' paged you, ages ago like,' The Boy moaned.

'Sorry kiddo. I'm only out the bed; I've got one of those mobiles now. I'll give you the number later—'

'Mam's dead,' The Boy cut in. 'The Guards… they called earlier and told Dad, then he fucked off to the pub.'

'What…? Are you alright? What happened?'

'I don't know.'

'I'm coming straight over. Go back to the house. I'll be there in a minute.'

Fallon hung up the phone and dialled The Big Fella.

'You're up early,' came The Big Fella's voice, warm, avuncular, cunning.

'I know yeah,' Fallon replied. 'Listen, we need to put that bit of business on hold for a few days. My Ma… she's dead… I need to look after the brother. Me old fella has taken to the pub, and you know what he's like…'

'Jaysus Fal, that's desperate. What happened?' The Big Fella said, stopping Fallon mid-sentence.

'I don't know. I'm going over there now.'

'You do what you need to do and give me a ring when you're sorted. I'm sorry, lad. Let us know if you need anything. I might give you a quick call in a couple of days to see where we're at, but there's no hurry. I'll make sure Tonto puts the kids to bed in the meantime and we can take care of the paperwork when you're sorted.'

'Sound,' Fallon replied, then hung up.

Chapter Four

THE BIG FELLA

THE BIG FELLA WAS A hard fuckin' man. There was no doubt about it. The eldest of three boys, he grew up in Barrameena Manor, Cork's toughest address on the Northside of the city. The Manor, a Bronx concentrate, had all the violence, crime and social neglect of an entire New York borough crammed into a cul-de-sac of twenty-four houses where you grew up fast, or you stayed a small boy forever. A great observer from a young age, he discerned that there were two types of people in the Manor: the victim and the punisher. He decided at twelve years of age, as he held a kitchen knife to his old man's throat and prised him from his screaming mother, that there would be no victims in his household. He marched his old man to the front door, stared him down hard and left him in no doubt that to ever return would be a terrible mistake. They never saw their old man again.

The Big Fella was determined to rise above this culture of pathogenic microbial fission. He would not be some standard reproduction spawned of hate and rejection and was determined to cut a path for his younger brothers, that they might escape the stigma of the 'Manor born'. A tall boy with an affected bad attitude, he was rarely challenged, but when required to step up to the mark, he bulldozed headlong in a blur of violence and fury unseen even in the Manor's darkest corners. He soon gained a reputation as a violent contender, the consequence of which was a free pass for the two younger brothers. At home, he exercised complete control over the boys. In the absence of a father figure, he assumed the role of patriarch with their mother working long hours at the care home in the city. When they arrived home from school, they were put to their lessons and soon, under his supervision, they excelled at their studies, a sacrifice that paid off in later years as both boys thrived in their chosen professions.

It was natural that The Big Fella would gravitate towards drugs and crime. He teamed up with the local big head, Bomber the Bastard, and soon they had complete autonomy over the Northside, driving the Southside gangs back across the Lee, venturing themselves across the water to try their luck at the lucrative dealing spots on the Southside of the city. By the age of nineteen, he was a notorious figure on the Cork crime scene and known, in certain circles throughout the country, as a young man to be feared and respected.

By twenty-seven, he had put his brothers through university and had already made headway into the world of legitimate business. He owned many properties and had heavily invested in several developments up and down the country. His reputation as a fearsome negotiator was known the length of the Island and although his involvement with crime and punishment was often rumoured within his new circles of influence, the topic was never raised in his presence.

Now in his forties, his title 'The Big Fella', was not only a nod to his position in the country's burgeoning crime scene but also an acknowledgement of his physical prowess, presence and established position of influence in political and business circles. His involvement with the underworld was handled exclusively by his two protegés, Fallon and Tonto. Tonto, the junior of the two, ran a crew of duckers and divers who dealt mostly with distribution and retribution, while Fallon, a few years his senior, dealt with the negotiation and logistics of the operation, acting as a buffer between The Big Fella and the underworld. Bomber, the bastard, had long since been put out to graze. Bomber now resided in a sleepy gated villa on the island of Tenerife, where he maintained links with the runners and riders on the continent, ensuring a steady flow of contraband to serve the crew's needs. In Bomber's mind, he was still the boss, but as with everyone in this close-knit family, Bomber was exactly where The Big Fella wanted him to be.

The Big Fella picked up his phone and rang Tonto.

'Our friend,' referring to Fallon, he never used direct information while talking on the phone, 'is gonna be out of action for a few days,' he said.

'Okay?' Tonto enquired. 'It better be fuckin' serious. The kids are in bed and waiting to go to school and the paperwork is with the kids, so this puts us in a very vulnerable position.'

'What do you mean, the kids are with the paperwork?' The Big Fella snapped. 'That's the number one rule you fuckin' muppet. You never leave the kids with the paperwork,' he added in astonishment, the back of his neck searing with rage.

'I'd no choice,' Tonto said. 'I'll fill ya in when I see ya,' he explained, trying to buy some time.

'Pick me up now,' The Big Fella demanded. 'I'm at my mother's place, and don't turn up in that fucking bright red BMW, you langer.' He hung up the phone.

The Big Fella sat back on the sofa in his mother's front room, ran his fingers through his hair, sighed and contemplated what kind of clown would leave the money and the gear stashed in the same place. *He'd better have a fucking good excuse or him and that other fucking bollix...* He stopped short. He couldn't bring himself to utter a bad word about Fallon. Fallon was different. He operated and thought on a higher level than anyone he'd ever met before. If the gear and cash were stashed together, it definitely hadn't been Fallon's idea. Of that, he was certain.

Ten minutes later, his phone rang.

'You outside?'

'Yeah,' Tonto replied.

'I'll be out in a minute,' The Big Fella said, then hung up the phone and called up the stairs. 'I'm heading off Mammy, I'll see you during the week.'

'Okay, love,' his mother called back. 'Make sure you go to Mass,' she added. A hint of hope and mischief in her voice.

'I'm going straight there now,' he lied, then opened the front door and strode briskly up the garden path, pulling his blazer tight across his chest.

'Fuckin' Baltic,' he uttered beneath his breath. Tonto waved sheepishly from the bright red BMW parked in the layby across the street. The Big Fella, noting the car, rolled his eyes and mouthed the word 'bellend', then stopped to let a motorbike pass. The bike slowed and approached him. He looked at it, confused, as it pulled towards him on this chilly Sunday morning. The passenger's arm came forward and The Big Fella thought for a second that he was handing him something and reached out to him, then recognising the gun too late, recoiled in terror as three shots rang out in the Sunday morning sky and The Big Fella folded in a crumpled heap to the kerb.

Tonto felt the blood drain from his face. He tried to move, to act, to do something but he couldn't take his eyes from the scene unfolding across the street. A warm pool grew in his lap and he jolted into action. He reached for the gear stick, his foot slipped on the clutch, the car lurched forward, then stalled. He fumbled with the keys as the getaway driver's mantra played over in his head, 'Car in first, foot on the clutch. Car in first, foot on the clutch…' When he looked again, the passenger was running towards the car with the gun extended. Five more reports rang out and Tonto fell sideways into the passenger seat, then faded to black.

Chapter Five

MORE BAD NEWS

FALLON'S BIKE THRUMMED INTO THE cul-de-sac. The Boy ran to the window and pulled the lace curtain to the side as Fallon parked the bike, then walked up the path, removing his helmet. The front door opened with a clang, and Fallon walked into the living room and held The Boy.

'Are you alright?' he asked.

'I'm grand,' The Boy replied sullenly, then burst into tears. 'The fucking Guards called earlier, then Dad fucked off to the pub, I paged you with the last ten pence I could find so I didn't even have enough to ring Nan and Granda so they don't even fuckin' know, there's no food in the house, I've been sat here for ages on my own, like a fuckin' fool. Of course I'm not alright,' he stopped gasping for breath, wiped his nose on his sleeve, then added a 'fuck's sake', for good measure.

'I'm sorry, I'm sorry, I'm really sorry,' Fallon said. 'I'm here now. We'll ring Nan and let them know now, alright? We'll grab a sandwich at Murphy's and head straight down to the hospital, okay?'

'Okay, okay, I'm sorry,' The Boy sobbed. 'My fuckin' head is done in, that's all.'

'I know. Don't worry, I'll take care of everything. You stick the kettle on. I'll give Nan a ring.'

The Boy put the kettle on the stove to boil. Outside, a motorbike prowled into the cul-de-sac. He listened as the engine throttled down, idled for a while, then it revved up and sped off down the road. When he'd made the tea, he went back to the front room, where Fallon consoled his grandparents on the phone.

'Love you too, see you down there,' Fallon said, then hung up the phone.

He took his tea from The Boy and sat down.

'Is Nan alright?' The Boy asked.

Fallon's phone rang in his pocket.

'What now?' he cursed, then noticing it was Beebo, he picked up.

'Howya Beebo? I was gonna ring ya later, listen, I'm outta action for a day or two…' he began.

Beebo cut him short with the news about The Big Fella and Tonto. Fallon stood up and spun in a daze. He couldn't believe what he was hearing. First his Mam and now The Big Fella. He walked to the window, pulled the lace curtain to the side and looked the street up and down.

'Are you sure?' he asked. 'I only spoke to him half an hour ago.'

'One hundred percent lad,' Beebo confirmed.

Fallon placed his arm on the back of the sofa to steady himself. A feeling, unknown to him, rose through his body – fear perhaps, he wasn't sure. He sat down. He thought about the kids and the paperwork. Three people in the world knew of their whereabouts, two of whom were now dead.

'I'll talk to you later, Beebo,' he said.

'Laters…'

Chapter Six

FEARGAL

'DON'T THROW IT LIKE A rock, ya fuckin' ape,' Terry shouted. 'The petrol will come out of the top and pour all over ya. You'll be up in smoke, and I'll have to explain to your ma what the fuck's been going on,' he shouted over the melee.

Feargal nodded, then fixed the bottle, the base flat against his palm.

'Like this?' he asked, holding it up for Terry to inspect.

'Kind of,' Terry shouted. 'Hold the side loosely with your thumb, and these two fingers close to the end, then put your two last fingers on the bottom of the bottle and swing it low away from your body pushing at the base, so the petrol doesn't pour out all over ya... Show it here.'

Terry took the projectile from Feargal and held it as described, taking time to show his teenage student exactly what he meant. He lit the rag, ensured a good flame, took two bounding steps, and with a practiced sweep launched the poor man's hand grenade high into the air. Feargal watched its arc in dreaded anticipation, first the rise and then the fall, beyond his control, now at the mercy of gravity's parabolic pull. Rocks and projectiles fell around him. One glanced his shoulder, but he paid it no mind as he stood with mouth agape watching the petrol bomb explode on the bonnet of a parked car, then jumped with excitement to the young boys' bellowed hoots and clamour as the young rebels ripped up their torn-in-two town.

'Got it?' Terry asked.

'Got it,' came the reply. Five goes later, and he had it… to an art.

It wasn't long before Feargal left petrol bombs and riots behind, graduating to handguns and armed robbery. Both he and Terry, five years his senior, developed a fearsome reputation as reliable and violent young soldiers of the Republic, their names soon synonymous with paramilitary activity throughout West Belfast. By the age of nineteen, under Terry's tutelage, Feargal was a feared lieutenant running a ten-strong company of hitmen, robbers and military tacticians, their names associated with the worst atrocities of the Troubles in Northern Ireland. They were ghost men, rumoured bogey men whose names struck fear in the hearts of loyalist soldiers and Protestant paramilitaries alike. If you heard Feargal and his squad were looking for you, it only meant one thing. They weren't the type of boys to conduct interviews. If they were on your trail, you'd already had your chances.

In his early twenties, word came down from the top that Jackie Brosnan, one of the Provos' highest ranking soldiers, wanted a sitdown, to be held at an undisclosed location. Brosnan's paranoia and reputation for high security was well known amongst the ranks. Feargal's crew were blindfolded and transported by sheep lorry on mart day to a bar in Portrush. It was Tuesday lunchtime. They'd emptied the pub and there were gunmen stood guard at the front and back doors with snipers positioned at the upstairs windows. Sitting by the fire drinking a pint of Guinness, Jackie Brosnan stood when the men arrived. He walked to them, removed their blindfolds and waited while Feargal and his crew stood squinting as their eyes adjusted to the midday light. Suddenly one of Feargal's lads piped up:

'Is this O'Neil's fuckin' bar in Portrush? I wish you'd a told me, my Ma only lives around the corner. I could've popped over to see her last night.'

The bar fell into silence, the tension in the room unbearable... Brosnan was the first to laugh. Soon, all present fell about in stitches. From that day forward, Feargal and Brosnan became inseparable, waging a bombing campaign across Ireland and the UK, the likes of which had never been seen before.

They were expert planners, disappearing like ghosts into the night to a network of safe houses and welcoming faces north and south of the border. They were frequent clandestine visitors to the house on Lovers Walk throughout The Boy's childhood. He remembered waking to see Feargal's black Capri parked on the drive; it was gone again in the evening on his arrival home from school. Or Feargal and his crew turning up by foot unannounced in the middle of the night at the back door. They would sit, play cards and drink tea for two to three days in the back room, curtains drawn, the room thick with cigarette smoke. Or Feargal's tense, huddled conversations with Daniel in the hall or back garden, both men careful not to be overheard. Or Daniel sat at the table smoking with Feargal, his crew bunched tight around a book illustrated with circuits and diagrams.

Now stood across his mother's grave, The Boy recognised his uncle Feargal. The years had been kind to him. He looked more like an elegant businessman in his tailored suit and overcoat than he did a paramilitary hitman. These days he was more likely to be seen on the six o'clock news stood at the shoulder of a senior Sinn Féin politician than he was to be found holed up in a ditch in South Armagh with a Libyan-bought firearm in hand waiting for a passing military convoy. Those days were long behind him now, though he still had the look of a man who didn't mince his words.

'Alright son?' Feargal asked The Boy later that evening at the pub.

'Hi uncle Feargal,' The Boy replied.

'How's your da? Have you seen him?'

'No, but I know where he is, though. He's in the St Legers. He's been there since the Guards called,' The Boy replied.

'He's a terrible man, your Da. Are you staying with your Nan and Granda for a while or what's the plan? I know they'd love to have ya.'

'No, I'm alright, I'll stay with me Dad. Fallon is nearby as well, so between the two of them I'll be grand,' The Boy explained. 'It's not like I saw much of Mam lately anyway, so not a lot has changed. I'll be fine.'

'Aye, I know, but at times like this it's best to have people around ya, if only for a few days like. I'm here as well until next week, so if you need anything, maybe I could give you a hand or whatever, maybe pop into town and pick up some new guddies or something.'

'Guddies?'

'Aye, guddies, sneakers, exercise shoes, you know what I mean.'

The Boy shrugged.

'Sure, let us know what you wanna do, I'll not push ya son,' Feargal added as he rose, tousled The Boy's hair and made his way to the bar before turning.

'I know you'll be alright son,' he said, 'but it'd be nice for your Nan and Granda to have you around. I think it would do them the power of good.' He let the thought hang a moment before adding. 'Will you think about it for me? You'd be doing me a massive favour,' he said, as he looked The Boy in the eye.

The Boy held his uncle's gaze, held it some more, and watched as a look of doubt spread across his uncle's face.

This wee fucker is staring me down, Feargal thought. Then The Boy cracked a gentle smile followed by a wink that said, 'I know your game Feargal, now away with ya.'

Feargal winked back and continued to the bar.

'Alright mate?' he said to Fallon, and the pair embraced.

Chapter Seven

MOTORBIKE

THE BOY WALKED TO THE food table. There were sandwiches and cakes of every description, some bowls with coleslaw and different coloured rice, two big silver things with tea and coffee, some cakes and pies, already sliced. No sausage rolls, he noted. Poor show.

'What are you looking for?' a voice behind him said.

He turned to see a youngfella, dressed like a waiter, not much older than himself, standing there.

'Nothin' I'm grand,' he said.

'There's more stuff out the back, that's why I'm asking.'

'More?'

The youngfella smiled.

'Any sausage rolls?'

'No, sorry. D'ya like curry?'

'I like chicken curry.'

'That pie is a chicken curry pie and it's proper good,' the youngfella said, pointing.

'Thanks,' The Boy said.

He took a slice of the pie, placed it on a paper plate, and walked back to his seat. He looked around the bar. People were acting and talking like normal. This could be an office party, he thought. He didn't know what to expect, he'd never been on this side of a funeral before. Somebody's child crawled out from under a table. Three of his granda's friends laughed at a fourth mimicking an awkward-looking golf swing. Feargal and Fallon, thick as thieves by the bar.

He couldn't make out what they were saying, but they were not in agreement. Of that, he was certain. Fallon's remonstrations as Feargal attempted to impart some avuncular wisdom left The Boy in no doubt that it was falling on deaf ears. They parted with an embrace, and Fallon thanked his uncle before joining The Boy at the table with his grandparents and some neighbours from Blackpool.

'She was a beautiful girl, Marie…' a neighbour started. 'Beautiful. I remember when I first saw her. I thought she was the most beautiful little thing I'd ever seen. You wanted to pick her up and squeeze her. She was perfect.'

'And clever,' another added. 'Brains to burn, smart as a whip God rest her,' she turned her face skyward, blessing herself.

'What a waste of a life, it'll be a while before we see another one like her,' added Mary Byrne.

'She's happier now, though,' her father said, his eyes brimming. 'What, with the drink and all that other nonsense, what life had the poor wee girl at all with the last few years?'

The Boy listened to his grandad's words. He thought about what he said. He didn't know the answer. He had no clue what kind of life his mother'd had with the last few years. He knew it wasn't great, nor was his own life for that matter, and he felt an irritation somewhere at the back of his head that he couldn't quite articulate, grow. Or maybe he could articulate it, but wouldn't allow himself to. Not yet anyway. In the pit of his gut he felt a roar, a desperate cry of agonising pain and he pictured himself alone down there in the darkness and he told him to be quiet. He felt a sting at the bridge of his nose, and blinked back a tear. He could cry, if he let himself. He wasn't sure what good it would do. He took a long breath, sat up in his seat and scanned the group. He picked the slice of pie up from the table and took a bite. It was good. Chicken curry pie, he thought. He looked to Fallon.

Fallon winked, then eyed the door. The Boy nodded discreetly, and they left unnoticed.

'We need a few quid,' Fallon told him. 'We gotta pay the removers and the priest, and you'll need to have some money for the next few weeks,' he explained as they walked to the motorbike. 'Granda said he's gonna pay for the funeral, but I'm not having it,' he added, taking his helmet and adjusting the strap.

'Well, I've got fuck all.'

'I know that,' Fallon said. 'I've got money. What I mean is we need to get it. Come on,' he said, handing The Boy the spare helmet. 'Get on the back. I need you to come somewhere with me. Do you know how to ride a bike?'

'A bit,' The Boy said, a mischievous grin forming on his face.

'Get on the back, ya little bollix.'

With The Boy on the back, Fallon put the bike in first gear and eased out of the car park. When they reached the main road, they turned right and headed for Blarney, then Fallon took a sharp left and soon they were in thick, unfamiliar countryside and The Boy lost his bearings as the terrain became increasingly remote. He thought Fallon was going around in circles when he noticed, for the third time, a sign for Fermoy, then they took an abrupt left up a steep lane into a wooded area where Fallon took a right then sped up another lane about wide enough for a single car. The lane, covered in thick moss and grass, told The Boy it had seen little traffic. Tall conifers either side of the route sheltered them from onlookers. Fallon stopped shy of a crest in the road, jumped from the bike and told The Boy to 'keep it in first with the clutch on, if any vehicles approach, take off, make three lefts and you'll end up back here again. I'll be watching out for you, so don't worry if you can't find the exact spot.'

The Boy put the bike in gear as instructed and waited anxiously as Fallon disappeared over the ditch. When he reappeared a short while later, he had a bundle of cash in his right hand. Fallon took the clutch in his left hand, and with his right, he passed the cash to The Boy.

'There's five grand there,' he explained. 'Tuck it inside your jacket until we get back to the house. Now push back,' he said as he nudged The Boy into the passenger position. The Boy secured the money inside his jacket and nudged Fallon to go. Fallon knocked his visor down and they sped towards the north side of the city. The return journey took less than ten minutes, and The Boy realised Fallon had been circling and delaying en-route to the woods.

Fallon eased up on the throttle as they approached the city. The telephone cables swooped by, dropping, then rising in a hypnotic loop from post to post, then lamp to lamp, shadow, then light, then shadow again. The Boy felt the stack of cash pressed against his body and in that moment he felt for the first time in days, months, maybe even ever, a sense of security wash over him as he held on tight to his brother's sides. Fallon slowed the bike to a crawl as they reached the cul-de-sac in Blackpool, then rolled to a stop outside their house. The Boy jumped from the bike, removing his helmet and started telling Fallon a story about some kid in school.

'There was this little kid, right?' he started. 'And these two older wankers,' he said as he stepped inside the gate. Fallon put the bike on its stand, removed the keys, flipped up his visor, and undid his helmet's strap as a motorbike pulled onto the street behind them, stopped for a moment, then sped towards the house. Fallon, noticing the bike, shouted at The Boy to 'get behind the wall!' He could see the passenger's left arm extended with a gun in hand and he instinctively ran to the right side of the motorbike, swinging his helmet as the first shot rang out. He grabbed the handlebars and pushed the bike towards the ground, then swung his helmet, landing two hard blows to the passenger's head and shoulder. The passenger fell to the road, dazed. Fallon turned his attention on the driver, landing some hard blows of his helmet on the driver's hands and arms as he struggled to right the bike and get it moving again. From the ground, the passenger fired two more rounds, and Fallon stumbled back as the driver repositioned the bike, ready for an exit. Fallon felt a searing ache raging in his side. The houses around him spun, and he collapsed to his knees. The Boy, frozen until now, ran instinctively to his fallen brother, who mouthed at him to 'run' as the passenger fired two more shots into Fallon's chest. The Boy continued to Fallon and took him in his arms as the passenger found his feet, raised his gun towards The Boy and took aim. Out of nowhere, a howling neighbour broke the gunman's attention, and he jumped then watched in horror as she approached at a pace from behind The Boy with a skillet brandished in her hand.

'Go on to fuck ya durrrrty little bastard,' Brida Scully bellowed. 'I fuckin' dare ya, ya little bollix,' she boomed as he pointed the gun her way and she let fly the pan, hitting him square in the shoulder, then continued her charge. She couldn't believe what she was doing, but she couldn't stop herself.

The driver revved the engine, a call or reminder to his passenger, who turned and ran to the waiting bike. Brida retrieved the pan from the road and launched it one more time, hitting the passenger hard between the shoulder blades as he mounted the bike and disappeared into the night.

The streetlights flickered, casting eerie shadows on the scene. Brida picked the pan from the road and stood sentry o'er The Boy, her weapon clutched tightly in her hand. Her heart pounded in her chest, a mix of grief and adrenaline coursing through her veins. She looked at the scene.

What in the name of Holy God? she thought as Fallon, cradled in his brother's arms, bled to death. The Boy's voice, a fragile whisper, echoed in the night's silence.

'They're gone Fal, it's okay, they're gone now… they're gone…'

Chapter Eight

DERRY

DETECTIVE INSPECTOR DERRY TWOHIG SAT reading *The Corkman* in the corner bar at the Metropole Hotel. As Feargal arrived, he peered out over his spectacles, folded his newspaper, sprang to his feet, and extended his arm as his old friend and associate approached. The men shook hands, stopping short of an embrace, though the deep-rooted mutual respect they shared was undeniable. Derry, a long-time sympathiser of The Cause, came from a strong lineage of active IRA men. His family's involvement could be traced back to the times of Pearse, Collins and beyond. Though not an active member himself, his position in the Garda had been a source of crucial information for Feargal and his gang for many years.

They took their seats and chatted as Caroline, the waitress, approached.

'Right Derry,' she said, 'your boyfriend has arrived. What'll I get ye?' and she gave Feargal a cheeky wink.

Feargal grinned politely before asking, 'Can I have a cup of tea please, and do you have any scones?'

'I do,' she said. 'Will I get ye a menu altogether?'

'No, no, I'll have tea and a scone. That'll be fine, thanks.'

'Are you sure?' looking at him doubtfully.

'Certain thanks,' Feargal replied, not sure how to take her.

'Righteo,' she said, writing. 'And what about yourself, Derry, bacon doorstop?' she asked suggestively, lips pursed, sticking her chest out, but not too much.

'Perfect love,' Derry replied. 'And a tea as well, for me, please.'

'Hang about,' Feargal added playfully. 'Nobody said there were bacon sambos on offer,' rubbing his hands together.

'Well, I did offer you a menu, but you were all "me want scones",' she said in her best caveman voice.

Feargal laughed. 'Will ya go on to fuck ya cheeky wee rap? I'll have a bacon sandwich and the scone. Have you cream and jam?' he asked.

'Where did you get this fella?' Caroline asked Derry, and they both sniggered, Derry rolling his eyes.

'I do,' she replied, to Feargal. 'And will I sit here and feed it to ya as well, pet?' she joked before disappearing to the kitchen, wiggling her arse as she went, confident both men were watching. She wasn't wrong.

'She's something else,' Feargal scoffed, then let the thought fade into an awkward silence. 'Thanks again for meeting me today,' he said to his old friend.

'Not a bother,' Derry replied. 'Shit circumstances, but unfortunately, it's the way sometimes.'

'It is, it is,' Feargal agreed. 'It's been a bad run alright, first Marie and now her young fella, a bad old run of luck alright.' He let the thought hang a moment before adding, 'Did you hear anything?'

Derry stalled, took a long breath, measuring his words before starting:

'You know Marie had been bad on the drink for a while,' he offered, half statement, half question.

Feargal nodded, and Derry continued.

'She hadn't been living with Daniel and The Boy for over a year, and the last I heard she was staying with some other poor crater, who was as badly off as herself above on Fort Hill. They were all but homeless and drinking what dole they got and popping any tablet or other old shite they could get their hands on.' He stopped to gauge his audience. Feargal nodded again and Derry picked up once more.

'There had been a few times in the last year where she'd had her stomach pumped at the infirmary and another where she was admitted with deep lacerations to her wrists.' Leaving that hang for a moment, he continued. 'I'm only telling you this so you might understand the situation, Feargal, and if you'd rather I spared you the details, please let me know.'

'No, no, go on… I'm grand Derry.'

'Anyway, on the night she passed, they'd been out drinking all day, Marie and this pal of hers. There had been some drugs… I think someone mentioned ecstasy, cocaine and some other bits and pieces, whatever they could get their hands on I guess… according to reports they went back to a party in Barrels Cross. Marie fell asleep on the sofa and in the morning when they went to leave, they couldn't wake her… they called an ambulance and sure by the time it got there she'd been dead about three hours.' Derry looked away, giving Feargal a moment.

'So, there was no sign of any carry on then?' Feargal asked.

'None,' Derry reassured. 'It was simply the lifestyle she'd been living finally catching up with her… I'm sorry, Feargal.'

'Sure, I know well,' Feargal sighed. 'And wee Fallon? What to fuck went on there? Did you hear anything?' he said more expectantly.

'Not a fuckin' dickie bird,' came the reply.

'Nothin'?' Feargal asked in disbelief.

'Not a whisper,' Derry said. 'Which is fuckin' odd, normally in these situations someone'll get word that something is going down and if we feel it's none of our business, we'll give that whole scene a wide berth until the event has passed but this time, we had nothing.'

'Jesus Christ,' Feargal said, shocked. 'I thought you'd have a name for me, and I'd be lining up a few lads to come down here and settle the account… nothin'?'

'It's not like before,' Derry explained. 'Where you had your different gangs battling for turf. Fallon and The Big Fella supplied the entire city. You still had the old gangs on the Northside and Southside, but the two boys supplied them all and for much cheaper than they could've ever got it themselves. We knew all about them and their operation, but to be honest, the set up suited us fine. There were no fights over dealing spots. If someone stepped out of line, The Big Fella got that Tonto lad to sort it out. It was self-policing. The only time the local drug squad got involved was if some Mammy from Douglas complained that some little bollix was selling gear on her street or some shite, and even then, they'd let Fallon and his lads sort it out.' He looked out the window and sighed before adding, 'I shouldn't be saying it, but having them lads running things the way they did made our lives a lot easier. I can tell ya the fallout from this is gonna take about five years to settle down again. The Big Fella almost certainly had some of our lads on his payroll. I mean, I can't say it for a fact, but I'd be very surprised if he hadn't. They've left a massive hole. There's no one with the skills or connections the lads had who could fill the void. It's gonna get very fuckin' messy Feargal, I can tell ya, but in terms of who's behind it… no one has a fuckin' iota.' He stalled for a moment, gauging Feargal before continuing.

'Until the incident involving Fallon took place, I'm almost embarrassed to admit that ninety-nine per cent of us would've put money on Fallon being the chief suspect. Not that he wasn't a good lad, it was generally agreed that he was a prince of a young fella, but there was no one else with the balls to make a move against the other two or anyone who might've gained as much from their demise.'

Derry allowed the thought to sink in, but Feargal was miles away, that old tactician's brain working overtime, weighing every conceivable option and advantage and hanging each hat on all the major players. Derry was right, no one in their right mind would've had the balls to make a move like this… but still and all… some fucker had, and with each passing moment, it seemed more and more likely he was getting away with it. *No…* Feargal thought, *cool your jets mate. He'll slip up*, he reassured himself. There was no point in making a move like this unless people knew about it. This game wee Fallon played was full of pricks and posers. Someday some prick will tell some other prick and that prick will tell a girlfriend, who's friends with some gobby wanker's sister who will open her big fuckin' mouth in the wrong place at the wrong time and then we'll work back along the chain breaking a few knees as we go and eventually it'll be, *Hello Mr Billy Big Bollix so you're the prick who shot my nephew?*

'One bacon doorstop for Derry,' Caroline announced, jolting Feargal from his daydream. 'And one doorstop and a scone with jam and cream for hungry bollix here,' she flirted. 'I'll be back with the tea in a second. Can I get ye anything else?' she asked, not waiting for an answer, waddling off.

'She's a right wee strap of a young one,' Feargal gushed in amazement, a bulge rising in his trousers. *I might stick around for a bit when Derry fucks off*, he thought. *I reckon I'm in here.*

Chapter Nine

CLIFFORD

FROM THE SUMMIT OF KILDUGGART Hill, Clifford Cromby surveyed his land. His heart swelled with pride as he eyed the lay of it. To the west, the estate stretched down to Cork City, stopping a few miles shy of Glanmire. To the east, magnificent landscapes rolled towards Midleton with Kilduggart Hill at the centre, offering picturesque views of Cobh, the city, and, on clear days, breathtaking panoramas all the way from Old Head to Ardmore. Perched on his quad, he watched from the escarpment, his new farmhouse standing proud in the west. At ten years old, she was settling well into her surroundings. The stark white walls and angled paraboloid roof, though futuristic at the time of construction, now felt as much a part of the estate as the centuries-old oak trees scattered in clusters throughout. His heart swelled again as he recalled his battle and subsequent triumph with the local planning officers. *Cunts*, he thought as he turned the quad east, slipped it into gear, gave it a taste of the throttle and let it roll down the mountainside towards the old, abandoned manor house far over in the valley below.

The old house, Kilduggart Hall, was a tumbledown Georgian mansion, its north end gloved in moss and vines as though some subterranean tendrilous beast had extended its claw and was drawing it slowly inch by inch to its lair deep in the valley below. The approaching lane and paths had long since yielded to ditch and field and the house was now only accessible by foot, quad or hoof. With its closest neighbour five miles to the north, this once fine home seemed, in every sense of the word, abandoned. Surrounded by a ten-foot-high, wood-panelled fence clearly signed DANGER. NO ACCESS ALLOWED, the house had not seen uninvited guests since the Cromby clan had deserted her some forty years ago.

Clifford navigated the quad through verdant farmland, the large pastoral meadows of Kilduggart Hill giving way to arable cropland, deep and fertile, that stretched for several miles until it reached the overgrown paddocks that encircled Kilduggart Hall with acres of hostile towering shrubs and brambles.

He approached the paddock from the west, then followed the peripheral stone wall until he reached the far end, where a crumbled section allowed him access. He manoeuvred his vehicle expertly, meandering through the acres of brambles and thorns, arriving a few minutes later at the boarded gates of the old house. He parked the quad out of sight behind an overgrown laurel hedgerow, where he unlocked an obscured side gate and stepped unnoticed inside the grounds. Moments later, he was at the old kitchen backdoor. Inside, he passed through its grand corridors that led to the magnificent ballroom at the rear of the main living quarters. He skipped across the herringbone floor until he reached the bookcase set into the wall at the far corner of the room. Peering over his shoulder, he pushed gently against the bookcase's extremity and stood back as it swivelled on its centre. He stepped through the opening, stood a moment at the top of the staircase and listened to the young boys chatting in anticipation below.

'Daddy's home, boys,' he called down the stairs, removing his gloves and tapping them on the handrail excitedly as he took each step down. He could hear them scuttle and fuss as each of them dropped whatever they were doing and ran to the bars of their cells, fawning and chatting wantonly as he passed, and he took each extended hand, kissing and fussing over them as he circled the basement, finishing the lap at dearest Raymond's cell. He stopped, took Raymond's face in his hands through the cell bars, and cradled it. Clifford's eyes watered as he recalled their many happy years together.

'Raymondo, Raymondo, Raymondo…' Clifford sang as he kissed his hands, then wiped his eyes dry with his handkerchief before wiping his own.

Raymond had joined him when he was twelve years old and although he resisted at first, in time he had grown to love old Cliff, as had all the guests who'd found themselves part of his dysfunctional family down here in the basement. There were four cells, and each faced a large central space that housed a kitchenette and two sofas. The cells, though compact, were adequately furnished with a bed, a chair, a sink, a toilet and some shelves. Each cell measured roughly fourteen feet by ten and had a portable television and games console with a wide range of all the latest games. There were four or five hundred books scattered among the cells and he encouraged his guests to read, and the older boys were particularly encouraged to study the Maths and English volumes to prepare for their graduation on their sixteenth birthdays.

That was the deal. Once you joined the family, agreed to cooperate and behave, you only had to stay until you were sixteen. Upon your sixteenth birthday, you were given ten thousand punts and the choice of going to a local college to further your studies or starting your new life as an apprentice plumber or electrician. Clifford would make all the arrangements, and his guests were always thrilled when their cellmates graduated, finally emerging back to the real world. Often, they would write telling of their fresh adventures and Clifford would regale the lads with stories of the graduate's exploits beyond the cells of Kilduggart Hall.

Raymond was graduating today. He had turned sixteen two days earlier. Clifford had been busy, so today was his first opportunity to perform the graduation ceremony. Clifford promised to make up for the delay with a bowling trip and a burger once they'd reached the city. Anticipations were high. Raymond had excelled at his studies over the last few months and, with Clifford's guidance, had decided he would attend a local college to further his studies. He had set his hopes on becoming a social worker. He longed to reach out to other young lads who, like himself, had fallen on hard times and needed a little help or guidance. Not every child would be fortunate enough to meet someone like Clifford, and after all, there were only four cells down here. Clifford couldn't possibly shoulder the burden of all the city's destitute waifs and strays. No… Raymond had decided that each of us must play our part. We must each help those less fortunate than ourselves. Clifford had advised Raymond that the path he'd chosen would not be an easy one, but assured him he would be there every step of the way, and even if it took ten years or more, he would bloody well make sure that Raymond reached his goal.

Clifford opened Raymond's cell and led him to the centre of the room. He washed him head to toe as the ceremony dictated, and they blushed at the cheers and whoops from the other boys as they shared an embrace on the sofa. But today was not about that. Today was Raymond's day, and as tempting as it was for Clifford, he would not put his desires before Raymond's entitlement. Raymond had waited long enough, and today he was moving to his flat in the city, where he would begin his studies at the end of the month.

Ringing the ceremonial bell, Clifford orated poetically about life and the paths we choose. How our love of some things and rejection of others is like a magical dance, and if we make the right choices, each of us can achieve our wildest dreams and beyond. Clifford presented Raymond with his IR£10,000 cheque and there wasn't a dry eye in the house when Raymond passed from cell to cell, hugging each boy through the bars. Stopping finally at little Eoin's cell, he held his friend for a long embrace. Eoin, the youngest of the group at seven years old, a departure from Clifford's own rules about age that no one understood, least of all Clifford, had been paired with Raymond.

Raymond, the group's elder, had been tasked with guiding Eoin through his first few months in the cellar. The two boys had grown quite close, and Raymond promised he would wait for Eoin to graduate and when he did, they would be best pals forever on the outside. Clifford advised Raymond not to promise to write too often as he would be very busy with his studies, and anyhow with a young lad like Eoin it was best to let him get on with things and sure wouldn't they meet again in a few years when Eoin graduated and t'would all be grand.

When he'd said his farewells, Clifford led a sobbing Raymond by the hand up the steel stairs, through the bookcase, on through the ballroom, down the corridor and into the kitchen, where he asked him to *stall the ball* a moment while he checked the coast was clear outside. Raymond, bursting with excitement, waited patiently, and when Clifford returned moments later, he was relieved to hear that there weren't any nosey neighbours, and they were free to head out into the world. It was dark outside.

'It's better this way,' Clifford explained. 'It'll help your eyes adjust to the brightness, Raymondo. After all, you've only spent the last four and a half years in an artificially lit dungeon,' he joked, and they both giggled.

As they crossed the yard, Raymond almost passed out with the intense headiness of the cool night air, fresh and fragrant with a charged bluster, the night alive with opportunity and adventure. The world, his, to be taken on and tamed. Tonight was the first of many great nights, and he would be forever grateful to Clifford for opening his eyes to the opportunities this beautiful world could bestow. They ran hand in hand to the quad bike, and as they donned their helmets, Clifford helped Raymond with his strap. Once mounted, Clifford showed his passenger how to hold on tight and, as they navigated their way through the thorny paddock, Raymond shrieked excitedly as a briar caught his exposed ankle.

'Are you alright?' Clifford asked, concerned for his passenger.

'I'm fine,' Raymond called above the engine's purr. 'A thorny bit scratched me... he-he!'

Free of the paddock, they sped south, with Raymond on sensory overload as he spied, for the first time in years, the stars and the clouds and the moon in the valley as bright as day, and car lights in the distance snaking along the coast road. *It won't be long now*, he thought as they drove, and soon they stopped by a ditch. Raymond thought he could hear the rumble and swish of the ocean below.

'Will you be okay to walk from here?' Clifford asked.

'Walk?'

'Yes, we can't take the quad on the road. I've got the car on the other side of this wood. The quad is only for fields and shit like that. We need to walk for a bit to the car. Come on, hurry, or the bowling alley will be closed,' he encouraged, placing his helmet on the saddle then helping Raymond to remove his. Clifford took a torch from his pocket and guided Raymond through the woods, taking great care not to mis-step on the rough terrain. A half mile into the hike, they stopped. Clifford removed his backpack, handed Raymond a water bottle, and they both drank.

'Are you okay with pressing on?' Clifford asked.

Raymond nodded, and Clifford handed him the backpack.

'Put the water bottle back in when you're done. I need a pee,' Clifford told him, and he walked to the side while Raymond fumbled with the zipper in the dark.

'Is it giving you bother?' Clifford asked over his shoulder as he removed his belt.

'Give it here,' Clifford said. Raymond held out the bag in the darkness of the woods. Clifford grabbed his hand, and with a sharp yank, spun him one-eighty. Raymond felt something slip over his head and he gave a nervous giggle as Clifford looped his belt about Raymond's neck, yanked it tight, then spun so they were back to back. He threw the belt over his shoulder and leaned forward until he felt Raymond's feet leave the ground and he held him suspended like that, ear to ear, as Raymond kicked and reared, clawing desperately at the belt. Clifford heaved and wheezed, then gave a few sharp jolts until he felt the neck snap, then waited as Raymond's arms and legs settled about him like heavy ropes, and he lowered him to the ground, shone the lamp in his face and wondered at what point had Raymondo lost hope. He held the torch to his face a while longer, as though he might ask him, then he took a knife from the bag and stabbed him twice in the heart.

'Raymondo, Raymondo. To be sure, to be sure,' he sang in a leprechaun lilt, then dragged the slumped body to a pre-dug grave concealed behind a fallen tree.

Chapter Ten

MOURNING

HE SAT BY THE WINDOW, in the front room of his grandparents' house in Blackrock, watching the driveway. *Muntins*, he thought to himself as he rubbed the wooden frame that divided the window into smaller panes. He didn't know how he knew they were called muntins, but he did. He often knew useless shit like that. His heart sank as he heard the door open behind him and he turned, expecting to find some long-faced prick, and smiled when he saw his nan poke her head around the door.

'Are you alright, pet?' Ann asked, closing the door to the mumbling din of the mourning. A rosary, a cry, a welcome laugh.

'I am,' The Boy said, turning back to the drive. He imagined Daniel rounding the corner and walking up to the house. *Any moment now*, he thought.

'I brought you a few sausage rolls,' she said, 'and a bottle of Coke,' and she laid them beside him. He looked at her again and smiled, then turned back to the road and waited.

'Will I leave you to it?' she asked him.

'I'm grand nan,' he said, turning to her. 'I need a few minutes away from that lot, that's all.'

'I know what you mean. Will I stay with ya, or would you prefer to be by yourself?'

'I'll be fine here. You go out and give Granda a hand, he's probably losing it.' He forced a smile.

'Okay, pet, if you're sure.'

'I am, go on,' he said, picking up a sausage roll to complete the pretence.

There'd been a steady convoy of mourners. Hair tousling, bear-hugging pledgers of 'whatever you need'. 'Anytime, anytime' they'd say, urging him to abandon hesitation then depart, their void soon filled by some such others waiting to spin him in misery and leave him cocooned, peering from his gloom, their departing voices like echoes in his haunted half-life, submerged in the black depths where grief abides to have its way with him.

And then they'd ebb, the rubbers of cheeks, and he'd take a breath until some fresh wave would have them pouring in the back door and the front door or down the fuckin' chimney, all long faces and limp wet palms crying and looking to him for what? And he'd find himself among them wondering how in the fuck he'd got there, and he drifted like that for days that turned into weeks until he rose one morning to the sound of birds, and he could feel the icy claws of sorrow release him as he rolled back the stone of his tormented days.

There is no stock but my own, he thought. *No stock but my own.*

Chapter Eleven

THE ST LEGER

FEARGAL OPENED THE FRONT DOOR and stepped inside. The habitual aroma of beer, smoke and piss masked with detergent, though not unique to the St Leger, was undoubtedly one he'd long associated with the place. It brought back many memories.

Daniel, sat at the bar in his usual spot oblivious to all others, was deep in conversation with himself. Actions to be justified, wankers in absence to be dressed down. He wasn't standing for this shit anymore… right? They could all fuck off… right? 'Bunch of cunts, ballbags all of 'em,' he snarled.

Feargal took the seat next to Daniel, pointed to the Guinness tap, then spread his thumb and index finger wide apart, indicating to Tony that he wanted a pint. Tony started the pint and set it to rest as Feargal laid a fiver on the counter. Tony took the fiver, rang it up, placed the change back on the bar, finished the pint, and placed it central on a beer mat Feargal had squared against the edge of the bar; then he gave Feargal a conspiratorial wink, not a word passing between the two.

Feargal had that gift. He could communicate with all manner of men from far-flung corners of the globe without uttering a word. Many years of weeks and nights holed up in silence had honed this gift to where he could not only impart his own expressions without words, but a simple squint of the eyes or a pursing of the lips conveyed without doubt that there was to be no speaking.

Feargal took a long draw on his pint, placed it again central on the beer mat and spoke at last to Daniel, all the while keeping his gaze fixed behind the bar.

'You didn't make it to Marie's funeral then,' he said.

Daniel jumped, almost falling from his stool, then spun in amazement, aware for the first time of Feargal at his side.

'Fuck me,' Daniel slurred. 'What in the fuck… Feargal? Jaysus Christ you scared the shite out of me,' he exclaimed, steadying himself.

'Certainly smells like it,' Feargal replied, his gaze still fixed behind the bar. 'I said you didn't make it to Marie's funeral then. Were you busy? Some pressing engagement, perhaps?'

'Fuck off,' Daniel spluttered.

'And what about your wee man? Wee Fallon. Didn't fancy popping over to pay your respects to him, either? And The Boy, do you even know where he's at?' Feargal asked.

'You're full of shit Feargal, you are full of fucking shit… Where the fuck have you been for the last few years? Nowhere, that's fuckin' where… no cuntin' where… So fuck off back to nowhere and leave us in fuckin' peace you pious prick.' Daniel's venom finally found an audience.

'You call this peace? Och, I've been around alright Daniel, and don't let on you didn't know where to find me, or how,' Feargal added, turning at last to eyeball Daniel.

'And what would I want with you? Is it thick you think I am? You are the reason we are in this fuckin' mess. You're a lying prick, a using bastard… I'd want to have been in a fuckin' bad way before I'd invite you back into our fuckin' lives. Why the fuck do you think your parents took Marie and moved as far away from you as the country would geographically permit? Well? Because you are fuckin' poison… rotten to the core, they knew it, and they got as far away from you and Belfast as they physically could. But you couldn't let it be you fuckin' arrogant wanker. You had to keep poppin' up here, poppin' up there… the scarlet fuckin' pimpernel…'

Stopping to catch his breath Daniel took a long sip from his pint then, changing tack, continued.

'One fucking job, you said one job, you fuckin' liar. That's what you fuckin' told us, Feargal. You're full of shit and you're a prick and a liar and Marie and Fallon are a product of the misery you leave in your fucking wake so don't walk in here and ask me where was I for the last few days Feargal… don't fuckin' ask.'

'You finished?' Feargal asked, not expecting a reply before adding, 'The Boy is with his Nan and Granda. Sort yourself out and go see him, or there'll be a third funeral, and you won't miss this one I promise you.' He sank his pint and headed for the door.

Daniel let himself stew a moment, then leapt from his chair and followed Feargal out into the street. He looked left and right, then spotted Feargal climbing into his car. Feargal eyed Daniel and stepped back as he approached. Anticipating the attack, he sidestepped the blow and Daniel fell forward, his own momentum knocking him off balance. Feargal, a seasoned bundler, caught Daniel neatly and flung him into the car across the driver's seat, making him land upside down in a heap on the passenger side with his head in the footwell. Feargal jumped in and drove at speed, braking and turning sharply to prevent Daniel from righting himself. A hundred yards up the road he pulled into an abandoned lot, pulled hard on the handbrake, sprang from the car, rushed to the passenger side and pulled Daniel by the seat of his pants out through the door and hurled him across the lot in the dirt. He took Daniel by the shirt collar and dragged him to an obscured corner where he pinned him to the wall with his forearm hard against Daniel's neck.

'What've you gotta say now big man? Go on Daniel, I'm all fuckin' ears! What else has been burning in your chest for the last few years that you're only finding the balls to bring up nigh, you snivelling wee bastard? Come on big mouth, let's get it all out now me old pal! Come on you fucking prick,' he shouted.

Tears streamed down Daniel's face. Feargal released his grip, and Daniel slumped to the ground, sobbing. Feargal paced over and back, foaming at the mouth, frothing as he seethed.

'You fuckin' knew what you were getting involved with – you fuckin' knew who we were and what we were capable of. I never asked you for shit. You came to me, and you told me about fucking pagers and remote triggers, mister fuckin' university lecturer, member of the fuckin' board, mister *National Geo*-fuckin'-*graphic*... *Science* cunting *Weekly*. I never asked you for shit, anything you gave to me, you volunteered, no one put a gun to your head,' Feargal, now on the verge of tears himself, stood back and wiped the spittle from his mouth.

Daniel rolled onto his side and started to sit up. 'But you took it with both hands, and you fucking ran with it though... didn't ya?'

'Aye, I did, surely. It was genius, son, a game changer. What did you expect? Come on, Daniel you're the smartest prick I know don't tell me you thought it was a one-time thing... even if I wanted to stop them using it I fuckin' couldn't have and you fuckin' know that. Once we had it there was no way we were ever going back.' Feargal took a cigarette from his pocket, sparked it up and passed it to Daniel, then repeated the process for himself.

'It fuckin' destroyed her,' Daniel blubbed. 'Every time she heard the news, she knew it was her introducing you and me that made it possible... easier.' He wiped the snot from his nose.

'Don't kid yourself Daniel,' Feargal responded. 'You're a smart cookie but some other prick would've worked it out eventually, it was only a matter of time for fuck's sake lad, give yourself a break... and look where we are nigh, months away from peace. Thanks to you,' he continued as he exhaled, took a long drag on his cigarette, then flicked it to the ground. 'Come on, I'll buy ya a pint. I think we need it,' he said with his hand extended.

Chapter Twelve

THE BOOK OF DANIEL

Part I

HE'D ALWAYS BEEN A BRIGHT lad, Daniel. 'Get the paper, son!' Fintan would call. Daniel, sat patiently with the *Examiner* in his hand, would hold it aloft as his father swept him up in his arms and they'd retreat to the comfort of the lounge, where Daniel would trace his Dad's finger, as Fintan read each article aloud. Then one day he stopped, looked at Daniel and said:

'You know that one, son.'

'The?' Daniel mouthed nervously.

'Good man,' Fintan encouraged. 'And the next word?'

'Par-liam-en-tary?'

'Good lad, and that one?' He pointed to another.

'Ass-em-bly... assembly.'

'Perfect,' Fintan praised the three-year-old Daniel. 'Bloody perfect... Mags get in here and listen to this!' he called out to the kitchen.

Next, they took on maths. They started with the times tables, but it was immediately clear to Fintan that Daniel knew the answers, not by rote, but by some deeper understanding of all that was in the world. It was perfectly natural for Daniel to conceive that twelve twelves were one hundred and forty-four. 'Sure, what else would it be?' his little face exclaimed when Fintan asked, 'Are you sure?' Daniel gaped back with a confused look that said 'Of course, I'm sure.'

His concept of time and distance was staggering. 'Two hours, eight minutes and fifty-six seconds to our destination if we continue at our current velocity,' he would exclaim from the back seat of their Morris Minor.

'We will need to make a few stops at crossings and stuff like that and there's a four-mile stretch with a speed restriction of thirty miles an hour,' Fintan corrected. 'So, it might not be exactly as you estimated but you're bloody close enough lad.'

'I've already allowed for stoppages,' Daniel replied, 'and the thirty stretch is for three point two miles, which I've also factored in. So, all things considered, I should be closer than you think, but let's see how we get on.'

Snotty little bollix, Fintan thought to himself, his heart bursting with pride.

'Man must *strive*,' Mr O'Hara continued to his wife looking up from page four of Daniel's essay 'Endeavour', stressing the word theatrically. 'Push our limits for that in which we believe, but we must not lose sight of our role in this game. We are but a speck on this earth. We belong to her and not she to us and when she is done with us, she will send the winds to set each man a-tumble about her great prairies until at last we are naught but dust, and so shall gather in vast clumps at her four corners and stack ourselves high atop our jet planes, our computers and our tanks, until these vehicles and triggers of doom too are dust and the elephants again will roam in their thousands whilst new beasts leap from the oceans and the seas to take their chance upon the beaches and beyond, leaving man to sleep beneath the fathoms, a vast crude puddle in waiting for some new being with their kelly bushings and their ledgers, and in time their guns and their pain until she sends her winds again.'

O'Hara folded the pages and sat back in his armchair as the light from the fire twinkled with the tear in his eye.

'He's eleven years old,' he told his wife.

'Eleven? Poor little fecker,' she exclaimed, 'worrying about shite like that at his age. His parents are probably a pair of feckin' hippies filling the little crater's head with a load of old shite.'

'I know them, they're not. His old fella works at the beet factory, and his mother is Carol Sweeney's daughter from across the field.'

'Which one, Mags?'

'Yes, Margaret.'

'That's Mags' lad?'

'That's him.'

'Fuck me, Margaret's lovely. Jaysus H Christ, he seems lovely.'

'He is lovely, but he's also gifted. The title of that essay was "The weather at the weekend". I've got twenty-five other essays about rain and walks with Mammy and Daddy. The closest any other kid came to a variation was Paddy Flynn who wrote that rain makes him sad because it makes the mound of earth that marks his mother's grave shrink and his Dad can't afford a headstone so he's afraid if it rains too much he won't be able to find where his Mam's buried.'

'Jaysus H Christ, will ya fuckin' stop, you're killing me,' the wife protested before continuing. 'Is he eleven as well?'

'No, ten.'

'What did she die of, his ma?'

'The big C, my dear, the big C. Went to the doctor on the Monday after she dropped the kids at school... she was dead three weeks later.'

'Kids?'

'Yeah, four in total. Eamonn is nine, Paddy is ten and there're twin girls as well... I think they are four.'

'Stop... for fuck's sake, will ya stop? Twin girls... holy suffering mother of Christ. Don't tell me any more. What's the husband like, the father?'

'He's sound. I don't really know him. He works. There's an aunt living nearby who helps. It's a mess, but they'll be fine. That's how it goes sometimes. My concern is Daniel, he's wasted in our school. He needs to be somewhere more nurturing.'

'Speak to the Head.'

'He'll do fuck all, he wants him to stay at St Pat's. He makes the school look good.'

'I don't know, maybe the parents wrote the essay.'

'He wrote it. It's not the first time he's written stuff like that.'

'Speak to the parents, see what they want. Maybe you could guide them with reading for the lad or something like that,' she said as she knitted one, purled the next, then placed her knitting down and headed for the kitchen.

'Maybe,' O'Hara conceded. 'You're a bit of a smart cookie yourself, aren't ya?' he said, and he chased her into the kitchen. 'Come here to me, ya little strap. Mr O'Hara wants a word…'

'Fuck off, ya pervert,' she squealed as he caught her up by the pantry door, gave her a squeeze, then turned and walked to the hall where he picked up the phone book, found Fintan's number and dialled. It rang three times.

'Hello,' came Fintan's voice. They spoke for some time about Daniel and his talent. O'Hara told Fintan about the essay, but Fintan had already read it.

'I want him to be normal,' Fintan said. 'No, not normal. He'll never be "normal", but I want him to be one of "the lads", for as long as he can be, anyway. Be a kid. All this is natural to him, ya know. He hasn't learned the things he knows, and we certainly haven't pushed him. God knows how he knows it, but he does. Do you know what I mean? He grasps all concepts, he sees all outcomes, he's aware of constellations and theories and computers and life cycles of beasts and creatures I've never even heard of, and he can quantify every blooming thing in the universe, and what's more is he's always right. It's not like we have a library of books in the house. I've bought some of them since, so they are there if he wants to read them, but the things he knows are beyond books. There'll be a time, and I've no doubt it'll be soon, when someone will get their talons in him and squeeze him for all he's worth – but not now. I watch him play with the lads on the street and my heart soars that he's not insular or unsociable. Do you know what I mean? I thank my lucky stars every day he's not some brainbox who can't string two friendly words together, and right now, encouraging that aspect of his personality is my priority. Do you know what I'm saying to ya?'

'I do, I do,' O'Hara replied.

'He takes to the bed sometimes. He says it's his tummy, but I don't know. I reckon it all gets too much for him, and he needs to shut down for a little break. I mean, I don't know, we've taken him to the doctor, and he's saying all the right things to convince the doctor but…'

'Okay, I hear ya,' O'Hara replied.

'What I'm trying to say is… thank you for thinking of him and I know your heart is in the right place, but I am aware that he's a talented lad and when he lets us know he's ready, we will make sure he gets the guidance and support he needs. But I'm not putting any pressure on him or pushing him in any direction. He'll find his own way, I'm certain of that.'

O'Hara let the words sink in, drew a breath to speak, then didn't.

'I'm sorry for ringing you like this,' he began. 'I… I… anyway, he's a great little fella, and he's clearly in good hands.' He was about to hang up when a thought came to him. 'Before you go… can I ask you one thing?'

'Of course.'

'What's a "kelly bushing"?'

'Fucked if I know,' Fintan replied.

O'Hara hung up the phone, feeling small.

Chapter Thirteen

LOVE COMES QUICKLY

July 1987

HE'D ALWAYS LIKED BOYS, THOUGH what that meant he wasn't quite sure. Words like 'faggot' or 'queer' first entered his consciousness during his teens at boarding school. Slants bandied about the dorm or locker room, like 'Rodders is a homo', 'Jasper you bender' and so on were never aimed at him. Never 'Clifford is a homo' – no one would've dared. A bright and flamboyant lad, he was also brawny and mean, capable of extremes. He'd had but two scraps during his time at Clongowes, both of which ended in hospital visits, though not for him. He was a charming and brilliant boy, but the bastard within was never far below the surface. Over-concerned classmate one moment, raging maniac the next.

At university in Cork there were some girls, there were also some boys. The latter of which were aggressive clandestine encounters, followed by the threat of violence if strict confidentiality did not ensue. He kept his sexuality a closely guarded secret from his parents. When they passed, both within months of each other, he was finally free to live his life as he chose, but the Cork gay scene – which mostly consisted of rent boys and landlords – fell shy of his bohemian expectations. He travelled further afield to Dublin at first, then London and New York, yet despite his many dalliances he was still left wanting.

On a hot Friday morning in July of '87, he left the farmhouse early for an appointment in the city. He had a meeting with his accountant on Patrick's Street, then on to Blarney to pay for repairs to the combine harvester.

Robbing bastards, he thought, *eight hundred quid for a fucking flywheel, on a combine bastard harvester. They're takin' the piss.* He was *gonna fuckin' tell 'em* he decided as he drove, singing along to Madonna's 'Who's that Girl?' The sun was up and he put the roof down as he glided along the lower Glanmire road. He felt good as he drove, and he could feel a shift in his emotions. It was a great day, he decided, and what the fuck did he know about flywheels or how much they fucking cost, he'd pay the fucking bill and be done with it.

'Life is too short for this shit Clifford old boy!' he said. That was it, his mind was made. The cunts could have their eight hundred fucking quid, small change to a man of his means. He might even tip the fuckers. They had done a top job, and it would be harvest time in a few weeks. It would be a pretty fucking difficult time of year without a combine harvester. He might play that one by ear, he thought. Maybe a tip was pushing it.

The meeting with the accountant was the usual 'how much, you fucking cunt?' followed by an explanation, an apology and an uncomfortable handshake. Feeling hungry, he nipped into the Long Valley Bar on Winthrop Street to grab some late breakfast, early lunch.

'A meal some might call brunch,' he said to the waiter, who looked at him with eyes that said, *cunt*.

After breakfast, he continued on to the Allied Irish Bank on Patrick's Street to pick up some cash before pressing on to pay those bastards in Blarney. He'd changed his mind again, *They should've asked before fitting the component*, he thought *I'm not a blank cunting cheque*. On the other hand, he had asked them to come out ASAP. He remembered using that exact acronym. Maybe he'd have to suck this one up. Live and learn, rack it up to experience. He settled on playing it by ear when he got to the repair shop.

Pulling into the yard, he parked the car in a space marked STAFF ONLY.

I dare the cunts to ask me to move, he thought as he swaggered into the reception with its mud- and straw-strewn floor, and its pictures of tractors and farm equipment hung upon the wall. Clifford looked around disdainfully as a receptionist in her early twenties looked up from her ledger and smiled.

'Good morning, sir,' she said as she beamed.

'Good morning. Clifford Cromby, Cromby estate. Is it you I speak to about this bloody bill?' he scoffed, unable to restrain the prick within.

'I can help you with your bill, Mr Cromby. Is there a problem?' she asked.

'Well, you tell me, its eight hundred fuckin' quid for a bastard flywheel, does that sound right to you?' Sensing the upper hand now he turned up the heat, flinging the bill onto the counter and adding, 'My estate manager said your lad was only there twenty minutes, by my reckoning that's two thousand four hundred quid an hour. Fancies himself, this lad of yours.'

'Oh, right?' she replied, untroubled by Clifford's wanker act. 'Let me take a look… The total here isn't correct Mr Cromby…' she continued, leaving it to hang for a moment, allowing him to make an even bigger prick of himself. He didn't disappoint. Before she could draw a breath, he was straight in.

'Halle-fuckin-lujah,' he bellowed. 'Finally, someone in this fucking place knows what they are doing.'

She gave a modest giggle, almost a *thank you* but not quite before adding, 'This total hasn't had the VAT added – if you give me a moment, I'll nip out the back and have that adjusted for you Mr Cromby sir,' trying not to burst out laughing as Clifford launched into a fit of expletives. The manager came rushing from the back office to see what on earth was going on in his reception. When Clifford finally relented his rant, the receptionist placed her hand on Clifford's forearm and spoke.

'Mr Cromby, why are you so upset? If you look here at the bottom of the page, it clearly says that there is no charge to the customer as the repair is a warranty item – however, we need you to sign for the repair as the owner so we can submit our claim to the manufacturer.'

'You what?' Clifford stammered. 'No charge?'

'Yes, Mr Cromby, your unit is still under warranty. I'm sure our lad would've explained that on the day.'

'He did not.'

'Not to worry though… sure we are all sorted now. Is there anything else I can help you with today?' She smiled.

'No, no, that's fine,' Clifford whimpered, as he signed, replaying the last few moments in his head, desperately searching for some scrap of dignity in the exchange but coming up empty as the yard door burst open.

'Is that your car in the staff area, Mr Cromby?' the yard manager barked.

'I'm not sure… did I park in a staff zone?' Clifford replied, crushed.

'Convertible jag? We don't get too many of them around here.'

'Oh, right, that's mine,' Clifford chimed apologetically.

'Can you move it, please? We've a delivery waiting outside. The trucks use that space to turn,' he added in a no-nonsense tone.

'Of course,' Clifford replied.

He walked to the car and climbed in, wishing the ground would swallow him whole.

A sudden indignant rage rose through him. *Who the fuck do they think they're talking to?* he thought to himself.

He opened the car door, swirled in his seat and placed his foot on the ground. The manager watched.

Where are you off to? Clifford asked himself. *Haven't you gotten us in enough trouble today?*

He froze, smiled at the manager, then slowly eased back into the seat.

He put the car in gear, reversed from the parking space, then exited the yard.

He needed a drink. *A cold pint of Heineken*, he thought, *it's fuckin' roasting and those bastards have me all a fluster.*

He drove into Blarney to Christy's bar, where he collapsed in an armchair and sank a pair of shaky pints in quick succession. Christy's daughter brought the pints, stopping to chat about the hunt and the weather and any other old shite that popped into her head. *She fancies me*, Clifford concluded. She was a bit female for his liking, though she'd do a turn.

'I might have some light supper before I head off,' he told her.

'Will I bring you the menu?'

'That would be wonderful. No point heading off now, traffic would be murder,' he said as though to himself, then watched as she scuttled off.

The clock above the bar read four fifteen. He would treat himself to a read of the paper while nursing two more pints and a sandwich, he decided. That would pass a few hours nicely, then he'd whizz up through Killeens down into Glanmire and straight out the road. 'Home in fifteen minutes,' he surmised. *Lovely jubbly*, he thought as he nestled in, his afternoon laid out nicely.

Shortly after six, he was half sleeping, half reading an article on fishing rights in the North Sea when Christy's daughter, clearing his table, brought him back to the room.

'Can I get you anything else, Cliff? I'm about to head off home,' she asked.

'Ah hello darling,' he feigned. 'Forgive me, I was miles away. I'll have a coffee and a few biscuits if you have any, and I'll settle up with you as well before you go.'

'I'll tell the girls to bring them over. It was lovely seeing you. Look after yourself and don't leave it so long before you come back again,' she said, then headed back behind the bar.

He drank his coffee. He liked coffee. Especially after a few pints, it almost wiped the slate clean, almost. Outside, the slanting sun shone hot and low. *Value in the evening yet*, he thought as he climbed into his car, put his sunglasses on his head and watched the polarised people passing by, the bar filling up behind him and he wondered, *have they been waiting for me to leave?*

'Don't be ridiculous,' he sighed as he fired up the car then pulled onto the road as the locals filed by in twos and threes – those whoring bastard communal conspirators – and the morning's exchange rose to haunt him… *cunts, cunts, cunts*! He put his foot to the floor and gunned the car through the town.

'Fucking peasants!' he roared, and the anger felt good.

He came upon roadworks in Killeens where a fat man, dusty in a yellow jacket, boomed above the din of the Kango.

'Head down towards town and pick up the Mallow Road below and cut over that way.'

'Thank you, my good man,' Clifford roared back, smiling, followed by 'dopey cunt' under his breath as he hit the road. Ignoring the advice, he took a left toward home via Dublin Hill on the city's Northside.

Lucky or what, he thought, and he swung by the cross, a local dealing spot, to pick up some gear for the weekend. As he crested the hill, he pulled over and parked his car by the ditch. There was a young lad sitting on a gate with a blade of grass hanging from his mouth. A good-looking lad, Clifford noted. He thought his name was Chubs, but he couldn't remember.

'Alright?' Chubs enquired, recognising Clifford.

'How are you?' Clifford responded.

'What are you after?'

'What have you got?'

'Hash, trips, yokes.'

'Yokes?'

'Pills from Amsterdam, they are the shit.'

'How can I say no?'

Chubs laughed. He hadn't tried one yet, but he wasn't telling Cliff that.

'How many have you left?' Cliff asked.

'I've got six ten spots of hash, ten yokes and eight trips.'

'How much for the lot?'

Chubs looked in the bag and made a quick calculation.

'Three hundred?'

'The money's in the car. Jump in while I count it,' Clifford said, and they walked back to the car where Clifford counted out the money and handed it to Chubs.

'Fancy a smoke?' Cliff asked. 'I live over the road. We could take one of those yokes if you like…' He put the car in gear and drove on down the hill before Chubs had a chance to answer.

Clifford reached into the bag and retrieved four of the yokes. 'Are these them?' he asked, holding them out.

Chubs nodded, and they necked two each dry.

'Fuck me,' Cliff shouted, at the acrid taste at the back of his throat. 'They taste like rat poison,' and he laughed out loud as the wind rushed by.

When they approached the lane to Clifford's house, he slowed the car down, then pulled over to the side.

'Get down in the footwell,' he instructed, 'there shouldn't be anyone here but get down to be on the safe side,' he added as he closed the roof of the car, then drove into the yard and parked by the back door.

'Stay here a second, while I make sure the coast is clear,' he told his passenger.

He walked through the kitchen, calling out as he went on through the house and out the front door. All the staff cars were gone, and he went and closed the yard gate before checking each of the outhouses. Satisfied they were alone, he returned to the car and led Chubs into the house, where he walked from room to room, eyeing up the valuables.

'Nice gaff,' Chubs remarked. 'Stick on a few choons there, boy will ya?'

'Choons?' Clifford enquired as visions of some working-class dietary staple like fish fingers or Denny sausages popped into his head. He really was unprepared for such company. There was a pheasant in the pantry, he recalled, as the buzz from the yokes came on strong and washed over him like a warm avalanche. A strange stillness took hold of him as each moment lingered then flashed to the next and he found himself wanting to hold Chubs in his arms one moment and in the next he wanted to take his head and smash it hard against the mantel over and over and then he was back in the room and he could hear the word *choons, choons, choons* and he thought *What the fuck are you talking about…*?

'Choons… tunes! Music, you gowl… stick on some music!' Chubs laughed, noting Clifford's discomfort.

'Of course… tunes as in musical tunes… yes I've loads of records, the stereo is in there,' Cliff replied, pointing to a room with two large sofas and a television. 'Put on whatever you want, the records are next to the stereo in the wooden box… I'll get us a drink,' suddenly conscious of his poor hospitality skills.

'These yokes are fucking amazing,' Clifford mouthed as he made his way to the kitchen, dancing Billie Jean style. 'Shamone… hee-hee,' he cried, slapping his knee.

He poured two large vodkas with ice and filled each glass with Coke, crushing two more of the yokes into Chubs' glass and giving it a stir.

'Yoka-me-bob,' he muttered. 'No, no, wait Yoka-me-Chub,' and he laughed out loud trying to hold the thought in his head for later.

'Your music is shit,' Chubs jibed, holding a copy of *Tubular Bells* in his hand.

'A lot you'd know,' Clifford retorted as he set the drinks down. Then he reached into the box and retrieved the Pet Shop Boys' album *Please*. He put the record on the deck and cranked it up on the Technics stack system as 'West End Girls' blared throughout the house, and they downed their vodka-Cokes then sang in each other's faces as they soared on the yokes with their free hands high in the air. Collapsing on the sofa they laughed as the song faded and the record continued on to 'Opportunities', track three on the album, and they jumped to their feet again dancing to the intro's mechanical beat leading to the solo keyboard then exploding with the opening line. They twirled, and they fell, then they got back to their feet and stumbled in sync with the music, mangled. Clifford removed his top, and they danced and they laughed into the wee small hours.

'Will I get the bong?' Clifford asked as he handed Chubs a trip and they downed them together dry.

'Bing, bang, bong,' Chubs replied, then crashed onto the sofa. Clifford took the bong from a box beneath the stairs and stacked the bowl high with a hash and ecstasy cocktail, and they smoked, and they smoked, and they smoked as Clifford tried to recall in vain his earlier play on words.

'Yoka-doodle… Yoka-majig…' he tried.

'Can you see that?' Chubs asked, pointing to the valley through the window.

'See what?'

'You say.'

'No, you say.'

'No, I want to know if you really see the same thing,' Chubs said.

'Okay, do you promise to be honest?' Clifford asked.

'Stick a needle in my eye.'

'On the crest of the hill, do you see where the light is forming? The row of people…'

'How many?'

'A hundred, maybe more… dancing.'

'Fuckin' mental, what's the big one doin?'

'He's picking up the smaller ones, and he's putting them on his shoulders, and they are diving into the crowd where they explode in a burst of lights and stars.'

'Fuck off… did I say this to you earlier?'

'No, what you said earlier was "that's the way I like my chicken". Do you remember?'

'Oh, yeah…' Chubs replied, then smiled.

Outside in the valley, the sun, fat, dewy and burnt at the edges, rose. Chubs, nestled in his host's embrace, let the sleep take him. Clifford's forearm and elbow lay supportive in the crook of Chubs' neck, and he kissed the lad's ear, and he thought how easy it would be to pull his forearm tight towards his shoulder and lock the lad hard against his body until the life drained from the wee lad's limbs.

On the Technics speaker, Jimmy Somerville ooh'd his ghoulish entrée then the *ooh* turned to an *aah* as Clifford felt his arm close tight about Chubs' neck, and he squeezed as his free hand clamped the offending wrist to assist the draw. Clifford threw his head back and locked his legs vice-like about Chubs' waist and pulled. Chubs struggled at first for breath, then realised in his half-sleep what was happening and tried to get his hands inside Clifford's forearm, then he kicked and flailed, but it was no use. The cushions from the sofa flew about the room as Chubs bucked and reared; Clifford turned his face away until he felt the lad's grip relent and then he turned the juice up, squeezing tighter and tighter, gyrating against Chubs' back as he pulled the throat harder and harder in a frenzied rhythmic attack over and over until he felt the neck break, and he released the lad. Clifford rolled onto his side and lay there for some time, heaving and wheezing with the foam frothing at the corners of his mouth.

Clifford pulled Chubs to him and held him a while, more gentle now, and he felt a warm rush rise at his feet. It surged through his legs, into his abdomen then it crashed like a wave about his shoulders, bubbling at the bottleneck, then exploded in his head, and he thought he might pass out as he lay there in his ecstasy, and still it flowed through him, euphoric and alone in the room save for the corpse and this unfathomed thing, this unholy communion of a keystone clunk. He knew in that moment who he was, who he had always been, deeper than bone, at his essence, in the space between his cells – he gazed at his soul and it was as black and blazoned as the earth's core, from where it was begot, and the tears rolled down his face as he turned onto his knees and raised his hands up to the sky, waking out there in the valley, as a burst of stars shot forth from his palms and filled up the room to the sound of Somerville's solicitations that his lover should not leave him in this way.

Chapter Fourteen

ROOM AT THE INN

IN THE MORNING, CLIFFORD LEFT the body concealed beneath the duvet, locked his bedroom door from the outside and left the house. In the yard, he stopped by the toolshed, took a pick and a shovel from the wall, strapped them tight to the quad, and set off east across the estate until he reached the woods at the far end of the Cromby grounds. He parked the quad out of sight and set off on foot until he reached a secluded spot, where the brush was thick, and set to work. He dug for hours, stopping occasionally for water or to catch his breath before turning once more to his work, losing himself to the scheme of it all, his residual glow affording a hum or vibration to his labour, no strain between the spades. His body but a tool, he dug ceaselessly, unyielding.

Later, he looked up from inside the grave, the edge high above his head. He stretched up with his hand. He could reach the ground with the tips of his fingers, but when he tried to pull himself out the earth broke free and fell in the grave beside him. He tried again on the opposite side, but the same thing happened.

'Nice job Clifford,' he said to himself.

'Don't be such a know it all,' he replied.

He tried again and again, but the result was still the same. He could feel his heart race. He needed a rest. He lay on the ground and looked up at the trees swaying from side to side. A peaceful feeling came over him, and he looked at the blue and grey sky passing above the trees, and he thought he might sleep a while.

He closed his eyes and breathed. He could feel himself go. It was a beautiful feeling, that moment before he nodded off, and he tried to stay like that, hold himself in that perfect moment for a little while… The wind rose. He jolted. He looked about at the cold damp reality of a deep deep grave.

He sat up, rolled onto his knees then stood. An urgency came upon him, and he tried once more to pull himself from the grave. More earth fell and he pulled again, this time more desperate.

'Steady, old boy,' he heard himself say and he looked at the heap of earth growing at his feet. He could at least keep pulling earth from the sides until he had enough to make a step or a mound, he thought, and he could use that to boost him up the sides – then he spotted the pickaxe.

After some consideration, he upended the pick in a corner of the hole and used it as a step to climb from the grave, then used the shovel to retrieve the pick. He threw the tools on the ground and stood there for a moment looking into the hole. He thought about jumping back in without the tools. He didn't know why, but he could've jumped back in that hole as easily as gone home, and if it weren't for Chubs' body back at the house, he reckoned he'd be down there now.

'Come on, shit to do,' he said to himself.

He covered the hole with branches, stashed the tools nearby, returned to the quad and made his way back to the farmhouse.

As he shot back west, he caught sight of the old Cromby homestead, Kilduggart Hall, to the north. He turned the quad and made for the old ruin. The afternoon sun caught the old house and Clifford marvelled at its magnificence as he stopped by its great gates. He'd never understood why his family had abandoned such a fine home. He climbed from the quad and ventured over the perimeter wall to the overgrown yet still impressive courtyard to the rear of the house. The kitchen door, pining on its hinges, swung as he approached and he took it as an invitation. In the kitchen, he pulled a chair from the dusty table and sat in the afternoon gloom of the mansion's east wing. A draught from the depths of the vast halls sucked the adjoining door shut with a slam and he rose, chuckling at the gaiety of it all. He ventured along the corridor that led from the kitchen until he arrived at the old ballroom, where his attention was drawn to a descending staircase in the far corner of the great hall. He took the stairs one at a time, squinting into the blackness rising at his feet. A cool damp pool of abandoned space gathered at his waist, then swallowed him whole as he took the remaining steps down. He took a match from his pocket, struck it, and held it to the darkness where he found himself in the expanse of the old wine cellar. There were four alcoves. Two on the left and two on the right that enclosed a large open space at the centre of the vault. The alcoves were shelved within save for the last where the shelves had been removed, and it called to mind the cells and dungeons from the movies of his childhood. Some old western or the *Count of Monte Cristo*, he thought, and he chuckled as he imagined the space filled with captives. Long-haired pirate types in loincloths, all withered and manged, pleading for *agua!* Or maybe they didn't have to be crusty voiced, mangey old bastards, he thought. What if the cells were filled with Olympic swimmers in their speedos and caps? Or full of young men like Chubs? All different types, but younger. Not too young, mind. Older than twelve, but younger than sixteen would be about right. *I'm not a total fucking pervert*, he told himself.

It made perfect sense to him. He could rescue homeless or troubled lads from the streets of Cork city and give them refuge within these walls. He would make the place nice, better than the streets anyway. They'd be queuing up to get in here. Of course it would have its advantages, he weighed. He didn't visualise or contemplate that aspect too much, he wasn't fully comfortable with that idea yet. But whether or not he liked it, he knew it was happening, and he could do fuck all about it. He was on autopilot now, at the mercy of some pedo homunculus within.

He left Kilduggart Hall and headed back to the farmhouse. He pottered about the house, making tea and tidying up from the evening before. After nightfall, he took Chubs' body from the room upstairs, concealed it beneath a tarp, then he placed it in a trailer attached to the quad. He checked the ropes were tight, then he set off across the estate until he reached the woods. He lifted the body from the trailer, walked it to the grave, and lowered it in. As he stood there in the moonlight, filling the grave, he marvelled at the expanse of the wood with its tree trunks standing proud against the evening's lunar hue, and he reckoned he could bury no end of bodies out there. He drove back to the farmhouse and slept.

In the morning, he rose early, went to the living room and lit the fire. When the fire was strong, he went back upstairs, where he shaved and dressed. Afterwards, he removed some vital documents from the home safe and put them in the estate office on the other side of the yard. He returned to the house, piled the fire high, and allowed it to take while he ate his breakfast in the kitchen. After breakfast, he went to the shed, took a rake from the wall and a gallon drum of petrol that he laid by the backdoor. He parked the Jaguar by the door, put the convertible roof down, then returned to the living room and raked the fire onto the floor and rug, then he walked calmly to the fountain in the yard, where he cleaned the rake and returned it to the shed and its place on the wall. He locked the front door of the house and watched through the window; the fire spread through the family room and into the kitchen. He climbed into his Land Rover, drove to Mass then continued on to Midleton for Sunday lunch.

He was making short work of a peach flan when the waiter came and placed his hand on his shoulder.

'There's a telephone call for you, Mr Cromby,' he told him, then led him to the reception.

'Hello, Clifford speaking… a fire? Is it the house or an outbuilding? Are there any animals trapped…? Yes of course… I'll be there in fifteen minutes…'

He paid his bill, jumped in his Land Rover and drove to the smouldering rubble of his former home, where he watched the Jag, parked to the rear of the house in a ball of black smoke, with glee.

Result, he thought, and smiled.

In the weeks that followed, he submitted an insurance claim and commissioned a new modern home to replace the burnt-out farmhouse. A battle with local planners ensued, from which Clifford emerged triumphant, and in the eighteen months that followed, an ultra-modern statement home rose from the ashes.

Kilduggart Hall received a new roof. Clifford insisted on reusing the old tiles. The roofers peeled back the ivy covering part of the old roof and replaced it after the repairs were complete. They made the old windows good where necessary. Clifford opted to paint clear varnish over the existing paintwork, ensuring the frames were watertight but kept their aged and weathered look, the intention to affect a neglected facade yet the house was sound within.

He transformed the basement into a four cell fortress. He secured each cell with a steel gate, then marvelled at his ingenuity as he held each cell door open, released it, then watched with sheer glee as it slammed closed under the force of its integrated spring mechanism. Time after time he would stand outside a cell, open and release the steel gate, marvelling at its satisfying *CLUNK* as it swung closed, then automatically locked tight. The gates had been supplied by Christy Joyce, a bare-knuckle boxing champ and master craftsman, and though Clifford had no hand in their crafting, he took great pride in their ingenuity, as if he'd made the gates himself.

A concealed entrance within the ballroom's elaborate bookcase secured the top of the stairs. The estate house was then ringed by a fence that was twice as high as the tallest man and marked as 'derelict and dangerous'. The paddocks surrounding the old ruin were planted with brambles, thorns, hollies and all manner of hostile shrubs Clifford salvaged from the estate's vast border and transferred one by one, making the paddocks impassable. Impassable, to the untrained eye, for indeed there was a pass if one knew where to tread. Clifford tended that meandering pass with such care and attention that one could easily get lost in its terrible maze if you weren't familiar with its twists and turns. He instructed all farm hands that the old stately home was in a ruinous condition and access was forbidden. When asked, Clifford would reply that he had secured the house as best he could and perhaps in the future he would look to renovate the old place, but for now it was too dangerous. In the months that followed, he allowed the ruin to settle into its new condition while he planned on how best to fill its vaults.

When enough time had passed and the old mansion had been obscured into its surroundings, Clifford stocked the cells one urchin at a time. Stalk by stalk, he filled his menagerie with Ireland's estranged and destroyed youth. He would watch the comings and goings of young boys in and around homeless shelters for troubled youths in Cork, Limerick and Dublin. He would at first befriend some lad who took his fancy or seemed an easy target, then over the weeks he would groom him, gaining his trust, constantly gathering information about them and their home life. Would they be missed? Are people likely to search for them? Had they a history of running away? Were their parents alive, if so, were they alcohol or drug abusers? Softly, softly, catchee monkey. Then, once he was confident the profile was a good fit for his project, he would drug the lad and transport him to his new and final home in the cellar of Kilduggart Hall.

When the new family member awoke in his cell, it usually took a few days to adjust, but eventually all Clifford's guests learned to play the game. The promise of a bright and prosperous future, once you'd reached sixteen, was usually enough to persuade the poor tormented and neglected souls that their current situation was better than their life on the streets, or with their previous foster families or orphanage cohorts. Some lads who'd come from abusive settings believed their outlook to have improved significantly down there in the cellar with the other boys. Sometimes even Clifford believed it too.

Chapter Fifteen

ENTER BANJO

'THOSE GATES, FIVE GRAND EASY,' Banjo said.

'Five grand?' Mossy gasped. 'Seriously?'

'All day long, and that front door, another two grand,' Banjo added.

'Look at that roof,' he continued. 'That's a good roof and dem windows. They might look old and worn out but dem windows is fresh. Not a single pane broken in the whole house. Some fucker's taking very good care of that house for some reason. God only knows what treasures are stored inside. Fireplaces, balustrades, chandeliers. There might even be paintings still hung on the walls or bookcases burstin' with first editions. They go for a fortune if you know where to take 'em. That's before we ever find Christy's gates.'

'Christy's gates?' Mossy asked.

Banjo shuddered as he recalled the night when he'd gone with his uncle Christy and his father to deliver four steel gates, by moonlight, to the mansion in the valley below.

'I told you. About ten years ago, we delivered them. I'll never forget it as long as I live.'

'You were there?'

'I was there, with me father and me uncle Christy, Halloween night 1989, a Tuesday night I'll never forget, and that hoor led us through that paddock below. And see dem towering bushes, they were only shrubs at the time and there was a long twisty path and he made us follow it, horse cart and all, and when we got to the house, he'd a ramp dug down at the side of it and he'd a section of wall knocked out of the gable end that opened up the yard to the basement. An eerie fuckin' spot, I'll tell ya. And the horse, when it got to the ramp, it bucked and reared and wouldn't take another step and we'd to drag the gates by hand one at a time down into the basement, black and cold as swamp water, and I swore that night, that I'd never set foot on this estate again as long as I lived.'

'Did you ask him what the gates were for?'

'Did I fuck, but Christy did.'

'And?'

'He turned to me with his hands out like Frankenstein and he said, "for keeping naughty boys in", and started towards me, and Christy put his hand on his chest real firm like and yer man laughed, a crazy laugh, and you could tell he wasn't afraid of Christy or anybody and he says, "anyway lads, back to business" and he took a fist of money from his pocket and tipped us well, then he walked us back to the road laughing to himself all the way.'

'Fuck.'

'Fuck indeed.'

'But why is it all boarded up with the danger signs?' Mossy asked, hoping to dissuade Banjo.

'That's the clever part,' Banjo said. 'Make it look like it's fucked and fallin' down but really it's a treasure ship, and we be pirates Mossy boy, we be pirates.' He grabbed Mossy in a playful headlock, wrestling him on the ground before correcting himself and remembering they were on a stakeout.

They'd been watching the old Cromby estate house on and off for weeks now, and Banjo and Mossy were convinced more and more with each passing day that someone was keeping something very dear to their heart within those walls. The apparent abandonment didn't stack up when put under scrutiny. The newish roof, the windows, the fella on his quad coming and going at quare hours, often staying late into the night, taking great care to lock up, picking his way carefully through acres of brambles when leaving.

It's all too… too what? Banjo thought as he lay in the hedge, Mossy by his side, staking the place out for the third time that week. For the want of a better word he settled on: 'Pretended, it's all too pretended.'

'Pretended,' Mossy concurred. 'Pretended.'

Chapter Sixteen

FIVE GRAND

SHE SAT AT THE KITCHEN table smoking her third fag. The clock above the cooker read nine-fifteen. She had her first fag each morning after Annie left for school at ten to, so that made it three fags in twenty-five minutes. *Not quite chain smoking but fair goin' all the same*, she thought. Not in a *well done* kind of way, but more of a *slow the fuck down girl* sort of thing.

The brown envelope, lying there in the middle of the table, really bothered her. She wanted to keep it. I mean, she needed it badly. Well, not 'badly', but she could do with it. It wasn't like they were starving or anything. Money was tight alright, but money was always tight, and she was definitely in over her head, but…

She picked it up, put it back down, then picked it up again and hefted the weight of it. It was a tidy bundle, she thought enviously. She placed it back on the table, looked at it for the last time, then decided. Her mind was made up, and that was that. She was gonna get the bus out to Blackrock and speak with him. She couldn't give it to Daniel. He was a disgrace. He'd spend it in a week and before you know it, there'd be some other crook round here on a motorbike looking for The Boy and sure, hadn't he been through enough, the poor crater? She'd do the right thing and give him back the money. Anyway, wasn't it only torture, lookin' at it.

She stuck on the kettle and sparked up a last tab. She'd wait until half past, then she'd walk down to the post office, pick up her giro and head out to see him.

*

On the bus, she realised she'd never been to Blackrock before. Not even the castle. I mean, every dope and his dog had been to Blackrock Castle. *Every dope but me*, she thought, *the story of my life*. She thought about her old fella and her husband and yer man at school with the big mickey… Benny… fuckin' Benny. She laughed. Three arseholes that fucked up her life. Poor ould Benny wasn't that bad, she conceded, but the other two. A rotten pair of yolks if ever there were two rotten yolks. She stopped herself.

'Not today, Brida,' she sighed. 'Give yourself a day off pet, one day… you deserve that.' Out the window she saw a sign for Castle Road. *Jaysus, that's me*, she thought, rising to her feet and calling to the driver. 'Let me off here for God's sake, I was miles away.'

'No problem love, do you know what stop you want?' the driver asked.

'Kind of,' she replied. 'I'm on the right road, but I'm not sure of the exact house. It's past the castle on the right. The third house, I think.'

'No worries, we're not quite there yet. Sit down a few minutes and I'll give you a shout when we get there.'

'Thanks love,' she said, sitting back down then checking her bag, the envelope safe within.

A few minutes later, she stirred from a daydream.

'This is us here now, love,' the driver said, pulling in. 'The houses here are spread out nicely, so you should find it easy enough.'

'Good man, and where do I get the bus back in later?' she asked.

'Walk back the road a bit. There's a stop before the castle, well… beyond the castle. Before if you're coming out from town and beyond if you're goin' in. Know what I mean?'

'I think so, thank you,' she answered, looking at him, confused.

She walked along the road, looking in at the first house. She'd know Albert's car if she saw it, she thought.

No car, great. The next house had a high gate, and she had to strain on her tiptoes to look over. Inside the gate, she could see Albert's black Mercedes. There was a bell to the side, and she pressed it, uncertain, then waited a few moments.

'Hello,' came a lady's electronic voice from a speaker on the wall.

'Hello,' Brida responded, casting her voice over the gate, not placing much faith in the technology. 'My name is Brida Scully; I'm a neighbour of Daniel and...'

'Ah Brida, how are ya?' came the voice. 'I'm opening the gate there now. Come up to the house.'

The gate opened slowly, and Brida walked up the drive, unsure of what she'd say next. Ann came to the door and stood there rubbing her arms, looking left and right about the garden.

'Hi Ann,' Brida called as she approached, her arms apart. She gave her a warm hug and Ann guided her through to the kitchen.

'Come in Brida, are you alright?' Ann enquired, genuine concern in her voice. 'Sorry about the gates, himself insists on keeping them locked until things settle down a bit, sure you know what it's like. Tea... or coffee... something else?' She winked, opening the fridge door and pulling out a bottle of Chardonnay.

'Tea's fine, Ann, seriously,' Brida protested as she watched Ann fill two glasses, regardless.

'You are a terrible woman,' she added as she took the glass from Ann. 'How are ye all getting on?' Brida asked, not sure what else to say.

'We are grand, sure you know yourself; there's good days and bad days and there's days that are neither good nor bad, which I think are the worst. At least when you're feeling like crap you can get on with it and push through, but a day where you don't know how you feel drags on and on, and you end up going over everything a hundred times. Should I have done this or that and all the what ifs? It's great when people call, and sure he's great company, the poor wee crater.'

'I know, I know – it sounds to me like the middle of the road days should be written off as bad ones, pet. Sure it's impossible not to keep goin' over it again and again. It's only natural. How's Albert doing?' Brida added, almost as an afterthought.

'He's busy with the shop. It does him good to have a routine. I mean the lads could look after the shop, but it's the familiarity that keeps him sane. I thought he was gonna go in the river when he got the news about our Fallon. He doted on that boy. He's nuts about the two of them but when he heard that the poor lad had been…' Ann put the tea towel to her face, wiped her eyes and shook her head. 'I'm sorry… when he heard what they did to him, I thought it would be the end of him. All those years he worried and fretted about our Feargal, and finally now when it seems like Feargal is out the other side this goes and happens. It knocked him for six, but he's doing a wee bit better now. He needs his routine so I'll not stop him going into the shop each day if it means he's not here traipsing about the place trying to make sense of it all.' She stopped, placed her thumb to her mouth and gnawed at a whitlow nail, her gaze fixed on the ragged flame in the fireplace beyond, casting her thoughts to the crackle and fizz, lost in a hypnotic disequilibrium that carried her aloft to some place beyond, Brida's voice a tether through the haze.

'We all have our own ways of coping,' Brida said, interrupting Ann's moment of reverie. 'And The Boy? My heart breaks for him. His mother first, then Fallon. He worshipped the ground Fallon walked on.' She lowered her voice, fearful he might hear.

'I don't think he's quite grasped it yet. He was bad for a week or more. He was going around like a little ghost. The doctor had to give him something to steady him. He seems better now though, but it's early days. I'd say he has a few bad days ahead of him yet. He was a bit better when Feargal was around, but since he went back, he seems a bit lost again. That young fella of the Mulcahys, Gordon, has been out a few times, though, and they play video games and walk up to the shop. He's up there now with him. Albert doesn't like them goin' too far though, in case… you know…' Ann let the thought hang, her attention drawn once again to the mantel's crackle and fizz, before she continued.

'Brida, I know Marie was very badly off the last while and I know she was a terror for asking friends and so on for money. God knows she'd a path worn to my door looking for handouts. If you knew of anyone that Marie owed money to or anything like that, would you let them know I'd be more than happy to put things right? I know only too well what it's like to be owed money you are relying on, and I would be heartbroken if I wasn't able to make amends on her behalf. I would hate for Marie's legacy with her friends or neighbours to be tainted by something like that… Do you know what I mean?'

Ann held Brida's gaze. Brida gazed back and held Ann's hands.

Hold on a minute, Brida thought to herself, *she thinks I'm here because Marie owes me money.* She was about to blurt some protestation when she stopped herself short, took a deep breath and replied.

'That's very decent of you Ann, if I hear of anyone, I will let them know. You are very kind,' meaning every word.

'Unless they are drug dealers,' Ann said, 'then they can feck off.' She slapped Brida on the knee, relieved that the crudity of finance was removed from the equation, before continuing: 'I really appreciate you staying with my boys after they were attacked, Brida. It would break my heart if I thought he was on his own and frightened. It was a kind thing you did staying with them until the Guards came. We really appreciate it, and we won't forget it. If there's ever anything we can do… I mean it Brida, anything.'

'Ah, will you stop? Anyone woulda done the same.'

'Anyone could've, but they didn't. There was a lot of curtain twitchin' and no action went on that night. You came straight out and let those rotten bastards have it and then you stayed with my boys, and that takes real guts. God knows what the poor crater might've done if you weren't there,' Ann said.

'Ah, will ya stop, anyway I'm glad to hear he's doin' better. I wanted to pop out and say hello. I was going to ring, but I didn't have a number,' Brida added.

'He's upstairs playing video games there now. Will I give him a shout, he'd be delighted to see ya,' Ann said, adding 'I'll call him there for ya,' shouting up the stairs. 'Will ya come down a minute love, Brida Scully is here to say hello.'

'Coming now, Nan,' The Boy shouted back, then he jumped up from the beanbag and scampered down the stairs.

'Hi Mrs Scully, how are ya?' he asked, poking his head around the kitchen door.

'I'm grand, don't mind me. How are you? You're looking smashing,' she said.

He tutted, looked at the ground and said, 'I'm grand, I'm going back to school on… is it this Monday Nan?'

'It is,' Ann replied. 'He'll travel into town in the morning with his Granda and get a lift out again in the evening.'

'Ahh, great, it'll be lovely to get to school and see all your pals,' Brida said as The Boy joined them by the fire, and they chatted. After a while Brida stood up, took her coat from the back of the chair.

'I'd better head back into town,' she started. 'Annie will be gettin' in from school at three. I've loads of time, but I don't wanna risk it.'

'Are you driving?' Ann asked.

'No, I got the bus out. They are fairly regular, so I should be alright.'

'Ah Jaysus, you shoulda said, I'll drop you in the road. Albert's car is there. He got a taxi earlier. He's going for a drink after work,' she said, rolling her eyes.

'You will not. Between us we've polished off that bottle. I'll get the bus in. It's no bother at all.'

'Are you sure? Jaysus, I feel desperate,' Ann said.

'I'm grand. I need to remember where the stop is, but once I've that worked out, I'll be on the road in no time.'

'I know where the stop is. I'll walk you down. Is that alright Nan?' The Boy asked.

'Of course it is love.'

Ann pulled Brida in and gave her a long hug. 'I'll give you my number,' she said, and she went to the sideboard, wrote it on a piece of paper, then handed it to Brida. 'You be sure and ring me if you need anything. Take yourself and Annie into my Albert's and get yourselves some new shoes… on me. I'll tell him to keep an eye out for ye. I mean it.'

Brida smiled, gave her one last hug, then left with The Boy.

They walked along Castle Road together in silence. As they rounded the corner, The Boy looked back over his shoulder, then turned to Brida.

'I'm sorry I didn't come and see you sooner, Mrs Scully. I've been a mess. I didn't mean to ask you to mind the money that night. I didn't think Fallon was gonna… I thought he was only hurt. The money was for Mam's funeral, and I thought the Guards would take it off me. I didn't think it was gonna be this long before I saw ya. I'm really sorry.'

'Don't be silly love, I'm not cross, I understand. I only called in case you needed the money back. I wasn't sure if it was yours or maybe someone was looking for it or you might be in some kind of trouble,' Brida told him as she took him by the hand.

'Thanks Mrs Scully, sound. The money was Fallon's. We had it to pay for Mam, but it all went arseways. Nobody's looking for me… or it. I hope you weren't worrying too much. I'm grand honestly…'

Brida stepped from the path into an archway, reached in her bag, retrieved the envelope and handed it to The Boy, who took it in his hands, looked over his shoulder, then tucked it expertly in his waistband.

'I need to sort out a few bits and pieces,' he told her. 'I don't know who paid for Mam or Fallon's funerals or what I'm supposed to do with this money now, but once I've got my head around all that I'll come and see you right... I promise.'

'What are you talking about?' Brida said watching her tone, careful not to upset him knowing his heart was in the right place. 'You don't need to do anything for me... look after yourself and don't be worrying about funerals or paying off debts. Your uncle Feargal and your Granda aren't short a few bob, so there's no need for you to be worrying about things like that... Do you hear me?' She looked him straight in the eye then gave him an old Mammy hug.

He nodded in agreement, as a tear formed in his right eye.

'Now, where's this bus stop?' she asked him.

'That's it there,' he replied, pointing across the road. 'Here's one now. This one'll take you all the way in.'

He hugged her once more, then he turned to the bus, and he waved it down.

'Look after yourself,' she said.

'I will... Thank you.'

'For what? Behave yourself,' she said, then she turned to the driver.

'Hello again, you worked it out, I see,' the driver remarked.

'I had a little help,' she said, waving to The Boy as the bus door closed. The Boy waited until the bus departed, then bolted down the road, up the drive, into the house and straight back up the stairs. Ann sat by the mantel's blaze chatting to herself or some other departed since, called to him as he passed.

'Are you alright love?'

'Grand,' he called back. 'Give us a shout when tea's ready,' and he turned to Gordon, pulled the five grand from his trouser belt, threw it on the bed and said, 'Wait'll you get a load of this...'

Chapter Seventeen

FUNERAL HOME

THE FIRST THING THEY BOUGHT was a games console. A PS1 and a blast of games. They'd had their eye on the PS1 for a long time, but the idea they'd ever own one had been a pipe dream. A pipe dream until Brida'd rocked up with Fallon's money.

'Where'd ya get that?' Ann had asked.

'It's Gordon's. His Mam said we can keep it here, cos he's over here so much and I've no games,' The Boy lied.

He remembered the sudden pang of guilt that had spread across Ann's face. He felt bad now as he recalled the memory, sat on the bed with Gordon at his feet playing *FIFA: Road to World Cup '98.*

It was brilliant. Gordon, a total football nut, was winning. The Boy was glad of the company and, even though he wasn't any good at it, he enjoyed the craic. There was a new game on the way though, and from what he'd read it would be right up his alley. *Grand Theft Auto.* He couldn't wait. He'd had sleepless nights imagining what this new game might be like.

Gordon jumped from the floor. 'Eat that motherfucker!' he shouted. He'd won. The Boy hadn't noticed.

'Right,' The Boy said. 'I'm goin' to town, are you coming with me or not?'

'Yeah, I'll come. I told ya I would.'

'Good, come on then.'

'Let's have one more game.'

'No… I'm goin' now and you're not stayin' here with my Nan.'

'Why not? I'm sure she'd be delighted to have me,' Gordon jibed.

'Weirdo.'

'Ooh Ann… are you sure Albie won't be home early? Let me lock the front door, to be on the safe side…'

The Boy laughed, rolled his eyes, then walked to the hall and called down to Ann.

'Nan! Gordon wants to stay here and kiss you while I head up to the shops.'

Gordon sprang to his feet. 'Shut up, you langer!' he hissed.

'What's that love?' Ann called up from the kitchen.

'We are heading up to the shop. We'll be back in a bit,' The Boy replied as they walked down the stairs.

'Okay, love, take your jacket. It's spitting rain out there – don't be too long. Will you take your key…? I might pop out myself.'

'Okay Nan, see you in a bit,' The Boy replied. Gordon winked at Ann as they passed. Ann, unsure, winked back.

On the bus, Gordon rattled on about his favourite subject, Manchester United, or more specifically, Roy Keane – Gordon called him 'Roy'. The Boy hated football. He hated all sports. It wasn't his thing. He wasn't sure yet what his thing was, music perhaps. Or clothes. He loved clothes. They both did. Gordon always had the latest Air Max sneakers and snazzy tracksuits. The Boy's Granda had a shoe shop in town, so he was never wanting of a good pair of shoes, but Gordon's Air Max collection did cause The Boy some envy. Not in a mean way. He loved Gordon and was happy for him, but Jaysus he loved his trainers too. He looked up as they approached the bus station.

'Right, this is us,' he said, rising to his feet.

O'Meara's funeral home was an old family business. A Cork City stalwart. They'd buried more than half of the Northside's dead.

'Let me do the talkin,' Gordon said as they arrived at reception.

'What? Will you sit down over there and keep quiet?'

'No, let me do the talkin' You're too upset. I'm happy to do this for you,' he added, looking The Boy in the eye.

'Sit down, you bender,' The Boy demanded as a tall, portly man in his fifties strode from the rear of the shop, put his two hands on the counter and asked in an exhausted tone, 'Right lads, what can I do ye for?'

The Boy, thrown by the exchange, stammered, 'I'd like to pay a bill, I…' then, losing his train of thought, stopped a moment as Gordon sprang to his feet.

'What my friend here is trying to say is that he'd like to know if there's any money owing on his…' he paused. He thought a moment. 'On his…' he repeated then looked to The Boy.

'On his…?' O'Meara said.

The Boy smiled.

'Are you Jimmy Mulcahy's lad?' O'Meara asked Gordon before turning to The Boy. 'Is he alright, I mean, in the head?'

'I'm not sure. I think he might have some ailment as yet undiscovered,' The Boy replied, and they both laughed.

'Right, right, right,' the undertaker said, pointing at The Boy, a look of realisation growing on his face. 'I have you now, you are Marie's lad,' clicking his fingers trying to recall. 'And… Fallon's brother.'

'I wanted to talk to you about the cost of their services and all that. I didn't want there to be any money owing or anything. I don't really know how it works, but I know it costs money, so…'

'So, you wanted to make sure it was all sorted and above board, that is very admirable. Normally I wouldn't talk about this sort of thing with someone as young as yourself but because you've brought your legal counsel with you today,' he said, nodding at Gordon, 'I think we can all speak like men, agreed?'

'Shoot,' Gordon replied. 'Now we are talking,' as he advanced towards the counter rubbing his hands.

'Right… Anyway. Your brother Fallon had an insurance policy

that took care of his costs, and your grandparents covered your Mam. I'm telling you this *mano a mano*, okay? So I don't want you going home telling anybody that we've had this conversation. You look like a good lad trying to do the right thing and I don't want you worrying about stuff like this, so…'

'Understood.' The Boy nodded before continuing. 'What about gravestones, and the like?'

'All sorted.'

'The flowers?'

'The same. It's all taken care of. Go home, relax. If you've got money to spend, then go buy some ice cream or something, but be careful not to give him too much sugar,' he said, then nodded at Gordon.

'This conversation never took place,' Gordon added, backing towards the door.

'Thanks Mr O'Meara,' The Boy said, and he offered his hand.

O'Meara took The Boy's hand and shook it. He looked him in the eye. 'You look after yourself son,' he said.

The Boy nodded, turned for the door and went outside.

'Right, where to now?' Gordon asked.

'The St Leger,' The Boy said. 'Are ya coming?'

'I hate the Leger. It stinks of piss.'

'We won't go in.'

The St Leger Arms was not a child friendly pub. Its patrons consisted for the most part of single men who kept to themselves. At the weekends the tone livened a little as couples and groups from the nearby estates stopped in for a few on their way to town, but, come Monday morning, it fast descended into stout-slurping loneliness. Its maroon carpets stunk of beer and piss and its wood-panelled walls had a thin sticky layer of tar and nicotine, and it was rumoured around the Blackpool estates that its patrons could oft be found licking the walls for the want of a fag on a Monday evening, as they waited in torment for their dole on a Tuesday.

Drink, you could get on tick, but fags were another matter. If you'd no coin for the machine you'd be going without.

They crossed the road. The Boy stood by the side door and motioned for Tony to meet him in the alleyway, with his index finger to his lips, followed by a wink. Tony threw his bar towel on the counter and made his way through the back of the bar to the adjacent alleyway, where The Boy waited by the back stairs.

'What's the craic kid?' Tony asked. 'I haven't seen you in ages, you alright?'

'Ah yeah, grand. I'm at me nan's for a few weeks. I'll be back soon enough. How's Daniel doing? I hope he's not giving you too much grief.'

'Will ya stop? He has me driven mad. He's grand though.'

'How's his tab goin?'

'Ah well, I've lost count,' he laughed, then looked back toward the bar.

'Seriously, how much is he in for?'

'I honestly don't know.'

'Three hundred?'

'Hmm…'

'More?'

'A bit.'

'Five?'

'You're getting warm.'

'A grand?'

'Somewhere around there. He gets his royalty cheque or something every December, so I don't mind letting it build up. And he always pays.'

The Boy reached into his pocket. He'd divided the money into one thousand punt bundles earlier that day. He pulled out one stack and handed it to Tony, then pulled out another and did the same.

'There's two grand there, that should keep him goin' a while. I'll be back in a few weeks to see how he's doin'.'

'Where'd you get this from?' Tony asked.

'Don't let that bother ya, it's his share, so don't worry, it's not my money. Tell your Mam I said hello.'

'I will, good man. Will ya have a Coke or something? I'll bring 'em out here if you like.'

'Nah, you're grand. I'm gonna head back out to Blackrock. My nan'll be freakin' out wonderin' where I am.'

'Good luck… thanks,' Tony said.

He hefted the money in his hand. He knew drug money when he saw it, and this was drug money all day long. He watched them cross the road and head for the bus stop. He felt bad for taking it, but there was something about The Boy. He had an authority or commanding nature that belied his age. He thought about running after them and asking if everything was alright, but he knew it wasn't. How could it be? Anyway, they'd only lie. A punter called his name, and he turned to the bar.

'Coming,' he called back. He looked to the road again. They were gone.

The punter called his name again and he turned and headed back to the bar.

Chapter Eighteen

LONELY

DANIEL STOOD UP FROM THE bar, steadied himself on the rail, let go cautiously, then stumbled back onto a table of locals.

'For fuck's sake Daniel!'

'Sorry lads, fuckin' hell, I didn't see ye there. Will ye… will ye have a drink?'

'No, you're grand. Are you going home or to the toilet?'

'What?'

'Come on to fuck,' the local said as he helped Daniel into his jacket, then walked him to the door. 'Will you be okay from here?' he asked, releasing Daniel like a cupped bird to the world, waiting at the front door.

'I am, I am, I am. Thank you kindly, kind sir. You're a good skin, I promise you faithfully…' Daniel mumbled, then he walked on past the chipper until he reached the cul-de-sac where he eyed his house across the green. The house spun like a kaleidoscope, and he ambled in its direction until he reached the gate where he stopped for a moment, sat on the kerb and stroked the ground where Fallon had ceased. He remembered Fallon in Marie's arms dancing in the high garden on Lovers Walk. Laughing and spinning around and around in fits of delight, safe in his mother's arms, each oblivious to the other's fate, happy in that moment, forever now in Daniel's mind.

He rose, stumbled for the gate, then fumbled his way to the front door. In the hall, he felt his way blindly along the wainscoting until he reached the kitchen, where he opened the back door and stepped onto the small porch that led out to the garden. In the porch's corner, he reached into the small wooden box and retrieved the rope. He placed the rope under his arm, then he positioned a plastic chair beneath the centre joist of the pergola. Sitting for a moment, he checked the noose, then stood on the chair and passed the rope over the joist. He passed the noose through a loop at the loose end and let it fall so it hung at his chest. The chair wobbled beneath his weight, and he used the rope to steady himself before placing the noose around his neck, then he pulled the knot tight to his artery. He put his hands by his sides and rocked the chair back and forth as memories of Fallon and Marie came flooding back and he sobbed there for a while. He steadied himself, wiped his nose on his sleeve, then stood on the chair, sniffling for some time. With the noose tight at his neck, he prayed for the backbone to kick out the chair and end it all in an instant. *That one flash of courage is all it would take to release me at last*, he thought. He stood a while longer until he realised that tonight would not be the night, then he wiped the snot and tears with the heels of his hands, loosened the noose, unlooped the hoop, stepped from the chair and placed the rope neatly back in its box where it nestled like a coiled snake, waiting.

Chapter Nineteen

THE BOOK OF DANIEL

Part II

'WHAT IS IT?' FINTAN ASKED.

'It's my project… for the Aer Lingus Young Scientist competition.'

'I know that, but what is it?'

'I told ya, a backwards clock.'

'What do you mean, a backwards clock?'

'It can reverse time, well theoretically anyway,' Daniel explained. 'It takes longer to reverse the time than the time you've actually reversed but in theory if we had a computer that could perform the reversal quickly enough then we could travel back in time.'

'But time is linear son, there is no such thing as the past, there's only now,' Fintan exclaimed, rather proud of himself but aware still he was no match for his son.

'How do you know?'

'Well, I don't but…'

'Exactly… don't get me wrong, I'm not saying that we can travel back and run with the dinosaurs. But what I am saying is… if we could make my quantum computer with enough processing power, we could, in theory, recreate the past. Doing it, however, would be another challenge, but in theory it's possible.'

'And this design of yours is what could make it possible?'

'Kind of… the only problem is… Do you see that bit here that says "Q.C."?' Daniel said, pointing to the diagram.

'Yeah… what's that?'

'That's the quantum computer that doesn't exist.'

'What does it do, the computer?'

'Basically… it calculates every parameter and force involved in the mighty unison of a single moment, then reproduces them in reverse and reverses them again and does that billions and billions of times per second, so the user experiences them in sequence.'

'Jaysus… that's amazing. Do you reckon it'd work?'

'Course I do, and what's more is I can prove it.'

'Fuck me pink! You need to write this shit down, son. Why don't you send it to that science magazine you read and have them look at it? You could be onto something massive here. Forget about Butlins, we could set up a time travel company. We could have the Viking experience or people could experience death, but then someone would travel back to before the event and stop them from repeating the process and travel with them back to the present.'

'You're melting my brain. Will ya stop? The assessors will review it at the Young Scientist, sure they'll know.'

'You'd be surprised. They're probably all as thick as shite.'

'I doubt they're thick as shite, but I know what ya mean.'

'Right,' Fintan committed. 'We are taking this to the Young Scientists. We'll fuckin' show 'em!'

Dr Christensen looked at Daniel's diagram. His pursed lips and flared nostrils suggested he was deep in consideration. His eyes looked at the drawing, then at Daniel, then back to the drawing. He repeated this action over and over then finally, after some time, opened his mouth to speak, closed it again then walked away wagging his finger as though words were being said in his head, but he could not form them on his tightly pursed lips. Daniel watched as he disappeared through a door marked 'Private'.

Ignorant prick, Daniel thought.

'Dr Beckett, I have a young man who claims to have invented the means to travel through time,' Christensen said.

'A time machine? This should be interesting.'

'Well, there's no actual machine, but there's an equation that is quite impressive. To be honest, it's beyond me. I was hoping you might take a look?'

'A "daddy" job?'

'Maybe.'

'No problem. I'll get down there in a bit. A certain politician's niece is in the competition, and he wants to bring her submission to my attention personally.'

'The fucking neck on some people.'

'I know, right?' Beckett replied, checking his reflection in the mirror. The white lab coat, the thick-rimmed glasses and scruffy mass of hair that stood outright from his head were all meticulously dishevelled. He was the real deal.

Daniel waited and waited. Christensen didn't return. At five o'clock, he overheard the lads from Roscommon at the table next to him talking.

'They're announcing the finalists,' they said.

'They're what?' Daniel asked.

'The finalists, they're announcing them now.'

'No one even looked at mine properly. How do you know if you're a finalist?' he asked them.

'They've already told them. I think they make the announcement so the non-finalists know they can fuck off home,' and they laughed.

'Fucking bullshit,' Daniel sighed, and he picked up his jacket and headed for the door. He'd been noticing it all day, the haze. He'd managed to keep it at bay, but now he knew there was no stopping it.

'Well?' Fintan asked, waiting in the car.

'No joy.'

'What?'

'They've chosen the finalists and I'm not one of them. Can we go? I feel sick.'

'Your stomach?'

'Yeah,' he replied, and he put his belt on and rolled to the side. He didn't understand what happened to him when the fog came and he needed to retreat from everything. There was no rhyme or reason to it. Sometimes there were triggers or signs, but normally he'd notice it coming a day or two in advance and then it'd be there, and he'd take to the bed until it passed, and it'd be like some long weird dream where he'd grumble and sigh when they'd ask if he was alright.

'My tummy is at me,' he'd tell them, and that would be that. They'd mollycoddle him for a few days and then one day he'd wake up feeling better and he'd get back to it, the slow climb out of it. This one was the same, although it had come on faster than usual. When they got home from Dublin, he took to the bed.

'Is he alright?' Mags asked.

'It's his tummy.'

'What about the competition?'

'They announced the finalists, I think, and he wasn't one of them.'

'You think?'

'That's what he told me.'

'Poor little crater. Bunch of thickos. They wouldn't know their arses from their elbows.'

'Thick as shit.'

Christensen put his coat on and watched Beckett put the finishing touches to the list of finalists.

'Are you happy with the choices?' he asked.

'I dunno. There are so many. I can't even remember half of them.'

'It's the same every year. Sometimes it's easier when the likes of our politician friend forces our hand.'

'I know,' Beckett replied, and they laughed.

'What did you make of our friend with the time machine?'

'The time machine… oh shit. I never made it over to him. Fuck. How good was it?'

'Well, I don't know but it was next-level maths, that's for sure.'

'Fuck, fuck, fuck. Is he gone?'

'Oh yes, they are all gone home. He'll be back in the morning, though. You can look then. We can hold off with the finalist list until after we speak with him.'

'Where is it, his display?'

'I'll show you as we walk out. It's on the way. Are we going for a pint, or do you have plans?'

'I'll go for a pint.'

'Come on then, I'll show you the time machine as we leave.'

Beckett looked at the formula. Then at Christensen.

'What age was he?' he asked.

'Fifteen, sixteen, I'm not sure.'

'This is serious maths, and it makes sense. I think,' Beckett said, then he went to the start of the equation again and worked it across. The individual components seemed to glow or come alive as he passed until at last he got to the end and the whole thing shone. Beckett took a step back and read it once more to make sure that he was seeing it correctly. His eyes filled with tears, and he had to steady himself on a table. He checked it again and then again. Each time, it became more and more clear as its potential dawned on him.

'Can you see it?' he asked Christensen.

'No, I cannot. I know it's brilliant, but I can't see it. What is it? Tell me.'

Beckett walked him through, explaining as he went. Christensen looked at him blankly.

'One more time, please,' Christensen asked. Beckett started at the start and walked Christensen through again. As they reached the end, Beckett heard a sharp intake of breath as Christensen gasped at the realisation, then fell to his knees.

'Do you see it?' Beckett asked.

'I do, I do!' Christensen said as he rose and hugged his colleague, and they looked at each other with the eyes of men released from blindness.

'This changes everything,' Christensen sobbed. 'Everything.'

'We'll speak to him in the morning.'

They had a jar of phosphorus, the boys from Roscommon. They'd taken it for the craic. They weren't even sure what they were going to do with it or what they could do with it, but they knew it was explosive, and that was all they needed to know. Eamonn had put it in his school bag and transported it all the way from Roscommon on the school bus to the RDS in Dublin.

'Ya mad fucker,' Donal said.

'I know, right?' Eamonn replied as he stashed it under the exhibition stand. They thought they could pinch off little bits and throw it at each other and they imagined it making tiny explosions as it hit them.

Donal giggled. It was going to be the best craic ever. They took it from the jar and wrapped it in tissue paper to dry overnight, then they slapped each other on the back for a job well done as they headed out the door in anticipation of the next day's high jinx.

It was a localised blaze, and short-lived. Donal and Eamonn's entry went up in smoke, then the fire spread to Daniel's display. Then it went out. The fire alarm didn't sound, the water sprinklers didn't kick in. In fact, no one even noticed until the next morning when Beckett, who hadn't slept a wink, went in early to gaze upon Daniel's equation one more time.

When Daniel didn't show, Beckett went to the admin desk and got his details. He rang the landline.

'Hello,' Mags said.

'Good morning. My name is Dr Beckett from the Young

Scientist competition at the RDS. Am I speaking with Daniel's mum?'

'Yes, this is Margaret speaking. How may I help you?'

'I don't want to alarm you, but Daniel's exhibition was damaged by a small fire during the night, now nobody was injured but Daniel hasn't turned up to man his display this morning, and we are ringing to see if he's alright or if you've heard from him since yesterday?'

'He's here now, Dr Beckett. He came home with his father yesterday evening. He's in bed. He was very put out, and he's resting upstairs with an upset tummy.'

Upset tummy, Beckett thought. That old chestnut. He'd used it many times himself as a young fella when it all got too much for him.

'Oh, no,' he said. 'I hope he's feeling better this morning. Could I speak with him?'

'Not now. Anyway, I thought he was out of the competition.'

'Why would you say that?'

'His father came in last night and said that Daniel hadn't made it through to the next round and that his entry hadn't even been looked at properly.'

'I think there has been a misunderstanding. If I leave my number, will you ask him to ring me when he's feeling up to it?'

'Hang on, I'll get a pen.'

Daniel stayed in bed for three days. He dreamt he was flying through space and there were people trying to catch up with him. Not in a spaceship or anything fancy like that. He was in his pyjamas hurtling through space, and the stars were numbers and every once in a while he'd hit an asteroid and it'd slow him down and the people who were chasing him would gain on him and he'd have to will himself to get going and he'd remind himself of the impossibility of this without propulsion but he knew it wasn't real and somehow he'd be flying again, and then one day he heard a familiar trill and he saw a hole in space and he flew through the hole and he landed in his room to the sound of the phone ringing. He got out of the bed and went downstairs.

'Hello,' Daniel said into the receiver.

'Daniel?'

'This is Daniel. Who's speaking?'

'Daniel, this is Dr Beckett from the Young Scientist competition. Is this a good time to talk?'

'Yes,' Daniel replied. 'About what?'

'About your exhibition.'

'Okay? How can I help you?'

'There has been a fire, Daniel, and your exhibition, along with the entry beside yours, was destroyed.'

'Okay,' Daniel replied. 'That's okay.'

'Daniel, your formula, could you reproduce it, or do you have other copies of it?'

'Yes, of course, but I don't understand. I thought I was out of the running.'

'The competition is over, Daniel. They have announced the winner, but that's not important. Daniel, your formula. Where did you get it from?'

'I made it up,' Daniel replied. 'Well, I didn't make it up, exactly...' he corrected. 'It has always existed, out there in the ether waiting to be arranged or cajoled in the right order. I only brought all the elements together, so it made sense to fit my requirements. Do you know what I mean?'

'I do,' Beckett replied. 'I do. And tell me, when you wrote the formula, what were you trying to achieve? What I'm asking is: what is it working out?'

'It's the sum of all things,' Daniel replied, and Beckett felt the hairs on his neck stand on end as his eyes glazed over.

Of course, Beckett thought.

'It's a formula that can recreate or quantify everything in the universe,' Daniel continued. 'Of course, you would need to vary the factors, but that is what the accompanying algorithm does. The algorithm identifies and applies the variance to the factors as required. But it's all theoretical, of course. You would need a computer, a quantum computer, to process the algorithm and the associated calculations over and over at a rate that simply isn't possible and probably never will be, but the equation and the algorithm, they are rock solid. Did you see what it does?' Daniel asked.

'Yes, yes, I saw it. Could you talk me through it, though?' Beckett asked. 'I'd love to hear your take on it.' He could feel himself detach from the world as he recalled the equation, simple and brilliant, and he listened as Daniel told of a raindrop and a footstep and how each could be applied and reproduced by varying the formula and as Daniel spoke, Beckett felt the world around him dissolve and he floated in some place where all was one, and his spine rang in some beautiful harmony with all there was in the universe and there was no him, nor it, and Daniel's voice echoed from some place far away and he was talking about true *pi* and how he'd worked out how to produce it, and that anything less in the formula would produce a world like Swiss cheese and he *couldn't express enough how important that was* and nothing was beyond Beckett's comprehension and he thought to pick up a pen to take some notes but the concept of his hand was like some alien thing and the people in the room around him faded into some place parallel and he felt tiny exquisite explosions go off in his mind, and then it sang and he couldn't quite place the source of this elation until he realised it was everywhere and he knew there was no turning back now and he could hear Daniel approaching the end of the equation and he wished it could go on forever until a voice echoed that it would and then he heard Daniel say 'and that's basically it'.

Beckett felt himself ease back into the everyday with all its little aches and pains as the surrounding sounds grew nearer once again and he could feel the phone pressed against his ear. It was some time before he could speak.

'Daniel,' he said. 'You have discovered a formula that is central… fundamental to all things. Do you realise this?'

'Well, I wouldn't put it quite like that,' Daniel said.

'Believe me, this is everything. This formula answers everything.'

'And so what? It changes nothing.'

'No, but it could mean one of two things. Either we are all living in some computer generated existence and nothing is real. Or the central unifying power or life source that binds us all, God, is a mathematical formula that you've discovered.'

'Or… there is no God, and it's all simple science. Or there is a God, and I've worked out the formula he uses or… None of it matters. Perhaps it's some teenage daydream doodle on the back of a homework journal that resonates with lots of different shit and that's all.'

'It's more than that and you know it.'

'Maybe,' Daniel replied. He could feel the haze looming, and he thought he should sit down. The next few days would be hard, he thought. It was always like that after an episode. He'd wake up and it'd be waiting for him like some ould boy sitting on a chair by the bed in his pyjamas waiting, and Daniel would have to choose.

'The hill or the haze?' he'd ask himself. Some days he'd choose the hill, the tough climb out of it and others he'd choose the haze, and himself and the old boy in the pyjamas would go back to the bed and that was about the size of it and there wasn't much else that could be said or done.

'I give lectures at universities around the country,' Beckett started. 'A lot of "what ifs" supported by science. "Imagine this" kind of stuff. It's popular and there's lots of healthy debate and that kind of craic afterwards. I've got six dates coming up over the next few weeks. Would you be interested in coming along with me? You could talk about your formula. It's usually a smart crowd, so they would definitely grasp it. What do you think?'

'I don't know.'

'We could meet up beforehand if you'd prefer. I could help you put together a presentation or whatever you feel comfortable with.'

In Limerick, they brought the house down. In Maynooth, they were chased from the auditorium. In Galway, the crowds queued around the block from mid-afternoon while a crew from RTÉ waited desperately to catch a few words from Daniel and Beckett as they took to the stage.

Beckett's years of disciplined studies gave format to Daniel's brilliance. Daniel could orate fantastically about a single atom and its potential applications for an eternity. Beckett mapped out their presentations and when Daniel spiralled down a wormhole Beckett would bring him back on topic with some well-spirited guidance or banter as the audience marvelled at their genius delivery and how it all made such perfect sense sitting there amid this breathtaking simplicity, witnessing in awe the universe and all its multitudes reduced to a single set of correlations. For that moment in time, the stars aligned and they felt, in the presence of such genius and purity, that everything was possible and they themselves could achieve the impossible if only they could carry the essence of these words with them out into the world and spread this word, this word... for it was the *word*, what else but the word could bestow such vision, such insight, such understanding without understanding – for the things that this young boy Daniel shared were beyond the capacity of any normal being, but when they came from his mouth there could be no misunderstanding, as the words were as natural to Daniel as wind to a valley and had the world fated him to be born to a place without words he would've fashioned them from rocks and mud and shared them among the people and impart to them with such understanding the meaning of these formations that not a man, woman nor child could have a single doubt as to his message, and they would be right. Their minds were clear, and as they left the auditorium with their heads full of dreams, they swore they would change their confused ways, and that night they made love and slept sound, safe in the knowledge that at last there was hope in the world.

They'd been invited to speak on the *Late Late Show*, where the host Gay Byrne proffered it was 'heresy'. Daniel smiled. He could sense the doubt in Gaybo's warble. He was right. Gaybo's heart wasn't in it, his bottom lip on the brink of a quiver. Daniel held Gaybo's gaze a moment more. He watched old Gaybo's eyes soften as his cheeks sagged. As a kindness, Daniel let Gaybo's gaze go. He wasn't up for the fight. Someone had advised him to take this position, or maybe he thought it was what his viewers wanted, but these words were not his own. Of that, Daniel was certain.

Daniel exhaled softly then he turned back to old Gaybo and told him of a billion broken hearts reunited in heaven if there was such a place, with a billion dead babies and of Mary's joy and fear when she held in her arms for the first time her boy-child, Jesus Christ, and of all the bonds that must be broken so the truth may be unchained and how we'd backed ourselves into a blind and dark alley, and the only way out was to tear the walls down, and once we'd started, sure we'd realise they were only a thin veil of our own making and we'd been surrounded by the truth all along if only we'd had the courage to reach out and take it. He told him about rocks and fish and time and space and of all the things seen and unseen, and at one point he realised he was holding Gay's hand and that the tears were streaming down old Gaybo's face and Christy Moore, sat next to him, rubbed Gaybo's back while Beckett jotted the whole lot down in a notepad he'd bought that afternoon from Eason's on O'Connell street. Then he told him of the first man's doubt and fear and how he'd cast his doubt out into the darkness and when it returned, it was a bright and shiny thing full of all the wonders of the world and how he'd wanted so desperately to take that bright and shiny thing and hide it from all others, that he might keep it for himself, but despite his greed he'd cast it out again in all its brilliance so that others might find their way and when they did, each one too would send it back out into the shadows and before long they had banished it entirely, the darkness and the whole world was ablaze with light. He told the folks at home of the dangers of doubt, and how the darkness had once again found purchase in the light and it was spreading fast and that each one of us must push it back and pull our brothers and sisters from it so that they too might feel the light and all its wonders. He spoke for fifty minutes straight of love and science and the possibility of everything, and when at last he'd finished a wave of realisation swept over him, and he thought he might faint as he took in the studio audience, each one of them, be they man, woman or child rising from their seats, clapping and roaring with the tears too, streaming down their faces.

'We'll go to an ad break,' Gaybo blubbed into the camera, wiping his nose on his sleeve. 'Join us after the break when we'll have music from Christy and more from Daniel.'

'Jaysus, that was beautiful,' Christy said. 'If I could put them words to music with a lash of the bodhrán here and there mixed with a bit of Connemara scat, Jaysus, I'd be a millionaire in the morning… what? Ho!'

After the show, Christy took them to O'Donoghue's bar on Merrion Row where Daniel sang a rebel song and danced with Anne Doyle while Beckett disappeared to the men's room with Gerry Ryan and BP Fallon reappearing some time later with the manner of a man who'd fist fight a fuckin' gorilla.

Luke Kelly sang a tale of love and lore while Christy waited patiently for his chance to try out a new song about the colour of a young wan's hair that some lad had given him at the Glasgow Folk Centre, or so the story goes.

Chapter Twenty

THE MIGHTY ARM

'THERE'S A MIGHTY ARM,' CLIFFORD started. 'And it sweeps. Back and forth, back and forth.' He swayed his hand in demonstration of its arc.

'Back and forth, back and forth,' he repeated, then looked the child in the eye. 'And it's invisible and it's soundless and sometimes it'll sweep right over your head, and you won't even know it's passed. Another time it might pick you up, carry you forward and set you down in such a place that you could only dream of, and when you find yourself in this new place of prosperity and wealth you might look around and think that you're the smartest cunt on the planet because you've done so well.

'But don't forget it sweeps both ways – it can pick you up on its reverse and set you back with some illness or financial ruin or the loss of a loved one. You might look about and scream, "why me?" But it's already gone. You are yesterday's news. Another time this sweeping arm or broom or however you want to imagine it might knock you down and snuff you out, and before you have time to think what has even happened your game is up, and it's already moved on, picking men up, knocking some down, setting some back or making some great. And it's indiscriminate, you know, this mighty arm. It doesn't give a fuck if you are rich or poor, black or white, tall, fat, skinny or squat. If it's your time, it's your time, every man will get his chance. Some might even get two or more. Back and forth, back and forth,' Clifford repeated, as he continued to sway his hand.

'Now you might think, waking up in this basement today that the mighty arm has picked you up and set you back a place or two... and that's understandable. But believe me now when I tell you that nothing could be further from the truth. Believe me, this day, when I tell you that this mighty arm has picked you up, and it has carried you aloft and set you down in this place of great opportunity and potential, and believe me also when I tell you that today is the first day in a tremendous journey that is going to be the making of a great, great man,' he said, poking the child's chest, softly.

Clifford stood up from the bunk, walked to the bookshelf, and picked up a copy of *Gulliver's Travels.*

'Can you read?' he asked the child. The child looked around the basement, then back to Cliff, then shook his head and said 'No.'

'Then that's where we'll start,' Clifford replied, then called over his shoulder to the other cells. 'Are we gonna teach our new member how to read boys?'

'YESSIR!' came the booming reply. The new child jumped at first, then smiled at the realisation he was not alone.

'Come on,' Clifford told him. 'Let's introduce you to your new friends,' and he took the child by the hand and led him to the centre of the basement as the others cheered and whooped, and as the basement filled with echoing thunderous applause, a tear formed in Clifford's eye. He looked down at his new guest and he smiled as the tear spilled over the brim and ran down his shiny cheek then slowed on the stubble of his unshaven jaw.

Chapter Twenty-One

BACK TO SCHOOL

'You can think about it any way you like, and I know there are lads here that know more about this than me or certainly will in time, but for now… for the here and now… as far as you are concerned… I am the all-seeing, all-knowing oracle for all matters relating to physics. Are we understood?'

'Yes, Mr O'Malley,' came the chorus.

'I don't want to hear any ifs, buts or maybes. I'm not interested in time continuums, I don't care about some programme on the telly about matter and space… we are not here to discuss anything that is not in your textbook because it will not be in your exam and I don't have the time to teach ye what is in the book, not to mind any other nonsense. So, am I perfectly clear? In school you learn what's in the textbook. At university you look for answers outside of the textbooks, so if any of you lads want to expand your minds and "think outside the box", then unfortunately you will need to wait a few years. Understood?'

'Yes, Mr O'Malley.'

'Okay lads… right, so we were on page ninety-seven yesterday and we were talking about potential energy?' Looking around the room, he noted, 'I'm not seeing much potential here today, lads. Late night?'

The Boy drifted in and out, in and out, in and fucking out. People had been different with him, he thought. They were all nice. Some were even kind, but they'd all been different to how they used to be. He'd catch them looking at him, then quickly look away again. Gordon said they were afraid of him. He didn't like that. He didn't want people to be afraid of him.

'You've been in a shootout,' Gordon had explained. 'A real live shootout… those saps are only jealous. You are like a hero of old, like Éamonn Ceannt.'

'Who?'

'Éamonn Ceannt!'

'Never heard of him.'

'Okay, Joseph Mary Plunkett then.'

'Mary and Joseph who?'

'Plunkett, they were a husband and wife duo. They hung them together in the one noose for their part in the Easter Rising. These saps think you are like Joseph Plunkett's wife, Mary.'

'Fuck off.'

'Butch Cassidy then?'

'Didn't he die in the end?'

'We don't know.'

'Whatya mean? Aren't they surrounded with no escape as the film ends?'

'Exactly! So, you can make up your own ending.'

'But in real life?'

'There's no such thing as real life. These boys are the stuff of legends. Many people believe they survived the shootout, and that's that. No one gives a fuck about what mighta happened or actually happened. They jumped off a cliff on horses and survived, laughing… so who's to say they didn't survive the shootout?' He wasn't finished, but he wasn't sure how to weave The Boy back into the conversation.

'You're fuckin' mental,' The Boy had said. 'So, are you telling me people are making stuff up about me?'

'No, I'm saying you are a fucking legend.'

Satisfied to move on, Gordon had finished with, 'To them, you are a fuckin' enigma, a mythical creature. They fear you and they respect you. Don't fill your head with paranoia and bullshit thoughts. If they are looking at you funny, it's because they don't know how else to act.'

'Do you understand me?' O'Malley called, eyeballing The Boy.

'Who, me?' The Boy blurted as he snapped from his daydream, suddenly back in the room.

'Yes you, are you following me?'

'Yes sir.'

'Okay… try to keep up lads, we will only go over this stuff the once. When it's gone, it's gone, as the man says.'

At lunchtime they sat in the bike shed smoking and chatting. There were more lads than usual today. Young fellas of all ages and denominations stood there puffing away, trying to make eye contact, start a conversation, be seen with him. Some of them were showing off, bragging, horse playing, acting the bollix. All of them talking about smoking dope or buying gear or sortin' a friend out with smoke. He found it confusing; he didn't understand any of it. That was Fallon's world. He'd smoked hash with Gordon a few times, but that was it. It wasn't something he wanted to do, day in and day out, and he hadn't enjoyed it. He didn't want it to be part of who he was, or represent him. He found that people who associated themselves with drugs became one-dimensional caricatures, almost. All other aspects of their persona were sidelined or diminished. Or maybe, he thought, people took drugs because they had fuck all else going on in their lives, or lacked identity. He wasn't sure, but he was sure that it wasn't for him. All this new talk about drugs confused him, and he wanted to get away from it all.

'Fancy some chips?' he asked Gordon.

'Cool, I'm fuckin' Hank Marvin.'

'Gaylord.'

'Wanker. Have you got money?'

'I've got a few quid.' The Boy winked.

*

In the chipper, the Italian lads were taking the piss as usual.

'Can I've a snack box?' The Boy asked before turning to Gordon. 'Snack box?' he asked.

'Yes, mate,' Gordon answered. He'd heard it on TV and liked the ring of it: *mate*. He played it in his head a few more times, *yes mate... yes mate...*

'Two "snack-ina-box" coming right up – you paying for your girlfriend, sexy boy?' Gennaro asked.

'Yes, please and two Cokes. Can you put ketchup on both as well, please?'

'No problem, sexy boy. Six-a-fifty please.'

'Keep the change,' The Boy replied, handing him seven quid.

'Big fuckin'a-spender, huh? Mafioso, keep da fuckin' change, huh? Unbe-fuckin-lievable. Next!'

They slid into a booth by the window. Outside, a behemoth of a man talking on his phone turned and looked through the glass pane. Distracted, he looked away again, then turned back quickly, eyeballing The Boy. He mouthed something into his phone, hung up, then put it in his pocket. Holding The Boy's gaze, the giant walked in the door, taking care to duck beneath the frame as he passed between the jambs. He approached the table, motioned for Gordon to move in, then he sat down opposite The Boy. His shoulders spanned the double seat, and Gordon had to lean to one side to accommodate his guest. The giant looked into The Boy's eyes and spoke.

'My name is Dave, Black Dave. I'm a friend of your brother.'

Chapter Twenty-Two

BLACK DAVE

HE'D REALLY FUCKED UP THIS time. Gone too far, even by his standards. The instructions had been simple. Take the money to the Rising Sun bar in Deansgate and give it to Tall Paul. Tall Paul would then give him a sports bag to deliver to an address in Didsbury. Once he'd delivered the sports bag, they would pay him one hundred quid for his troubles, and everyone could go about their business. But what did David Patrick Muldoon do instead? He only looked inside the envelope and upon realising there was a couple of grand in there, seven grand precisely, thought,

'Fuck it, I'll keep the money and head over to Ireland and no cunt will ever find me.'

He jumped in a taxi, stopped by his house to pick up his passport, continued on to Liverpool, then hopped on the next ferry to Dublin. As he stood at the stern watching the docks fade in the distance, a moment of doubt and fear gripped him like a vice. He thought about jumping overboard and swimming back to shore before a moment of swagger and strut engulfed him and he turned his back on the docks, walked to the bar, slammed a twenty on the counter, and settled into a pint of Guinness. I'd better get used to the black stuff, he told himself. I don't wanna stick out too much when I get to Ireland.

He stuck out like a sore thumb. The Dubs, they loved him, and he didn't experience any hostility or racism. The opposite, in fact, was the case. He soon gained notoriety 'round the drinking haunts of Dublin's inner city. He became a minor celebrity of sorts. After two weeks of drinking and scutting up and down O'Connell Street and beyond, Dave realised he needed to get out of Dublin. He jumped on the first train headed south and four hours later he awoke in sleepy Cork City.

Cork was a different dynamic to Dublin. You could get your head around Cork easier. There was less to take in, but it was still all going on. The university and regional hospital had many African doctors, students and lecturers, so the sight of a young black lad in and around the city centre didn't draw attention in the same way it did in Dublin. He rented a flat on Shandon Street and soon found work as a bouncer in the city's many night spots. He worked out hard every day, stayed away from the pub and before long he was in high demand all over the city with clubs and pubs paying way above the odds to have Dave working their front door. He set up his own firm and within a few months had a team of bouncers working the club doors throughout the city. It wasn't long before he caught the attention of The Big Fella. A business deal was struck and soon Dave was living very comfortably indeed.

The Big Fella was clever, Dave could see that, but the way he operated was archaic. London and Manchester gangs had adopted the 'never touch' policy decades before and Dave was shocked to see that Cork criminals still drove around with bags of drugs in the boot of the car and other ancient practices that were a surefire way of landing you in jail for a very long time. He schooled The Big Fella on best practice and slowly helped him to adopt a code of conduct that put as much distance between him and the criminal element of his business as possible. Within a few short years, The Big Fella, under Black Dave's tuition, ran one of the tightest operations in Europe. The two men embarked on a mutually beneficial enterprise that saw both their status and wealth rise astronomically. In time Dave schooled Fallon and Tonto, who in turn schooled their subordinates and before long the codes of practice adopted by the team became so watertight that the local Drugs Squad gave up on all attempts to bring them down, allowing the operation to self-govern with the occasional meet up with The Big Fella to set some ground rules when the local Guards felt it necessary.

Despite Dave's unquestionable status and position of influence within The Big Fella's organisation, he remained independent. He ran his own crew supplying drugs and security to the city's nightclubs and bars. He was The Big Fella's inner counsel and was often referred to as 'the consultant'. His expertise and cunning were second to none, and he was the negotiator of choice when a situation arose between rival gangs, usually from opposite sides of the river. His negotiation style was simple. Both parties involved would be called to Dave's office on Shandon Street, where he would sit them down opposite each other before delivering his opening gambit.

'Right… Welcome fellas. Thank you for coming today. I think we all know each other, so let's not waste any time fuckin' about with introductions or any of that poncey bollocks, agreed?'

'Agreed,' they said together.

'Okay, so you both know that the business you are involved in is supplied by the same source and although you are from different sides of the river and historically that meant something, nowadays it doesn't matter anymore. It's some ancient territorial bullshit you are allowing to cloud your judgement. So, keeping that in mind, are we all agreed that I am an independent adjudicator here and my decision is final? Do you both understand and agree to that?'

'We do.'

'Good, so as I understand it Carl, you sold one kilo of hash to Mucky's customer for one hundred punts less than he had been charging. Is that correct? And I don't give a fuck about any other details, so the answer is a yes or no. Keeping in mind that I already know the answer? So, yes or no?'

'Yes… but—' Carl replied, about to explain, before Dave cut in.

'Yes or no, remember? Okay, Mucky, in response to this you

knocked on Carl's door and when he answered you pulled him onto the street by his ridiculous looking fringe and punched him in the face five times, breaking his nose. Again, I would like a yes or no answer.'

'Yes… four punches,' Mucky corrected.

'Yes or no! What is the matter with you wankers?'

'Yes.'

'Fucking finally! You both know about the baseline pricing agreements that are set out by your supplier. The baseline prices are set for this exact reason. You can sell for as high a price as you like, but you cannot sell it for less than the baseline price.' He looked up over his glasses from a piece of paper he was pretending to reference, before continuing.

'Carl, you not only tried to undercut Mucky, but you also sold the hash for one hundred punts less than the baseline price – bit naughty. This customer was a long-time client of Mucky's so Mucky was selling to him at baseline as a reward for the customer's loyalty and commitment over what I understand was many years. Again, I would like a yes or no answer. Carl, do you accept this synopsis of events?'

'Yes.'

'Good, okay. My finding is that Carl must apologise to Mucky and pay him a bag of sand in compensation for undercutting him and trying to steal his customer. This bag of sand will be deducted from Mucky's outstanding bill with your supplier and added to Carl's. Agreed?'

'Bag of sand?' Carl asked.

'A grand.'

'A thousand quid?'

'A thousand quid, agreed?'

'Agreed,' they both affirmed.

'Carl, when you're ready. Please offer Mucky his apology.'

Carl, scorned, looked at Mucky with a crushed hatred in his eyes. Teeth bared, he hissed a cursory 'Ssssorrrreee'.

'What the fuck was that?' Dave asked. 'Are you taking the fucking piss? Do you want me to bang your head off every fucking wall in this office, then take you downstairs and throw you in front of a bus, you arrogant little cunt? Yes or no answer, please.'

'No.'

'Right then, shape up and apologise like a man.'

'Sorry.'

'Louder.'

'Sorry.'

'To him, not me, and say his name.'

'Sorry Mucky.'

Mucky held out his hand, savouring the moment. Lapping up every second, he replied 'Thank you, Carl,' with a Cheshire grin spreading from ear to ear.

'Right, sit down, you pair of wankers. I'm not finished yet. Carl, after Mucky broke your nose, how did you feel? This is not a yes or no question, but neither is it a session at the shrink. I don't want to hear about emotions or any of that soppy bollocks. What I want to hear is what you wanted to do to Mucky. Take your time, in your own words… Shoot.'

'I wanted to kill the bollix,' Carl started. 'I wanted to knock on his door and put a fuckin' bullet in the cunt's head.'

'Understandable,' Dave cut in. 'Okay, we are getting somewhere now. Right, so you've told me you wanted to shoot him. That's murder. What does murder do? It attracts press attention, and it attracts police attention. Not local police or press, but national, the kind we can't control. That's bad for business, you pair of cunts. Think… fucking think!' He tapped his temple.

'Mucky, if you'd come to me or the boss before attacking Carl, I would've awarded you two grand today. Your violence has cost you a grand. You are as much of a fuckin' twat as Carl is a sneaky wanker. Either of you jeopardise the boss's business again and you're both out. Now fuck off you pair of cunts.'

*

Ten years after he first arrived in Cork City, Dave was now a wealthy and successful businessman, and although the passing of The Big Fella and Fallon had been a personal blow, his independent status ensured that his enterprise was largely unfazed by their demise, and his personal wealth afforded him the luxury of time when deciding who, if anyone, would be his next supplier. Sitting across the table from The Boy in a chipper on Shandon Street, he marvelled at the striking resemblance The Boy bore to his late brother Fallon.

'Hello Dave,' The Boy replied. 'How can I help you?'

Dave looked at The Boy, his eyes welled up, and he took The Boy's hands in his.

'I'm really sorry for your loss, son. Your brother was a great little man. He was a loyal friend to me. He was clever, kind and without question a beautiful soul. I know you must miss him terribly, but I want you to know what a wonderful person he was and how his kindness and intellect impacted so many other people's lives. We were very lucky to have known him.'

'Thank you,' The Boy responded, unsure of what else to say.

'That's beautiful,' Gordon added, then asked. 'Do we call you Dave or Black Dave?'

Dave looked down at Gordon before turning to The Boy. 'Is he alright? In the head like?'

The Boy laughed. 'I don't think so,' he replied.

Dave pulled Gordon in for a warm embrace. 'I'm messin' you little wanker,' before adding, 'Can I get you boys some chips or something?'

'No, thanks we've ordered. It should be here any minute,' The Boy told Dave as Gennaro eyed them suspiciously from behind the counter.

'No problem, boys,' Dave added as he pulled a notepad from his pocket, wrote his number on a page, ripped it out, and handed it to The Boy. 'If you ever need anything, come and see me. You boys wanna go to a nightclub or whatever… ring me up and we'll tear it up big style, hit the town hard.' He elbowed Gordon playfully.

'You do know we are still at school,' Gordon replied, matter of fact.

'Alright Mary Poppins, don't get your knickers in an Oliver Twist,' Dave jibed. As he stood to leave, he motioned to The Boy to follow him outside.

'I know you've heard it a hundred times, but I mean it, son. You need anything, come and see me. I'll be keeping an eye on ya, so don't feel like you're on your own. You need school shoes or books, a new bike, somewhere to stay, money, whatever, ring me. I'm at your disposal, son.'

He shook The Boy's hand and pulled him in for an embrace before finishing with, 'Go on, ya little fucker,' patting him on the back as he departed.

As The Boy took his seat, Dave noticed through the window Gennaro eyeing The Boy suspiciously. Dave opened the door and shouted across the counter.

'Oi nosey bollocks, mind your fuckin' business and make sure you give these boys some extra chips. Come on, chip-fuckin'-chop!' Then he winked at The Boy, closed the door and strutted his way down Shandon Street, city-bound.

Chapter Twenty-Three

CLIFFORD AND CARL

'I NEED MORE?' CLIFFORD TOLD Ginger.

'How much more?'

'I'm not sure, maybe a thousand pills, a couple of kilos of hash?'

'I can get 'em… Cash?' Ginger asked, his greedy eyes lighting up.

'Do you take cheque?' Clifford replied sarcastically.

'I meant cash or tick. When you need 'em by?'

'As soon as, and cash.'

'Alright, let me see what I can do. I'll ring ya on your mobile. What's your number?'

'I'll come back. When will you know?' Clifford asked, reluctant to give this prick his number.

'Swing by tomorrow about midday. I'll know then.'

'How much?'

'I'm not sure. I need to talk to somebody who needs to talk to somebody else… Ya know how these things go?'

Clifford nodded knowingly, though he had no clue how these things went. He was up for learning new skills, though. Week after week, he would buy ecstasy and hash for his basement family, but each time he did, it increased the likelihood of him attracting the attention of the law. He needed to reduce the frequency of these purchases yet continue the supply. His solution was to buy in bulk.

*

When he returned the next day, the usual pricks were hanging about. The usual pricks but one. A handsome lad, of about twenty-five years, Clifford guessed. Handsome, though not conventional for a boy. He had high cheekbones, big Bambi eyes and full, blushed pouting lips that formed a perfect 'O' like a blow-up doll. The 'O' about big enough for a dick at a squeeze, Clifford thought. He wore his fair hair cropped tight at the back, top and sides, with a long fringe that fell across his eyes and face. No black crop top, sallow skin or goatee for this lad. He bore no hint of the typical blue eyed Mexican that inhabited the hills on the Northside of the city.

He flicked back his fringe with a toss of his head to the side, ran his fingers through it five or six times before letting it fall again in his face, then surrendered with a final flick to the left.

'At ease, gents!' Clifford announced.

Ginger looked up from the card-game. He had one eye closed, a cigarette hung from his mouth and his hands were full of game-cards. He raised his chin in acknowledgement, pointing the cigarette at the handsome lad.

'This is Carl,' he said out of the corner of his mouth. 'Have a chat with him, he'll sort you out.'

Carl stepped from the table and threw his cards in a pile at the centre. 'Good timing,' he said as he approached Clifford with his arm extended.

'Clifford, nice to meet you,' Clifford said.

'Alright Clifford, Carl… sound,' Carl replied, shaking his hand. 'Ginger says you wanna have a chat.'

'That's right, is there somewhere we can go?'

They drove out through Gurranabraher and Fairhill, estates well known to Carl, the stomping grounds of his youth, then turned onto Knocknaheeny. Carl smiled at Clifford's face, awash with shock, as he watched a group of children who by his estimation should certainly be in school, chase a flaming lorry tyre roaring by, in a wasteland to their left. Ahead, another group rode bareback beasts, bridled with bailing twine, their unshod hooves gliding the tarmac, and they banged on the bonnet of Clifford's open top Jaguar as he passed them on the road. Carl sighed with relief as a chorus of insults receded behind him, and soon they were driving down green country lanes.

'Turn down there,' Carl said. 'Keep going until you get to the gate on the left, then pull in.'

Clifford parked by the gate, and sighed. Carl took a joint from his pocket, eyed it up and stepped from the car before sparking the end. Clifford followed, unsure as Carl exhaled, then turned. A plume of smoke engulfed him.

'How do I know you're not a cop?' he asked.

'What?' Clifford said in disbelief.

'A cop, a fucking Guard… How do I know you are not a fuckin' *Garda Síochána*?'

'I don't have time for this shit,' Clifford sighed. 'Get back in the car. I'll drop you back to the pub.'

'Don't be so hasty, kiddo,' Carl replied, offering Clifford the joint. Clifford took a long draw, inhaled deeply, held it for a while, then exhaled and repeated the process.

'If I was a Guard, I wouldn't be standing here smoking a joint with you in the middle of a cunting field. I'd be in Anglesea Street filling out parking tickets or some other bollix. Now are you gonna sort me out or do I have to drive to Dublin for this gear, for fuck's sake?' He handed the joint to Carl.

Carl laughed as he took the joint.

'No worries, relax boy, we'll get you sorted alright. It's five and a half grand for the black and the yo-yos are ten quid a pop. So, work it out.'

Clifford considered, 'Okay, I'll take the two kilos and five hundred pills. I'll give you ten grand for the lot.'

'No can do, ten and a half, that's it.'

Clifford considered for a minute before replying,

'Okay, no problem. Thanks for your time, but I'll pass. Jump in. I'll drop you back to the pub.'

Carl took two more drags on the joint, thought a moment, exhaled then replied, 'Ten three, that's it.'

'Ten grand... not a penny more.'

'I can't do it, seriously I'd like to help you out, but I can't do it.'

'Okay, ten three, but you deliver it to a place of my choosing in Glanmire.'

'I can do that,' Carl said, extending his hand. 'Deal?'

'Deal.'

Clifford couldn't get Carl out of his head. He was like a giddy schoolgirl. It was dangerous; he thought. If Carl had asked Clifford for twenty grand for the gear, he probably would've paid him. What the fuck was he thinking? He started looking for excuses to meet up with Carl again. They'd exchanged numbers, and Clifford found he had to force himself not to ring his number over and over like some lovesick puppy. They'd arranged two more meetings, once when Carl dropped off the gear and then there would be a follow up meeting the next day when Clifford would hand over the money. On the day of the first meeting Clifford showered, shaved, put on his black chinos and polo neck, then he stood in front of the mirror for an hour fixing his hair and plucking his nostrils and eyebrows. He put on his leather jacket and decided to attend the meeting on his motorbike. *It's more macho*, he told himself. It was a special edition Kawasaki, who wouldn't be impressed by such a bike? Clifford mused.

The drop off point was a picnic area in Glanmire. It was near Clifford's house and there was an exit at both ends if a speedy getaway was required. Clifford pulled into the picnic area shortly before seven. As he parked the bike, his mobile rang.

'Hello,' Clifford said, giddy with excitement.

'On your left, there's a bench with two seats. Can you see it?'

'Bench with two seats, yes I see it.'

'Behind the bench, there's a bin.'

'Yep, I see the bin.'

'What you're looking for is beside the bin in a green bag.'

Clifford pointed the headlight of his bike toward the bin, put the bike on its stand and walked towards the bag.

'I can see it,' he reported as he continued his approach. 'Okay, I have it.'

'See you tomorrow,' Carl said, then hung up.

Clifford took the backpack, put it over his shoulder, hopped on the bike, secured his helmet and exited the rest area at speed, keeping the revs low. His heart pounded in his chest, and it took a moment or two for his disappointment at not meeting Carl to surge above the adrenalin of the deal. He kept his pace steady until he was certain he'd cleared the danger area before dropping a gear and accelerating along the byroads, home to the safety of the Cromby estate.

The next day he rose with the birds, put in a good day's work on the estate, then finished early to prepare for his meeting with Carl that evening, to hand over the cash. He pained for hours over what to wear before settling on a casual T-shirt and jeans combo complemented with some Timberland boots and a black leather jacket in a biker style. He arrived at McDonald's on Patrick Street early, ordered a Big Mac meal and took a seat by the door. He checked his reflection in the window, strong against the outside darkness. Looking good, he thought as the door opened, and Ginger bounded in alone.

'What's the craic?' Ginger asked as he took the seat opposite Clifford, then helped himself to some chips.

'Not too bad,' Clifford replied. 'Are you alone?'

'I am. Have you got some paperwork for me?'

'Paperwork?'

'Money!'

'Yes, of course… paperwork,' he mumbled, his face reddening. 'It's in the bag on the seat beside me.'

'Can I have it?'

Clifford passed the bag of cash to Ginger.

'Thank you very much,' Ginger said as he stood to leave.

'Aren't you going to count it?'

'No. See you later,' Ginger replied, then walked out the door, leaving Clifford alone with his Big Mac and fries.

Clifford binned the meal and headed to the car, dejected. It was great, of course. He now had a steady supply of drugs to keep his guests compliant but the very handsome Carl with whom Clifford was now hopelessly in love had fucked up all his plans. He wanted to impress and seduce Carl. He wanted Carl to like him, love him even, but it was clear that Carl had no interest in Clifford. He was most likely repulsed by him, he thought. Clifford supposed Carl viewed him as some middle-aged creepy pervert who bought drugs in large quantities to assist with his depravities, which, to make matters worse, was the truth.

He went to the basement of the old house every night that week. He had a boy in each cell and each of them took it in turns. Each playing their part, some more willing than others. Some even hoped to be selected. Clifford didn't like that. He liked to see the fear in their eyes; he liked to detect the hesitancy behind the pretence. If he could not detect it and felt the little perverts actually enjoyed it, then these boys graduated quickly to the woodland ceremony. He would make some excuse to the group, saying the lad's parents or foster parents had been in touch and they really wanted to contact him. Clifford extolled that it was only right and they should go together to meet with them. He owed them that, he would suggest. The lad would agree and one fateful night he would be led to the woods and never seen again. On Clifford's return to the group, he would explain that the lad had returned to his old life, and they would speak at length about how much they would miss him until shortly afterwards he was replaced and then forgotten.

In the weeks that followed, Clifford had all but put Carl from his mind. He would need to make contact eventually to arrange a new delivery, but his obsession had considerably waned.

He'd travel to Dublin or London a couple of times a year, rent a suite at some upmarket hotel and spend the weekend buying champagne and plying the young and available boys of the city with drugs and shopping trips. Sat in his booth in The George in Dublin, he was holding court, surrounded by hangers-on, when he noticed a young, handsome man standing at the bar on his own. *I know that little bastard,* Clifford thought through his cocaine haze. He closed one eye to focus, but that made it worse. Had he shagged him the night before, or maybe the last time he'd been up here? If only he could fucking focus. He picked up his glass of champagne and downed it in one. As he turned his gaze again to the bar, he recognised the flick of the fringe and those lips…

It can't be, he thought. *No fucking way… Carl, a fucking poof, what the fuck?*

When Cliff looked again, the lad was chatting with some equally handsome bastard who was obscuring Clifford's view. He reached into his pocket, pulled out his phone, and dialled Carl. Over the din of the bar, he could hear Carl's phone ring and his elation rose as he watched him remove it from his pocket and place it to his ear.

'Hello,' Carl shouted.

Clifford listened to the voice as he watched Carl struggle to hear over the noise of the packed boozer.

'Hello,' Carl shouted again, then hung up.

Clifford smiled, then called the waiter to his table. 'Could you give those two handsome bastards at the bar a bottle of Moët from me?' he asked. The waiter, who was no stranger to Clifford's epic benders, returned to the bar, removed a bottle of Moët from the fridge, popped the cork, placed the bottle in a bucket of ice and slid it, complete with two glasses, to a confused Carl before nodding toward Clifford's table. Clifford raised his glass as Carl turned to thank his benefactor, then smiled, recognising Clifford immediately.

Busted, he thought as he picked up the bottle and glasses and made his way to Clifford's table, leaving his new friend at the bar.

'Hello matey boy, fancy meeting you here?' Clifford nudged as Carl joined him, leaning in conspiratorially.

'Alright? Up for the rugby?'

'Something like that. Great to see you. Fancy a little livener?'

'I'm okay a while, maybe later.'

'Do you come here often?' Clifford asked, and they both laughed.

'I've been here before, shall we say.'

'Are you alone?'

'I was…'

'We are about to head over to a new club in a bit. We've got a VIP booth. Fancy joining us?'

Carl looked about at Clifford's rabble. *A feckless mixed bag*, he thought, then considering the invite, replied, 'I'd love to.'

They spent the next two days at Cliff's penthouse suite, getting smashed in every way imaginable.

'Look at the state of you,' Clifford remarked, as they woke late Monday morning, both of them feeling a lot worse for wear, with his left eye stuck closed and a beer mat fastened securely to the side of his head.

'You don't look much better,' Carl replied, eyeing him in the mirror.

'How are you getting back to Cork?'

'I was gonna get the train, you?'

'I've got the car. You can travel back with me. I'll be leaving shortly.'

'I'm alright, I like the train. I can sleep on the train, get a drink.'

'You can sleep in the car. We can bring some drink with us.'

'What if I need a piss?'

'I can pull over.'

'You sure?'

'Yeah, come on, I'll buy you lunch.'

In the car, it didn't take long for their talk to turn to Carl's line of work.

'Are you telling me that one guy controls all the drugs in and out of Cork City?' Clifford asked in amazement.

'Yep… one guy controls the lot. I mean, he's got people working for him, but if you are involved in drugs in Cork, it will have come from him.'

'What if you brought in your own and started selling them?'

'There'd be no point. My cousin sells pills for the Gilley gang in Dublin. I told him how much I pay for gear in Cork, and he can't believe how cheap it is. He sometimes buys pills off me if there's a drought in Dublin because I can get them cheaper than he can.'

'This Big Fella guy must buy them in bulk or import them himself, unbelievable… What's he like? Have you met him?'

'The Big Fella?'

'Yeah.'

'He's a legend, he's a normal kinda fella from the Northside, but sharp as fuck.'

'Good looking?'

'He's got something… he's not pretty, but he's attractive, ya know what I mean?'

Clifford nodded. He knew exactly what he meant, and he rather fancied the idea of people describing *him* in such a manner. 'A mysterious allure,' he imagined them saying. He looked at Carl and smiled. He'd never have imagined as he drove to Dublin a few days earlier that he'd be driving home today with Carl in his car. Handsome and dangerous Carl. He smiled again. He felt quite smug.

Carl rubbed the leather seat of the car. He could get used to this life, he thought. He reckoned he could get used to Clifford as well. He had something. Money was the immediate answer, and Carl wasn't too proud to admit that to himself. He found money attractive, and he was comfortable acknowledging that, but there was more. A vulnerability of sorts. Clifford had an unloved air about him, and behind the bravado and the big daft oafishness was a child screaming to be accepted, maybe even loved.

They spent the next months in and out of each other's company. Both men were busy, and although they shared a relationship of sorts, each was determined to guard their secret fiercely. The idea of a public relationship was out of the question, a feeling that was mutually shared. When Carl would ask Clifford about his need for such large quantities of pills and smoke, Clifford would explain that they were for his friends in Limerick and Dublin who had difficulty with a 'reliable' or 'discreet' supplier, which was partially true. He had supplied some associates in both cities, but the true destination of his large drug orders was much closer to home.

Reliable and discreet, Carl thought, a surge of pride rising in his chest. *That's me.*

His guests at the old house had been keeping Clifford busy. There had been two graduations of sorts followed quickly by some new recruits. Some of the latest lads hadn't worked out too well. There had been a biting incident, and another had challenged Clifford in front of the rest of the guests. He could not tolerate this behaviour. The biter was taken to the woods and beaten within an inch of existence with an axe handle. He was then resuscitated and buried alive, slowly. Clifford tied the little fucker's hands and legs together, taped his mouth shut and with delight he watched the little shit's eyes plead fiercely as he piled the earth slowly, spade after spade.

The other mutinous rag, Barry, had spurned Clifford's advances in front of the other guests. Clifford passed the scene off as a joke and when his attempts to rescue the situation with playful banter had failed, Barry had aggressively pushed Clifford away.

'Fuck off, you faggot,' Barry shouted. 'Get your fuckin' hands off me, you filthy bollix.'

Clifford reached in his pocket and offered the lad an ecstasy tablet.

'Come on, you,' Clifford quipped. 'Does somebody want more disco biscuits?' he suggested, in a sing-song voice.

'Stick 'em up your hole, you cunt,' Barry replied, pushing Clifford again hard in the chest. Clifford stumbled to the ground, and Barry advanced, chancing a swiping blow of his foot to Clifford's head. Clifford anticipated the kick and rolled to the side. Like a cat, he sprang to his feet then bounded for Barry, collapsing the lad in a heap beneath him. He sat on Barry's chest and pinned his arms beneath his knees, schoolyard style. Clifford considered for a moment as the lad struggled in vain before landing the first blow to Barry's head, then the second, then the third, aiming for the soft spots. The nose, the throat, the ears and so on, delivering a volley of blows, counting each one out loud as they landed. The other boys watched in horror from their cells. Some turned away as the beating intensified. One lad wept.

'Twenty-nine, thirty, thirty-one, thirty-two and thirty-three, the age of Christ!' Clifford shouted then exhaled, exhausted, shaking out his aching hands as he looked to the lads in the cells now for the first time, the rebel lifeless beneath Clifford's weight.

'I'm sorry lads, I'm really sorry. We have rules here,' Clifford heaved, breathless. 'If you break the rules, then you gotta go. I'm sorry you guys had to see this, but he attacked me.' He stood up and made his way to the tap, where he poured a long drink before returning to the lifeless lad.

'Come on, let's get you to the hospital,' he said, as he bent to peel Barry from the floor. He sat the lad on the sofa in the middle of the room, then he checked the lock on each cell door.

'I'm gonna take Barry to the hospital, guys. Be good. I'll be back tomorrow sometime,' he said as the remaining boys looked on, trying desperately to come to terms with the scene unfolding before them.

Eoin looked across the basement to Patrick's cell. He felt sick. His eyes welled.

'Don't look,' Patrick mouthed, and he closed his eyes then turned his face to the ground, that Eoin might understand. Clifford lifted Barry from the sofa and walked to the stairs, a trail of blood streaking behind them. Patrick looked to Eoin's cell; he was staring at the ground. His little chest rose and fell with each sob. Patrick felt a rage grow inside him. He balled his fists; he wanted to kill Clifford. He thought about it, killing Cliff, and he felt his rage roar, then dissolve, soon replaced by crippling fear.

He looked again at Eoin. He was so young; six or seven, he wasn't sure. Eoin opened his eyes and chanced a peek as Clifford struggled with Barry's body on the stairs. Patrick held his finger to his lips. He waved his head from side to side. Eoin's chest rose and fell. He stifled a sob. He didn't understand what was happening. He wanted to rewind, go back, undo what had happened only moments earlier. He looked to the ground, the trail of blood up the stairs. The deep red pool sitting proud of the floor where Barry's head had been. His body hiccupped, then again. His hands clawed, the tension spread up his arms into his neck and head. Hiccupping sob after hiccupping sob followed. He began to shake.

Patrick watched from across the basement. He looked to the stairs as Clifford disappeared through an opening at the top, then looked back to Eoin. He wanted to run to him. Take him in his arms and tell him it was okay.

'Psst,' he said, watching the stairs.

Eoin in convulsions now, didn't hear.

'Eoin!' Patrick said. 'Eoin!'

Eoin looked at him helplessly, as though from the depths of

madness. His body shook. He looked to Patrick with pleading eyes. Patrick shook his cell gate, then again, louder this time. The rattle echoed through the basement. Eoin's eyes whitened at the noise. Patrick shook again. Dust fell from a light fitting above his head. The lad in the next cell came to the bars and looked toward the sound.

Eoin looked to Patrick, his own panic abating with this interruption to his aberration. 'Stop,' he mouthed, then looked to the stairs. He gave a series of shuddering sobs, then slid to the floor.

Patrick watched as Eoin took a long shuddering breath then exhaled.

'Again,' Patrick whispered. Eoin took another long breath. Patrick watched.

'Again,' he said. Eoin breathed and they sat like that for some time looking at each other, Patrick's gaze the faintest tether between Eoin and madness.

Outside they heard the low thrum of an engine coming to life. They looked to each other, then up the stairs. They were safe for now.

Eoin let out an agonising wail and rolled onto his side.

Patrick sighed with relief at the sound of Eoin's cries as they filled the basement in some great release, a deflation or bleeding of grief.

That's better, he thought, as a stillness came over the space and he looked to the child, calm again, and watched him pass into sleep. He sighed.

Clifford took Barry to the woods, where he removed his head with a battery-powered jigsaw. He'd been curious for some time if it was possible, and he was rather pleased at how easily the neck muscles gave way to the blade. The trick was not to apply too much pressure, he discovered. There were a lot of nerves and sinew in the neck. If you advanced the blade too fast, it got clogged and stalled the motor. *Slow and steady wins the race*, he logged for the next time.

He dug Barry's grave by lamplight, then raced across the estate, making it back to the farmyard in the morning, caked in blood and muck, with seconds to spare before the first of the estate workers arrived for the day's toil. He would need to return to the grave again in daylight to camouflage the area, but it could wait. Hurrying upstairs, he called the estate secretary from his mobile. She picked up on the second ring.

'Good morning, Mr Cromby.'

'Good morning, Kathleen, I hope I didn't disturb you. Can you talk?'

'Yes, of course, Mr Cromby. I'm leaving my house now. Is everything alright?'

'Yes, yes, nothing to worry about. I'm a bit under the weather, is all. I'll be at home all day. Can you ensure I'm not disturbed? I didn't sleep very well last night. I'm going back to bed now, so if you could ensure I'm left in peace for the day, I'd really appreciate it.'

'Absolutely Mr Cromby, if you need anything, ring the office. Would you like me to call Dr Harvey to see if he can fit you in later today?'

'No… I'm fine. A few hours' sleep and I will be back on form.'

Clifford took a long hot shower, necked two diazepam with a tall drop of scotch, and fell onto his bed, exhausted.

Chapter Twenty-Four

BLOW BY BLOW

He woke to the sound of a rutted tractor. The smell of gears grinding in the byroad filled his room, and he walked to the window and watched with disdain as the farmhands struggled to free the machine from the ditch.

'Cunts,' he hissed.

Some beagles bawled. Their cry struck a chord somewhere deep in Clifford, and he had to sit down as the night before came rushing back. Had he locked the cells? Had he hidden the shovel and pickaxe? He imagined a trail of blood from the old house right to his bedroom door, and he thought about his bloodied clothes and the quad and the back door handle. The list was endless, repeating over and over. He stumbled to the bathroom cabinet, downed two more diazepam, followed them with a large glass of scotch, then retched as he forced down a glass of water.

The bastard attacked me, he remembered. Never more than two lads out at once. That was the rule. Two, he could handle, but last night was close enough with the one. He would need to be more careful. He wondered what had made Barry so brave? Had he done something? Hormones, he surmised. It must be hormones. When he turned on his mobile, there were two missed calls from Carl. He'd ring him back later. He needed to eat.

In the kitchen, he fried some eggs with toast. He poured a tall mug of steaming tea and watched the yard outside, busy with the comings and goings of the day, through the window. No one waved to, or acknowledged him as they went about their business. Good girl Kathleen, he'd ring her in a bit, he told himself. He could feel the diazepam taking hold now. He could see clearly the events from the night before in an ordered sequence. He had stashed the shovel and pick by the fallen tree. The blood and muck-stained clothes were in a bag locked in a cupboard upstairs. The quad was clean and parked in the garage attached to the house, safe from view, and he remembered entering the house through the garage, checking his footprints and the handle… all were clean. He'd locked the cells, the old kitchen door, and the obscured entrance. A calmness came over him. He would need to return to the burial site to disguise the disturbed ground with leaves and debris in the daylight, but it could wait a few days. The wood was on private land and remote. Even if somebody did venture in there, the chance of them discovering the burial site was next to impossible.

His phone rang again – it was Carl. A smile spread across Cliff's face. He was starting to like Carl. Not that he'd admit it to himself, but he had to admit that being with Carl was better than being without Carl and he'd sometimes find himself thinking of him fondly as he drove in the car, a joyous smile stretched across his face; then he would check himself in the rearview mirror. *You silly twat*, he'd say to himself. *Get your bloody shit together.*

He answered the phone.

'Good afternoon,' he heard Carl say.

'Yes, it is… I wasn't feeling great last night… so I went back to bed earlier. How are you?' Clifford replied.

'Good, I've been called to a meeting.'

'Meeting?'

'About the incident.'

'Okay… with whom… and where?'

'It's with Mucky and Black Dave at his office on Shandon Street.'

'Would you like me to come along?'

'No, it's only around the corner from me. I'll walk down.'

'How do you think it's going to go?'

'Should be fine. The Big Fella built his reputation on undercutting and fucking people over. So he should see my side. Plus, Mucky used premeditated violence against me before looking for mediation. They come down hard on that shit. It's bad for business.'

'Don't let them take the piss, remember his customer came to you and not the other way around. Are you sure you don't want me to come?'

'Certain, I'll ring you when I'm done.'

'Okay then, call by later if you like. This place should be quiet after seven.'

'No worries, laters.'

'Good luck.'

'Sound,' Carl said and put his phone in his pocket.

Clifford showered and dressed, then walked across the yard to the estate office. Kathleen, as ever, was busy chatting with some of the farm workers.

'Good afternoon, Mr Cromby,' she said, making no mention of their earlier conversation in front of the staff. *Discreet and reliable… good old Kathleen.*

'How are you, Kathleen? How's it all going today?'

'Great, Mr Cromby. Alan and Peter were telling me the repairs to the border fence are complete as far as Darcy's Cross and they hope to be finished entirely by the end of next week. They also estimate the repairs will come in under budget by about seven hundred punts. Isn't that right, lads?'

Alan and Peter nodded and mumbled some inaudible reply, of which Clifford picked out the words 'like', 'boy' and 'fence post'. The rest made no sense to him.

'Well done fellows, marvellous job, I say. Marvellous bloody job.'

He always spoke like an English gent when conversing with the staff. He couldn't control it. It was involuntary. He'd open his mouth, and some English Brigadier would bellow from within.

'If you need me, Kathleen, give me a ring on my mobile,' he said. 'I'll be in the house taking care of some paperwork.'

'How are you feeling?' Kathleen mouthed inaudibly.

Clifford responded with a wink and a thumbs up before departing to the main house.

He spent the afternoon pottering about. He shuffled here and there, back and forth. There seemed to be no real purpose or intention to his movements. He stood for an hour by the glazed wall of the mezzanine, gazing blankly to the valley beyond toward Kilduggart, where the rutted tractor had struggled earlier that day. Another half hour was passed absently cleaning the kitchen island with a dry cloth over and over the same spot. Round and round he went until he turned his attention to hoovering the hall and lounge with great purpose and alacrity.

Shortly before six, he found himself sitting in a cold bath crying intensely to Mariah Carey's rendition of the Harry Nilsson hit 'Without You' on repeat. He could remember running the bath, but he had no recollection of removing his clothes or getting in the bath, nor did he remember a single moment spent in the bath while it was hot.

In the bedroom, his mobile trilled and he jumped from the water and ran, hoping to catch it in time.

Carl's number flashed on the screen.

'Hi, how'd it go?' Clifford asked.

'Shit,' Carl said, then proceeded to fill Cliff in with the news from the meeting.

'Alright… calm down. Where are you? I'll come and get you.'

'I've gotta meet someone in a half an hour, but I'm free after that. I can get a taxi out.'

'No… I'll pick you up. Ring me when you are ready. Are you hungry?'

'Starving. I'll get some Chinese on College Road. Can you collect me there at seven?'

'Cool, see you then.'

*

Clifford racked up two lines on the shaving mirror in the bathroom. He hoovered them one after the other, then stood back and checked his reflection in the mirror. His frontal lobe throbbed. It felt good.

'You fuckin' beauty… you fuckin' beauty… you fuckin' beauttttaayy! Look at you… look at you… look at yoooouuuuu!!' he roared in a Richard Burton style, beating his bare chest.

'Who's the man? Who… is the man? Who's the man? It's fuckin' you,' he sang in a Joe Dolan lilt. He turned to leave the room, then twisted on his heel sharply and pointed to himself in the mirror.

'I'll see you later… who, me? You talking to me?' he asked himself with a smile.

The man in the mirror smiled back. 'Feeling better?' he asked.

Clifford nodded.

He smashed out two more lines, jumped in the car and headed for College Road. When he got to the Chinese restaurant, Carl was waiting by the door.

'Alright?' Carl asked, jumping in.

'Fuckin' right I'm alright, where to, guvnor?'

'To the farmhouse, old boy, and don't spare the horses.'

Clifford held up the bag of coke.

'Livener?' he asked.

'Do I ever,' Carl replied as he dipped a wet finger in the bag, rubbed his gums greedily then bumped four or five pinches in a row, cautious of his broken nose.

'Carl is back in the room!' he exclaimed loudly as the ache in his nose abated. 'That is the shit, that is the fucking shit squire,' he said as he reached for the radio and cranked it up. Billie Ray Martin's 'Your Loving Arms' blared through the Blaupunkt speakers. Carl took a Hong Kong chicken ball from its container, dipped it in the bag of coke, and offered it to Clifford.

'This MSG is fuckin' more-ish,' he joked. Clifford downed the chicken ball in one, then tilted his head like a hatchling and cawed

'More! More!' Both men were in hysterics as they drove back to the farmhouse where Carl continued his rant about Mucky and Black Dave.

'Then the fuckin' wanker threatened to throw me under a bus,' Carl explained, as he settled into the sofa.

'He what?'

'If you don't shape up, I'll bang your head off the wall then throw you in front of a bus, guvnor me laddie,' Carl said, imitating Dave.

Clifford laughed, then lined up the coke, four lines each, as Carl continued to mock Dave's accent in hysterics.

'You both agree that I am an independent party and my decision is final,' he mocked, then turned intently to the lines of coke. He threw his head back before continuing. 'I wish I'd shot the fucker… bang…' motioning some phantom pistol in a gangland style. 'One shot in the back of the fuckin' head. Good night, ya cunt.'

Clifford loved this side of Carl. He knew he was a nasty fucker, but this talk of murder was something else. 'You could still?' he suggested.

'Too late now. They'd know it was me. I'd have Tonto and that other little wanker Fallon on my case. Tonto's one nasty bastard. I've missed my chance, I shoulda done it after he attacked me. Followed the wanker home and finished it there and then. It went on too long and The Big Fella got word of it. Anyway, it'll come back around again. I've got a plan. I'll have my fuckin' day. All I need to do is sit and wait. Sit and wait.'

'Fuck that.' Clifford hissed. 'Shoot 'em all right now. Bang, bang Big Fella,' he said, then snorted a line. 'Bang, bang Fallon,' he wheezed as he exhaled, then bent once more and snorted another. 'Then finally, bang, bang Mucky… problem solved,' he said, exhaling, then sniffed at a third line. As he sat back on the sofa with his eyes closed, he mouthed the words, 'Establish a new supplier and you take over. Job done.'

Carl looked at Clifford, not quite believing what he'd heard, then he took the rolled-up note in his hand and said as though to himself, 'Not Mucky, not yet. We leave Mucky a while. In fact, we let him thrive. Then when the time is right, we make the cunt suffer.' He turned to the coffee table and snorted the remaining two lines. 'We'll need money,' he said, exhaling.

'How much?'

'Hundred grand?' He rubbed his nose.

'Done.'

'You can get it?' Carl said and he blinked Clifford into focus.

'I can,' Clifford replied. He'd been keeping a large supply of cash at hand since he'd started having guests at Kilduggart. He had an exit strategy in place. It involved a bag of cash, a fake passport, a boat and a remote beachside property in Morocco.

'We'll need shooters and getaway vehicles. High-powered bikes, preferably. I can get both,' Carl said vacantly, not to anyone in particular, as he took the bag of coke and tipped a heap onto the table.

By morning, they'd charted their course. Fallon and The Big Fella would go first, then they'd wait. They'd watch as contenders rose above the parapet and as each one rose, they'd take them out until at last there were none but them, and Carl would take the throne.

Chapter Twenty-Five

JANIE LANE

AT FIRST, THEY THOUGHT THEY'D never spend a whole three grand, but when the first thousand went they soon realised that the money would not last forever. There were no extravagant splash-outs. They'd spent it mostly on takeaways, video games, a couple of games consoles and taxis. They'd started smoking weed. Beebo, possibly the only man in the city with drugs, albeit a dwindling supply, was taking care of their needs.

Gordon would recount verbatim tales of Agamemnon and Odysseus with The Boy hanging on his every word, interrupted only by pangs of hunger, upon which they would set forth by starlight in search of satiation. Pizza was their number one choice.

'Food of the ancients,' Gordon would exclaim, holding aloft a slice. 'I kid you not. King Superbus and the Etruscans marched upon the soldiers of the Republic in the Silva Arsia, their bellies filled with pepperoni pizza!' he'd roar as The Boy, in stitches, rolled another joint.

'We've got two hundred and eighty-seven punts left,' The Boy reported.

'That should see us through to retirement,' Gordon joked. 'It's a bloody fortune boy, a bloody fortune,' in his best Peter O'Toole.

'Well, given that we've spent the other twenty-seven hundred in about four weeks, I reckon it should last us about three days.'

'What about Tony? Do you reckon he's got any change for us?' Gordon asked and they burst out laughing.

'If we buy an ounce of smoke from Beebo for one hundred, that leaves us with one hundred and eighty-seven quid. After that, we are officially skint.'

'We'll get jobs. Are you any good at giving head?'

'Fuck off, you wanker. I'll be your pimp. I can rent your scrawny arse out down the Coal Quay. Although I can't see there being too many takers, the state of ya.'

'You'd get employee of the month. The only complaint you'd get is "over-keenness". Your appraisal would read "Approaches his work with great alacrity. He has a voracious appetite for cock and has been known to take his work home with him,"' Gordon said as they rolled on the floor in hysterics.

'Fuck off, you prick,' The Boy howled.

'Seriously though, is that all the money that's left?'

'That's it.'

'We need more. I think I'm addicted to pizza. I'll start robbing grannies' handbags to buy margheritas if we run out.'

'Could you borrow your aunt's motorbike?' The Boy asked.

'It's a Honda-fuckin'-fifty for fuck's sake. I wouldn't be seen dead on it. Anyway, she sold it. She bought a car.'

'How much are they?'

'A car?'

'No, you dope, a Honda-fuckin'-fifty.'

'I don't have a clue. Janie Lane has a load of them. What do you want one of them for?'

'I'm not sure. I have an idea,' The Boy said, then stood and headed for the landing.

Gordon grabbed his coat from the bed and followed him out.

'Where are we going?' he asked.

'I'm not sure. Janie's first. Do you trust me?'

Gordon nodded. He could tell by the way The Boy was acting that this was serious. He had that faraway look in his eyes that he got when something was brewing, and Gordon didn't wanna miss out.

*

Janie Lane's yard lay two miles out on the old Mallow Road. It had wide steel gates with a rusted logo that read 'Lane and Sons'. It was, on inspection, legible. However, no more info could be gleaned from the sign. It made no mention of how Lane and his or her sons had made their living or what trade they'd plied or may have plied in days gone by within the boundaries of their fenced venture. The yard was strewn with machinery in various states of decline and disintegration. There was a tractor on jacks with a rear wheel removed and the engine pulled from its guts, entrails left hanging. There were several cars in a similar state of disrepair. Some on their sides, one upside down and another stood upright leant against the gable end of an outhouse. There were steel beds and hospital equipment in a row that ran the length of the east boundary, flanked by a row of pallets upon which Janie had stacked batteries and motors of every kind, waist-high.

Janie, from what they could work out, was either Lane or son, though there were no other Lanes thereabouts. A skinny man of about fifty, he had appeared so for twenty years or more. He sported two days' growth of beard. His nostril hairs, that sprang from his nose like a busted mattress, met in the middle, awning at his wet upper lip. His right eye was glass and his left eye invariably had one tear formed and brimming at its inner that hung suspended, glinting in the sun, his oculus bejewelled with some ancient sadness he'd all but let slip, sitting there now and for an eternity alone amidst the rubble of his inherited yard.

When Gordon and The Boy arrived, Janie was sitting at the desk in the Portakabin to the yard's rear. There were two men sat opposite and as they approached, the men rose from their seats. Janie thanked them for their time and instructed them to return in a week, when he would have everything in order. When the men departed, Janie turned to Gordon, looked him up and down and said,

'What is it this time?'

'Nothin' much, thought you might need some company.'

'You came all the way out here in a taxi to keep me company. In all my life, I don't reckon anyone's ever pulled up at those gates in a taxi before. It must be some important business you boys got goin' on if you're getting taxis about the place.'

'So, you don't need our company, then?'

'What I need is somebody to stack those batteries over there on pallets. You reckon you can do it?' he said to Gordon, then eyeing The Boy, he added. 'You never told me you got married. She's a cutie.'

'We need a Honda 50, you got any?' Gordon asked, ignoring the slant.

'You know I do.'

'How much?'

'Depends which one.'

'We need a reliable one that's not too flashy.'

'I can guarantee it won't be too flashy… but reliable… how much you got?'

'Enough. Show us what you have.'

'They're in the shed. Take a look and let me know which one you want.'

'No papers?'

'No papers? Hmmm, I knew you was trouble soon as I saw that taxi pull up outside. Whatever you boys are up to, I want no part. I'll get ye a bike, but after that I don't wanna know. Understood?' he looked them both square in the eye, considered a moment, then relented. 'Okay… come with me.'

They walked to a shed behind the main house. Janie pulled open the barn door and ushered them inside. Seven bikes stood in a row along the side wall and Janie motioned to a red Honda at the end.

'No papers, runs like a dream. I'll fill the tank. Two-fifty.'

'Has it got a key?'

'It's in it.'

'Helmets?'

'I'll get ye something… two helmets will cost ya three hundred all in.'

'Two-fifty the lot, that's all we got.'

'Stack them batteries I mentioned on the pallets and you've a deal.'

'Now?'

'Now.'

Gordon looked at The Boy. The Boy nodded and Gordon offered Janie his hand.

'Deal.'

'Don't stack 'em too high. I'll get you girls some helmets.'

They stacked the batteries five high. There were batteries of all shapes and sizes, and the trick was to stack 'em so they 'slope slightly in towards the centre,' Gordon explained. He had form. He'd worked for Janie before and there were always batteries to be stacked. You stacked them, then you wrapped them in film and moved on to the next pallet. If you stacked them right, a pallet with four times four batteries per layer stacked five levels high weighed roughly a ton. Janie got paid by the ton, so he liked to see them stacked so.

As they were stacking the last pallet, they watched Janie wheel the Honda from the shed and put it on the kickstand. He pulled out the plug, held it to the sun, gave it a wipe and put it back in its hole. He checked the oil, picked up a gallon drum from a shelf by the side wall and poured petrol through a rag until the tank was full. He fired up the bike and watched as a plume of smoke escaped the exhaust. He gunned the throttle a few times and watched as the smoke eased, then let her idle a few minutes more while he went inside the house to get some helmets. When he returned, he dropped the helmets next to the idling bike and strolled toward the boys.

'You lads about done here?'

'Got this last few, but after that, we're done.'

'Leave 'em, I'll finish them in the morning. The bike is running for ye over there. How much did we say, two-fifty?'

The Boy counted out the notes and handed them to Janie.

'Thank you, boys. Now I'm not saying you gotta go, but you can't stay here. Your bike is over there, and the road is that way.'

With The Boy at the helm, they drove aimlessly for fifteen minutes. First down into Blackpool then out towards Blarney, then beyond until the road gave way to countryside and Gordon wondered if they were lost until at last The Boy noticed a sign that read Fermoy, and he pulled a sharp left up a country lane into a wooded area. After a short distance, he took a right and sped up a lane that was about wide enough for a single car. On the left, he spotted an opening in the ditch, and he pulled in and cut the engine. He walked the bike along the side of the ditch, concealed it from the road, then pulled a fallen limb across it to secrete the bright red panelling from view.

'Where the fuck are we?' Gordon asked.

The Boy raised a finger to his lips as he removed his helmet and motioned Gordon to follow him. Gordon removed his helmet and followed. When they were a safe distance from the lane, The Boy turned to Gordon, took his helmet from him and motioned him to duck down.

'I think there's money hidden around here somewhere. I'm not sure where exactly, but Fallon took me here to get some dough a while back.'

'The five grand?'

'Yea… I think it's further up the lane, but I wanted to hide the bike while we searched.'

'Cool.'

The Boy stashed the helmets in the ditch, and they headed back out to the lane. They walked to the crest of the hill where The Boy jumped over the ditch, taking care not to crush the grass or brush.

Then he pulled himself over and motioned Gordon to follow.

'Be careful not to leave tracks,' he whispered.

Gordon rolled his eyes. 'Okay kemo-fuckin'-sabe,' he mouthed as he followed, taking great care not to disturb the area, then he jumped over the ditch, and they sat there in the duff and looked about the place. The Boy tried to recall if Fallon had gone left or right on that fateful night, but he couldn't remember, and his mind began to wonder until Gordon pulled him from his rumination.

'Well?'

'What?' The Boy asked, startled.

'Well, what now?'

'I don't know. Look about the place, keep low. He wasn't gone that long, so if it's here, it's nearby.'

They divided the area and agreed to meet back at the same spot in five minutes. Gordon followed the ditch along, looking about as he went. After three steps, his foot sank between some branches, and he crashed into the dirt hard. As he hit the ground, he heard a crackling plastic sound from beneath the branches. He pushed himself back instinctively to his feet, then he tripped again, fell back in the ditch and rolled in the dirt. He tried to right himself and as he did so, eyed a green refuse bag protruding through the shrub at his foot where he'd tripped. The Boy ran to his side, helped Gordon to his feet, then pulled at the branches greedily. There were ten green bin liners lying side by side in the undergrowth. The sun reflected up from the bags at their feet and their faces, imbued with an emerald sheen, shone, and they looked at each other speechless, then turned with crazed eyes to their treasure and tore at the bags without grace or shame, panting with foam forming at the corners of their mouths.

Two bags were stuffed with cash, six were full of parcels of hash tied four bars in a bunch, each bar stamped with a Mercedes logo.

Another two had fifteen individually wrapped plastic bags, each containing one thousand ecstasy pills embossed with what looked like some kind of bird on either side of every pill, and a last bag beneath the rest was wrapped tight with eight hard blocks neatly packed inside. Each block was about the size of a house brick and was wrapped in cellophane.

They looked at each other. Gordon made to jump in the air, shouting, but The Boy raised a finger to his lips, swaying his head from side to side. They pocketed one bar of hash and a four-inch stack of bills. The Boy righted the stash and led them back to the bike through the woods, keeping low all the while. They rode to the city in silence. When they got to Blackrock, they parked the bike a few streets from Albie and Ann's, then continued home on foot.

'What the fuck? There must be a million quid there,' Gordon said as The Boy counted the stack.

'There's five grand here exactly,' The Boy said.

'There must be at least a hundred of them stacks,' Gordon added. 'What's that… five million?'

'Five hundred thousand,' The Boy corrected.

'Not bad… And what about all the gear? There's gotta be millions there.'

'Fuck the gear. There's enough cash there to set us up for life. What the fuck would we do with all that gear?'

'Smoke it.'

'Or burn it.'

'One joint at a time.'

'This could be really awesome or really fuckin' bad. We need to get our shit together, and quick. This could get us killed. I need sensible Gordon, not fuckin' Gordon the mental bastard… okay?'

'Sure.'

'We can't tell a soul. Agreed?'

'Agreed.'

'Seriously, we cannot tell a fuckin' soul.'

'I agree… How we gonna sell all the gear though if we can't tell anybody?'

'We are not selling the gear. We wouldn't know where to start. We'd end up in jail or dead.'

'So, we burn it? That's your answer?'

'I don't know. I need to think about that. That's the hard part. The money will be easy. I think we should move the money first. Take it deep in the woods and bury it until we decide what to do with the gear. At least if we fuck up getting rid of the gear or someone finds the stash, the money will be safe.'

'Smart.'

'Right, we go back out tomorrow evening with a shovel and stash the money separately, then we move the gear back from the road a bit until we decide what we are doing with it. Are you in?'

'Are you sure you want me in?'

'Absolutely, fifty-fifty all the way, but I need you to keep your shit together. Can you do it?'

'Abso-fuckin-lutely, what's half of five hundred grand?'

'Loadsa fuckin' money, now roll a joint you wanker,' The Boy said in an attempt at humour.

He hadn't anticipated the find. He'd hoped they might find more money, but how much, he hadn't contemplated. Another five grand would've been fine, beyond fine, but this? This was beyond comprehension. On the outside he'd won. His ship had come in, prayers answered, his dreams come true, but inside he felt a rumbling doom, like an echo of some distant storm forming out on the ocean, heading their way.

Gordon peeled the cellophane from the bar of hash. It was bigger than his hand. He looked at The Boy, smiled, held up the bar and gave it a triumphant shake, like a match winner, then kissed it.

The Mercedes emblem glinted in the light of the bedroom. It looked posh, harmless, like some exotic chocolate they'd been gifted by a rich and mysterious uncle back from his escapades abroad.

When he thought about the money, he saw pizza, video games, new trainers and fun, but when he thought about the drugs his mind went blank. He saw nothing. It was as though he was staring into a Stygian abyss, silent but for the faint rumblings of some desperate malevolence approaching at pace, way off in the darkness.

Chapter Twenty-Six

DIGGING

'I THINK IT'S GRANITE,' GORDON wheezed, then collapsed to the ground next to the hole.

'Stop being a pussy, let me at it,' The Boy said as he took up the spade and set to work. The spade clanged on the hard ground and reverberated up through his wrists and into his elbows.

'It's hard enough alright,' he said. 'This spade is making it even harder. Let's fill it back in. We'll come back tomorrow with a proper shovel, a triangular one. You know what I'm talking about?' The Boy asked.

Gordon looked at him, drew hard on the joint, exhaled, then launched into a rant.

'If this was London in the sixties and we were a couple of Irish navvies, McAlpine's Fusiliers, and there was a wife and babbies at home, depending on us, they'd be going hungry tonight. Where's your fuckin' pride, man? Get your back into it. Come outta the way to fuck you spineless prick. Let me at it,' Gordon said, inspired now. Taking the spade from The Boy, he launched himself at the task, some fresh wind in his sails. Three spades in and he was all puffed out.

'To be fair,' he wheezed. 'McAlpine would have a proper fuckin' shovel and a pick. Let's come back tomorrow when we're tooled up.'

They returned the next day with a proper shovel, and a pickaxe. Gordon took a compass from his pocket, held it out in front of him, then swayed left and right like a man at some great act of calibration, setting the world gone awry to right. The Boy looked at him confused as he held the compass up to the sun, then to his ear, then set about walking in circles until at last he stopped and smiled.

'What's the compass for?' The Boy asked.

'You'll see.'

They set about their work methodically. First, they wrapped the cash in twenty grand bundles, then they bagged the bundles in groups of five. There were six bags in total. Five bags with one hundred grand and one bag with ninety. They dug six holes scattered throughout the woods. Each hole was approximately two feet cubed. The Boy would pickaxe the ground first, then Gordon would dig out the earth until the hole was the right size. They then lowered a bag into each hole, filled the hole back in, then jumped on the earth to compact it before concealing the dig site with duff and debris scattered about the area.

The location of each site was easy to remember. They established a starting point, then using the compass Gordon had brought, walked fifty paces north, buried a bag at the foot of a tree, then fifty paces east and buried a bag at the foot of another tree, then north again and so on until they'd buried all the bags. They identified the trees by breaking off the second branch from the ground on the opposite side of the tree where they'd buried the bags.

'Whatya think?' The Boy asked as they lowered the last bale.

'I don't care how broke I get, I am not digging that shit up again for at least a year,' Gordon said, pocketing the compass.

'It's hard work alright,' The Boy said. 'Pizza?'

'Pizza.'

Chapter Twenty-Seven

MARIE

'WHAT DOES HE DO OUT there?' The Boy asked.

'Who?'

'Janie.'

'Deals in scrap mostly.'

'He does now, but "Lane and Sons", what's that all about?'

'Oh that, they were undertakers.'

'A one-eyed undertaker? Will you ever fuck off?'

'Seriously, they were undertakers, and no regular kind. They were the *crème de la crème*. State funerals, shit like that.'

'How do you know?'

'My old man told me.'

'Why did they give it up?'

'Had to. It's the rules.'

'What rules?' The Boy asked, tiring of the conversation, but intrigued.

'They'd done their seven generations.'

'Their what?'

'Seven generations. Undertakers can only ply their trade for seven generations. After that, they must leave the trade for two. It's called the fallow period.'

'What? Why?'

'You wouldn't believe me if I told you.'

'Chance me, I'm fuckin' stoned.' They both laughed.

'It was found in ancient times,' Gordon started, 'that all

incidences of reported vampirism could be traced, without exception, to the burial of an eighth-generation tradesman – like a blacksmith or a carpenter, or any of the guild trades for that matter – by an eighth generation undertaker, and so, it was decreed by a Masonic order that all undertakers must cease trade after their seventh generation of practice.'

'Jaysus H Christ,' The Boy roared in astonishment.

'A perfect example. He was an eighth-generation carpenter, entombed by an eighth-generation undertaker, and how did that work out?'

'You are something else,' The Boy exclaimed as he reached for the pipe.

He held the lighter to the bowl, toked hard, watched the embers glow then recede, held his breath tight and watched the glow dwindle. He pulled once more, forcing another draw, then again watched the embers rise in response as his lungs inflated. Beside him on the sofa, Gordon continued with his tale then meandered as The Boy held his breath hard, lips pursed, his mind unbridling, cast down a vortex where his Mam sat Sabbath, outcast, cold out there in the waiting and he placed his coat about her shoulders then lingered in her essence, speechless, until he was forced at last to release his breath, draw air and ache in solitary sadness as her presence ebbed, giving way to Gordon's bellowed tale of Atlantis mermaids and where you might find one.

Chapter Twenty-Eight

DIGGING DEEPER

'STILL NOTHING FROM BEEBO?'

'Nothing,' Gordon replied.

'Did you call to his house?'

'I've been ringing and calling and swinging by the pub. If something *has* happened to him, I'll be the chief suspect.'

'Will you shut up?'

'What? I will.'

'If something has happened to him and the Guards are looking for suspects, they are hardly going to think that the fella who's going around asking everyone if they've seen him has anything to do with it.'

'Why not?'

'Because if you knew where he was or what happened to him, you wouldn't be looking for him, ya thick—'

It had been two weeks since they'd stashed the gear, and the idea of selling it instead of destroying it had germinated in The Boy's brain, and with each day that passed had grown stronger by the hour. God knows why. They had loads of money and knew fuck all about selling drugs, but for some reason, beyond any logic or comprehension, they simply had to sell the gear. They'd dreamt up some imagined fantasy where they were looking over their shoulders and fist bumping criminals in some lawless world where it was cool and respected, and there were aeroplanes and backpacks and skin of yer arse situations that they ran from, laughing. A clueless pair of pricks, if ever there was a pair.

Beebo had been their natural choice to help shift the gear, but he'd vanished. Fuckin' vanished. He was everywhere one minute, then nowhere the next.

'What about this other guy, you know? Can we trust him?' The Boy asked.

'Ah yeah, he's sound.'

'Remind me. How do you know him?'

'He's a friend of me cousin's, salt of the earth.'

'For a drug dealer.'

'What does that make us?'

'A pair of mugs.'

'Seriously, though, he's been dealin' for a while, I think. He's the perfect candidate for us to get rid of all this gear. We give it to him a little at a time, he sells it, and we pocket the cash. When it's all gone, we tell him we can't get any more and we are quids in. Retire to East Cork. Job done.'

'Let's give Beebo another few days. If he doesn't turn up, then we go with your cousin's friend. Alright?'

They waited two more weeks for Beebo to resurface. He never did.

Out on the old Mallow Road, beyond the high bridge, there was an old rat run that took you down to the River Bride, where, behind an old oak tree, Beebo kept his private stash. Twenty feet from the stash lay Beebo, face down in the river.

He'd been sitting on a big rock by the bank smoking a joint, listening to the Stone Roses on his headphones one evening at dusk.

'You lucky fucker,' he told himself, as he thought about The Big Fella's stash. He was certain he could work out where it was, and once he'd sold all his own gear, he intended to find it. It was in one of four, maybe five places, he reckoned. He knew the general areas and the method of concealment, so he was pretty confident he'd locate it with ease. For now, he was content to chill out and enjoy the calm. 'I Am the Resurrection' blared in his headphones, and he felt the joint take effect. *Life is good*, he thought as he stubbed it out on the rock, flicked the roach in the water, then turned to head back up to the stash.

He couldn't believe his eyes at first when he saw the two dark figures shimmering in the evening's half-light. They looked about six or seven feet tall, clad head to toe in black, skin-tight leathers, and their shiny black helmets with the visors down gave off a series of soft, orange dusky glints. They looked like a pair of fucking aliens emerging from the bush, he thought. He took his headphones from his head, half hoping these unearthly beings might make some terrestrial sound or communication, but all he could hear was the river and the swirl of the blood rushing in his head. He mouthed the words, 'what the fuck?' as they set upon him and he knew in that moment they were human, and he was fucked.

They wrestled him to the ground, dragged him to the river, and held his head beneath the water until he drowned. Then they rolled the big rock into the water and placed it on his back to weigh him down. He's down there still.

Gordon reached out to his cousin's friend Charlo, a handbag-snatcher from Mayfield. They'd arranged a meeting to hand over the first consignment in the car park of the Commons Hotel. When they arrived, they saw the white Honda Civic parked behind a tour bus out of sight from the main road. A tall lad in his early twenties stepped from the passenger side of the car and lit a cigarette as they parked and dismounted.

'Alright?' Charlo said as they approached.

'Yeah sound,' Gordon replied, removing the backpack and setting it on the ground.

'Are you Fallon's brother?' Charlo asked The Boy, looking him up and down. 'You're a skinny little prick, aren't ya? You could do with putting some meat on dem bones, boy,' he said, and he shook The Boy's hand. A little rough, The Boy noted.

'So what's the craic with this gear you want me to help you with?' Charlo asked, in a manner that suggested he could take it or leave it.

The Boy looked at Gordon, then paused.

'Help?' he asked, and he let the word sit there a moment.

'Yeah, Gordon was telling me you need a hand moving some gear.'

'We both know there's no gear in Cork City or any other city between here and Dublin. So, I'm not sure we're gonna need any help. The only reason we are meeting you tonight is because Gordon told me you were on the level, and you'd be a good choice for us to partner up with. Now if you wanna start gaining the upper hand from the outset, that's your choice, but I can see through your schoolyard bullshit. So, we can start again if you want, or we can fuck off right now.'

Charlo sniggered and stepped back as he relit his cigarette. He let the fag sit in one corner of his mouth as the smoke escaped the other.

'You're Fallon's fucking brother alright. I'll give you that much,' he said as he eyed The Boy slyly. 'Okay, let's do this,' he said, clapping his hands. 'We agreed five kilos and a thousand pills at a time… Twenty grand all in with two weeks' credit. Yeah?'

'Okay,' The Boy replied, then he nodded at Gordon, who reached for the bag.

'Whoa, whoa, whoa!' Charlo protested. 'Don't tell me it's in that fuckin' bag,' he said, looking around the car park nervously.

'Okay, I won't,' Gordon said as he slung it over his shoulder.

Charlo jumped in the car and rolled the window down. 'Follow us out the road,' he said, 'and keep a safe distance. If we get any heat, stop following… Jaysus Christ.' Then they sped off.

The Boy looked at Gordon, rolled his eyes, climbed on the Honda and followed. When they caught up with Charlo, he'd stopped in a boreen on the outskirts of the city. He leaned out of the window, pointed to a post by the roadside, and shouted over the car's engine.

'Put the gear behind the lamppost out of sight and follow me back into town. We need to have a serious chat.'

Gordon placed the bag in the undergrowth behind the lamppost, climbed back on the bike, and they followed Charlo, with The Boy throttling the shite outta the Honda, trying to keep up. Charlo pulled into a disused forecourt, stepped from the car, lit a joint and waited. As the boys pulled in, he motioned them to stop, then he stormed forward, jabbing his finger in The Boy's chest, shouting.

'If you two ever pull a stunt like that again, I'll fuckin' bang yer cuntin' heads together. From now on, we arrange a drop-off point. You put it there and I pick it up when we are sure it's safe. Never bring a bag of gear directly to me again. Are ye fuckin' thick or what? If this is gonna work out, you two better get wise fast… I'll ring ye in two weeks. Now fuck off, before we really fall out.'

The Boy held Charlo's stare.

'If you've half a cunting brain, then whatever it is you're about to say… don't fuckin' bother. Go tell whoever the fuck gave you this gear about the stunt you two pulled and see if they think I'm overreacting,' Charlo shouted.

The Boy stared Charlo down, put the bike in gear, then pulled out of the forecourt.

Chapter Twenty-Nine

THE BOOK OF DANIEL

Part III

MAGS STOOD BY THE OPEN fridge. The cool air blew past her face. She could've stood there all day. She took the pie from the middle shelf and placed it on the counter.

'Fourteen dates in America?' she heard Fintan say. She'd already discussed the trip with Daniel earlier, and didn't envy him trying to sell the idea to his Dad.

'Fourteen dates in America,' Daniel replied.

'America?' Fintan said, turning to Mags, as though they were both hearing it for the first time. She walked to the Aga and checked the temperature.

'America,' she heard Daniel say.

'Fourteen days?'

'Yes Dad, fourteen days,' Daniel sighed.

'I dunno, son,' Fintan replied. 'You're only sixteen. Is Beckett definitely going?'

'Of course he's going.'

'How will ye get around?'

'There's a tour bus.'

'A tour bus?'

'Yes, there's a bus… there's a driver and a tour manager and we are getting paid. It's all legit, and we get to speak to the publishers about the book they want us to put together.'

'A publisher?'

'I know yeah… there's talk about doing some talk shows and

radio appearances if the campus tour goes well. It's blowing my mind.'

'You're telling me,' Fintan sighed.

At the airport in Shannon, the operations manager Tony Ryan escorted them to their seats.

'I liked your talk on *The Late Late* Daniel, it was fuckin' awesome,' Tony told him as he led them to their upgraded accommodations in first class.

'Thank you, Mr Ryan,' Daniel replied.

'You've got your head screwed on son, I'll give you that. If you could think of one thing to improve how airlines are managed, what would you suggest?' Tony asked, leaning in conspiratorially.

'Employ algorithms,' Daniel replied as he handed Tony his jacket.

'What are they… fuckin' robots?' Tony asked, confused.

'What?' Daniel said, even more confused.

'Al-go-whatever the fuck you called them. What are they, fuckin' robots or something?'

'An algorithm… no, no, no.' Daniel laughed before continuing with a wink. 'It's essentially a formula for success. Find yourself a mathematician, tell him what you want to achieve. If he's any good, he'll write you a few algorithms that'll pitch the odds in your favour.'

'Fuck me pink, that sounds deadly. A mathematician? Where do they hang out?'

'You won't find better than Dr Beckett,' Daniel said, motioning to Beckett settling into his seat.

'I'll write you an algorithm,' Beckett said. 'Meet us when we come back in a few weeks and we'll make a plan.'

'I'll fuckin' hold ya to that boyo, what'll ye have to drink? On the house.'

'Champagne, my good man,' Beckett replied.

'We've fuckin' loads of that shite. Darren!' Tony hailed the head flight attendant. 'Make sure these two get the presidential treatment… no… fuck the president, give these lads the papal treatment.'

'Does the pope drink?' Daniel asked.

'He does when it's free, the tight fucker,' Tony replied, then burst into laughter as he headed for the exit.

'See you when we get back, Mr Ryan,' Daniel called.

'I'll be waiting on the whorin' tarmac.'

Daniel slept. When he woke, he could feel the words forming, like some realisation from a place far beyond yet deep within him. 'The hill or the haze?' it asked, and before he could answer, he heard the captain's seductive velvet timbre announce:

'Cabin crew, seats for landing.'

A light pinged overhead, and the cabin came alive with a thousand bustles, clicks, yawns and questions. Then it settled as fast and he looked to Beckett, deep in a drunken slumber and he turned his thoughts inward and answered, *the hill.*

When they landed, the bus waited to whisk them to Boston, their first stop, where a coven of witches from Maine, fat hairy-chinned bitches, one and all, had set up vigil outside the auditorium with their **DANIEL 7:23** banners raised high. They chanted his name and screamed in tongues, with tongues pierced. Inside, Daniel spoke, and the crowd flew. Atop a wave, each man and woman rode strong, shoulder to shoulder, and when he was done, he set them down gently with love on the banks of sense and reason, reborn, and they felt the freshness of their rebirth, and the world was their canvas, and they would paint it anew, unburdened of ideas old.

In New York, they brought the house down. In Washington, there was talk of a visit to the big house… Daniel declined. Philadelphia to Chicago, then on to Minneapolis and Seattle, where the audience refused to leave the auditorium for two days after Daniel and Beckett's performance. Next on to Portland, then San Francisco, where as Daniel took to the stage, he saw in the distance a tumbling white haze one hundred feet high approach him at a pace. He stood there powerless as it absorbed him whole and he sank to his knees and surrendered to the inevitable.

No one could reach him… he'd retreated to the recesses in the abyss of his magnificent mind. They flew back to Shannon where Tony Ryan waited on the tarmac as promised. He carried Daniel in his arms to his waiting father. Fintan took his broken child from Tony and placed him gently in the back of the car, where Mags ran her fingers through her little boy's hair as they drove in a dream back home.

The phone rang nonstop.

'Jaysus H Christ Mags, will you plug that fuckin' thing outta the bloody wall?' Fintan howled.

'Will you calm down, love, for God's sake? It'll all stop soon. They'll get the message and stop ringing soon. Have patience Fintan,' Mags told him.

'Patience? I've the patience of a bloody saint. To be fair, it's a lot to take in, Mags. I mean… Elvis Presley rang here yesterday… Elvis bloody Presley. Can you hear what I'm saying? It's not gonna stop any time soon Mags, I can tell ya that.'

Mags looked at Fintan. He was right. She knew he was right, but Daniel was her focus now, he had to be. The phone was a lot. It hadn't stopped since Daniel's return. Call after call. Stranger after stranger injecting themselves into their lives.

'Why don't you go for a pint,' she said.

'My fuckin' head is spinning.'

'I know pet, but we've been here before. Right?'

Fintan nodded. He was on the verge of tears. She could tell he needed space.

'Go on,' she said. 'Go for a few pints. I'll get the tea on.'

'Okay,' he said, and he walked to the hall and took his coat from the stand.

'Don't talk to any reporters. Fintan, did you hear me?'

'Reporters?' he said. 'For the love of God, will ya give my head peace?'

Mags watched as he passed by the window. *Poor man*, she thought. He wasn't built for this. It was hard enough for him trying to comprehend Daniel's complexities at the best of times, but this, this was too much. The phone rang. She wanted to pick it up and scream *FUCK OFF!* down the line. She gave it some serious thought. She imagined how satisfying it would be. It stopped ringing.

'Thank Christ,' she said.

A few more days, she told herself. In a few more days he'll be right as rain. This time was no different than any other time. She could feel the tension in her head dissipate. She walked to the fridge. A cool air blew past her face as she opened the door. It felt good. She took a chicken, a bag of potatoes and two bottles of milk from the middle shelf of the fridge and placed them on the kitchen table, then walked back to the fridge, placed her head on the cold shelf and breathed ten long breaths. When she was done, she closed the fridge door, stood back and looked around the room.

'You're okay, Mags,' she said. 'You're okay.'

Beyond the haze he hears their voices, Fintan, Mags, some others. They come and go, come and go, ebb and flow. Christy's voice one day caused him to stir, and it was almost enough to pull him from the haze. He tried, he really fuckin' tried to make a move, but it felt like a hundred whoring bastards with pillows were pushing him from every angle and he forgot about Christy and the voices ebbed once more and he thought again in ones and zeros and they poured down around him and piled up high above his head and soon he was swimming in the fuckers. Ones and zeros every-fuckin'-where, and he could eat them – when he ate a one he'd float up and when he ate a zero, he'd sink down, and when he ate them by the dozen his eyes would spin, ring up like a cash register and the net result would see him rise or fall. He'd float like this for days on end until some old shite would catch him drifting and he'd be drawn for a moment beyond the haze.

Then one morning he awoke in his bed to the sound of the birds. He sat up, swung his legs over the edge, and called down to his mother. 'Ma… Ma… Ma, can you hear me?'

'Jaysus, love, I can, are you alright?' Mags cried, running at him, throwing her arms around her lovely boy. 'Sit down, love, Jaysus Christ, how do you feel?'

'I'm grand. What's the matter with ya? I need to ring Beckett. Has he been in touch?'

'He's been ringing every day, son. Every day without fail. He's been worried sick about ya.'

'Don't worry about me Ma, I'm grand. Every day? How long have I been in bed?'

The tears came streaming down Mag's face. She could hardly bring herself to tell him.

'Three weeks,' she sobbed.

'Three fuckin' weeks, Jesus H Christ Ma… what the fuck?' he said, rubbing the hair on his head. 'Did I eat at all? I'm fuckin' starving.'

Mags could barely bring herself to speak through the tears.

'I need to ring your Dad. Come downstairs. I'll get you some grub, ya poor crater. Are you sure you're alright?'

'Will ya stop? I'm grand Ma, I'm fuckin' starvin' though. Any chips?'

Chapter Thirty

MORE DIGGING

'CHARLO'S BEEN IN TOUCH,' GORDON said. 'Nine tonight, same spot again. They'll drop the money there shortly beforehand. We pick up the money and leave the gear at the same time.'

'I don't like the way this prick is calling the shots. Does he want the same amount?' The Boy asked.

'He wants more, but I told him we couldn't get it. I thought it might keep the pretence alive, that we have a supplier.'

'Good thinking.'

Gordon tapped his temple and winked at The Boy. 'Downstairs for dancing, kiddo, down-fuckin'-stairs for dancing.'

'You're a gowl.'

They'd been back out to Janie's yard a few days earlier to upgrade the motorbike. They'd hoped Janie would take the Honda back and let them exchange it for something bigger, but he didn't wanna know.

'You wanna what?' Janie'd spewed, his not great, 'good eye', bursting from its socket, his veined cheeks reddening.

'Not a fuckin' chance,' he continued. 'God knows what fuckin' shenanigans you two hoors have been up to on that bike. Not a fuckin' chance in fuckin' hell to fuck. I'll get ye a *new* bike alright. But I don't want that fuckin' Honda within ten miles of me. Are we clear?'

Gordon looked at the Honda parked by the gate. He also noted the impossibility of the ten-mile rule in a small city like Cork, but thought better of pointing it out.

'No worries, keep your knickers on,' Gordon began. 'We need something reliable and fast, but not too flashy. About 400cc should do the trick. Reasonably new and again, no papers.'

'No fucking papers.' Janie sighed. 'I need my head seeing to, gettin' involved with you pair of wankers. This is all gonna end bad. I fuckin' knew it, first day I laid eyes on ye, I fuckin' knew it.' Gordon noted the misuse of the plural but again opted not to bring it to Janie's attention.

He ushered them to the shed at the back of the main house. Janie opened the barn door, where the usual row of bikes sat by the left wall, waiting. In the centre of the outhouse, veiled in a black dust sheet, a lone bike stood. Their eyes sought it out instinctively, as if by some mystic insight Janie had foretold their desire and this lone centrepiece had sat in eager anticipation of The Boy's arrival.

Janie pulled back the dust sheet, like a matador revealing some magnificent beast he'd brought to heel, orating proudly as he did so.

'Kawasaki ZXR 400, custom matt black finish, fast as fuck, reliable as fuck and not too flashy. As long as you two don't boot about the place like a pair of eejits, no one will even bat an eyelid as ye roll on by. You need to make a swift exit? This little beauty will not let you down.' He folded the dust sheet, tucked it beneath his arm, and stood back with the other arm outstretched, to complete the revelation. Their eyes bulged as they beheld the bike in all its unburnished beauty, bible black, dusk's raven, cut from the night.

'How much?' Gordon asked as The Boy, trance-like, walked to the bike and circled it with the manner of a man approaching some smouldering rock begot of the heavens.

'Thirty-two hundred. If ye want, I'll get rid of the Honda for ye, but it'll cost an extra two hundred.'

Without a word, The Boy counted the money, handed it to Janie, then proceeded once more to circle the bike, his fingers brushing the matt black finish, marvelling at the sensory response as he passed his hand over its surface, coarse and smooth and haunting.

'We're gonna need some proper helmets and jackets. Can you help us?' he asked.

'I can.'

'Plain black, no stripes or markings. Non gloss, if possible.'

'Call into Fogarty's in town, ask for Barry. Tell him I sent ye. He'll get ye whatever ye need.'

'Thank you,' The Boy added before continuing. 'When can we take it?'

'Get yourselves sorted with helmets and whatever else ye need, then pop back out. I'll tune her up and make sure she's running proper for ye. I get the feeling ye won't wanna be breaking down somehow. Bring the Honda and the old helmets with ye. I'll have 'em ground to dust before ye've left the yard.'

'See you in a few days,' The Boy said, and he shook Janie's hand.

Janie didn't disappoint. Three days later, they drove the Honda out to his yard and left in style on their new Kawasaki.

To prepare for their meetings with Charlo, the boys had readied five parcels, each containing five kilos of hash and one thousand pills. They'd hidden them at different locations along the rural byroads of the city's Northside, ensuring they would not need to return to the stash for at least a month. They pulled the rest of the stash further into the woods, concealed it beneath a green tarp, and covered it with earth and forest debris.

At eight forty-five, they put on their helmets, climbed on the Kawasaki, and sped across the city, stopping to retrieve one parcel. The Boy kept watch as Gordon jumped from the bike and pulled the parcel from the ditch before continuing to the drop off. When they reached the boreen, they drove past the post, continued to the end of the lane, then returned, confident the area was clear. When they reached the post again, Gordon leapt from the bike, exchanged the packages, jumped back on and they sped across the city towards Blackrock.

They counted the money for the third time.

'Fifteen grand,' The Boy reported.

'Are you sure?'

'Course I'm fuckin' sure. You counted it as well. How much did you count?'

'Fifteen.'

'Exactly, the wanker has stiffed us for five grand and now he has another twenty grand worth of our gear. Come on, we are goin' for a walk. I'm ringing this cunt now.'

They walked down the stairs and out the front door. They crossed the road, and The Boy took his new phone from his pocket and dialled Charlo's number. After two rings, Charlo picked up.

'Story?' Charlo asked.

'"Story" my hole. You were shy on your end earlier. What's going on? That's not what we agreed?'

'No worries, kid, this is normal practice. I've got one or two loose ends that should be tied up tomorrow or the day after. I'll see you right once it's sorted and the slate will be clean except for the recent pick up. This is how it always goes down. If we're gonna make this work, we need to trust each other. Thursday morning I'll meet you for a cup of tea and we can have a little chat and balance the book… okay?'

'No, it's not okay. I've got people haunting me for this gear. It happens my way or I move on to someone else. Tomorrow evening, meet me at the petrol station from a few weeks ago at seven o'clock and have the money. Any more of these stunts… you're out and I pass your debt on to my supplier, and you can explain to them how this is normal practice.'

The Boy hung up the phone and turned to Gordon, playing the conversation over in his head.

'How'd I sound?'

'Does it matter? It's said now, I guess you sounded calm and in control. He either goes for it, or he doesn't. What if he tells us to get fucked?'

'I'm not sure.'

Charlo had been busy in the weeks since his meeting with The Boy. He had capitalised greedily on his unique opportunity. As the city's only dealer with a steady supply, he had doubled the price of ecstasy tablets from fifteen punts to thirty. He was selling a sixteenth of an ounce of hash, which traditionally cost ten punts, for twenty, which in simple terms meant he stood to recoup fifty-eight grand for his twenty grand investment every fortnight.

His enterprise, however, had not gone unnoticed. In a car, overlooking Charlo's dealing spot on Cork's Northside, Clifford and Carl sat and watched the steady flow of punters first disappear round the back of the terraced houses, then re-emerge surreptitiously at the opposite end moments later, their faces concealed beneath hoodies or baseball caps as they scurried to nearby cars or motorbikes where their drivers awaited, vehicle in gear, clutch applied ready to go.

'Who is he?' Clifford asked.

'Some wanker called Charlo Kelly. Last I heard of him he was robbin' handbags on Patrick Street. Now he's selling gear hand over fist. I've no idea where he got it from or who he's connected to,' Carl replied.

'What should we do about him?'

'He might've stolen the gear somewhere – he might be back robbin' handbags in a few days once he runs out. Let's give him another week. If he's still here next week, then we action our plan as discussed. You cool with that?'

'I think we should shoot the cunt now,' Clifford replied, a wry smile growing on his face.

'Now? Like right now? We can. If you want,' Carl replied, his taste for blood baited by Clifford's response.

Cliff thought a moment, put the car in reverse, and backed slowly from their vantage point.

'One more week,' he replied. 'We action our plan in one more week.'

The Boy woke early the next day. He had two missed calls from Charlo. One from late the previous night and one from seven that morning. He regretted the previous evening's exchange and wished he'd not been so gung-ho. He went downstairs where Ann, sitting by the mantel smoking a fag, looked up.

'Morning love,' she said. 'Will I get ya some breakfast?'

'Cheers Nan, can I have Coco Pops?'

'No, too sugary. I'll get you some porridge with bananas and a cup of hot chocolate. How does that sound?'

'Can I have eggy bread?'

'You can. I've lovely eggs there your Granda got at the market. Gimme five minutes and I'll have you sorted, pet. Will you have a hot chocolate as well?'

'Thanks Nan,' he replied, forgetting himself, regressing too easily to her little boy, then back again as fast. 'Gimme a shout when it's ready,' he told her.

He walked to the back of the house and sat on a bench beneath the bower to the rear of the garden, where he sheltered from the rain. He removed his phone from his pocket and dialled Charlo's number.

'Good morning, sunshine,' Charlo chimed. 'Are we in better form this morning, petal?'

'I've missed calls from ya, whassup?'

'Nothing's up, it's all going down, actually. About that outstanding paperwork. I'll get it to you next week. I've got a prior arrangement tonight, so your seven o'clock rendezvous won't be possible.'

The Boy bit his tongue. *Not a word*, he told himself, *do not engage with this shit.* Some seconds passed before Charlo chimed back in.

'Are you still there?'

'I'm here.'

'Well?'

'Well, what?' The Boy's heart pounded in his chest. He could hear it in his ears. He was certain Charlo could hear it through the phone.

'So, I'll ring you next week?' more question than statement.

'I'll be waiting at seven o'clock tonight. If you don't show, I told you what I'd be doing. I haven't changed my mind.'

'What do you think this is, a fuckin' Western? Are you thick or what? I told you already that I need to round up some loose ends and I'll sort you out. What's the fuckin' problem? If you weren't so fuckin' green, you'd know that's how this shit works.'

'I know how much you've been selling that gear for, and I know you're selling it yourself from a spot up the Glen. All cash, no tick, no middleman. If you've got rid of the first batch already, by my reckoning you've got somewhere between fifty and sixty grand in your back burner, so don't fuck me over with this loose-ends coming up shy shit. You've got the money and then some. You're trying it on, and we both know it. Tonight at seven, I'll be expecting ya.' The Boy hung up.

Chapter Thirty-One

FORECOURT

THEY ARRIVED TEN MINUTES EARLY, drove past the forecourt, circled around, then drove past for a second time. When they returned for the third time at two minutes to seven, Charlo was nowhere to be seen.

'He's got five minutes, then we are outta here, agreed?' The Boy asked.

'Whatever you say, boss.'

'Don't gimme that "boss" shit. We agreed… if we can't trust this prick then it's better to cut our losses. Yeah?'

'Absolutely.'

'What time is it now?' he asked.

'Seven o'clock.'

'Right… three more minutes and we go,' he said. He felt pathetic even giving him three minutes. He knew he wasn't coming, but he needed something definite. Some finite act from where he could draw a line.

'What then?' Gordon asked.

'We speak to Black Dave. Get some advice. Maybe he can get our money back. I dunno.'

'Do we tell him about the stash?'

The Boy looked at the ground. He didn't know the answer. If he was telling Dave about Charlo then he'd have to divulge some information, but how much he was comfortable with, he wasn't sure.

'I don't know,' he said. 'He might know someone more reliable to help us get rid of the gear.'

Gordon nodded.

They smoked an anxious joint and waited. Gordon spied in the distance a small red car approaching.

'Is that him?' he asked.

'How the fuck do I know? He drives like an old woman if it is him. This fool's going about ten miles an hour.'

'Maybe it's a drive by,' Gordon joked. Realising his stupidity, he tried to retract the words, but The Boy cut in.

'What time is it now?'

'Seven-O-four,' he said, in a DJ-style.

'We let this car come and go, then we are outta here.'

'Jaysus Christ, we'll be here all night.'

They watched the red Nissan Starlet approach the garage, pull alongside, then mosey on down the road. The Boy flipped his visor down, twisted the throttle, released the clutch, and sped off in the opposite direction.

The Boy marvelled at Black Dave's bulk. He was enormous. Taller than the chilled drinks cabinet and easily as wide, he noticed, as Dave helped himself to a Coke then joined them at their table.

'Let me get this straight,' Dave said as he sat back down. 'You know where Fallon's stash is and you've been selling it to this joker, Charlo? Charlo hasn't paid up and you're not sure how to go about getting your money? Fuckin' hell, son, you're a dark horse. Talk about fuckin' feet first.'

'Do you know who I'm talking about, this Charlo?' The Boy asked.

'I've never heard of him, but I know all the lads from the Glen and the Northside. It won't be too hard to find out who he is. Without a doubt, he'll have your money, and I can get it back, but it's working out how to do it. If I pick him up from his dealing spot, he won't have the money on him. He might get spooked and run, so we need to do a little detective work. It won't be a problem though, so don't worry. Is the gear all gone?'

'No, there's some left.'

'What's the plan?'

'I wanna get rid of it.'

'What have you got left? Roughly?'

'About eight thousand pills and fifty kilos of hash,' The Boy recalled, not mentioning the white powder blocks.

Dave exhaled loudly. 'Fuckin' hell mate… I can help you get rid of it if that's what you want me to do. The pills… I can have somebody collect them from you this afternoon. I can get them sold for top dollar through my lads in the clubs. Obviously, everyone who touches 'em gets a cut, but I can safely guarantee you ten quid a pill. The hash is not really my bag, but I know a good lad who worked for your brother. He's honest as fuck and hard as nails. He was tight with Fallon, so there won't be any funny business. You can work out a price with him yourself, but I know he's keen to get back to work. I reckon he'd be ready to rock and roll right away. He might even help with the Charlo situation. Do you want me to put you two together?'

'Okay, yeah cool… About the pills, do you mean take them in batches or take the lot at once?'

'Whatever you're comfortable with.'

'The hash I definitely want to do in batches. If this guy gets busted, then I'm fucked. At least if it's in smaller amounts, I only stand to lose that amount.'

'Good point. Fifty kilos of hash is fuckin' bulky. And the pills?'

'Let's do two thousand pills to start with and take it from there. This is all new to me… I don't wanna leave myself exposed. How long will it take to get rid of two thousand pills?'

'They'll be gone by tomorrow and the money will be back after the weekend, Tuesday or Wednesday at the latest.'

'Fuck me, that's fast.'

'We don't fuck about, sonny boy. The following weekend they should be cool, but the Monday after, my boys should be ready for another two thousand. Sound okay?'

'What's your cut?'

'The guys work for me, so I'll get my cut from them. The ten quid I mentioned will be all yours. If they sell them for more… your cut goes up, but I'll stipulate a minimum price that will guarantee you at least a tenner a pill. Whatya think then, sonny boy… are we doing this or what?'

The Boy looked at Gordon.

'He's gotta be better than the last guy… right?' Gordon said, and he laughed.

Dave smiled.

'I think that's a yes,' The Boy said.

'Right!' Dave started, gathering his thoughts. 'Ring me on my mobile from a payphone later today once you've got the pills put to bed and we can arrange for my boys to pick 'em up. I'll start looking into this Charlo lad. My mate will ring you about the other bit of business. His name's Mucky, and like I said, he's a top geezer. You probably know this already, but no direct calls between mobiles. I will never ring your mobile from mine, and you do the same. If you need to ring me or anyone you're doing business with, then use a payphone. We don't want any links between us established in case this old plan of ours goes south. Cool?'

'Okay, cool,' The Boy replied.

'Right, I'm off then. Laters,' Dave said as he stood up from the table, walked to the counter, and paid for their drinks. Pocketing the change, he started for the door, all the while watching Gordon staring blankly at the car park.

'Is he alright?' Dave asked. 'In the head like?'

'Ah, he's grand. I think. He gets like this sometimes.'

'I'm watching two dogs… over there,' Gordon explained, pointing to the car park. 'They're stuck together. The dirty bastards probably spent the entire morning tryna get the ride and now the poor fuckers are stuck and can't get away from each other. I guess it's true what they say, careful what you wish for.'

Dave looked at The Boy. He had a confused look on his face.

'You seem like a popular kid,' Dave said. 'I bet you could have no end of proper mates,' he said, then reached across and ruffled Gordon's hair playfully.

Gordon shrugged him off.

'Laters,' Dave said, then he exited the caf.

The Boy suddenly felt defensive of Gordon. He wanted to run after Dave and explain that he was only joking, that Gordon was only joking too and he was really great, but it was too late.

He meant it though. Gordon was great and if not for Gordon he would never have had the guts to do this alone, nor could he think of anyone else alive he would trust enough to stand shoulder-to-shoulder with, or back-to-back if it came to it, in this situation. He was lucky and he knew it.

'Will we walk round to HMV and see if there's any new games out?' he asked.

'When is that one about the fella robbin' the cars comin' out?' Gordon asked.

'Soon, I think. Will we check?'

Gordon nodded.

Chapter Thirty-Two

CHARLO!

He enjoyed having stuff, Charlo. He'd never had shit. Fuck all is what he'd had, in fact, fuck all. His old man was a pisshead cunt, his Mam was a pisshead cunt and his grandad who'd raised him and his sister was a dirty old pedo pisshead cunt.

He'd done a few spells at the borstal in his teens, and he was keen to avoid a return to the gaol system at all costs. His recent explorations into the world of organised crime had given him a taste for luxury. He could see the allure. It was almost worth a spell in the old clanger. He had tea bags and cans of beer, milk in the fridge, packets of ham, eggs, bacon, and crusty bread. Crusty bread, he thought. You knew you were doing alright when you were buying fresh crusty bread every morning. Some wanker had even turned up at the dealing spot with a stolen Technics stack system two nights back that he'd bartered for two ten spots, so now Charlo had some decent choons boy! He could go to the pub to have a few pints, then leave safe in the knowledge that he could buy more if he wanted to. Gone were the quiet days of desperately drinking every penny in fear of not getting another chance to have a sup for a while again.

'Drink up, drink up for this may be the last sup,' the dole boys would chant on a Tuesday binge, their wives and hungry babbies waiting patiently at home for the bread-winner's return.

He had a block of hash, five new T-shirts, two new pairs of jeans, three new pairs of trainers, a black jacket, a green jacket, petrol in his motor, and money in his pocket. Life was fuckin' great, and it was all thanks to Fallon's cocky little cunt of a brother. Who did the little bollix think he was? He could fuck right off. Supplier? My hole… What prick in his right mind would give that snotty little bollix all that gear? The little prick has been selling off his dead brother's leftover gear.

Charlo was convinced of it. The dopey little bollix had gone round Fallon's gaff, lifted a mattress and there it was, or some similar scenario. *Well, thank you very much*, Charlo thought. *I'll take that off your hands.* He was only sorry he'd paid him back the fifteen grand. He reckoned he could've left a bag of rocks for the dopey cunt and he'd not have noticed til he got home on his shitty little Honda 50.

Ah well, he was quids-in now, so fuck him. He'd sell this last load of gear, then it was *adios amigos*. He reckoned he'd have about a hundred grand in cash once he'd finished. More than enough to join his sister in Santa Ponsa.

Twenty-two grand, she'd said… twenty-two grand to buy the apartment and about another forty grand to buy her boss's taberna. It was that simple, buy the flat and the boozer and still have about forty grand to fuck about with. His sister would run the pub, and Charlo would look at investing the other few quid if the right opportunity presented itself. For the time being, though, he would chill.

About two more weeks, he guessed, before he'd be ready to rock and roll, two more weeks. The gear was flying out the door hand over fist like shit off a shovel. All cash, no tick. If you wanted tick, you could fuck off… in fact you could fuck right off, right off to fuck with ya. His only overhead was a hundred quid a night to use the dealing spot.

It was Doolan's spot. Doolan had no gear, so Charlo asked if he could use his spot in the meantime. It had excellent cover, with lots of places to stash the gear. There were lots of escape routes, and a network of nearby safe houses ensured he could deal with peace and security. When he'd first asked for the spot, Doolan's natural reaction was to tell him to fuck off, but he thought better of it when Charlo offered to pay fifty quid a night for the privilege then doubled it to one hundred after Doolan's initial refusal.

'Okay,' Doolan said. 'A oner a night, but you're outta here as soon as things are back up and runnin'. Agreed?'

'Agreed,' said Charlo. Then he set up camp, and the money rolled in.

Chapter Thirty-Three

SHIT HAPPENS

'Let me get this straight,' Carl started. 'We don't shoot him at the dealing spot, right?'

'Correct.'

'We wait until he's finished for the evening, follow him home… Then we ambush him along the way?'

'Kind of,' Clifford replied. 'We wait until he dips back into the ditch to secure the stash, or whatever he does in there. Anyway, when he pops in tonight, we'll be waiting for him.'

'And we shoot him?'

'Not this time. I'm bored with shooting people. He deserves a more personal touch, this Charlo.'

'Whatya mean personal touch? We're not gonna ride the fucker, are we?' Carl asked, confused.

'No, no, not at all. Heaven forbid. However…' He paused for effect. 'I think we should… gut the fucker.'

'Gut him? Whatya mean *gut him*?'

'One of us grabs him from behind. The other sticks a knife in his navel and pulls it up sharply until it hits his sternum, then we stab him twice in the heart before slitting his carotid artery, *et voilà*!'

'Navel? St-stern… whatever the fuck?'

'Sternum, his breastbone.'

'And this artery?'

'How about you grab him, and I'll do the rest?'

'How about we shoot him?'

'We could, but where's the fun in that? Come on, let me show you how to restrain him without getting your hands in the way. We don't want any hunting accidents now, do we?' Clifford said as he grappled Carl in a playful headlock.

'How do you know all this shit?'

'It's common sense really. Regular folk don't think about it though, that's the difference. However, we need to think about it, so listen up, this is important. When you grab him from behind…'

Dave hissed, then reached back instinctively to where the razor had snagged the pimple at the nape of his neck. He inspected his bloodied finger. The third one this week. He would need to ease up on the dose, he thought. He'd been cycling steroids for as long as he could remember. Occasionally he would notice some minor side effects, but never any of the horror stories from the tabloids like sagging breasts, or roid-rage. There was never any of that shit. The worst he'd experienced was the occasional acne breakout on his shoulders and neck, a problem easily remedied by adjusting the dose.

He continued to shave his head in sweeping motions from front to back, stopping short of the neck, then proceeding cautiously, his finger surveying the site before advancing further the blade. He then swept the razor over his ears in parallel lines, stopping at the crown before turning at last to his face and neck, completing the ceremony.

'You are one handsome bastard,' he remarked, turning his head left to right, admiring his handiwork in the mirror.

'Right, Charlo,' he practiced. 'You picked the wrong boy to fuck over.'

A bit clichéd, he thought, then tried again.

'You've been a naughty boy Charlo my friend.' *Better*, he thought, *much better*, before continuing: 'You have a little bill outstanding with an associate of mine.' *That'll work*, he thought. 'Well, I say a little bill, but… it is in fact a substantial amount of money…'

'Not bad,' he said, dressed, then headed out.

It's a blustery fucker of a night, Dave thought. The air was full of a strange charge, blowing this way, then that, then still for a time until it picked up again and buffeted against the cars as they passed him on the street. He rehearsed in his mind again his opening gambit, but he couldn't quite regain his earlier authority. *Why am I so fucking edgy about this lanky string of piss*? he thought. He'd put bigger fuckers than this prick straight a hundred times before. He had a bad feeling about it. He wasn't sure why, but something wasn't right. He'd watched Charlo working hard these last few nights, racking up the readies. He'd noted the comings and goings. What time he started, which way he arrived, which way he left, who brought the gear, et cetera. The method had varied slightly each night, but it had always ended the same way. A motorbike would turn up three or four times throughout the evening and take a stack of cash from Charlo. At ten thirty it would turn up for the last time, take the cash, then Charlo would leave alone on foot and head along the path at the back of the houses to a waiting car on Glen Avenue. It was a five-minute solitary walk, and it was on this walk that Dave planned to lay down the ground rules.

Dave walked the fifteen minutes to Glen Park, took up his usual stalking point and watched as Charlo sold The Boy's gear to a queue of begrudging yet grateful punters that stretched all the way down to the North Ring Road. It had to be handed to him, he was making a good go of it, Dave thought.

At a quarter past ten, Dave heard the low purr of a high-powered motorbike. He checked his watch. It was too early for the final pick-up. He watched as two dark figures climbed from the bike, cut the engine, pushed it the final few hundred yards before concealing it amongst the sheltering trees that lined the path in the valley below. He continued to watch as the figures carefully placed their helmets in the brush next to the bike, then scurried across the park to the hedge at the far side. He could almost make them out. It was two men, he thought. One of them was vaguely familiar, but he couldn't be sure. Fucking bike thieves, he surmised, stashing the bike out of sight to use for a robbery or some other sneaky business that was none of his fucking business.

He turned his attention once more to Charlo as he wrapped up the evening's affairs. Like clockwork, at ten thirty, the motorbike arrived. Charlo handed over the cash, then turned on his heel and began his brisk walk along the back lane to his pick-up car waiting on Glen Avenue. Dave gave the few remaining punters a moment to disperse, then he started at a trot along the treeline to where he'd planned to intercept Charlo.

He wasn't gonna fuckin' make it, he thought as Charlo reached the planned intercept point. Dave still had fifty yards to cover, and he watched as Charlo walked from view. Dave broke into a sprint. As he reached the path, he watched Charlo disappear through a break in the ditch and into the thick bushes that lined the path on either side.

Where the fuck is he going? Dave thought as he watched from the cover of the treeline. He was certain Charlo hadn't seen him. What the fuck was he doing? Dave didn't like it. His bad feeling returned, and he waited it out to see if Charlo emerged.

At about ten fifteen each night, Charlo would feel the first rumblings. It would start with a feeling of wind passing internally. A fart of sorts, but no release. The next sensation would be a filling of the lower intestine. It was unmistakable and the urge to shit, although not unbearable, was certainly undeniable. A few moments later and his ring piece would be doing all it could to stop the inevitable. At ten thirty, the urge would be unbearable, and he knew with absolute certainty that he would need to take a shit soon. He'd shut up shop, turn on his heel and head for the pick-up car waiting two streets over.

Halfway along the path, where it swerved behind the cover of trees on either side, he would disappear over the ditch, drop his trousers and shit his heart out. The relief was bliss, and he would close his eyes as tears of pure relief streamed down his face at the realisation he'd made it through one more night. He was one more stack of cash closer to his early retirement in Santa fuckin' Ponsa, baby. There were only a few nights left. If he could hold it together for a few more nights, he'd be done.

Tonight was no exception. At ten thirty, he handed over the cash, turned his back on his pleading punters, and began his brisk walk along the back lane. As he approached his dumpsite, he glanced over his shoulder, took a sharp left over the ditch, continued for three more paces, then dropped his trousers, closed his eyes and cried as the shit poured out of his arse and a rush of wellness started at his sphincter and soared through his body to the top of his head as he realised again he was one night closer to his dream.

Cliff and Carl, frozen in secret disbelief, eyed each other in amazement as Charlo dropped his trousers and began to sob and shit, a snot bubble forming at his right nostril. Carl swung his head left to right. He wasn't grabbing this dirty bastard from behind. Clifford rolled his eyes, mouthed 'you cunt' then stepped from seclusion, drove the blade of his knife to the hilt in Charlo's closed eye and clamped his hand over Charlo's mouth to stifle the scream while simultaneously stabbing him repeatedly in the chest and neck with his free left hand.

In a moment, they were both upon him in a frenzy of stabs and slashes. He had fallen on his back, and they set about stabbing his crotch, thighs, stomach, chest, face, and throat until there was no place left to inflict a wound. Clifford then flipped Charlo's body onto its stomach, and the attack began once more. They stabbed the dead body lying there helpless, prone in the ditch with its trousers about its ankles over and over until, at last, Carl stopped to catch his breath.

Clifford nodded. It was enough.

They stood. Carl's head spun. He surveyed the scene as his frenzy eased. He felt sick. He looked to his partner, unsure. Clifford, giddy with excitement, gave him the thumbs up, then disappeared through the back of the ditch to the motorcycle waiting in the valley below. Carl looked at the body one last time, then followed.

What the fuck is he up to in there? Dave thought. *The dirty bastard is probably knockin' one out. Maybe he's clocked me and done a runner.* He stepped from the tree line and edged along the path until he reached the point where Charlo had entered the ditch. Peering into the darkness, he could hear footsteps exiting on the opposite side. *Sneaky little fucker,* Dave thought and started over the ditch in pursuit of the fleeing footsteps. Three steps in, he slipped and landed on his arse. The stink of shit coupled with a metallic tang caused his eyes to water, and he realised he had fallen in a warm puddle or oil spill of some sort. His hand sank into a wet, viscous gunk and he recoiled instinctively, then slipped again as he tried to right himself, this time landing with a crunch on what he guessed in the darkness to be a dead dog or a bag of kindling.

He rolled to the side, reached into his pocket, retrieved his lighter, held it aloft, and sparked the flame. Dave squinted as his eyes adjusted, then kicked back in horror as the flickering light cast thereabout revealed his deathly companion. He put his free hand to his mouth, crawled to the opposite side of the ditch, and watched the two dark figures as they reached the hidden bike. There was something about one of them, but he couldn't quite place him. He was too far away. Who the fuck was he? His gait, the way he flicked back his hair before he put the helmet on… he knew that cunt, he knew he fuckin' knew him, but who was he?

He rolled back inside the ditch, taking stock of his situation. He was lying in a ditch, feet away from a freshly dead body covered in the victim's blood and shit. This was not good. He needed to get the fuck outta here and fast. He watched as the bikers departed, then made his way down to the dirt path that followed the park around until he hit the North Ring Road. He waited as a car passed, then advanced from the darkness to the phone box on the opposite side of the road. The blood had absorbed in his black clothes, presenting no contrast, and he turned his back to the road as he dialled Frank, his head doorman and trusted associate.

'Hello,' came Frank's groggy voice.

'It's me. Listen carefully. I'm on the North Ring Road. Drive past the phone box then take a left at the cross. There's a layby about one hundred yards on your right. Pull in there. I'll be waiting on the other side of the ditch. Come immediately and bring some black plastic bags and a complete change of clothes for me. I'll explain when I see ya,' Dave said, and he looked the road up and down for vehicles.

'You what?' Frank said.

'Hurry, for fuck's sake, and bring me a smoke and some diazepam.' The diazepam was a tall order but if he came good, it would be a result.

'You what?' Frank repeated.

Dave felt his anxiety rise. He was gonna need the diazepam. He took a deep breath. A car passed by. He turned from its beam.

'Say "you what" one more time, I fuckin' dare ya, Frank. Now listen carefully, North Ring Road past the phone box, left at the crossroad, layby on the right. Bring clothes, smoke, diazepam and large plastic bags. Now hurry the fuck up!'

Chapter Thirty-Four

NEWS REPORT

TONY HELD THE GLASS BENEATH the Guinness tap. He looked out at the pub; it was mobbed with a good early morning crowd. It wasn't even dole day. He wasn't complaining, days like this were few and far between.

'Carpe-dime,' he thought to himself. 'Carpe-dime.'

'Two of the same please, Tony,' a customer called, shaking two empties.

Tony nodded. He pulled two glasses from under the counter, and started two more pints of Guinness.

There'd been another murder, up the Glen. Some youngfella called Charles Kelly. The locals were referring to him as Charlo. Tony didn't know him. He wasn't one of his regulars.

'Ireland's Murder Capital,' the newsreader had said, referring to Cork, on the radio earlier.

It's certainly gettin' that way, he thought.

He topped two pints and slid them across the bar. 'Two Guinness,' he called. 'Four-forty, please.'

'Cheers Tony,' the customer said, and counted the change into Tony's hand.

'It's on,' another shouted. Tony spun to see a picture of the Kelly boy, Charlo, a typical local-looking lad, on the TV screen.

'Turn it up!' someone shouted.

Tony scanned the bar for the remote, picked it up and pointed it at the television. He turned up the volume, then placed it on the bar again. A chorus of 'shh,' rose among the crowd as the reporter's voice filled the bar.

She was up the Glen, and when she reported her location a cheer spread throughout the pub.

'Shh!' Tony said.

'There he is now. Go on Pat,' somebody shouted, recognising the local politician stood at the reporter's shoulder. She pointed the microphone at his chin; they hadn't heard her question.

'Fine Gael bollix,' another called out.

'Will ye shut up?' Tony said. The pub fell into a silence. The punters leaned forward and listened as the politician spoke about local services 'working closely together' and how the Gardai were 'following leads' and 'appealing to the public for information'.

'Dirty snitches,' someone shouted.

The reporter was talking again now; they couldn't hear her.

'Shh,' Tony said, and then they were back in the studio, where another reporter, a man, continued the story. Behind him on the screen, a picture of Fallon flashed, followed shortly by The Big Fella and Tonto, side by side, wearing vests, muscles on display. A table of younger lads at the back of the pub cheered followed by a series of gasps, then silence again as a picture of the local youngfella, Eilee's lad, Eoin, seven years old, missing for the last few months, filled the screen. You could've heard a feather's fall.

'Poor lad,' a punter at the bar said to Tony. 'I know his mother, Eilee.'

'She used to come in here, back in the day,' Tony said.

'What age is he, the little boy?'

'Six or seven. I'm not sure.'

The newsreader spoke again; all ears and eyes trained in his direction. The television went black followed by an orange and yellow flash in the centre of the screen that faded with a faint hiss. The pub erupted in protest, chairs slid back as men stood, a glass hit the floor.

'What the fuck?' Tony shouted, turning to see Daniel, remote in hand. He'd come in the side door, they hadn't noticed. Daniel placed the remote on the counter, the scene about the pub as though he'd hit some magic pause button; men half stood up, mouths open mid shout, pints inches from thirsty mouths, all eyes on Daniel now.

A customer sitting in his seat picked his drink from the bar and moved along. Tony took a glass from beneath the counter and started a pint as the punters turned back to their glasses and the conversation picked up once more.

Chapter Thirty-Five

FRIEND DOWN THE ROAD

Sounds of people and vehicles coming and going in the street below. Town, maybe city sounds, he surmised, though not familiar. The cars came closer, the people stopped, chatting to one another. Not the usual hurried, distant city sounds he was used to. He could pick out individual voices with a more rounded lilt. The room, red as a womb through his eyelids, loomed and enshrined him in its stillness. He made to rise from the bed, but his body betrayed him. He tried in vain to open his eyes… *fuckin' diazepam*, he recalled.

He tried again to open his redundant eyes, and he passed once more to the slumbers where he dreamt of a ship of slaves ablaze on the Atlantic. The captain and its crew were exacting their escape aboard its only lifeboat. The cargo, chained, sat motionless within, their eyes closed to the terrors about them, as the ship listed, then groaned and began its doomed descent beneath the waves. Dave swam from one to another, pulling at their chains in some desperate bid to free even one soul. Their icy, shackled hands were frozen within their bonds as bubbles escaped their nostrils like rats from a scuttled schooner, when a giant hand from above snatched him by his scruff and cast him up above the surf to bob amidst the jagged swell and watch the giant propel with ease among the breakers, with a young slave girl atop his back, naked and crying.

When he woke, he recognised the red, hunt-themed curtains of the Beehive Hotel.

'Fuckin' hell,' he gasped as the horrors from the night before came screaming back.

He dressed quickly, ran downstairs to the payphone and dialled The Boy.

'Hello?' The Boy answered.

'It's your mate, how you doin'?'

'Have you seen the news?'

'Don't say another word. We need to speak. Can you come and see me?'

'Of course, where?'

'Remember, I told you we had a "friend down the road?"'

'I remember.'

'Come to that town, ring my mobile from a payphone when you get here. Our other friend in the news… did you ever ring him from your mobile?'

'I'm not sure, I think so. He rang me for certain.'

'Did you ever ring me on that number?'

'No.'

'Never?'

'Never.'

'Okay, is your phone pay-as-you-go or is it linked to you?'

'Pay and go.'

'Okay, get rid of it. Remove the sim card and burn it, then throw the phone in the river. What about your weird little mate? Does he have a phone?'

'He does.'

'He needs to do the same. Are we clear?'

'Crystal.'

'Cool, ring me when you get here. Be sharpish mate, things have changed significantly.'

*

Dave walked back to the hotel room. He shuddered as the previous night's terrors returned in flashes. The shit, the blood, Charlo – what was left of him – face down in the dirt. Who the fuck were those cunts on the motorbike? He'd seen that one with the hair somewhere before, but he couldn't place him. He'd been too far away to make his face out, but his poncey gatch was unique. It would come to him. He cringed as he recalled his escape.

'Too fuckin' close,' he muttered. 'Too fuckin' close.'

He ordered a club sandwich and a Coke from the room service menu, then showered while he waited for The Boy. He'd almost rang Charlo in the days leading up to his death, he remembered. The hot shower beat at his temples, then his neck and back as he cycled his head in rhythmic fashion, his left hand on the mixer valve inching one micron at a time towards cold. Three or four times he'd thought about ringing the cunt, each time settling to confront him face to face. He'd be in a right fuckin' jackpot now, he conceded, had he rang the wanker. His left hand inched ever more towards cold, his neck and head cycling left to right as the water pounded.

'Focus on the breath,' he told himself. 'Focus on the breath.'

The shower's torrent, icy now, pounded about his ears, his left hand twisting until it reached the cold stop. He drew in a long calm breath then exhaled, in again then out, repeating the process over, counting each cycle until at last he reached ten and he turned the shower off. He stepped from the enclosure to the sound of his phone ringing on the bed.

'Good morning,' came the familiar voice. 'Did you sleep okay, my little flower?'

'Yes mate, are you coming to see me?'

'I'm downstairs in the bar. Come down when you get a chance,' said *our friend down the road.*

Our friend down the road, as he was known, had long been an associate of Fallon and his crew. Existing on the fringes of the group, he ran his own micro-empire in the towns and villages of North Cork. A charming, impish little cunt, he had a knack of worming his way into your head. So much so that if you spent even a few moments in his company, you felt like you'd known him all your life. He had a trustworthy face, a firm handshake, a comic wit and an emotional intellect that made the little wanker impossible to dislike. He contacted the crew when he needed gear, always paid cash up front, and when they needed to vacate the city for a few days, he was the first man they thought of, and he never let them down.

Dave noticed his friend sitting in the snug nursing a Guinness.

'Will ya have a drink?' he asked, wrapping Dave in a warm embrace, throwing his arms around Dave's shoulders. He was a huggy bastard.

'I'm alright,' Dave replied, then changed his mind. 'Actually, I'll have a brandy and port.'

'A large one?' His left brow raised. The little imp was very persuasive.

'Yeah, yeah,' Dave replied, meaning 'no, no' but it was too late now as his friend walked behind the bar, started a Guinness, then put it to settle as he fixed Dave a brandy and port. Dave marvelled at his fluid movements as he danced between the bar staff, not a single eyelid batted at this intruder in their midst. This ghost-boy fixing and flying in their area of trade with such banal expertise. He finished the Guinness, slipped the head barman a sneaky fiver, grabbed the brandy and a packet of crisps and before Dave knew it he was sitting by his side with his arm round his shoulder, snuggling his cheek, telling him it was alright, that he was with his little friend now. Though Dave would never admit it, those soft, soothing words coursed straight to his soul and in that moment he had not a care in the world.

'I spoke with the manager,' Dave's friend began. 'You checked in yesterday at six. You ordered steak and chips at the bar at seven. I have two witnesses who will place you at the bar here between the hours of seven o'clock and midnight. I have a local taxi driver who collected you from the old Mallow Road at five o'clock yesterday afternoon and drove you and your fishing rods straight here to the hotel. There are no cameras on the road between your pick-up point and your drop-off here at the Beehive, so you should be safe and sound.'

'You're some fuckin' operator,' Dave sighed, his relief evident. 'Cheers mate. I owe you one.'

'You actually owe me two grand,' his friend replied. 'Unfortunately, corroboration like that does not come cheap. I've taken care of it, so don't worry for now. Drink up for fuck's sake, you look like you need it. What about your mobile phone? Did you use it at the scene?'

'No, it was off. I turned it off so no cunt would ring me and give the game away.'

'Touché.'

'You're tellin' me.'

'When was the last time you used it?'

'About six o'clock yesterday evening.'

'In the city?'

'Yes mate, at the flat.'

'Okay… so your phone places you in the flat at six yesterday. We might need to adjust our story slightly, but we are close enough.'

Dave jumped as his phone beeped on the table.

'Fuckin' phone.' Dave hissed, then coolly answered, 'Hello.'

'It's me, I'm here.'

'Whereabouts are you?'

'Not sure, by the train station.'

'Come into town. There's a hotel on your left called the Beehive. We're in the bar. There's a snug at the back.'

'We?'

'It's our friend. I think you two should meet.'

'We'll be there in a few minutes.'

'We?'

'I brought my weird little friend.'

'Great…'

When The Boy arrived with Gordon in tow, eating a McFlurry, Dave wasted no time in getting down to business.

'These two wankers who attacked The Big Fella and Tonto and then you and Fallon – I think they might be the same guys who paid a visit to our mate on the news. Can you describe them to me, this pair of jokers?' he asked The Boy.

'Biker gear, both thin. They had their helmets on so it's hard to tell you any more, but they were lively. Young, I think. The passenger was definitely young.'

'How could you tell?'

'The way he moved, he had a spring about him. He was there, then he was gone. I can't really describe it,' The Boy said, struggling to find the words.

'Don't worry mate, I know exactly what you mean. These wankers last night, there was two of them 'n'all. I recognised one of them, but I don't know from where. It'll come though. As soon as I see him again, I'll know him. It's from one of the clubs or somewhere. The way he carried himself… it was unmistakable. As soon as I clock that cunt again, I'll fuckin' have him. In the meantime, we need to be really careful. I'm gonna stick around here for a few days until the dust settles, but you two need to stay indoors. How you getting on with Mucky?'

'Great, we've agreed on a price. It's all put to bed. We've got a plan in place.'

'He needs to be careful. I'll make contact and let him know our suspicions about these biker cunts. In the meantime, keep your head down, son.'

'I will, Dave, thanks,' The Boy replied.

'You need a piece?'

'A piece?' The Boy asked.

'Yes, we fuckin' do,' Gordon said.

'A shooter,' Dave explained, ignoring Gordon.

'I'm not sure,' The Boy said, shocked by the option, though not ruling it out. He imagined a gun in his hand. It didn't feel out of place, but could he shoot one? He wasn't sure.

'Okay no worries. Anyway, like I said, heads down for now. I'll keep Mucky up to date and I'll be in touch in a few days once the dust has settled.'

Chapter Thirty-Six

CANNIBAL

'I can't imagine you fat.' Clifford laughed as he ran a hand over Carl's chiselled torso.

'I'm not lying,' Carl replied. 'Fat as fuck, I was.'

'I'm not suggesting you are lying for one second, but to see you now… it's hard to imagine you as a pudgy little fucker.'

'The looks I used to get. Utter disgust. The slagging, you wouldn't believe.'

'Oh, I would. Kids are cunts.'

'My old man hated me because of it. He was this big GAA head. I had no interest in sport, and I was "fat and lazy". The things he said,' Carl sighed, then continued. 'I'm a twin, you know?'

'Really? Oh my God.'

'Well, not an actual twin, but I was a twin in the womb. "Vanishing twin syndrome". There was a twin on one scan, on the next, it was gone. My Mam had been having pains or something in the first few weeks, so they scanned her early. The doctor told them it happens, and it's harmless. The second twin gets absorbed by the other.'

'Absorbed by the other?'

'That's what my old man said, though there was disgust in his voice.'

'Wow.'

'Do you wanna know how I found out?'

'Go on.'

'I was eight years old. I was playing with my cousin, Kieran. We were playing Mammys and Daddys, and you guessed it… I was the Mammy. Anyway, I tried to kiss Kieran, and he started calling me a faggot, so I beat the shit out of him. He told our parents, and my old man brought me home and beat the living shite out of me. Called me a useless, fat, queer.'

'The rotten cunt. Is he still alive?'

'No, he died a few years back.'

'Lucky for him.'

'Anyway, he sends me to my room, and I can hear him downstairs roaring and shouting at my Mam. "That useless fat cunt, all he wants to do is eat shit and watch telly and now he's a fuckin' queer" and so on. And my mother's screaming, "Don't say that about him, it's puppy fat. He'll grow out of it". But he's having none of it and he screams back at her, "Puppy fat? Puppy fuckin' fat? Do me a fuckin' favour. He was born a greedy prick. The fat fucker ate his own cuntin' twin in the womb, for fuck's sake."'

'What?'

'I know, unbelievable. Right?'

Clifford put his arms around Carl and held him tight.

'What a monster,' he whispered in Carl's ear, but in his mind, he was proud of the hungry little bastard. 'All this talk of eating babies is making me hungry,' he said.

Carl laughed.

'Bacon buttie?' Cliff suggested.

'Oh yeah, and a cup of tea.'

'Good shout,' Cliff said. 'Give me five minutes.'

'I'll give you a hand.'

'Stay where you are,' Cliff said as he pulled a house coat about his waist and headed for the stairs.

He walked to the kitchen, opened the fridge and took a packet of bacon from the shelf. He put the pan on the range and turned on the heat. He reached behind his ear, took a half-smoked joint, placed it in his mouth and bent to the gas flame. He took a long draw then stepped back, peeled some bacon from the pack and placed it on the pan. The smell of bacon filled the room, and he walked to the stairs and shouted up to Carl.

'Do you want an egg, as well?' He took two long draws on the joint while he waited.

'What?'

'An egg, do you want an egg?'

'No, thank you.'

Clifford walked back to the pan and turned the bacon.

A figure passed by in the yard, followed closely by another dressed in yellow.

Clifford turned. He froze. It was the Guards. He ran to the stairs, took them two at a time, burst into the bedroom and grabbed some farmery-looking clothes from the closet.

'You alright?' Carl asked.

'The Guards are downstairs. Stay here, and don't make a fucking sound.'

'The Guards?' He started for the window.

'Get back from the fucking window, for fuck's sake.'

Carl stopped in his tracks and ducked. When he looked again, Cliff was gone.

Clifford ran to the extractor fan and put it on full, then he grabbed a can of air freshener from beneath the sink and doused the room.

His doorbell rang. He turned the bacon off the heat, walked across the kitchen, closed the door behind him as he entered the hall, then walked to the front door. He picked the keys to the yard office from the keyboard, took a long deep breath, then opened the door.

'Hello,' he said with a confused look on his face. 'How did ye get in here?' He walked past the Guards to the yard and looked at the gate at the end of the lane.

'Mr Cromby?' the older guard asked.

'Oh, forgive me,' Clifford said, turning. 'I'm shocked to see you, that's all.' He offered them his hand. 'When I heard the doorbell, I assumed it was one of the staff, come to borrow a trailer or something. They often do at the weekend. Is everything alright?' he said, shaking the older guard's hand before taking the other.

'Are you Mr Cromby? Mr Clifford Cromby?'

'Yes, I'm Clifford. Is everything alright? You've got me worried now.'

'Oh, forgive us Mr Cromby, but we tried the bell on the gate a few times and got no answer, so we thought we'd walk up the drive and try the door. It's some place you've got here.'

'Thank you, but how can I help?'

'We're investigating the gangland stabbing of a young man by the name of…'

Clifford felt his head spin. His knees buckled and he felt himself start to go. The yard spun, the voices became distorted.

'Mr Cromby? Are you alright, Mr Cromby?'

Clifford snapped back into the yard. 'What?' he heard himself say.

'You looked like you were taking a turn Mr Cromby. Are you alright?'

'Gangland stabbing?' Clifford heard himself say. 'Out here?' He laughed. 'I'm sorry,' he said. 'I haven't eaten today. I'm actually recovering from a rather nasty cold. Are you sure you're in the right place?'

'I'm sorry Mr Cromby, as I was saying. A motorcycle suspected of being involved in the murder of Mr Charles Kelly was spotted on CCTV on the Midleton road below on the night of the murder, but then seems to disappear. Now we suspect it may have turned up this laneway and we are conducting house-to-house enquiries to see if anybody noticed anything unusual.'

'Well, I don't know,' he said. He watched the young guard walk toward the outhouse. 'What night are we talking about?'

The older guard consulted his notebook. Some inaudible transmission emanated from a speaker on his shoulder.

'Go ahead,' the guard said. Some equally inaudible transmission followed.

'Copy that,' the guard said. 'On our way.'

'Did you hear that?' the younger guard said. She was back by his side now.

'We've to go, Mr Cromby. If you think of anything, will you give us a call,' he said and he handed Clifford his card.

'Yes of course,' Cliff said, then watched them depart. The weakness in his knees returned and he placed his hand against the wall to steady himself. He took a long slow breath, walked to the hall, clambered his way to the mezzanine and watched the squad car snake its way along the lane in the direction of the city.

Chapter Thirty-Seven

LUCKY MUCKY

Mucky was a different animal. He was grateful to be working with The Boy. Nothing was a problem. His attitude was relaxed. There was no tension, no need to second guess or keep on top of his every move. The gear went out, and the money came back. Week after week, Gordon and The Boy watched as the stack of gear in the woods dwindled and the number of holes at the foot of trees increased. It was easy. Dave was taking the pills, Mucky was taking the gear, and the boys were getting rich.

It had been some weeks since Charlo's demise, and although Clifford had taken pause in the immediate aftermath of his visit from the Guards, he was starting to regain some of his old confidence and bloodlust. But it had rattled him.

'Where's he getting it from, the gear?' he asked Carl as they watched Mucky liaise with some well-known underworld associates in the car park of the Blackpool shopping centre.

'I don't know,' Carl replied.

'And these pills in the clubs. Dave?'

'Dave, without a doubt.'

'Fucking Dave, we should've left that Yardie cunt lying in the street with the first two,' Clifford scoffed. 'Might he be involved with this other cunt?'

'I don't know.'

'Right... well, we have little choice now. They both have to go.'

'We can't take out Mucky yet. It's too soon. The entire city still knows I've got it in for him. If we take him out and people make any association between me and the hit, then it won't take long for them to track us all the way back to The Big Fella and before you know it we are up to our necks in heat and shit. Don't forget Fallon's connection to the RA. Trust me, we don't want them cunts on our case.'

'The fucking RA. Do you mean those arseholes selling that fuckin' newspaper on Patrick Street… *An fucking Poblacht* or whatever it's fucking called?'

'That's exactly who I mean, and those lads are the tip of the iceberg. Trust me, that's a cage we don't wanna rattle.'

'Are you getting scared, petal, wind picking up a bit, my love? Grow a pair. We are taking out the Yardie and this other cunt. What's his name?'

'Mucky.'

'Yes, fuckin' Mucky, he's not long for this world either. We can keep an eye on him and see if taking out Dave stops his supply. If it does… lucky Mucky. If it doesn't… then I'm afraid Mucky's gotta go, me old China, and let the chips fall where they may.'

Carl had to admit; he'd enjoyed the last few weeks. The break had been nice. Seeing Clifford flustered had been a welcome respite from the chaos. He was all for taking over the city and doing what needed to be done, but there was something about the Charlo situation that went beyond the necessary. Not that any of it was necessary, but if they were to be successful then certain people had to go. He was okay with that. The Charlo escapade, not so much. It was as though Cliff was doing this for sport, and now he'd set his sights on Mucky.

'You alright?' Clifford asked.

'Never better.'

Chapter Thirty-Eight

LANDLORD

Tony cast a forlorn eye about the bar, then sighed. He'd always assumed it would be his, one day. His mother thought different though. She was selling up and Tony was going to uni. *Fuckin' uni*, he thought. *What the fuck am I gonna do in uni?* He loved the bar life. He was good at it. It had been in his blood for generations. It's not like she needed the money. The old whore was loaded. She owned flats all over the city, she owned a half share in a bed-and-breakfast in Killarney with her sister Niamh, not to mention the fortune his old fella'd left her. What was she thinking? She'd lost her mind. That was it. He settled on the notion that she'd lost her fuckin' marbles when he noticed movement in the corner of his eye and turned to see The Boy waving to him from the barrels in the side alley.

'What's the craic boy?'

'Grand, how's Daniel?'

'He's grand.' He checked over his shoulder. 'He strolls in about two-ish these days and sits in the same spot, minding his own business.'

'How's his bill going?'

'Grand, he's no bother. I'll ring ya when it gets down. Is that all ya called for?'

'Ah no, I was riding by, and I thought I'd check in on him. How are you?'

'Ah, I'm grand. My old one's selling the place, so I'm a bit fucked off about that, but…'

'Jaysus, what are you gonna do?'

'Ah, I'm not sure. She wants me to go back to uni and study law like my old fella. No fuckin' chance.'

'Is it on the market yet?'

'No, but she's had Morris & Collins out earlier and they've valued the place at two-sixty, so it won't be long. Keep it to yourself though – I've got a few lads with tabs that need settling. If the word gets out sure I'll never see the fuckers again!' He laughed.

'No worries. Sure, who would I be meeting?'

'You're looking well, boy. Have you won the fuckin' pools or what?'

'I wish. C'mere to me. Would you be interested in stayin' on and runnin' the place if someone was to buy it and they needed a manager?'

'Fuckin' too right, boy. Who've you got in mind?'

'I'm not sure yet. I'll let you know.'

'Sound.'

'No bother Tony, look after Daniel. I'll be in touch.'

The Boy rode up towards Shandon Street, stopped at a phone box by the cross and called Dave.

'How would I go about buying a pub?' The Boy asked.

'Hello Dave, how are you?' Dave replied sarcastically. 'Will they take cash?'

'I doubt it.'

'It'll be hard, but it could be done. How much we talkin?'

'Two hundred and sixty grand.'

'You couldn't buy it yourself, but if you knew someone who'd be happy to front the purchase, I know a man who could make it happen. It might end up costing you a few quid on top in the end, but it would be legit, and no cunt could touch it.'

'Cool. Will you set the wheels in motion?'

'Whose name are we gonna use?'

'Daniel.'

'You're a crafty little shit, you know that. Let me guess… The St Leger?'

'Exactly. Morris & Collins are representing Mrs St Leger. Will you get your man to approach them and make a full price offer as long as it never goes to market? Stress that his client is very strict about confidentiality.'

'No worries, mate, how soon can you get the paperwork together?'

'I'll need a day or two.'

'I'll speak with my man this afternoon.'

He rode back down to Blackpool, stopped the bike across the road from the St Leger, then sat there eyeing up his intended purchase. *It's perfect*, he thought to himself. He could run all the money through the pub, pay the tax on it and in a few years' time he'd be one hundred percent legit.

Across the street by the post office, he noticed Brida Scully. She was talking with Quigley, the moneylender. The Boy watched Quigley snatch a fist of notes from Brida's hand, then lean in menacingly. Brida backed up, put her purse in her bag and marched off toward the cul-de-sac. Quigley spat on the ground, then stood there counting the money. The Boy rode back to the phone box and dialled Dave's number again.

'Hello,' Dave greeted.

'It's me again.'

'Fuckin' hell mate, you're keen.'

'No… it's about something else. Can you find out what the relationship is between Quigley, the shark, and Brida Scully?'

'Brida Scully?'

'My old neighbour.'

'Right? I can ask, shouldn't be a problem.'

'Thanks Dave. Can you let me know as soon as possible?'

'I'll have news by the end of the day. I spoke to my man about that other bit of business. He's on the phone with them now, so we should have news there as well today. I'll keep you posted.'

'Nice one Dave, laters,' The Boy said, and he hung up the phone.

From where he stood at the top of Shandon Street, he could see all the way down to Blackpool, out across the river to the Southside and, if he moved a few steps, he could see along the harbour out to the port and Blackrock. He'd never thought of the city in that way before, as many things and places. He'd only ever considered what was right in front of his nose, and for the first time in his life he felt part of something bigger, something beyond him and his situation, yet still within his control. He liked how it felt, that feeling of control. He walked to his bike, put his helmet on and headed for Blackrock.

Chapter Thirty-Nine

TROUBLE IN THE SOUTH

THERE WAS HOPE AT LAST of peace in the North. That's what they kept telling him. There was talk of disarmament, a 'cessation of violence', it heralded. Promises from Downing Street met with suspicion from the Belfast Boys. Feargal was very clear about his stance. They could all fuck off as far as he was concerned, but he played along, for now. He'd seen it too many times before, the same old bullshit. His switch had been flipped a long time ago and once you'd flipped that switch, there was no flipping it back and it would take a lot more than some catchy terms like 'the Belfast Agreement' or 'multi-party agreement' to cajole Feargal. But times had changed, and he too would have to change, or at least pretend to put on his happy hat and shake Mr Blair's hand.

'Fuck it,' he sighed. It was a hard pill to swallow.

The phone on his desk trilled. He jumped in his seat, fumbled, knocked the phone from its stand, then searched in the darkness as the receiver scuttled about the floor, a faint 'hello' echoing from the earpiece.

'Yes, hello… I'm here… gimme a moment to fuck,' Feargal called out as he righted the phone, then placed it to his head.

'Feargal, it's Derry, can you talk?'

'Hi Derry. Talk-talk or talk?'

'I'm not sure which is which, but it's about that business in Cork.'

'Probably not best on this number. Are you at home?'

'No, I'm at a pay phone. I'll give you the number.'

Feargal wrote the number down.

'Gimme a few minutes,' he said.

He placed the phone back on the office table, grabbed his jacket from the hatstand and ran out the door. He couldn't fuckin' believe it. He'd almost given up hope of hearing anything from Cork about Fallon or The Big Fella's murders. *What the fuck could it be...* who *the fuck could it be*? he thought. His heart raced as he bounded down the stairs three at a time, until he reached the lobby doors, where he raced across the street to the phone box by the park, then hesitated.

That shower will have this phone tapped, he thought, as he turned and hailed a taxi down.

'Drive around the corner a wee bit until we see a phone box,' he instructed the driver.

'What?' the driver asked incredulously.

'A phone box, I need a phone box...' then, pausing a moment, 'Russell Street, take me to Russell Street.'

'You'd walk there in two minutes.'

'Here's twenty quid, now will you ever drive to fuck like a good man?'

They drove to Russell Street. The driver stopped by the chipper and Feargal jumped from the car, then raced to the phone box. Fumbling in his pocket, he removed the number and dialled Derry Twohig.

'Hello.'

'Hello, sorry about the wait. I was looking for a phone box.'

'No bother. How are things?'

'Grand, grand, you said you had news?'

'I do, I do. A certain somebody, code name "big black bamboo", has a large supply of roundy whites and a known associate of his has a large supply of black... brown.'

'Big black bamboo has a load of roundy whites, and his mate

has black and brown… what the fuck are you going on about, Derry?' Feargal asked.

'A certain somebody who's not white has the roundy whites. Are you following me?'

'Not really mate.'

'I thought you were head of intelligence in your outfit; don't you lads talk in code?'

'Aye, we do alright, but we don't talk fuckin' shite. I've driven halfway across town to get a number that's secure and you're talking like Frank fuckin' Zappa. Spit it out, for fuck's sake.'

'Does the name Black Dave ring any bells?'

'It does.'

'Up to his neck in pills, and he has a known associate who has a steady supply of hash – it's strongly rumoured that Dave is the source.'

'Okay… and do we think Dave is involved in the other shenanigans with the lads?'

'I've not heard that, but here's the thing. All the pills that Fallon and The Big Fella supplied had a "double dove" logo, and all of their nine bars had a Mercedes sign stamped on them. Now, the pills and hash in circulation in Cork at the moment all have that exact same branding.'

'Maybe they have the same source, and they are picking up where the two lads left off.'

'Maybe… but a source of mine has made contact with an old friend of the lads on a certain Spanish island who assures them that he hasn't put them in touch with this gear, and the only possible source of these particular brands would be him, or else it's the gear that he arranged for the two boys shortly before they met their demise.'

'I'll be down tomorrow.' Feargal placed the phone on the receiver, stepped from the phone box and hailed down a passing cab.

Black fuckin' Dave, he thought. *Well, fuck me.*

Chapter Forty

A VISIT FROM THE NORTH

DAVE WAS FEELING AWESOME. HE'D had a great session at the gym earlier, hit the sauna and pool afterwards, been for a nice bit of lunch and now he was heading home for a quick shower and a change, then it was straight back out for a few pints with his cronies before hitting the pubs on Patrick Street later that evening. He hummed to the tune of 'Walking on Sunshine' as he took the stairs two at a time. His key slotted straight in the hole, the door opened with ease, and he slipped inside.

As he removed his jacket, he felt the door stop in its closing swing and turned to notice two large lads with shoulder length hair and moustaches, sporting faded double denim, follow him into the hallway, close the door expertly behind them then bundle him to the ground in a swift and effortless motion. He struggled in vain until a voice from inside the lounge called to him.

'Relax Dave, you're a big lad but we do this for a living. We only wanna ask you a few wee questions, then we'll be on our way.'

Dave stopped struggling, the two goons helped him to his feet and as they did, he realised they'd cuffed his hands behind his back. *I'm dealing with pros here*, he thought. Not cops, but not regular wankers. They marched him to the lounge, where Feargal sat comfortably in an armchair, eating what appeared to be a bowl of nuts.

'Fuckin' RA cunts,' Dave sighed, recognising Feargal. 'Make yourself comfortable, lads,' Dave said, attempting to regain a modicum of control.

'I'm sorry about all this, Dave,' Feargal started. 'Allow me to introduce myself.'

'I know who you are,' Dave said, cutting Feargal off. 'Now what the fuck is all this about?'

'Why don't you humour me and take a guess?'

'Don't fuck about Feargal. Spit it out. What bullshit have you got in your fuckin' head?'

'Sit down, Dave,' Feargal instructed. Dave sat opposite Feargal uncomfortably. 'I'll untie your hands, Dave, but if there's any fuckin' about, it won't end well for you. Like I said, I've got a few questions for ya, and then I'll be on my way.'

'Don't you mean we? I hope you're not planning on leaving the fucking gorillas behind?'

'Very well Dave, *we* will be on our way,' Feargal replied then chuckled to himself, motioning to the gorillas to uncuff Dave's hands before continuing.

'Dave, you're selling pills that were given to The Big Fella and Fallon shortly before they died. You've been selling them for weeks now, so you've got a sizeable quantity of these pills. Would you mind telling me how you came about having such a large quantity of these specific pills?'

'I got them from your nephew.'

'Convenient that…' Feargal started, popping a Brazil nut in his mouth triumphantly before continuing. 'Convenient, given he's now no longer with us to corroborate your story.'

'Not that nephew.'

'I'm sorry?'

'I got them from The Boy.'

'The Boy?' Feargal asked, then motioned to the gorillas to wait outside. Dave waited until the gorillas were out of earshot before continuing.

'He found Fallon's stash and asked me to get rid of it for him. I agreed – it's a large quantity of drugs and the cash would set him up for life. He tried getting rid of it himself, but he got ripped off.

I agreed to help him. I thought I was doing the right thing. He'd been through a lot, and I felt he could use a break. You know what I mean? Doing it himself, he'd have wound up dead or ripped off.'

'He's only a kid for fuck's sake.'

'That's why I'm helping him.'

'And the hash?'

'Not my bag, but I've put him in touch with one of Fallon's mates. He's in safe hands.'

Feargal sat back in his chair, ran his hands through his hair, and breathed a massive sigh of relief. 'How much we talking?'

'Not sure. He's in the process of buying a property in town that's valued at three hundred grand. He reckons he has the cash on standby.'

'Property?'

'The St Leger, you know it?'

Feargal knew the St Leger only too well.

'Legers, the pub, three hundred grand?' he said and looked at Dave with a what-the-fuck face.

'Two sixty, but by the time the money is processed and shit, it's gonna work out somewhere around the three hundred mark,' Dave explained.

'Who's handling the purchase for him?'

'Sullivan from Kinsale, you know him?'

'I know him, I'll ring him tomorrow… his rates are extortionate. Cheeky bastard.'

Dave nodded. 'Robbin' bastard,' he said.

'Fuck me, Dave, I'm sorry about all this. Can I buy you a pint?'

'Leave it out mate,' Dave said, relieved at the finality in Feargal's tone. 'I'd expect no less. I'll pass on the pint, though. I've got a prior arrangement.'

'Aye no bother, son. Let's keep this conversation to ourselves for now, alright?'

Dave nodded.

Chapter Forty-One

BOOMERANG

'GOOD NIGHT MAM,' ANNIE CALLED from the hall.

'Good night love, come here and give us an old fonda, will ya?' Brida chanced.

'Ah, will ya stop?' Annie protested as she walked to the kitchen and surrendered to her mother's arms. She was only nine, but she had an old soul. She'd been here before, many times, and she could read her mother like an open book. Her Mam needed a cuddle. She didn't quite know why or what ache was breaking her tonight, but if an old cuddle was all she was asking for, then who was she to deny her that?

'Will I stay up and watch a bit of telly with ya?' Annie asked.

'Ah, you're grand love, go on away up. I'm heading up soon enough myself,' Brida replied as she kissed her on the forehead, gave her one last squeeze, then let her go.

'Can I leave the light on?'

'Leave the hall light on. I'll turn it off when I go up?'

'Good night Mam, love you.'

'Good night, love.'

Brida listened. When she heard the toilet flushing and the bedroom door closing, she reached for the box above the cooker, retrieved the half fag she'd saved from earlier, sparked it up and inhaled deep. She loved that first draw. It was all downhill from there, but that didn't stop her. She hit the switch on the kettle and sat back down at the table. She played the numbers over in her head for the hundredth time that day.

Four hundred and eighty for the electricity. Two hundred and ten to Murphy's for groceries. Four weeks behind on the rent, and eleven hundred and fifty to Quigley...

Her blood ran cold at the thought of him. How could she have let it get this bad? *What was I thinking taking money from a fuckin' money lender*? she thought. It started off as three hundred quid at Christmas, but now, because of missed payments and whatever other shite he'd come up with, she currently owed Quigley the Bollix eleven hundred and fifty quid. She squeezed her eyes tight and smacked herself hard on the temple. Four quick blows.

'Stupid bitch, stupid bitch, stupid bitch,' she hissed. She wanted to scream and pull the cupboards from the walls. She wanted to push the cooker on its side, pick up a chair and smash it over the table, pull the tap from the wall and let the place flood around her as she smashed windows, doors and every bastard thing, culminating with her taking a sledgehammer to the walls and surrendering to the inevitable as the house collapsed about her, swallowing her whole.

The kettle trilled. She leapt forward and hit the switch for fear she'd wake Annie. Her face a stream of tears, she wiped them on the tea towel, put the bag in the cup, poured the water, then paused a moment as the mix infused.

She'd tried all day not to let her old fella into her head. She'd busied herself about the house, but then without realising he'd be there playing over and over, again and again, that smarmy bastard, leering and laughing. The rotten bollix with his big red head stood there howling, cartoon-like.

There were no words, at least none she could remember, but he didn't need to say anything, for the laugh said it all. *You are a useless yolk. You fucked it up like I knew you would. I knew you'd be back at my door with your hand out. Go on and say it, 'Daddy, I'm a tramp and a whore and I amounted to nothing. You were right and now I need your help. I should never have gotten with that useless wanker of the O'Malleys. They are nothin' but knackers and I'm sorry for not listening to ya. Please forgive me, Daddy'.*

She could see it now, she almost believed it, she was that low, the scene playing out in her mind for the millionth time. She took three long draws on the fag, stirred the tea bag and poured a splosh of milk until it turned the right shade of brown, then sat at the table and weighed again for the thousandth time all options available to her. No matter which way she laid the planks, the arrow inevitably pointed her straight back to her father. She'd go to him tomorrow and throw herself at his mercy, she resolved. She would take what was coming, for Annie's sake. This was no time for pride. She'd return tomorrow, cap in hand, and tell him everything. She'd start at the start and let him have the entire story, warts and all, ask him for a loan and be done with it.

She stubbed out the fag, sank the dregs of the tea and walked to the sink. She rinsed the cup and sat it to dry, ran the fag end under the tap and dropped it in the bin beneath the sink. Defeated, she walked to the hall, closing the kitchen door behind her. The landing light cast its beam down the stairs, across the front door into the little foyer, and it drew her eye to a small white parcel on the ground. It hadn't been there earlier, she thought as she bent to pick it up. She hefted it in her hand, its bulk familiar, and her heart raced at its potential contents. She sat on the bottom step of the stairs to steady herself, opened the envelope, peered inside and sure enough, it was stacked tight with ten and twenty-pound notes. At a guess, she thought there must be a couple of grand. There was a note inside and her eyes brimmed, then spilled down her cheeks as she read:

Brida,

I've come into a few quid and want you to have this as a way of saying thank you. Please don't try to give it back to me. I hope you can accept it. There is also a job for you at the St Legers three mornings a week (cash in hand), tidying up and doing the bottles if you want it. Starts at ten and finishes at two so you can fit it in around school. Call in and see Tony if you fancy it. My friend Dave will pick you up in the morning to go with you as your witness to visit Mr Quigley.

Brida held the envelope close to her heart as her lids brimmed once more and the tears spilled over and flowed down her cheeks. Her heart soared as she thought about the poor little fucker with all his troubles and how he'd still found it in his heart to think of her amidst all his own shite. She thought about new shoes and a coat for Annie, and she cried out loud then laughed through the tears as she pictured Quigley's face when she handed him his fuckin' money.

'Never again,' she swore, 'never again'. He was a little diamond, she thought as she imagined herself heading to the St Leger for her new cash-in-hand job. A smashing little fella. She started up the stairs to tell Annie she needn't worry her little heart anymore, that they were alright again, but she thought twice and decided to let the little crater sleep. In the morning, she would give her lunch money. She couldn't wait to see the look on her little face, and she cried some more as she took the stairs two at a time, the envelope and its contents clutched tight to her breast.

Chapter Forty-Two

GONE FISHIN'

He loved to fish, Dave. He craved for the way of it, like a calling. The clothes, the tackle, the earthy smell of the surrenderings of rocks and rubble cast up from the riverbed to linger, fall, then flow and settle. Four or five times a year he'd pack the boot with his rods and tackle, head out the old Mallow Road, then cut over the Nagle Mountains until he hit the Blackwater where she passed beneath the bridge at Killavullen.

He parked on the main street outside Harney's bar and lounge, climbed from the car and stuck his head in the bar door.

'Alright gorgeous?' he called. The barmaid looked up from a Guinness she was topping, and she beamed as she took sight of him standing in the doorway.

'Jaysus H Christ,' she said, trying to act cool. 'Look who's back, the big bold bollix himself. Are ya having a pint?'

'I am, to be sure,' Dave replied in his best Irish accent.

She picked a clean glass from the shelf, pulled the first draw then set it to rest.

'Are ya down for the fishin?' she asked.

'And the company,' he replied, giving her a cheeky wink. He could be an awful flirt.

She smiled. She liked Dave. Everyone did and she knew his blaggarding was harmless.

'Are you stayin'?' she asked.

'I was hoping you'd have a room for a day or two?' he asked, more official now.

'I'll have to check the book, but I'm sure we can squeeze ya in. What's the plan?'

'Walk the river today, fishing as I go. I should be in Mallow by about teatime… bit of dinner and a few pints, then get a taxi out here for the last few later. If you have room for me,' he said, taking the pint from her and sinking down half in one thirsty gulp.

'I'll send one of the lads in to collect ya,' she said. 'What time do you think you'll be ready?'

'Don't worry about it,' Dave replied. 'You lot'll be busy. I'll be out about ten-ish. I'll get a taxi from Golden's.'

'Golden's at ten… I'll have Patsy collect ya and that's that,' she told him as she leafed through the B&B bookings. 'I've got room two next to the phone in the hall free tonight and tomorrow night. Do you want it?' she asked, peering over the top of her reading glasses.

'That'd be lovely,' he replied, finishing his pint, then adding, 'Are you doing sandwiches today?'

'I am.'

'Lovely. Can I get a chicken mayo and a packet of King crisps?' he said, placing the empty glass on the counter. 'And another one of those, my lovely.'

'Sit down there and I'll bring it over in a minute,' she told him, motioning to the seat by the window.

He sat by the window and watched her as she went about her business in all her majesty. *She's a decent woman*, he thought. He watched as she wiped her forehead with the back of her hand, then blew air upwards as she swung her fringe from her eyes. He chuckled like a schoolboy at the wobble of her breasts as she held the loaf firm and cut the coarse crust with her work-dulled blade. She looked up and caught him gawking.

She smiled.

He looked away and blushed.

She's a decent woman alright. A decent woman, to be sure to be sure, he thought to himself.

The second pint went down as easy, and the sandwich and crisps hit the fuckin' spot. She brought him a scalding mug of tea, and a ham and egg doorstop rolled in newspaper for the fishing. She had a fear of the hunger and the thought of it catching up with him later was more than she could bear.

Fuck me, he thought. *She's some fuckin' woman.*

'Do you want a bottle of milk?' she asked. She was always offering him milk. He could never understand it. Was he to take it with him? How would he keep it cool?

'I won't,' he replied in his best country accent. 'I've a bottle of water, sure that'll be grand.'

'No bother, tis there if you change your mind,' said she.

'Thank you,' he said, took his sandwich from the table and he headed outside.

'Golden's at ten,' she called, and he gave her a cheeky wink.

Outside, he took his rod and tackle from the boot of the car, put the tackle in his backpack, slung the pack on his shoulder, pulled the boot door closed and headed for the river. At the bridge, he stopped a while to watch the salmon steady against the current in the water below. Their little noses fixed, their shiny backs flickering in the flow, and he lost himself to the sound of the water piling and crashing about the abutment, the river quickening as she passed between the piers – yet the salmon stood their ground, and he watched in wonder until a passing Massey pulled him from his absence and he stepped back from the parapet to watch it pass, trailer, hay and all. When he turned once more to the river, with a swish and a shimmy the fish darted upstream, and when they'd gone he wondered if they'd been there at all. He walked the bridge back, threw his leg over the deck and walked the wing-wall to the water's edge.

His plan was always the same. He'd follow the river upstream for an hour until he reached Fitz's Meadow where the Blackwater snaked about the high ground, and he'd break by the bend, set up his rod and cast across to the far bank where the willows awned the water.

He stood his rod up, checked his leader and fly line, followed the backing line into the reel, and saw that she ran straight. He picked his way between the reeds until he saw the rock, the first of four, that sat about six inches proud of the water. They were the remnants of an old stone bridge, razed to the river bed, back in the days when the whole country'd been at war. The four bridge stones lay perfectly on their sides with a metre's jump between each that took you about a third of the way across the river. From the fourth and widest rock, you could cast your line to tickle the tension without breaking the surface until you let the line lie. He stopped here each time without fail and he'd land a few easy ones before making his way on along.

He stepped from the bank onto the first rock, steadied himself a moment, gauged the distance to the next, then leapt with ease to the second. He stopped again, steadied himself, leapt to rock three, then with one last bound landed on the fourth and final rock. The water parted about the stones, and he stood for a while to gather his breath and his thoughts. He listened to the river sounds about him – the swirl, the babble and flow – rise and fall, and sometimes it was all he could hear and other times he had to strain to hear it at all and he could never understand how that was and yet it was always that way. He sat down, crossed his legs beneath him, laid the rod across his lap, closed his eyes and breathed. He focused on his breath at first, then he focused on the river sounds, a cricket or a bird or a dragonfly's hum as it swirled past his head. Then he heard the fat flops, and when he opened his eyes, he could see the waves where the salmon had landed and he stood himself up and cast out his line.

He was pulling them out fast, the fish. One salmon after the other, he landed them home, then released them back to the water as fast, laughing at their little faces as he put them back in, their heads craned in disbelief with a look that said, 'are you sure mate?' and he'd wink back at them and smile.

'Go on, you little fucker before I change my mind,' he'd say, then he'd place them back in the water, holding the tail with one hand, the other hand placed gently behind the gills in front of the soft belly, and he'd hold them like that until he felt the cold water seep between the fish and his hand, then he'd let them go, watch them fade into the water and then they'd be gone.

He reached in his pack for a Mars bar, tucked it in his shirt pocket, then reached once more for a pre-rolled joint. He placed the joint in his mouth, turned his back on the breeze, and held his lighter to the end until he saw her glow bright in the shadow of his cupped hand. He inhaled deep, held it a moment, exhaled, then repeated the process three times more. He stubbed the joint out on his heel, placed the rest in his shirt pocket and retrieved the Mars bar. He downed the bar in two bites, wiped his hand on his trouser leg, and pocketed the wrapper. He watched beneath the willows carefully for the flops and he thought about casting again before a rustling in the reeds by the water's edge behind him caught his attention. He turned to see a black mink eyeing him curiously from the bank. *What the fuck*? Dave thought, as the mink stood on its hind legs and swayed its head from side to side like a snake before the pounce, then dived like poured ink beneath the water, to reemerge on the first rock where it pawed its whiskers, eyed Dave for the second time, then submerged again, before appearing at rock two. Dave watched in shock and amazement the mink cross rock two, then dive again beneath the water. A moment later it burst from the water at rock three, stopped for a breath, squinted at Dave, then leapt from its perch, and swam with intent in Dave's direction. Dave, in a state of panic and disbelief, leapt from rock four to three as the mink passed beneath his feet, landed and without stopping continued to rock two, where he turned to see the mink perched on rock four, seeking him out. Realising Dave's deceit, it jumped back in the river and torpedoed in his direction. Dave bounded the final two rocks as a girly yelp escaped his mouth, then landed awkwardly on the bank, where he fell among the reeds. Over his shoulder he caught sight of the mink, atop rock one, searching. Dave scrambled to his feet and ran. He sprinted along the bank until his legs burned, and he could run no further, where he stopped by a willow tree to catch his breath. His legs ached, he could hear the blood pumping in his head, and he looked back along the path. The mink was nowhere to be seen. Dave placed his palms flat on his knees and wheezed out a series of long, hefty breaths before breaking into laughter. Tears ran down his face, and he laughed so hard he had to steady himself against the tree.

He took the half-smoked joint from his pocket, sparked it up and continued along until he reached Lovers Leap, where the water widened and slowed about a stony bluff and the river ran deep beneath the surface all the way to its foot. It was from here, in the past, that Dave had pulled home the keepers. Once, he'd swam the river across to the cliff face, put his hand to the rock and followed it down. He swam down and down and down and when he could hold his breath no more in the depths, void of light, he let go of the cliff face and, with a swish of his legs, he swam up and up. Halfway to the top, he felt a face, cold and pointed, brush against his hand, followed by a slow scaled body that tapered to a tail like none he'd ever felt before and it had no fear down there in the abyss. It must've been six feet long and at its centre measured two feet across. Alone in the depths and the darkness, the fear struck Dave's heart, and he swam hard. As he broke the surface, he felt it brush once more brazenly past his feet, and he swam like a madman for the bank. He shuddered with excitement and fear now as he recalled that mighty fish.

He removed his backpack and set it on the bank. From the side pocket, he took his bottle of water, twisted the cap free, and sucked hard. He kicked off his shoes, put his phone in the pack's pocket and rolled his trousers above his knees. With his rod in his hand, he checked the line once more, then waded into the water, mindful of the drop. The cold bed of stones shifted under his feet, the give and the settle grounding him at once with the river, ever changing. He stood a while wondering, then he caught himself drifting, checked the fly lines and cast the rod out, landing shy of the cliff's stony face. He pulled in a few beauties, then returned each one to the water. *Go on, ya little fuckers*, he thought, and he patted each one with a wet hand and stopped shy of kissing each catch goodbye. He was unhooking a ten pounder when, over his shoulder, he heard the reeds rustle and he turned on his bare feet, wondering.

There, on the bank, with a pistol by his left side, stood a tall figure clad in black leathers and a motorcycle helmet, his visor down, face concealed. He jumped at Dave's unexpected turn. Dave noted the surprise, and he let go the rod and charged at his attacker. The biker stepped back, slipped on the wet bank, and fell. As he fell, he pointed the gun at Dave and got off one round. Dave felt a blow to the side of his head. The bullet knocked him back into the water and he sank down and down and down. As he drifted down, he heard more blasts above the surface and the bullets fizzed and dropped about his head and then he felt his eyes close and he heard the sounds no more and he felt the big fish brush past his hand and he took her by the tail and she led him downstream and landed him safely by the bankside bleeding.

Dave touched his face where the bullet had glanced him. It was bleeding hard, but he'd live. He heard a motorbike start in the lane and he climbed to the bank, peered over and watched his young attacker flick back his fringe, put his helmet on, then climb on the back of his getaway bike. Dave's eyes bulged in disbelief, and it took all his will not to burst from the bank and rain down all his fury upon his attackers, but his head swam, and he felt himself go again as he let slip the words.

'Carl, you sneaky fucking cunt…'

Chapter Forty-Three

BROKEN FACE

HIS CHEEKBONE WAS BROKEN, HIS jawbone was broken, his head looked like a fuckin' melon. The bullet had collided with his cheek bone, split his face open and knocked him out cold. He stared in horror at his reflection in the hospital mirror. 'Look at the fuckin' head on you,' he thought to himself as he touched the stitches on his face then winced. It was a deep cuntin' ache right to the middle of his fuckin' crown. The hospital's painkillers hadn't even touched it, but Mucky was bringing him some proper gear and once it arrived, he'd be knockin' 'em back wholesale.

It hurt to talk; it hurt to sleep, it even hurt to think, but thinking was all he could do. He kept running it over and over in his head. Fuckin' Carl. What a silly cunt to go for a headshot. And then… and then! Dave laughed, it hurt a lot. *And then he took off the helmet and I saw him.* He felt the smile forming at the corner of his mouth. He looked to the mirror in panic as the smile spread across his broken face. He almost passed out. He held the basin with both hands as the rush of pain washed over him. The room spun, and he felt himself go. He rode it out, lowered himself to the floor, and slid on his arse to the safety of his bed. He slept. When he woke, Mucky, The Boy and Gordon were in the room. *What a fuckin' crew,* Dave mused.

He went to sit up, and The Boy motioned for him to relax. Dave pointed to the notepad by the bed. The Boy passed him the pad, and he wrote the word *TABLETS???* then turned the pad to Mucky. Mucky reached abruptly into his pocket, removed a pill pot, handed it to Dave, who promptly popped two of the pills. Dave lay back on the bed and he slept some more. The crew looked at one another and shrugged. Gordon giggled and soon they were all stifling sniggers.

When Dave woke again, he sat up in the bed and looked about the room. He picked up the notepad and wrote:

No disrespect, not your fight. Please wait outside?

He turned the pad to Gordon. Gordon started to protest but Dave took his hand, looked him in the eye, waved his head from side to side as he painfully mouthed the word 'no'. Gordon nodded. He understood. He was about to leave when The Boy spoke up.

'He stays. We are in this together. He stays.'

Dave looked at The Boy, thought a moment, then nodded his consent, picked up the pad, wrote Carl's name and showed it to Mucky.

'Carl did this?' Mucky asked.

Dave nodded, then turned to The Boy. He patted his left hand, then mimed a pistol shot.

'Yes,' The Boy replied.

Mucky turned to The Boy, confused.

'Fallon's shooter… he was left-handed,' The Boy explained.

Mine too, Dave wrote, then continued, *Carl killed Charlo.*

'You sure?' The Boy asked.

100%, Dave wrote, then continued, *must act fast, eyes on him 24/7.*

The Boy stood up from his seat, ran his hands through his hair, and let out an exasperated breath. He was about to say that Carl would be long gone when he read Dave's next note.

He doesn't know I saw him.

Chapter Forty-Four

THE BOOK OF DANIEL

Part IV

FINTAN CONSIDERED FOR A LONG time. He looked hard at Daniel. Rubbed his chin, looked to Mags for guidance, rubbed his chin some more, then repeated.

'Trinity College Dublin?'

'Yep,' Daniel replied for the third time.

'No fuckin' touring or auditoriums, do you hear me, son? I know it's been over a year now since America, but you need to take things much slower. Are you listening to me?' he pleaded.

'It's nothing like that,' Daniel promised. 'I'll be studying, researching, stuff like that.'

'And your accommodation's paid for?'

'Everything. I'll be getting a grant. You won't have to worry about a thing.'

'What about Beckett?'

'He works there, so…'

'What do you think?' Fintan asked, turning to Mags.

Mags looked to Daniel, then to Fintan, then back to Daniel again. She shrugged her shoulders and raised her palms.

'Do you promise you'll ring us at the first sign that things are getting too much for ya?' she asked.

'Of course I will Ma. I'll be going to classes and helping Beckett with research projects or whatever else he's got going on. That's it.'

'When does it start?'

'Whenever I want, but officially September.'

*

Dublin was electric. Beckett was his in, his man on the inside. There were girls and discos and partying and late-night ramblings followed by early morning walks of discovery and shame and everything was new and fresh, and his mind was wild with ideas and possibilities and it all made sense to him now and he could taste it, whatever it was life had in store for him was close. There were television appearances, radio interviews, and science articles where they referred to him as 'eminent', 'revered' and 'brilliant'.

They wrote Tony Ryan's algorithm, and he thanked them sincerely and warned Daniel of the 'evils in this fuckin' town, boyo' and they laughed and rolled on to the next glittery event where the illuminati filled their glasses and tried in vain to tap them dry. And then one day he saw her, and the earth stood still as his heart burst in his chest, and he knew he was ended as he watched her burn and beckon, and something inside of him beat a desperate retreat of no avail, and some young girl in her company called out her name and it rung in his heart and his fate it was sealed… 'Marie.'

She'd seen him on the *Late Late Show*. She'd cried as she'd watched this young boy soothe the nation's soul. He was brilliant, dangerous, beautiful and doomed and in her gut some primordial call told her to run and find herself one of them nice lads who drank five pints on a Saturday and played hurling on a Sunday, and worked on his father's farm the rest of the week and raised animals and ploughed land, land they'd build a home on some day, but she couldn't have stopped herself even if she'd tried. Their fates, they were sealed, and all the will in the world could not undo their tragic trajectory.

Daniel wrote articles for *Science* magazine and worked as a special adviser. It made him laugh, 'special adviser'. He sat on review committees and advised senior executives on strategy and other bollix that at first seemed daunting, but when he opened his mouth, the right words flowed, and people took notes and they paid him for his time. Clergy leaders called on him, he gave them all the same answer and each to a man left their meetings with their faith shattered and restored in equal measures.

Marie studied sculpture at the College of Art. Her work was inspired, moving and haunted. When she graduated, she worked in exhibition design, and it didn't take long before established design houses invited her to work for their brands. They were on every guest list, invited to everything by everyone. There was no door closed to them in the city. They shopped on Grafton Street and lived on Leeson. They ate in great restaurants where head chefs fought for the opportunity to present their food and regale them, if only for a moment.

They moved to Cork and got a mortgage. It was all very civilised they joked, and soon they were married and a baby boy followed and there was music, love and revolution in the air.

'I don't want Feargal bringing guns into the house,' Daniel told her.

'He won't bring any guns, Daniel. They need somewhere to get their heads down and they'll be gone again in the morning. Haven't you got your meeting?'

'Yeah?'

'Great. When you get home tomorrow afternoon, they'll be gone. Alright?'

'Grand.'

They waited in the kitchen as Marie arranged open sandwiches, olives, capers, and other delicacies for her guests.

'They won't eat this spread,' Daniel told her.

'Of course they will, they'll love it,' Marie protested.

'Revolutionaries on the run eating a fucking smorgasbord. Have you gone clean mad? They'll want stew or chips and beans with sausages, not fucking mushroom and olive tapenade. They'll fuckin' shoot us on the spot when they see this array.'

Marie let a smile cross her face, followed by a giggle. Daniel gave her a cheeky wink as he popped a Parma prawn, then fell to the floor in a feigned execution when three low knocks came to the back door. Daniel jumped to his feet and motioned for Marie to answer.

'Who is it?' she asked in a soft, pathetic voice. Daniel rolled his eyes, as a faint voice from the garden grumbled an exasperated, 'Jesus H Christ'. The back door opened and soon they were inside drawing the curtains and speaking in hushed lilting tones.

There were three of them, all three wore double denim, had shoulder-length hair and sported Teddy Roosevelt moustaches. They moved with proprietary confidence about the kitchen, looked at the smorgasbord doubtfully, then devoured it whole. One minute it was there, the next it was not. Feargal turned to Marie, took her by the hands and said, 'You're looking smashing love. Any chips?' Daniel shot her a triumphant glance as he turned on the chip pan, then peeled some potatoes. They ate, they smoked, they drank, and they left. Daniel dropped them by the cross at Drompeach, where they climbed over a ditch and then they were gone.

Freedom fighters, Daniel told himself. *There but for the grace of God… and all that shite.*

The next time, there were four. Unannounced, they walked in the back door and they stayed for three days. Jackie Brosnan had an intellect. He took Daniel on a journey of six hundred years of occupation and subjugation. They spoke about genocides and land-grabs and, for the first time in his life, Daniel was speechless. They sat into the night as Brosnan schooled him hard and left him wanting. *Freedom fighters*, Daniel told himself time after time and though the violence was unjustified, in his mind he understood why these raw men felt it was their only option and when he opened his mouth, his magic mouth that always knew the right words, he was left wanting. Daniel proffered. Brosnan laughed. He placed his hand on Daniel's shoulder, gave it a squeeze and said,

'You're alright son, you're al-fuckin'-right but see these cunts here we are dealing with? They don't want fucking peace. They want all of us here dead, and the only way they'll ever agree to fuckin' peace is if we give them fuckin' hell by comparison, and that's my job. So, I hear what you're saying but I've heard it all before.' In the morning, they were gone.

When they weren't working, they were drinking. There was always some place to be, something to do, somewhere. They both liked a sup, and they could put it away. Marie was the toast of the town. Daniel, in all his brilliance, paled by comparison, and he was happy to let her shine. She went from shining magnificence to warm basking glow, then back to magnificence, and then one day the light went out and she was nowhere to be found. She'd followed the black dog down the dark alley and closed the gate behind her. Daniel tried to coax her round, but she was beyond gone.

'She gets these wee turns, son,' Albie explained.

'She hasn't had one for a long while, but she gets wee turns like this,' Ann added.

'Turns?' Daniel asked, hoping.

'Aye son, turns, she gets a bit down, like,' Albie said.

'Oh, right!'

'Sometimes they're a day or two, but often they are longer.'

'Okay,' Daniel replied as he turned to Marie and took her in his arms.

'I'll give Dr Heffernan a wee ring. He knows what she needs. If that's alright with you, son,' Albie asked, but Daniel didn't reply.

His own haze, as ever, loomed. He'd learned how to keep it at bay with the booze and the drugs but some days he'd welcome it like a blanket, and she'd do the same, and the child would stay with Ann and Albie and when they'd picked themselves up sure all would be grand and they'd take the child home and Marie would shine and Daniel would blaze and they'd set the world straight until again it would crumble.

*

'Twins,' she told Daniel, bursting, and they leapt about the kitchen howling like fools. The next scan revealed one of each and they referred to them affectionately as 'The Boy' and 'The Girl'. Daniel readied the nursery. He painted one half blue and the other half pink. They bought two cradles from Cash's on Patrick Street, and the Bishop Michael Murphy blessed their fine home, and he placed his big hairy hands on Marie's belly while he said a little prayer for the two wee babbies growing inside of her. When the babbies were born in the Bon Secours, the nuns fell about the place fussin' and frettin' over the two magnificent specimens and all the young nurses would swoon when Daniel passed by and then they brought their babbies home to a life complete on Lovers Walk. At night when they'd put the twins down, they'd sit on the balcony with Fallon by their side and they'd watch the boats roll in and out on the harbour below, listening to the grunts and the groans, the coos and the moans of their new boy and girl as they drifted to sleep.

She loved them so much that her bones would ache. When they weren't by her side, she thought that her heart would explode in her breast, and she couldn't let them out of her sight for two minutes. She watched through the big bay window Daniel and Fallon return from their walk. Daniel had the big old bunch of rusty keys he'd found on a hook in the pantry. The keys opened a door in the back wall of the garden where they'd discovered a pathway that ran all the way down to the banks of the Lee. They'd been down and up every day since they'd found them. Fallon marvelled and grasped at the limbs that hung low, and he'd call from Daniel's shoulders to 'duck down Daddy, duck down' as they brushed across his face. He'd laugh with fear and excitement as they followed their secret path down to the banks, and they'd stay a while there, skimming stones and watching the birds.

Marie ran the rolling pin o'er the pastry. She had an eye on the garden and an ear in the nursery. She heard The Boy coo, and she took the fag from the corner of her mouth, sat it on the draining board, folded the pastry across the pie, forked the edges, egged the crust then placed the pie in the oven. She ran her hands under the tap, checked the time on the clock above the door, then she dried her hands on the tea towel and headed up the stairs to her napping pride and joys in the blue and pink nursery.

Daniel placed Fallon on the ground, kicked off his shoes and undid the buttons on Fallon's Jacket. Above their heads, a sound, an agonised bawl rose. He'd never heard anything like it, the scream. It was in him, around him, the air was thick with it. He could feel his bones rattle and amidst it all he heard his name… Marie was calling his name. He took the stairs, three at a time.

'Daniel! Daniel!' she bawled. The Boy watched on, oblivious, from the blue side of the room as Daniel burst through the door, took The Girl in his arms and placed his mouth to hers whilst Marie howled. The ambulance came, but it was too late, and she tried and tried in the days that followed to chase her blessed baby down into the darkness and each time she tried, Daniel would pull her back, and she'd beg him to let her go with her poor little crater alone in the unknown, and they cried and they fell and there was no coming back from this one and you couldn't fuckin' deny it.

Chapter Forty-Five

EILEE

Eilee looked at her checklist. O'Keefe's Walk she'd done last week, but this was O'Keefe's Terrace. They all looked the same. She wasn't sure anymore. Some of these streets she'd done immediately after he went missing, and back then, her record-keeping hadn't been as good as it is now.

She walked to the first house, number seventeen. She wasn't sure. She knocked.

A woman's shape moved inside the hall. Eilee took a deep breath. The door opened.

'Oh,' the woman said.

'My name is Eilee—'

The woman cut her off. 'I know who you are Eilee. We met, last week. You were here last week.'

Eilee looked at her checklist then to the street. 'It was O'Keefe's Walk I did last week. This is O'Keefe's Terrace.'

The woman sighed. She could've cried for her. 'Do you remember I told you last week that O'Keefe's Terrace runs into O'Keefe's Walk? They are the same street.'

Eilee looked behind her again. She wasn't leaving. She couldn't. She'd made a pledge to him, her little boy, that she'd check every house in Blackpool until she found him, and she wasn't taking this woman's word for it. She steeled her eyes. She hated this bit, the standoff.

'Come in,' the woman said, and she walked into the kitchen.

Eilee followed.

'Have you ever seen them before?' the woman asked, pointing at her kettle and toaster set.

Eilee felt her face flush. She scrunched her eyes. A few tears seeped between the lids, and she felt them warm against her cheeks.

'I'm sorry,' she said.

'Ye'r grand,' the woman said, and she placed her hand on her shoulder and gave it a gentle squeeze.

'Argos. Fifty-seven ninety-nine. A bit pricey but I said fuckit,' Eilee said. She had the same set. They'd spoken about it the previous week when Eilee'd searched the house and hadn't found her little Eoin.

'Will I put the kettle on?' the woman asked.

'No thanks,' Eilee said. 'I've imposed enough.' She walked to the door.

'How long has it been now?' the woman asked.

'Six months, four days, three hours and…' She looked at her watch. 'Twelve minutes.'

The woman's eyes welled up. 'I hope you find him,' she said.

'Thanks,' Eilee said. 'I will.' She left.

It was a cruel walk home, but she couldn't bring herself to knock on another door. She simply couldn't. She didn't have it in her. She reckoned it'd send her over the edge, and she couldn't go there. She'd start again tomorrow.

'Tomorrow, with gusto,' she committed as she turned into her estate. She looked ahead. Mrs Turner. She felt sick. She couldn't face her. She couldn't listen to her asking the same question every fucking day. It was too late to turn back. She wanted to. With all her heart she wanted to turn around and walk back down the road, so she didn't have to hear this silly woman and her fucking question.

Don't make eye contact, she told herself. *Don't make eye contact.* She watched Mrs Turner put down her brush – she was brushing the garden – walk to her front gate, lean on it, open her big stupid mouth and speak.

'Any sign?' she asked.

Eilee stopped. She put her hand to her forehead. Her eyes scrunched again. A series of thick fat teardrops fell on the footpath at her feet. She could hear them land. She wanted to scream. She imagined herself scratching at Mrs Turner's eyes. She could do it. She could easily do it. She took a long shuddering breath.

'Are y'alright pet?' Mrs Turner asked.

'There's no sign Mrs Turner. No sign. Now will you please do me a favour, a kindness even, and never ask me that question again?' Eilee sobbed. 'If there's any sign I'll let ya know. I won't go to the Guards, I won't tell the school or the paper or my mother or anyone else. I'll come straight here and let you know first, ya—' The words 'nosey old cow' sat inside her mouth, they were past her tongue, teetering on her lips even. She could've said them so easily.

Mrs Turner looked at her, mortally offended. 'Ah pet, I'm only…' she started, but Eilee was already walking on.

She walked to her front door, put the key in the slot, then fell into the hall. She lay there for some time. She needed to sleep. She sat up, crawled to the stairs and took them one at a time on her hands and knees to the landing. She crawled across the floor to Eoin's room, Buzz Lightyear everywhere. Posters, bedspread, his little rug.

She could smell him, Eoin. She crawled to his bed, pulled his duvet from the mattress, curled herself up in a ball and she slept.

When she woke, it was cold. The room was cold. She looked at her watch. The heating should be on by now, she thought. She put her hand to the radiator. It was ice cold. She walked to the hall and placed her hand on the radiator at the top of the stairs. It was hopping. She walked back to Eoin's room and checked the valve on the radiator. The arrow pointed at the zero mark, and she reached down and twisted it to five. A faint flowing noise emanated from the valve and she put her hand to the pipe and waited as it warmed. She followed the heat into the radiator and placed her hand to the top and kept it there until she felt it warm. A low creak followed by a series of clicks rose from the radiator and she sat back down on the floor and waited as the heat filled the room. She took the duvet from the floor, shook it out then dressed the bed.

'That's better pet,' she said, and she tucked the end in by the frame. She walked to the door, looked back at the room and sighed, then she walked down the stairs to the kitchen.

Chapter Forty-Six

GUN SCHOOL

He could talk more easily now, but it still hurt to smile and eat. Eating was a fucker. He loved food, and he was a big old unit. He needed a lot of calories. The fuckin' shakes and soup weren't even coming close. He could feel his stomach rumbling now. Boiled eggs, he thought in a light bulb moment, and he raced to the fridge, took a half dozen eggs from the shelf, filled a pot with water and set them to boil. Soft-boiled eggs with salt, he told himself, and he salivated. He was daydreaming about buttery toast when the doorbell rang. He checked the spyhole to see The Boy standing in the hallway, picking his nose. 'Dirty little bastard,' Dave laughed, then paused a moment. He was only a kid. He watched as The Boy scratched his nose, rubbed the back of his neck then knocked again. He thought about not answering. All he had to do was stay still and wait until he left. He'd go eventually, he told himself and he watched the child in his hallway, in over his head and he sighed. The Boy banged the door again and Dave reached for the handle and opened it.

'Alright?' The Boy asked, eyeing Dave's busted head.

'Yeah, cushty,' Dave answered, rolled his eyes, then turned and headed to the kitchen.

He looked old. A bit doddery, The Boy noted. His swagger depleted. He'd lost weight as well. It didn't suit him. Dave put his hand on the wall as he passed through the door, and turned.

'You ever used a gun before?' he asked.

The Boy shook his head, then looked at the floor.

'No worries,' Dave said. 'Somebody's gonna pick you up tomorrow, early doors, and go through some basics with ya.'

'Basics?'

'How to hold it, shit like that. You cool?'

'Yeah, cool.'

'About five-ish… in the morning. In fact, it won't be about five-ish, it'll be five sharp.'

'In the morning?'

'I know… it'll be worth it, trust me. We'll track dickhead's movements, so by the time you're ready we'll have a watertight plan in place. You know you don't have to do this, mate,' Dave added. 'I'll take care of this shit in a heartbeat, and we can get on with things as before. There is no pressure on you to get involved with this bit, believe me.' Dave's voice was almost a plea.

'I want to do it,' The Boy said.

Dave looked at him. He wasn't messing. 'Okay mate,' he said. 'I wanna be certain… that's all. Anyway, five o'clock. Yeah? He'll pick you up at the pub.'

'I'll be up,' The Boy said and there was no doubt in his head that he could do it. He could picture it, he could feel it, in his mind he'd done it a thousand times already. He didn't think for one second that killing Carl would make all the other feelings of loss and grief disappear. They were there. They were real. They were his, who he'd become, there was no getting rid of them, and he didn't want to. But killing Carl would be the mesh that tethered them down, and he was ready.

Chapter Forty-Seven

RECON

THE CARPET'S PATTERN COMPRISED BLACK, orange, and yellow swirls. Not quite paisley, but some distant relative, for sure. He often wondered how they knew, fabric designers. How did they know what would be acceptable to the psyche in that unique era or time frame? How could they possibly predict what the trend would be? How could they pinpoint with such accuracy these fleeting whims of an entire nation? It was beyond him. He remembered when they'd bought it, the carpet. The neighbours had called for weeks to see his Ma's 'good room'. They'd stand at the door and look in. No one could actually set foot in the room. She'd never allow that, so they'd all stand at the door and tell his mother how beautiful it was. He was so proud of her. He loved his old Mammy, did Carl. Then slowly over the years, one mishap at a time, the room was relegated to regular use. A drunk uncle at Christmas walking shit into the room, cigarette butts being dropped, his sister Clare puking on the wallpaper; and so on, until nobody gave a shit anymore. Carl smiled, flicked his fag ash in the mantel's direction, walked to the lace curtains, yellowed by the years, and checked the street up and down. A motorbike passed outside. He could see the driver's wrists – they were black for sure. He was certain of it, but he was also certain of the last bike he'd seen. *Snap out of it*, he told himself, then slapped his face hard. He walked to the front door, stood on the threshold, poked his head around the opening, looked the road up and down, then stepped onto the path and headed up the road. A motorbike sped towards him. As the bike passed, he recoiled in anticipation. He stayed contorted for a few moments with his arms clutching his head, one knee raised to his chin with his back curled, like a man crammed in some tiny space with the leg hanging over the side. He released his contortion one tendon at a time, then opened his eyes and looked about the street foolishly. *Get a fuckin' grip*, he told himself.

Dave and his crew watched as Carl crossed the road, then disappeared down Levitt Lane.

'Keep your eyes on him, boys,' Dave instructed over the radio. 'Follow at a safe distance. Do not approach, I repeat, do not approach.'

The next day was the same. He left his mother's, crossed the road, went through the lane, followed the main road up to the cross where he stopped into the bookies, then went to the shop to buy fags and a cold drink.

He was a creature of habit, Carl. The next day was the same routine, then the day after that. They would pass within feet of him, then keep going. Each time, they would watch him flinch, gather himself together, then continue on his route.

He could sense them, he could feel their baleful eyes upon him. He could sense these men who would do him harm, watching, and yet he did not see them. He told himself to 'cop the fuck on', 'snap out of it', but it was there, and it was a real thing, and he knew for certain that his days were numbered. But still, he stayed.

'Don't be a silly cunt,' Cliff had said. 'We've got work to do, you can't be fuckin' off with sheaves yet to bind…' whatever the fuck that meant.

Every passing car, every bike that thrummed, he feared might be the last sound he ever heard, as Dave and his crew watched and noted, watched and noted, watched and noted.

Chapter Forty-Eight

KILLER EYES

THE BOY THREW HIS LEG over the edge of the sofa, sat up and looked around the room. He took a moment to get his bearings. The alarm clock blared on the mantelpiece, and he stood, walked across the room and silenced it.

'Four fuckin' thirty,' he said to himself, then stretched out a long yawn.

He walked to the kitchen, filled a bowl with Coco Pops, poured milk over them and walked back to the sofa. He could've easily laid down and gone back to sleep. He wanted to.

'Come on,' he said. 'Come on.'

He spooned some cereal into his mouth. Instant satiation roared to his brain, and he suddenly felt awake. He stood from the sofa and walked to the window, eating his breakfast as he went. He thought about Ann. The look on her face when he said he might move back home with Daniel. He felt bad. The poor woman.

She'll be grand, he told himself. He finished the cereal and walked to the bathroom. He looked at himself in the mirror. He sighed then looked away again. He looked back at his reflection. He felt bad for himself – or maybe not himself, he wasn't sure how to articulate it in his mind. It was as though he'd left himself behind and the old person he used to be was sat frozen in some solitary limbo of loneliness, and this new version of himself was moving on without him.

He pushed the thought away. He ran the tap, brushed his teeth, rinsed under his arms, got dressed and walked back to the kitchen. He took a bottle of Yop from the fridge then went back to the front room and waited.

Shortly before five, he watched a black, sporty-looking car pull up outside the pub and he grabbed his jacket from the rack and headed down the stairs.

The man spoke like uncle Feargal, was about forty years old, wore flared denim jeans, a denim jacket and white Adidas trainers. His pale boney face sported a head of wiry shoulder length red hair. He had a beautiful moustache that curled up at the ends and The Boy wanted to reach out and twist it in his fingers but thought the better of this and resisted.

'Alright?' the man said as The Boy climbed into the passenger seat.

'Alright,' The Boy replied, and the man put the black Opel Manta in gear and headed at speed for the Cork and Kerry mountains.

They drove for hours. The Boy drifted in and out of sleep and when he woke for the last time the man was standing at the rear of the car, and was getting undressed.

'Alright sleeping beauty?' the man called. The Boy sat up and looked about the woods, confused.

'Get these clothes on you,' the man instructed, and he threw a green bag towards the open car door on the passenger's side. The Boy climbed from the car. He was about to speak when the man walked from the rear and punched him hard in the guts. The Boy doubled over, and the man elbowed him between the shoulder blades. The ground spun, The Boy fell, then heaved up his breakfast and looked up, confused. There was a tear forming in his right eye.

'Don't think because you're bringin' a gun to the fight that it's a foregone conclusion, wee man. Come on, get dressed and quit your greetin' or I'm calling this whole thing off,' he said, and he threw a photo of Carl on the ground next to The Boy.

The Boy hated Carl instantly. He was all cheekbones and fringe. Killing him would be easy, The Boy thought.

'You look at that photo at least one hundred times a day for the next few days. I want you to burn that image onto your brain. Are we clear?'

The Boy nodded, got dressed in silence, then they set off on foot. They hiked for half the day, stopping to grapple, and the man explained each time what he was doing and why and how The Boy should improve his response. As the day progressed, The Boy could feel his instincts hone. He began to anticipate the attacks and sometimes he even out-fought the man, but it was always a trap that led to some lesson. Then they'd hike some more with The Boy licking his wounds.

They had thirty-five fights that first day. When they reached the camp at nightfall, they ate a meal of cold beans and sausage, then they curled up for the night and slept. In the morning, they drank from the stream, fought for an hour and then had breakfast. After breakfast, the man showed The Boy how to clean and load his new guns. They fought for another hour, after which the man tested The Boy's knowledge of his guns from earlier, then he showed him how to hold the gun, how to point the gun and how to squeeze the trigger. They ate a mid-morning snack, fought for an hour, and when The Boy threw the man on the woodland ground, he could see a smile forming at the corner of the man's mouth.

'Good,' The Boy heard him say. They ate, practised some shooting techniques, fought some more, and then they slept.

When The Boy woke, he could hardly move.

'Take two of these,' the man told him, and he threw him a packet of pills. They walked for a while, fighting intermittently as they went. When they reached the mountain top, the man told The Boy to sit with his legs crossed and take in the view. The Boy sat and looked out over the valley. He'd seen nothing like it before.

'Close your eyes,' the man started. 'Close your eyes and bow your head. Take five deep breaths and focus on each one clearly.'

The Boy, anticipating a blow, winced, and the man told him they'd finished with fighting for now. His voice was calm and convincing, and The Boy relaxed and took the first breath.

'Deeper next time,' the man told him as The Boy exhaled and with the next deep breath he felt swirly and light, but it was good, and he surrendered to the process. After the fifth breath, the man told The Boy to imagine he was standing at the top of ten stone steps and to imagine the top step, cold and wet beneath his feet. The Boy could feel the step and the man told him to take the steps down one at a time, and The Boy could feel each step cold and wet beneath his feet as he descended. As he approached the last step, the man told him that when he reached the bottom, he would be stepping onto warm dry sand at the ocean's edge. The Boy took the last step and looked out at the ocean with the warm sun setting, and he heard the man's voice, low and soft, call out to him as if from some distant place across the ages.

'Repeat after me,' the man said. 'I am a killer.'

'I am a killer,' The Boy echoed.

'He will die by my hand.'

'He will die by my hand.'

'Can you see him?' the man asked, and The Boy nodded. 'Can you feel the gun in your hand?' The Boy nodded again. 'Then repeat after me as you hold out the gun, I am a killer, he will die by my hand.'

'I am a killer. He will die by my hand.'

'Now squeeze the trigger,' and The Boy squeezed.

They repeated the affirmation ten times, then the man walked The Boy back up the cold and wet steps, talked him through five more deep breaths and told him that when he was ready, he could open his eyes. When The Boy opened his eyes, he could see the same valley stretched out below him, even more beautiful now than before, and as he looked out upon it, he knew he was not seeing it now as he had before, for now he was seeing it with a killer's eyes, and he was okay with the change.

They fought and shot for the rest of the day, then they hiked and drove back to the city through the night. When the man dropped The Boy in Blackpool on that fourth day, there was no embrace or goodbye. The man told The Boy to repeat the meditation three times a day, then he drove off. The Boy climbed up the back steps of the St Leger, fell onto the sofa, and slept.

Chapter Forty-Nine

A MURDER

Carl opened the front door of his mother's house, looked up and down the road, then he stepped outside. *He did not recognise me*, he assured himself. *The helmet was on my head the whole time and it's got a tinted visor, there's no fuckin' way he knows it was me*, he said to himself, then he examined his run back to the bike, remembering how he removed the helmet in the afternoon heat. Uncertainty set in now and he checked the road up and down, then up again before stepping from the relative safety of his mother's porch.

Get a grip, you twat, he told himself. *You shot him. He fell back in the water and drifted down the river. There is no way he knows it's you… or does he?* The doubt rose again. He jumped as his phone trilled in his pocket, fumbled clumsily, then watched as the phone fell in the road and broke into pieces.

Mucky watched the doubtful steps followed by a moment of pause as Carl picked up the pieces of his phone, reassembled it, waited a moment while it rebooted, then dialled.

'I dropped it,' Carl explained into the mouthpiece.

'You what?' Clifford asked.

'My phone. I dropped it. That's why I didn't answer. You alright?'

'Yes, fine, fine… and you?' He sounded concerned.

'I'm grand. What's the plan?'

'I'll collect you at the shop. What time will you be ready?'

'I'm walking down there now. Should be there in two minutes. Where are you?'

'En route, it'll take me about five or ten minutes to get over to you. Why don't you wait, and I'll ring you when I'm nearby?'

'I'll walk down. I wanna nip in the bookies, and I need to get some fags. Do you want anything?'

'No, I'm fine… are you alright?' Clifford sensed a lack of the usual swagger.

'I'm a bit jumpy. I don't like loose ends.'

'It won't be a loose end for long. We will put this problem to bed imminently, now pull yourself together. You're giving me the heebie fucking-jeebies.'

'No worries, see you at the shop.'

Mucky picked up the radio and pressed the transmit button. 'The fringe is on the move, over.'

'Copied,' came the reply.

'Heading toward the bookies on foot,' Mucky added as he watched Carl duck into Levitt Lane, then disappear from view. 'He's cutting through the lane. Keep an eye out for him at the other end, number two.'

'Will do,' Gordon responded.

Carl could feel the panic rising in his feet. It surged through his legs, then into his gut where it paused a moment before continuing to his chest and arms, culminating at his temples. He shook like a shitting dog, then he stumbled against the wall, fell to the ground and empty retched. When he stopped heaving, he realised he was sobbing, and he lay there on the ground, and cried until the panic subsided. He sat on the ground and looked the lane up and down. He took a long deep breath, wiped his eyes and stood.

'No sign of the fringe at this end,' Gordon reported. 'Has he doubled back number one, over?'

'No sign at this end, either. Will I go check it out?'

'No, hold position. We can't risk him seeing us. He must be

having a smoke or something. I repeat, hold positions. Let's not lose our shit here.'

'Copied.'

The Boy listened patiently in his earpiece; he felt the comfort of the gun tucked tight inside his waistband. He unzipped his jacket, slipped a hand inside, and placed it on the stock.

'Fringe on the move at this end,' Gordon reported. 'Turning right towards the bookies.'

The Boy nudged Dave. Dave slipped the bike into gear and eased off slowly toward holding point B.

Carl, unsure on his feet, felt another wave of panic grip him and he stumbled to a nearby bench where he sat, exhausted, and looked the street up and down. It had all been too much for him. *Cliff is a fuckin' animal*, he thought. He needed time to gather his emotions and process the last few months, but every time he tried to set it all down, Cliff would come up with some new angle of attack. Dave had been a mistake, a bad fuckin' mistake. He'd fucked up badly. They should've got out of town, but Cliff wouldn't have it. He should be lying low somewhere, watching what Dave's next move might be. He made up his mind. He was getting out of town for a few days. He would tell Clifford when he met him. He couldn't live like this. He would get out of town, get his shit together, then come back and finish Dave and the rest off, proper.

A car whooshed by. He jumped. He wiped his nose and eyes. He'd been crying again. He hadn't noticed.

'That's it,' he said to himself. 'That's it. Enough.' He felt better. If Clifford didn't understand, then maybe it was time for a break from Clifford too, he thought.

He stood from the bench and continued towards the bookies. Stopping to cross the road, he looked left, then right, then left again before stepping from the kerb. A motorbike approached at speed, whizzed by him, and disappeared over the crest of the hill. Carl took a deep breath, then continued across the road.

'He should be by the shops any minute now,' Gordon reported.

'In position at the top of the hill,' Mucky added. 'I've a good view of the shops and the car park. No sign of the fringe yet. Are you in position number three?'

The Boy positioned the mouthpiece and spoke for the first time. 'In position B, standing by. Over.'

Clifford pulled on to Barrow Road, dropped the car into third gear, and eased in the accelerator. He joined the traffic, gauging his speed amidst the morning flow.

'I've got an eyeball on the fringe now,' Mucky said, cutting through the anxious silence. 'Number three, do you copy?'

'Copied.'

The Boy nudged Dave again, and they pulled from the side lane to join the traffic as it progressed up the hill. Cliff watched oblivious from the wheel as The Boy and his driver slipped past him in the outside lane, heading uphill towards the shops. The Boy spotted Carl fifty yards in front; he squeezed Dave's sides between his knees in anticipation. Dave dropped a gear and sped towards the intersection as The Boy repeated his affirmation over and over in his head.

I am a killer, he will die by my hand.

Carl stepped from the road onto the path – Dave pulled alongside. The Boy, his gun already in hand, lifted his visor and called Carl's name.

'Carl!'

Carl turned to see The Boy's gun trained at his heart. He looked from the gun to The Boy's face and listened in disbelief as The Boy spoke.

'This is for Fallon.'

Two shots followed. Carl fell backwards on the path, confused, then sat upright looking around him. The Boy jumped from the bike, walked calmly to where Carl sat and looked him in the eyes before delivering two more rounds. One to the head and one to the heart, then he strolled to Dave, pocketing the pistol, climbed back on the bike, and they were gone.

Clifford rounded the top of the hill in time to witness The Boy deliver the final two rounds. He watched in horror: his fallen lover and partner collapsed in the street. He broke from the stream of traffic, turned the car in the road and calmly departed the scene.

The Boy's head felt light, his legs and arms numb. He knew what had happened only moments earlier, yet some strange anticipation of the event he'd pictured in his mind for so long lingered as though it was still ahead of them. He watched, over Dave's shoulder, the road approaching in slow motion, to his left and right, green ditches whizzing by. He felt the bike slow. Dave pulled into a yard and accelerated toward an opening in a row of abandoned service units. He pulled inside out of view, put the bike on the kickstand and they climbed off. A barrel fire, crackling in the corner, shot sparks into the morning. A man The Boy hadn't seen before, one of Dave's crew he guessed, removed the fake plates from the bike, threw them on the fire, then jumped on the bike, and waited. Dave removed the gun from inside The Boy's jacket, handed it to the man then watched as the man departed on the bike.

The Boy looked at Dave.

'Clothes off,' Dave said.

He could hear the words, but he didn't know what to do. He couldn't move.

'Your clothes,' he heard Dave say. 'Take 'em off. Are you alright mate?'

Dave had his clothes in his hand. He walked to the fire and threw them in, followed by his helmet. He walked to The Boy and looked him in the eye.

'Come on mate,' Dave said. 'You can do this.'

The Boy looked at Dave, the morning's events racing at him now. Carl's face, climbing on the bike, accelerating away, the city, the country lanes, turning into the yard. He looked around him. *This yard*, he thought, and he jolted forward as a wave started at his feet, shot up through him and out through the top of his head. He heard Dave's voice, sharp and clear now. A wind roared through the building, sparks and flames flew up and out of the barrel, carried away on the wind. He heard birds and traffic outside on the road, a siren way off in the distance sent forth a *nee-naw* and suddenly he was back in the game. He remembered the drill. They'd been over it a hundred times.

He pulled his clothes off and threw them on the fire followed by the helmet.

'There he is,' Dave said. 'That's my boy.'

Dave handed him a football jersey and trackie bottoms. They dressed and climbed in the blue Corolla idling in the corner. Dave drove across the yard then eased onto the road.

'You alright?' he asked The Boy.

The Boy nodded. 'We did it,' he said. 'We fuckin' did it.'

'Yes, we fuckin' did mate. Yes, we fuckin' did.'

Chapter Fifty

EOIN

CLIFFORD PULLED INTO THE FARMYARD, parked his car in the garage, and entered the house through the side door, unnoticed. Inside, he went to the bathroom cabinet, removed a bag of charlie, cut two lines on the shaving mirror, rolled a note and bowed to the task. As he righted himself, he took sight of his face in the mirror.

'Cry, you cunt,' he told himself. 'There's nobody here but us. You loved him, admit it.'

His reflection stared back, defiant. 'Love him? Get to fuck you soft cunt,' he said, then noted the betrayal in his own eyes. He racked up two more lines, then two more, and then another two. When he'd snorted the last pair, he fell through the en suite door, picked himself from the floor and sat at the end of his bed where he caught again his reflection's plaintive gaze.

'Fuck off, you cunt!' he told himself, looked away, then looked back once more. 'What?' he shouted. 'Yes, I loved him. What do you want me to do… start fucking crying? You cry… cunt… go on… see, it's not so fuckin' easy, is it?' He picked up the phone and rang Kathleen.

'Good morning, Mr Cromby,' she answered.

'Kathleen, I'm not to be disturbed today, feeling unwell.'

'You don't sound great, Mr Cromby. Will I call Dr Harvey?'

'No, Kathleen, because he would disturb me. Remember a second ago, when I said I did *not* want to be disturbed? Well, I haven't changed my mind… I repeat, not… to be disturbed. Not to be disturbed. Mr Cromby is not to be disturbed.'

'Of course, Mr Cromby, you will not be disturbed. If you need anythi—'

Clifford hung up.

He rose from the bed by some involuntary force and turned once more to the mirror.

'Who the fuck is behind this?' he asked himself.

'Black cunting Dave,' came the reply.

'Why Dave?'

'He recognised Carl.' The name drew a sting at the corner of his eyes that spread across the bridge of his nose. 'Carl,' he mouthed desperately as the tears formed, hung for a moment, then spilled down his cheeks. 'Carl,' he repeated, then again, over and over, each time a little louder, until at last he screamed his name aloud, his face awash with tears.

'He recognised him?' he asked himself, then nodded solemnly in response.

'How?'

'The river. When Carl came back from the river, he wasn't wearing his helmet. He saw him. Somehow, he saw him.'

'But not you?' he asked the man in the mirror. Even he was not beyond suspicion. He waited. When no answer came, he cocked his head then raised a doubtful brow.

'No, not I,' came the reply.

'Why not you? What about the bike?'

'It's stolen. We destroyed it afterwards. I wore my helmet the whole time. You know this.'

'Carl told someone?' he said, pointing a finger as though it was *his* Carl and not *their* Carl, admonishing this version of himself. He could live with that.

'Never!' he heard himself say.

'Never?'

'Never!' He had to admit that he agreed.

'Then how?' he asked.

'I fucking told you. He removed his helmet. He fucking saw him. It's the only way.'

'Has he told anyone about you?'

'He hasn't told a soul for fuck's sake,' he snarled, approaching the mirror menacingly. 'Are you fucking listening to me? He hasn't told any-fucking-body.' The word body drew him back to Carl's slumped form by the roadside and he collapsed once more to the bed and howled.

In the evening, he watched from the mezzanine as the last of the estate workers left the yard. He followed the little convoy of lights as they tracked their way up the country lane, then disappeared off towards the city. An emptiness consumed the big house, and he found himself without explanation in the outhouse and not long after, he was riding the quad bike fast across the paddocks en route to the old house and the companionship that awaited him there.

Clifford's guests scurried and fussed, fixing their hair in shave-stained mirrors, some sniffing their pits. As Clifford descended the stairs, the more seasoned among the gathering noticed at once his crazed eyes and knew from experience that tonight would be long and uncertain.

'Boys, oh boys, my little boys, gather around me and raise me up, for tonight I need a friend!' He sang, and he bowed his head in defeat as his captives raced to their gates extending their arms as he passed from cell to cell taking each hand in his and kissing each one as he went, each boy fawning and fussing desperately, hoping they could placate him enough to keep the beast at bay. The beast was no stranger to these parts, and each had seen him many times. Each time they'd hoped it would be their last, but tonight 'twas clear Clifford had not brought the beast – the beast had eaten Clifford whole and had come here hungry of his own volition, and before the night was through would've eaten his fill.

Clifford jangled his keys, spinning on his heels, giving it the old 'eeny, meeny, miny'. Patrick couldn't believe his eyes or ears, and he watched in horror as Clifford included Eoin in the pointing game, landing on him now with the 'miny', then continuing.

Patrick ran the rhyme in his head. If it landed on Eoin, he vowed, he would pull the gate from its hinges and kill Clifford this very night.

'Catcha,' he heard Clifford say. Two syllables, one point. This changes everything. *It might be me*, he thought. He was okay with that. Anyone but Eoin. He watched Cliff, a little unsteady on his feet, and he reckoned if it landed on him tonight, he could get the better of Cliff and he imagined pinning Clifford beneath his knees as he knelt on his chest punching him over and over. He reckoned he could do it. He could see it in his mind. A fear rose in him but he pushed it down and prayed it might be him.

'If he screeches, let him go,' Clifford said, his finger flying wildly around the room paying no heed to the beats of the rhyme.

Four words, seven syllables were all that remained. Patrick scanned the room then ran the maths. It might be Eoin. Clifford spun, the words slurred as they left his mouth. There was no rhyme or reason to his pointing. Patrick felt the fear rise inside again though not for him. He closed his eyes, pushed it down and listened as Clifford completed the rhyme.

'Mo,' he heard Clifford say.

Patrick opened his eyes. Clifford had his back to him, and he was pointing. His hand swayed, between Eoin and Justin's cells. He staggered to the side a little then back the other way before settling on Justin.

Patrick sighed with relief.

Justin smiled.

Clifford unlocked the gate and led poor Justin by the hand as his other hand cupped the nape of the child's neck, and he pulled him to his chest and wept.

Patrick sat back on his bed. He looked to Eoin, white with fear. Patrick smiled at him then made a close-your-eyes motion.

Eoin nodded, then looked to the pair stood in the centre of the opening.

'I couldn't have known. Could I?' Clifford pleaded with poor Justin, and he gazed hard into Justin's eyes and saw there was no answer there.

'Oh, you poor child, I should not trouble your young mind with such woes…' He looked about the room, picked up his train of thought, released the child from his grasp and started.

'How could I have known boys, well? How could I have known this would happen? Is it my fault?'

'No,' came the response, all voices but one.

'True. It was a bitter game we played, and we both knew the fruits may not be so sweet, but this?' Justin inched slowly from his reach, watching Clifford's every move, poised.

'Justin? Where go you, child? Return here at once. Am I a fool not to have seen that this might be the way? Was I so blinded by lust and greed, so focused on the end that I could not see those about me who conspired to take me down?' He removed the bag of coke from his pocket, buried his face up to his cheeks and breathed, then he handed the bag to Justin.

'Fix me some lines, for goodness' sake, would you have me behave in such a manner as this, when 'tis clear tonight I am with the snake's belly? Did I not inform you upon my arrival that I had needed to be raised, and yet you watch me bury my face like a pack horse half-dead from the day's riding? Rile me not, child, rile me not.'

Justin scurried to the kitchenette, removed the mirror from the wall, and hurried to the table. He placed the mirror down and set about preparing seven lines while Clifford remained centre stage and wept openly.

'Have you readied my lines, child?'

'Yes, do you have a note? I have none, m'lord.'

'I have none,' he said mockingly. 'Yes, I have a note,' and he threw his whole wallet at Justin. 'And forget you not. I like the note rolled tight and the lines fat. And no fucking lumps. If I see one cunting lump in my chang, I'll lump you good from head to toe. Are you fucking listening to me? Are you?'

'Yes.'

'Yes, what?'

'Yes, I'm listening.'

'Yes, I'm listening what?'

'Yes, I'm listening, m'lord.'

'M'lord indeed, now carry on and hurry the fuck up.'

Justin regrouped the charlie, chopped and pressed, then chopped and pressed again before dividing it once more into seven lines, watching intently for lumps as he did so.

'Well? Are you ready?'

'Yes m'lord, all perfect,' Justin replied, shitting himself.

'It had better be. Are you listening?'

'Yes m'lord. It's perfect.'

'We'll see,' said Clifford, taking the note from Justin's hand, then attacked the lines, polishing off three in one greedy hit. He threw his head back, held his breath, and let his eyes bulge. He sat forward and searched out Justin in the room.

'Not bad,' he remarked as he exhaled. 'Have a line, old boy.' He handed Justin the note. Justin took the note and bent over the counter to start a line. As he did so, Clifford slammed him in the back of the head with his fist, smashing his face into the mirror. Justin stood up from the blow and staggered back from the counter, stunned. Clifford was on him in a flash, landing blows to his face and neck. He kicked him in the balls, and as the child doubled over in agony, Clifford drove his knee with all his might into Justin's face.

Eoin held the bars of his cell tight as he watched the horror unfold in front of him. He wanted to roar 'stop', but he couldn't. He opened his mouth to scream, but there was nothing there but the evil in the room, rushing down his throat, and he closed his mouth and his eyes, put his fingers in his ears and jumped on the bed. Behind him a loud pop filled the basement, followed by a snarl. Something ripped, he wasn't sure what, followed by a series of grunts and slaps that went on and on and on, then stopped.

'I told you no lumps,' he heard Clifford mumble, rolling from the heap for the last time.

'No lumps, I was perfectly clear about that and still you present me with this… this… this gravel, this shingle, this grit for want of a better word. Is my blinding your aim?' He looked about him now, each lad recoiling as he caught their gaze.

'Boys? Turn you not away in fear, my boys. You have no reason to fear me. It is I, Cliff. Can you not see the predicament he beset me? Would you too have me blinded? Eoin? Eoin? Arise from your bed child and quit your sobbing at once.'

Clifford stood from the ground and staggered from cell to cell, pleading with each child as he passed.

'Look at me, look at me, damn you. I am not a monster. He would have me blinded this very night. Am I to take from your silence that you too are complicit in his aims most foul? Turn you not from me, you bastard ingrate fucks, or I'll turn each one of you loose to the streets. See how you fare beyond the comfort of these walls? Is that your desire? Well? Is it? Is that your desire, for that is a lamp easily rubbed, and a wish so effortlessly granted?'

He picked the bag of coke from the table, buried his face up to his nose and breathed deep. He exhaled, breathed again, then repeated the process over and over until the room spun and he collapsed sideways on the floor. He reached across and touched the corpse on the ground beside him.

'No lumps,' he mumbled. 'I did tell you no lumps.' The cells spun, the room passed by again and again and he coiled in a foetal pose and squeezed his eyes tight until it passed.

He stood, looked at Justin's body on the floor and sighed. He thought about the hole he'd have to dig. He rolled his eyes. It could wait. He dragged the body to its cell, threw a blanket across it then locked the gate. He staggered around the basement, mumbling to himself, checked each cell was locked, then made his way up the stairs and out of the old house.

Chapter Fifty-One

CHERRY ON THE CAKE

CLIFFORD SAT TO THE REAR of the café, his back to the wall. He felt a little uneasy in his baseball cap and sunglasses, although they weren't out of place in this establishment. He spoke to no one, and he made no eye contact. When the waitress arrived, he ordered tea and a sausage sandwich by pointing to the menu, then settled in discreetly, unfolded his paper and started the crossword. From where he was sitting, he could see the front entrance to Dave's office building.

All quiet, he thought, *nothing to report*. The waitress set the food down. Cliff took the ketchup from the table, gave his sausage a squirt, put two sugars in his tea, stirred it twice, then turned his attention once more to the building across the street. He picked up his tea and sipped the cup cautiously. When he looked back across the street, he noticed the front door ajar, and beyond in the hallway's darkness he saw a large, dark figure sorting through the mail rack. Clifford pulled his sunglasses down his nose and squinted at the movement looming inside the hallway, then he watched as it turned and stepped from the darkness of the foyer into the bright morning sun on Shandon Street. It was Dave. Clifford placed his glasses back on his nose and raised his paper to shield his face.

Look at the size of that cunt. He's a fucking giant, Clifford marvelled to himself, *as was the getaway rider*. Cliff watched as Dave turned left and headed down Shandon Street towards the city. *The cocky fucker didn't even look over his shoulder*, he thought. *This is going to be easier than I imagined.*

Cliff picked up his sandwich, wrapped it in tissue and pocketed it. He left a handful of coins on the counter, exited the café, turned right, and followed Dave down the street on the opposite side. Clifford checked the gun in his waistband. He put his hand on the stock and cocked the lever, then made to cross the street. A motorcycle pulled up beside Dave. The driver handed Dave a helmet, and he jumped on the back, and they sped up Blarney Street then disappeared towards Sunday's Well. In an instant they were gone. Clifford replaced the gun in his waistband and headed for his car. It had all happened too fast for Cliff to register, but he recognised the skinny prick on the bike, albeit in the rider's seat this time.

Cliff was certain he had his hit team. He jumped in his car and shot up Blarney Street, then veered off towards Sunday's Well in pursuit. When he caught sight of the bike, he killed his speed and tailed them from a distance until they joined the Lee Road and the bike accelerated from view. Clifford swore as he put the boot down to no avail. They were gone.

He continued along the road in search of a turning point when he saw the motorbike pull into an abandoned factory lot on the far side of the road. He slowed down, pulled over to the side, and watched the men dismount. He let the car roll behind a ditch out of sight where he parked, climbed the ditch and peered over the top.

Dave and The Boy slapped each other's backs boisterously as they chatted. *These fuckers haven't got a care in the world*, Cliff thought. *Who is that second arsehole*? he wondered as The Boy stood with his back to him, laughed and slapped Dave playfully.

'How long will you be away for?' The Boy asked.

'A week or two, I'm gonna lie low for a bit, chill the fuck out. You need to do the same.'

'I'm moving in over the pub for a few weeks until things settle down,' The Boy replied.

'Good plan.'

'There's a flat upstairs with a back entrance. I'll keep my head down until this blows over. Mucky is sorted and your lads have enough to keep them ticking over, so I'll keep it on the lowdown for a bit. I can send Tony down to the shops if I need anything...'

'And Spain? Are you sure you want me to contact them?'

'Do it,' The Boy replied without hesitation.

'Okay, you're the boss. You could get out now and live off what you've racked up.'

'Let's do a couple of runs and get ourselves set up proper, then we'll let the crew take over when the time's right.'

'If you're certain.'

'I am,' The Boy answered, and he was. Something had changed in him. Something beyond comprehension or reason. It was like a drive or a compulsion, but to him, it was the right thing to do, of that he was in no doubt.

'Okay,' Dave said. 'I'll ring Murray and set it in motion.'

'Murray?'

'Murray Morris, Bomber's assistant, our man on the continent. You should see these two. They are like an old married couple, always bickering, but inseparable.'

The Boy laughed. 'Do it,' he repeated. 'A couple more runs, then out.'

'You sure?' Dave asked.

The Boy nodded. He'd thought about it. They had money, but not *money* money. A couple more runs and they'd be set up for life. He'd risked too much, lost too much, to settle for the mediocre. Now that they'd eliminated Carl, he reckoned there was nothing standing between him and a future filled with abundance, and it was a dice he was willing to roll.

'Alright,' Dave said. 'Let me speak with Murray.'

Cliff felt for the gun in his waistband. They were close, he measured, though not close enough to take a shot. He thought about rushing them, but a tall metal fence that bordered its entirety enclosed the yard. He looked to the exit at each end and followed the fence with his eye weighing up attack options. A lorry trundled by and The Boy, startled by the noise, turned.

Clifford felt the blood drain from his face. The hairs on the back of his neck stood on end at the vision of what he thought was Fallon's ghost in the yard before him. Then he recalled the crouched wretch by the kerb in Blackpool with his dying brother Fallon in his arms.

Of course… he thought, *it all makes perfect sense now.* The avenging runt sibling. Why hadn't he thought of this sooner, how could he have been so fucking stupid? And he remembered that cunting woman and her fucking pan. He should've shot them both dead when he'd the chance.

Cliff snapped from his daydream as The Boy's bike thrummed to life and headed for the exit at the opposite end of the yard. Cliff rolled from the ditch, ran to his car, threw it in gear, turned one eighty in the road and joined the traffic unnoticed as it made its way into the city.

His knuckles whitened on the wheel as he roared, 'Cunts, cunts, cunts!'

Over and over he roared. He had his men, though, and now it was a simple game of watching and waiting. He would have his fun with the young one. The big one – he would need to be careful with him, but the young one… he'd have fun with the young one. He played the scene over and over in his head. The little one would be fun, the cherry on the cake. It was all very exciting now, he told himself as he drove to Kilduggart, laughing all the way.

Chapter Fifty-Two

MURRAY MORRIS

It was busy in the plaza, Murray noted. Busier than usual, there was a bustle to the place. The cool weather had that effect. The locals, normally confined to the shaded protection of their villas, would swarm in droves to the *tabernas* on such days, or they'd sit and eat ice cream on the abutment that surrounded the square. Bomber the Bastard was playing pétanque with some old boys from the village. He was losing. He liked it that way. It was their game, and he felt privileged to be part of this ancient tradition. To beat them would be an insult, though sometimes he would win despite his best efforts. He would buy them beer and tapas and when the throwing was done, they would sit late into the evening and talk about the world and its ways. Some men would speak of fish and the Atlantic, another who'd worked the quarry all his life would tell of great rocks lain dormant since the dawn of time pulled from the valley, and he would point to the keystones and kerbs about the plaza and tell each one's tale. And a soldier, a proud son of the revolution who never spoke a word, would listen in silence nodding, as his tales were told by others until at last he would rise, touch each man on the shoulder and take his leave.

Murray watched as Bomber threw the boule high in the air with a deft flick of his wrist. The boule rose and spun, dropped like the dead, rolled back an inch towards Bomber and he spun on his heel clapping his hands, then walked in a half dance back to his seat.

The waiter placed his hand on Murray's shoulder. 'Señor Murray, there is telephone call for you.' He motioned with his chin to the desk.

Murray walked to the reception, picked up the phone and listened.

'Hello?' Murray said. 'Okay,' he continued, then listened again. 'I'll ask the question. Ring again same time tomorrow.' Then he hung up the phone and walked to Bomber, sat on the abutment waiting his turn to throw.

'That was Cork,' Murray whispered in Bomber's ear.

'Okay?'

'They are ready to go again. They are ringing again tomorrow. Can we arrange it?'

'Let's talk later. Ring Ronnie and make sure the docks are still open. Could you get me another beer? It's my turn to throw.'

Murray walked back to the reception, held up two fingers, then pointed to his beer and winked at the waiter. '*Dos*,' he added, to be sure, then he turned the phone towards him and dialled Cork.

'Hello,' a voice called over the booming decks at Uno's bar.

'It's Murray, will you get Ron?'

'Who?'

'Murray.'

'We are all merry here, boy.'

'Will you get Ronnie, please,' Murray shouted, getting annoyed.

'Who's this?' The voice came clearer now as the man stepped outside the door.

'It's Murray.'

'Hi Murray, I'll get him now.'

Murray waited as the music blared in the background. It was always the same. They'd answer the phone inside, realise they couldn't hear you, then they'd step outside with the cord from the payphone stretched behind. He could picture them now. He laughed to himself.

'Long time, double M,' came Ronnie's voice after a brief wait.

'Hi Ron, long time indeed and a sad one.'

'Indeed.'

'Are we open?'

'We are… for who?'

'Black Dave.'

'Okay, let me know when.'

'I'll have to okay it with the Bastard first, but I think it's on.'

'Okay, I'll wait to hear,' Ronnie said, then hung up.

Chapter Fifty-Three

TO THE ATLANTIC
(Harbour of Souls)

THE DIRT ROAD MEANDERED TIGHTLY between the overgrown hedgerows. In sections, Dave had no option but to let the car scratch that dry scrape, some resonant relative of bone that set the marrow rippling as the car creeped between the boughs. At the crest of the hill, Dave caught sight of the ocean's swell and his heart rose in his chest as he took in the view. He cursed himself and vowed not to leave it so long between visits. He parked by the gable end of the stone cottage, stepped from the car, stretched out a good stretch then examined the scratches to the bodywork. *Not too bad*, he thought, giving it a rub of his sleeve, then turned like a child to the wind and water's roar.

He'd first visited the cove six years earlier. An employee, one of his doormen, had a caravan a few miles back along the coast and Dave had gone to stay with him and his partner for a few days. On an early morning jog, he took a left up the dirt road where he'd chanced upon the old fishing hut. He remembered walking to the ocean, sitting on the sand, closing his eyes and listening as ten thousand howls and cries rolled in upon the breakers to settle and crash about him in this harbour of souls, each one some friend of old, beckoned thereabouts to drift no more amidst the waves, their days of hiss and fizzle behind them now as they settled there with him at last among the dunes.

*

As he lifted his bag from the boot, he caught sight of his face in the window's reflection. It was getting there. He'd have a scar for sure, maybe even a cool one, but he didn't care. He looked his face over left and right. *Still a handsome fucker*, he told himself. The sand blown up from the beach piled high against the back door. He took the spade from the hook on the sidewall and scooped the doorway clear. He thought about the journey that had brought this sand to his backdoor, and a pang of guilt swept through him as he took the brush now and swept it from his path. He slid back the large glass-panelled door, pushed the drapes back, stepped inside, and breathed in the stale air. He slid the doors all the way back, pushed the curtains all the way to the corner of the room, then walked to the bedroom and repeated the task. He ran the taps clear, then walked to the fridge, took a beer from the shelf, checked the date on the bottle, and crashed to the sofa. The tiny house flooded with the sea air swirling about him, and he listened to the waves breaking their lament on the shore as they chorused him gently and welcomed him home.

The house was but four walls when he'd found it. There was a bit of a roof, but not enough, and the sand piled high against the south wall where she led on to the beach. He knew at once that he had to have it. To the north, he saw smoke rise a few miles off across the fields and he set off jogging in its direction. *It can't get more primal than this*, he thought, *chasing fuckin' smoke signals. You are a fuckin' legend*, he told himself as he ran. When he reached the farmhouse, an old boy stood with his mouth agape as he watched this giant of a man, bare-chested and black, approach him at speed through his old spud field.

'Holy mother of sufferin' Christ,' the old boy gasped. 'What fuckin' boat did you fall off? Do you want me to call the coast guard? Come in to fuck and I get ya a shirt, ya poor bollix. When, and in what country did you last eat?' the old boy continued, taking Dave by the arm and leading him to the farmhouse. 'Do you speak English?' the old boy'd shouted.

'Leave it out mate, I'm not Shaka fuckin' Zulu,' Dave panted, catching his breath.

'Ahhh,' the old boy exclaimed, delighted. 'You speak English. Thank fuck for that, I thought I was under siege. When I saw you running across the field there, I thought, *I'll be in the big pot tonight if this whore gets his hands on me.*' He clapped his hands together, gave a toothless howl before continuing. 'What in the fuck are you doing out here with no clothes on ya mad whore ya?'

'I'm jogging and I have clothes. I'm wearing shorts and my vest is in my pocket,' Dave replied, patting his leg.

'Jogging? Are you fuckin' lost or what like, the nearest road is three miles back the way.'

'I'm looking for the owner of the derelict cottage by the beach straight back that way,' pointing south.

'The one with the red roof?'

'Are there others?'

'Well, no… but…'

'Then yes, the red roof one.'

'What's wrong with it? Is there a problem down there or something?'

'No, not at all. I was wondering if it was for sale. That's all.'

'It might be. What do you want it for?'

'I would like to do it up. Use it as a getaway.'

'Right, and how much money have you got?'

'I've got whatever it costs, within reason, mind.'

'Come into the house and we'll have a cup of tea and a chat. I need to ring somebody, but I think we might work something out.'

The old boy led Dave across the yard to the kitchen. He set the kettle on the hob, took the matches from a drawer on the side and set one to flame as he turned on the gas. When the hob was lit, he shook out the match and pocketed it.

'Sit down there and make yourself comfortable,' he told Dave. 'I'll make a quick call and be back to you in a minute.'

Dave could hear the old boy's soft muffled tones rolling up the hall. The kettle shrilled, Dave removed it from the flame, turned off the gas and set it to the side as the old boy returned and instructed him to sit down.

'What kind of host would I be now if you were to make your own cup o' tae,' he added.

'No problem,' Dave replied. 'Happy to help.'

'That was my brother on the phone. The house is his own. What's your plan for the place, he asked me?'

'I would love to fix it up and use it as a holiday home. I'd come back here when things are quiet… every other weekend. Maybe stay longer in the summer. Stuff like that. Is he interested in selling it at all?'

'Not really.'

'Fair enough. It's beautiful down there, though. It would've been nice.'

The old boy sat a tray on the table with mugs of tae and scones and butter and cream and jam. Dark red jam – Dave knew by the look of it that this was the good shit.

'Get stuck into that there,' the old boy told him.

'Thank you very much.'

'How long would it take you to fix the place up, do you think?'

'A couple of months.'

'There's bad access down there. You'd need to route all your materials through the farm on the tractor. There's electricity and water down there, but you'd need to plumb and rewire the whole place. It'd be no small job.'

'I'd be up for it.'

The old boy looked at Dave square for a moment. 'Here's the way of it. What the brother doesn't want is some blow-in from town buying the site below and sittin' on it. 'Tis sittin' down there doing fuck all as it is. Sure, why would he sell it to some lad to let it continue in the same way? Are you following me? Money wouldn't be enough of a motivator, if you know what I mean.'

'What kind of motivator might change his mind?'

'To see the old place with a bit of life in it again. To look down of an evening and see a light on below or a stream of smoke up out the chimney. Are you following me?'

'I'd get straight on it if that's what you mean. I wouldn't fuck about, I'd have the place in good nick by the end of the year.'

'Okay, how about this... you've got six months to get the cottage fixed up and habitable. If you do it in six months, then she's yours to keep for forty thousand. If you don't, then the deal's off. What do you reckon? Are you up to it?'

'Fuckin' right I am,' Dave replied.

'The site is an acre and a half, when you're finished your tea, I'll take you back down and show you the boundary. After that, if you're free, we'll head into O'Leary in town, and he'll put the contract in order. Did you say you had a shirt?'

'I do.'

'Good man, actually I might get you to leave the shirt off altogether. I can't wait to see the head on the old bollix when I walk into his office with you in tow.' He threw his head back and let out a mighty uproarious boom of a laugh, spraying scone and tea across the table and Dave.

'I don't know what to say...' Dave started.

'Say nothin'... there's an old barn at the end of the lane here. I'll show you as we head out. She's not safe anymore, and we built a new one at the far side over. Anyway, the old barn she's got some beautiful oak joists and rafters, and one side of the roof still has all her tiles. You can take what you want from it to fix your roof below and when you're finished with it, we can level her and use what's left for the fire.'

Dave looked around the room. He couldn't believe the old boy's generosity. Forty grand was a steal. For the first time in his life, he was speechless. He opened his mouth in an attempt at gratitude when the old boy cut him off.

'That said, you might do fuck all with it and I might have to turf you out in six months' time.' He burst into another round of laughter. 'Seriously though,' he continued, 'at our age it'd do our hearts a power of good to see the old place with a bit of life in it. 'Tis a shame we let it get the way we did. If you tell me you want to make use of it, then I say more power to ya, boyo.'

Dave knocked out the big back wall that faced the ocean. He made good the gable walls at either end, spanned the two with steel beams to take the weight of the joists and rafters and made good the roof with the oak and tiles salvaged from the old barn. With the roof on, he plumbed in a bathroom and a kitchen, poured some concrete floors and divided the space into a lounge and a bedroom with an en suite, both with floor to ceiling glass doors looking out upon the Atlantic Ocean. With the little house wired, floored and painted fourteen weeks after Dave had first set eyes on the place, himself and the old boy transferred contracts, popped a bottle of champagne and sat on Dave's new veranda sipping Dom Pérignon as the sun called time on the day and headed off west to raise some new boys from their beds, her work never done, ever fading.

He went to the bedroom and unloaded his bag. In the toilet, he pulled the light on and stood by the mirror. The wound on his cheek caught his attention, and he felt the fear rise in his gut, settle for a moment, then pass. He'd been lucky, and he knew it. So fucking lucky, he thought. If he hadn't charged at Carl and flustered the cunt, he'd be a dead man now. He thought about the huge fish in the deep waters by the leap. Had he imagined the big fish? He wasn't sure, but he was sure of one thing… he was one lucky cunt to be alive. Fuckin' Carl, cheeky bastard. Cheeky dead bastard. *Who was driving the bike?* he asked himself, *who was the cunt with Carl?* Probably some wannabe numpty, some hired driver without ambition or purpose who'd slink off into the background never to be heard from again. Perhaps…

He picked up his beer, walked to the water's edge, sat cross legged on the sand, closed his eyes and focused on his breath as a million lost souls rolled in off the Atlantic, settled there about him and welcomed him home.

Chapter Fifty-Four

THE BOOK OF DANIEL

Part V

THE BELFAST CREW CONTINUED THEIR calls. 'How in the fuck does this one work, Daniel?' Feargal would ask, holding a schematic to the light as Daniel, in his drunkenness, schooled these men of arms while The Boy toddled by.

'Now that my good man, is a piece of shit,' Daniel would slur, turning his nose to a fat little line before continuing. 'That might well work but why would you bother? A much more efficient option would be...' and Feargal would note.

It was little things at first. It started with some radio tomfoolery.

'Tell me, Daniel, how would a man tune this bastard radio to an undetectable frequency?' Or, 'Is it possible to adjust this whoring radio so I can hear what the peelers are saying?' and he'd guffaw drunkenly, embracing Daniel in some act of camaraderie. Daniel would amaze them with his intellect and understanding, his bespoke solutions blowing their small minds. Not only would he show them how to transmit on a discreet frequency, but he'd teach them how to sync their radios and scramble their communications, so they were totally undetectable.

'There can't be that many things you've got to say,' he started one night.

'Whatya mean?' Feargal asked.

'When you are on manoeuvres, it's not like you're chatting about what was on the telly last night or what you're having for tea. There must be a group of communications you use over and over.'

'And?'

'So make a list. For example, "unit b proceed",' Daniel mocked in his best Belfast tone, 'or whatever you say when you're up to your antics.'

'I'm with ya, go on.'

'Right, well, make a list of all the things, and we'll attribute each one to some covert correspondence. Each recruit to your group gets taught the list of communications, so when you're out and about on the radios, not only are your transmissions scrambled but you're also communicating in code.'

Feargal's mind was blown. All he had to do was mention a problem and Daniel would spit out a solution straight off the top of his fuckin' head. Access to Daniel's mind was like having their own technical division. He showed them how to remap car engines so they could outrun any pursuit vehicle. He designed an auxiliary fuel tank, so their cars could run for three times as long, so even if the police could keep up with them, eventually they'd run out of fuel. Simple, practical little cheats that consistently gave them the edge. Feargal's unit thrived.

Jackie Brosnan took the device from the boot of his car and walked discreetly to the waiting minibus. The minibus, used to transfer locals from a nearby estate to their place of work at Palace Barracks in County Down, was to be their latest target. They would set the device to go off at seven in the morning, a good half hour before the first workers arrived, but enough time to send a friendly message. It was a small device, but big enough to rise them from their beds and let them know these boyos meant business. The lookouts, positioned at either end of the road, gave the all clear and Brosnan disappeared from sight beneath the bus. He took the device from his satchel, fastened it to the exhaust, and set about arming the ignition. He checked his watch; it was two thirty. Four and a half hours, he told himself, as he set the timer and hit the start switch. The lookouts watched in disbelief as the minibus lifted from the ground and Brosnan's shattered body scattered out across the road in pieces.

Feargal was inconsolable. They'd checked everything twice. He was certain of it. They'd used this method a hundred times. It was foolproof, and Brosnan was no fool. He sat on the sofa on Lovers Walk and cried like a child. For days, he sat there looking out to the garden, drinking Hennessy and playing the what-ifs over and over in his head. It was his crew now. With Brosnan gone, it would naturally fall on Feargal to lead his men. It would need to be confirmed by the Senior Council, but he knew it was coming. He was determined it would never happen again. Not to his crew. They'd go back to the drawing board, set up a double, triple, quadruple checking system. It would be watertight, bullet proof, belt and fucking braces from now on, he told himself.

'No more fuck-ups, okay? No more fuck-ups,' he repeated over and over.

'Do you think he's alright?' Daniel asked.

'I don't know,' Marie replied, worried.

'How long is he gonna sit there? We've got the party on Saturday. I mean, he's welcome here anytime you know that, but…'

'Why don't you have a chat with him? He listens to you.'

Daniel looked at Marie doubtfully, then walked to the back room. Feargal, stood by the big window, jumped as Daniel approached.

'Fuck me Daniel, I was miles away,' he confessed, then laughed nervously.

'Sorry, I'm gonna start the tea. What do you fancy?'

'Ah… anything, mate. I'm not bothered.'

'Pasta?'

'Aye lovely, pasta.'

'Or a casserole?'

'Aye a casserole.'

'Lamb or chicken? I've got both.'

'Whatever mate. Check the dates.'

Daniel took the meat from the fridge and held it up to the light. 'Chicken to be used by… what date is it today?' He checked his watch. 'Twenty first, that's today – right, chicken it is then. Will you have a drink?'

'Aye mate, stick a wee drop in there,' Feargal said, holding out his glass.

'No problemo,' Daniel replied, taking the glass. He opened the freezer box and slammed the ice tray on the counter. The ice cubes slid about the surface, and he scooped them up and tipped them in the tumbler before adding two fingers, then he handed the glass back to Feargal.

'Are you not gonna join me?' Feargal asked, taking the drink.

'I will actually,' Daniel replied, then repeated the task.

Feargal stood by the back window. He could see all the way down to the harbour and beyond. He liked to watch the docks after dark, and he would sit there often, watching the ship lights come and go into the wee small hours. It reminded him of his time in Tripoli and those live-or-die days of his youth.

'I don't know how it happened Daniel,' he started. 'I can't think what he did wrong.'

Daniel put the knife down on the chopping board, took a long deep breath, picked up his drink, sank it in one and turned to Feargal.

'Ye need a new strategy.'

'Strategy?' Feargal snapped indignantly.

'It's fuckin' suicide, arming a device while you're stood next to it.'

'Whatya mean?'

'Look at the average working stiff turning up late for work. Nine times out of ten, what excuse does he use?'

Feargal looked at Daniel blankly. The concept of shift work beyond his grasp.

'My alarm didn't go off!' Daniel exclaimed. 'That's what they all say, now half the time they are bullshitting, but the other half they are telling the truth. So, what does that tell us?'

Feargal, struggling for an answer, looked at Daniel blankly before the realisation sank in and he sat back down on the sofa.

'Mistakes happen,' Daniel continued, 'and setting alarms or arming mechanisms with timers are one and the same. It was only a matter of time…' The terrible pun went unnoticed to Feargal. 'You need a way of arming and triggering the devices remotely,' Daniel explained and as the words left his mouth he could feel a helpless unravelling as some distant signing of contracts played out in his mind, and a greedy clawed hand scratched at some ancient scroll as his fate was sealed beyond damnation, and he knew in that moment that each foot forward would be a step of decline, until at last he stood afore the fiery gate, and he felt the good light leave him. Feargal, like some chancellor of the dead plying his ancient trade in the fiscality of souls let slip but one word:

'Continue.'

Chapter Fifty-Five

HIDE AND SEEK

On Pope's Quay, Clifford crawled the Corolla to the kerb. The rain bounced on the roof and bonnet in fat, whomping drops, then it streamed down the windows and side panels to gather in vast pools. He took the gun from the glove box, checked the magazine, then tucked it in his waistband. Tonight would be the night. He could feel it in his bones. Each night he'd waited, each night he'd watched, each night he'd gone home empty-handed. He'd walked from club to club, stalked the office block on Shandon, suffered his vigil at the cul-de-sac in Blackpool, lay motionless in the Blackrock brambles whilst creatures and demons advanced from the dark to tear at his tattered soul, taunting, taunting, taunting.

They had vanished... Dave and his boy had slipped the cunting noose. The rain stepped it up a gear, deafening now. Its torrent sprayed a billion tiny blinding lights, refracted all about him in advancing headlamps, then beat its hissing retreat on swishing wheels and a taillight's fizzling dwindle.

He stepped from the car into the rain, pulled his peaked cap forward, stopped a moment as the traffic passed, then he crossed the street and disappeared towards Rita's Villas. He followed the terrace around, keeping his head down as he scuttled the back lanes cloaked in darkness – silent in the rain, he passed unnoticed. When he reached Dave's office, he ducked into a lane that ran along the rear, where he backed into an archway, stood motionless, and watched. The building, silent but for the drains, gurgled, and he stood there for an hour, watching and waiting. Nothing moved at the block on Shandon Street. Cliff stepped from the archway, followed the lane to the main road, turned right on Shandon and headed up the hill towards Blackpool.

In the Blackpool cul-de-sac the rain soaked through his hat, ran down his face, slowing as it passed beneath his collar, then flowed down his back and chest in streams. Daniel's house, in lightless silence, betrayed no secret dwellers within, no hint of man nor boy about. Cliff followed the street around, then walked along the lane to the rear of the houses, counting each one as he passed.

'Eleven, twelve, thirteen and fourteen,' until he reached Daniel's back gate. 'Hello, you fucking beauty,' he hissed maniacally over the fence at the house abandoned.

The smell of poor men's dinners broiling wafted down the lane whilst some Mammy busy by a burning stove sang of the low fields of Athenry, chorused by the rain's erratic rattle on roofs of rippled iron. Some young buck in the house next door, fresh from the day's toil, took his woman in his arms and kissed her hard by the kitchen sink, while some other, two doors down, sat by the dinner table, schooled his young as his neighbour ran the roller with pride and a heart full of hope in his new home, glistening.

The tears rolled down Cliff's cheeks, warm against the rain as he watched two young boys on the bed bouncing, and he laughed at their scamper as their mother called them to the table. He cast his mind to his stolen basement boys, and his hand brushed once more his gun as he called to mind their vacant little graves dug neatly in a row at the woodland, waiting.

Chapter Fifty-Six

THE BOOK OF DANIEL

Via Dolorosa

'THEY SAY THE LORD WORKS in mysterious ways,' Daniel started. 'And if he does, then so too does the devil, his best apprentice. And if it's true that the Lord does indeed work in mysterious ways through some sleight of hand or some such roguery brought to bear by his wispy bedfellow the Holy Spirit, then so too is it true that the devil has a spirit all of his own. And this spirit too has reach and influence like a vapour released, spreading out to every far-flung corner and it goes by the name of the "demon drink".'

'Like a fart?' Tony joked. He'd heard this spiel before, many times, but he didn't like to stop Daniel when he was on a roll.

'At first it's all soft thumbs and kneading,' Daniel continued, 'right where it's wanted. A lilting voice and a warm embrace right when it's needed. And you might not even know your ache or pain, not yet anyway, but it knows, and it's all over it like a soothing balm. All warm-lipped luxury, rolling and kind, easy on the brakes, slowly round the corners, soft hands massaging, all shoulders and lower back and then one day it'll slip ya the cheeky finger and you might not notice at first, and the dirty bastard'll give it a sneaky sniff and pocket the offending digit. This is the moment, the most crucial point where it can go one way or the other and if you let it go, if you let that cheeky finger go, then there's nothing surer than he'll be having his way with ya by sun up. You need to call him out on that first finger, look him straight in the eye and say, "what in the fuck was that, ya dirty fucker?!" And if you do, then there's some chance for ya, but few do, few do indeed. And he'll be all pseudo-offended. All "how could you" and shite like that. "I'm a man of wealth and taste," he'll say, and he might move on to someone else in the hope he might make you jealous, but you've to reach over and pull his hand out of his pocket and smell that cheeky finger and if it's your own hole you're sniffing then you fuckin' have him boy – as sure as I'm sitting here if you call him out and prove him wrong about that cheeky finger—'

'One second please, Daniel,' Tony said, then turned his attention to a waiting punter. 'Evening, what'll I get ya?'

'Ignorant fucker,' Daniel said, then pushed back from the bar, turned and took in the scene at the St Leger. It was heaving. Fuck this shit. *Fuck this shit, this place and all these cunting people*, he thought. Tonight, would be the night. He'd had enough. This whoring bastard of a town could go and fuck itself, and he made for the door.

'Are you off Daniel?' Tony called.

'I may be some time,' Daniel replied over his shoulder as he picked his way through the Saturday night punters. When he got to the door, he looked back at the bar one last time, then he pushed the door open, and went outside. On the street, the cars honked their horns at passers-by and he turned to greet each one, but none were for him, and he pressed on. He passed the chipper, and somebody called his name but when he turned there was no one there. He fixed his collar to the evening breeze, and made for home.

When he got to the house, he walked to the back porch, took the rope from its box, placed the chair beneath the centre joist and he looped the noose over as he'd done so many times before. He pulled the rope down, checked it was tight, then he stepped from the chair, took a cigarette from his pocket, turned from the wind, and lit it up.

He thought about all that had gone before him: Mags and Fintan, Marie, Fallon, and the Girl. Then his mind turned to

The Boy. He'd be better off without his old man, he told himself. Everything he'd touched had turned to rat shit. The last thing The Boy needed was Daniel in his life, of that he was certain. He thought about Beckett, and a tear came to his eye as he recalled their last conversation.

'Call me anytime, Daniel, no matter what, no matter when. If you need me, call me.' But he never had. The thought crossed his mind that he might ring him now, but it was too late, he told himself, and he let the cigarette fall from his hand, stepped on to the plastic chair, placed the rope about his neck and fixed the knot tight to the side.

Tonight, he felt strong. He knew he could do it. In his heart, he knew he could kick the chair out from beneath him and he positioned his feet to the front, teetering on the precipice. He thought about Beckett some more. A smile crossed his face as he remembered Marie and Beckett dancing in the ballroom in Killarney, and Fallon and The Boy climbing the dunes at Inch Strand.

'Come on Dad,' they'd say. 'To the top of the next one.'

'We need to head back, boys,' he'd tell them.

'One more Dad… please…' He saw their little faces, plaintive in the wind as it swept their fringes, side to side. 'If we don't, it'll catch us.'

'No, come on, enough now. We need to get back,' he'd reply, and he remembered the words, the lazy lie, for there was nowhere to get to and he hated himself for letting 'it' catch them, whatever 'it' was. And it was close tonight. He could feel it, that looming doom his kids foretold, and he pushed it away and he forgave himself in these his final moments.

He turned his mind to the blasted victims, Jackie included, and for the first time in a long, long while he let them all in, and he held them close as the warm tears rolled down his face and he sobbed there like a child. He reached out and touched their faces, burns and all, and they smiled up at him – the whole backyard was alive with forgiveness and for a brief spell he even forgave himself. His shoulders rose and fell with each sob and he wiped his nose and eyes with his sleeve and as he looked about the empty yard, he recalled those early days when his mind was crystal with ecstatic clarity. Suddenly a flash roared through him and he saw, for the first time in twenty years or more, the world for what it was, a simple set of correlations.

It took him by surprise, and he had to steady himself, but he could see it all so clearly, and in that moment, he knew there was work yet to be done. His computer was more possible now than ever before and there was time still, to put it right, to be there for The Boy, fix things with Beckett and between them they could build the computer and maybe even go back and stop all the madness, the fucking madness.

He knew he was getting away with himself, but he couldn't stop it. He thought again about the Mammy and her babbie, the fat accountant and the hundreds of nameless others and in that moment, he solemnly pledged to honour them with his work. He would take his medication, make the right choices, steer clear of the drugs and the booze and rebuild the pathway to a richer and fuller life for everyone who'd ever put their faith in him or his ways. It was all so clear to him now. He knew exactly what he needed to do and how to do it. He could see each step aligned and he could feel the sear of his bygone brilliance burning in his brain. His pathway was sure, and true, and he resigned to put his world in order, and he would live his best life from this moment forward.

Watching from the shadows, Clifford stepped from the darkness, snatched the chair from beneath Daniel's feet, placed it on the porch, picked the cigarette from the dirt, took a long drag, and rested for a while as he watched Daniel writhe.

Chapter Fifty-Seven

TAKEN

IT RAINED ALL THE MORNING, in thick heavy whomps that sucked and gurgled in the gullies and gathered in vast pools about their feet. In the afternoon, the thunder started, and the day turned to black, interrupted by sporadic flashes of fat yellow lightning forked against the charcoal sky. When they lowered Daniel down, the rain picked up and the grave pooled with water, halfway up the side of the box. The priest mouthed the words for the dead and when he was done, the small crowd picked their way between the water and shuffled on back to the pub.

Gordon held tight as The Boy shot out the road and dropped him by the back lane that led up to his house. Clifford followed, keeping a safe distance. When he reached the house, he pulled over and watched.

'You gonna be alright?' Gordon asked. He knew the answer. How would he ever be alright? His mother, his brother and now Daniel. He felt silly for asking.

'I'll be grand,' The Boy answered. 'I'll give you a ring later, or call down to the pub if you're not doing anything,' he said, then slipped the bike in gear and drove off toward the city. Clifford put the car in gear and followed. Soon the traffic picked up, and he watched The Boy snake between the lines of cars and disappear from view. Clifford turned his car in the road and headed back to Gordon's. He parked by the back lane, and watched the house. He could see through the kitchen window, and he surmised with some certainty that the house was empty but for Gordon.

This wasn't part of the plan, he thought. He didn't even know who this kid was. Until a few days ago he hadn't even known The Boy was involved. He looked to the kitchen window again and thought. They were close, these two. Very close. If he couldn't get to Fallon's brother himself then he would get to him by whatever means possible. He'd come too far to start growing a conscience now. He thought about his situation, and the truth was, he simply didn't give a fuck anymore. He wanted revenge and this was how he was going to get it.

He took a deep breath, stepped from the car, took the home hostage kit from the boot, slung it over his shoulder, then walked to the front of the house. He looked through the windows as he passed. When he reached the front door, he tried the unlocked handle, stepped inside, and closed and locked the door gently behind him.

Gordon, not accustomed to violence, stumbled backwards in horror as he watched this grown man set upon him, wrestle him to the ground and restrain his hands behind his back. Clifford taped Gordon's mouth shut, dragged him by the scruff and bundled him discreetly into the boot of the car waiting by the back gate.

Chapter Fifty-Eight

THE BOSS WANTS TO SEE YOU

He hadn't heard from Gordon since the funeral. He was worried. He couldn't admit that to himself, but there was something in the background telling him he needed to be concerned. He took his phone from his pocket and dialled Gordon's number for the fifth time that day. It went straight to answerphone. He sighed. He tried to recall what they'd agreed when he dropped him home. He thought about Carl: could somebody have hurt Gordon? He pushed the thought from his mind.

He's fine, he thought to himself. He resolved to call to his house later and see if he was there.

His phone rang. He turned it in his hand, hoping, then sighed when he saw Mucky's number.

'Alright?' he said.

'Yeah, you?' Mucky asked.

'Yeah, I'm upstairs in the pub. Are ya calling round?'

'No, I've got some shit to do. I'm ringing you for a reason, though. The exiled king wants to see you.'

'Who?'

'Actually…' Mucky reconsidered. 'Let's meet up, it'll be easier. Not the pub, though. I can pick you up outside in a few minutes. We can talk while I run a few errands. Is that cool for you?'

'Cool… park at the shop. I'll keep an eye out here.'

'Any word from Gordon?'

'Nothing, you?'

'Not a thing. His phone is off. Have you called to the house?'

'No, that's the next step. I don't wanna freak his Mam out though.'

'Okay, see you in a minute.'

The Boy walked to the window and watched the street below. *What the fuck was he going on about, exiled king?* he thought.

'Who's the exiled king?' he asked, turning to Tony.

'Whatya mean?'

'The exiled king... that was Mucky on the blower. He said the exiled king wants to see me.'

'Oh right, that'll be Ronnie. Fuck me. Did he say what he wants?'

'No, should I be worried?' he asked. He'd heard of Ronnie, everybody had. Everyone knew the tale of the mythical king dethroned by The Big Fella and his crew, but to The Boy's mind, it was irrelevant. It was a done thing; the past was the past and so on, until he got the call.

'I don't know. It's been years since Ronnie was involved in your craic. Maybe he wants to offer his condolences.'

'Maybe. What's he like?'

'I dunno, probably a fuckin' nutter. They all are. No offence.'

The Boy looked at Tony, then out the window again.

'Should I go and see him?'

'I dunno. Speak to Mucky, see what he wants. If it sounds cushty, go and see him. If you smell a rat, tell him to get fucked. To be fair, he probably had some shit going down with The Big Fella, and now that it's quite clear that you are the new bigfella – albeit a little bigfella – he probably wants to see if things are still schweet.'

'Hmmm.'

Mucky tooted on the street below. The Boy grabbed his jacket and made for the stairs.

When he got to the laneway, he looked the road up and down. He spotted Mucky's souped-up Honda Civic. He couldn't understand why they all drove such distinctive cars. It made no sense to him.

They should be driving non-descript cars that fade into obscurity. This was something he'd be addressing once things had settled down. He walked to the passenger side and climbed in.

'Alright boy?' Mucky asked.

'Alright Muck, what's the craic?'

'No craic at all boy, this lad has got a message to me that Ronnie wants to speak to ya. That's all I know. He said Ronnie has some information he wants to share with ya and that was it.'

'Whatya think?'

'You're grand. We'll get Dave to go with ya. You'll be fine, anyway Ronnie's in another league. He's not bothered with what we do. He's well set up. When The Big Fella took things over, they came to an arrangement that set Ronnie up for life. I dunno what it was, something about dealing-spot levies and some property. I don't know exactly, but Ronnie doesn't need or want what we have.'

The Boy let the information sink in. Dave was off the grid and there was no way of contacting him. He didn't need this shit right now.

'Dave's off the grid until further notice,' he said. 'Did this Ronnie say where or when he wanted to meet?'

'No, but everyone knows where to find Ronnie.'

'Everyone except me!'

'Uno's.'

'Can you take me there?'

'Now?'

'Now.'

'Cool, let's go.'

Chapter Fifty-Nine

UNO'S

RONNIE WATCHED THE CAR PULL up outside Uno's bar. Mucky, he recognised, and although he didn't recognise his passenger, he knew it was The Boy. His resemblance to Fallon was incredible, and if the reports were anything to go by, it wasn't only his looks that he shared with his late brother. If what Ronnie'd heard was true, this little fucker was a right operator. He watched the two converse in the car. *Would he have the balls to rock up unannounced?* Ronnie asked himself. He'd clearly got his message, but had he the bottle to walk in the front door, bold as brass? *It would be true to form, alright,* Ronnie thought, *but still...*

'Ronnie? Ronnie...? Ronnie, are you fuckin' listening to me?' Noddy asked, annoyed.

'What?' Ronnie replied.

'Are you fuckin' listening, or what? This is important.'

'Of course I am Nod, sorry about that. I was watching the car outside,' he said, pointing to the Civic through the smoked glass window.

'Who's that?'

'That, my friend, is our prince regent. Now shape up, it looks like he's gracing us with his presence.'

The Boy stepped from the car, looked the street up and down, stepped back to let a cyclist pass, then rounded the bonnet and made for the door. He entered the bar unnoticed, or so he thought. It smelt like the St Leger, that unmistakable odour of beer, smoke and piss. Ronnie, deep in the pretence of conversation, side-eyed The Boy as he rounded the bar, walked to the pool table, took in the faces, then turned and headed back towards the bar again. The keeper set his paper down, looked at The Boy and spoke.

'I think you might be in the wrong place, son.'

'I'm looking for someone,' The Boy replied.

'And tell me now, have you found them? Because, like I said, I'm pretty sure you're in the wrong place?'

'I'm in the right place, alright,' The Boy replied, 'but maybe I should come back later.'

'Or maybe not at all… Huh?' the keeper added with a hint of menace, the 'fuck off' eyebrow raised.

'I think he might be looking for me, Paddy,' came a husky-voiced boom from the far end of the bar. The Boy looked towards the voice as Ronnie rose from his seat, then turned to face him where he stood. He was fuckin' huge, The Boy noted. He was built like a fucking tank with the air of a retired rugby player. Standing at a solid six feet or more, he had a well-built frame with a barrel chest that tapered down to his waist. He wore a sharp, fitted blazer he'd matched with a navy sweater, stylish jeans and a pair of smart loafers. He had a thick brow, Neanderthal-like, above deep-set hazel eyes and a wide toothy smile that did little to console The Boy.

Ronnie leaned on the counter. The Boy watched the bar bow beneath his bulk then rise again as Ronnie walked towards him with his enormous arm extended. The Boy took the giant hand in his and Ronnie pulled him in close, then spoke in his ear.

'My name's Ronnie. I'm guessing you're Fallon's brother?' he said, before withdrawing his face to take in The Boy's response. The Boy looked hard in Ronnie's eyes and, detecting a kindness, relented with a nod.

Ronnie returned The Boy's gaze, held it a moment, then nodded and motioned to a corner seat by the window.

'Sit down here my friend, we can have an old confab in peace,'

Ronnie said, and he sat The Boy down, then turned to the barman, who was waiting.

'Can I've a pint please Paddy and a…' He let the thought hang as he turned back to The Boy. 'What can I get ya?'

'I'm grand,' The Boy replied instinctively.

'Ahh, don't start that shite, for fuck's sake,' Ronnie said. 'You're my guest. Let me get you a drink.'

'I'll have a Coke… thank you.'

'So, a pint for myself and a Coke for my friend, please, and a pair of brandies as well, as a chaser.'

'Is that a double or two singles, Ron?'

'Two singles please Paddy,' Ronnie said, then turned to The Boy with a screwed-up face, half smile, half reassuring gurn.

Paddy started the Guinness and set it to rest. He turned to the brandy, fixed two small ones and placed them on the bar for Ronnie to approve. He grabbed from the fridge a bottle of Coke, popped the cap, let it fall expertly to the waiting receptacle as he retrieved a glass from beneath the bar, set it on the counter then called out to The Boy, 'Ice and a slice?' Ronnie turned, his eyebrow raised, waiting for an answer, the afternoon in suspended animation as The Boy considered, and when at last he consented the music picked up. Not a moment later, the glass clinked with two cubes, followed by the lemon and the Coke poured over the two, but only enough to make the ice cubes float, and he slid the bottle and glass forward to join the proud brandies. Before you could blink he was finishing the pint to complete the quintuplet as Ronnie passed him a score and the deal it was done.

'Keep the change Paddy,' he said, no hint of condescension.

'Sound, Ron.'

Ronnie corralled the drinks in his massive hands and navigated his way to the table.

'There's a Coke for you, my friend, and a pint for myself,' he said as he screwed up his face again, then continued. 'There's a drop of brandy there as well for ya. If you fancy it.'

'Jaysus no,' The Boy protested.

'You might change your mind,' Ronnie suggested, as he lifted one knee between his locked hands and rocked on his stool gently.

'I knew your mother,' he started. 'She was a good girl.' He paused a moment to think, then started again.

'She used to knock around with my cousin Sheila, when they were young like... and your Dad, I didn't know him as such. I knew *of* him, the whole country knew of him at one stage... so I suppose... well, it's a small town. What can I say?

'Your brother, though, now he was a one. I never met anybody like him, and I've seen 'em all. From gunslingers to pop singers, I've seen all kinds of apery and majesty, but I've never seen the likes of him. Not before and not since. He's a big loss.'

A butterfly, resting a while in the light fitting, fell, flew, or fluttered down and danced about Ronnie's head. Ronnie eyed it kindly, held out his massive index finger and cooed it to land.

'Look at you, ya little beauty. Have you been cocooning up there in my lights?' he asked. 'Jaysus, if you could talk, huh? I should charge you rent,' he joked, then stood and walked it to the door, where he held his arm aloft and watched proudly as she took to the sky.

'Lovely, fuckin' lovely, did ya see that Noddy?' he said.

'I did, Ron. What was it?'

'A butterfly, you cunt,' Paddy piped from behind the bar, and the punters laughed. Ronnie shot Paddy a daggery glance, then answered Noddy calmly.

'A Painted Lady, Nod.'

'This time of year?'

'I've seen them earlier.'

'If you say so, Ron.'

Ronnie took his chair at The Boy's table and picked up the conversation.

'He was a real gentleman, your brother,' he continued, settling back down. 'And he knew everything, every cunting thing. He could talk about anything, and funny, he'd have the entire place in stitches. A great little fella, a great little fella. You've had a rough run, son, no doubt about it, you've had a bad run. Yet here you are. He'd be proud of you, would Fallon. He'd be proud of you alright.' Ronnie picked up his pint, sank back half, placed it on the table and wiped his lips dry.

'I never saw it coming, ya know, and I see everything. Nothing gets past me, and I don't mean that in any big-headed way, but I know the inevitable like the back of my hand. I can see what's coming, but I didn't see that. Not a fuckin' clue. I know why now, but at the time I had no fuckin' clue.'

The Boy, sensing some grand news imminent, picked up the brandy and sank it in one. He was gonna need it, he could tell. Ronnie picked up his, sank it, then shook the empties at Paddy.

'Two more please Pad,' then turning back to The Boy. 'Do you want some crisps or something? They have toasties. Have you eaten?'

'I'm grand, thanks,' The Boy replied, feeling the heat of the brandy rise in his chest and settle at the back of his neck as Ronnie picked up the story once more.

'People think that The Big Fella and his boys staged some kind of war or a coup of some description, but the truth is far less exciting, I can assure you. They came to me about… Jaysus, it must be at least a few years ago now and they asked me if I'd like to come on board, join forces, so to speak. My brothers were either dead or in jail and at the time, it made sense to team up, but I didn't want to. I simply didn't fancy it so we sat down here,' pointing at the ground, 'where we are sitting now and we came to an arrangement, an understanding, if you will. We shook on it, and they left. There was no taking or giving, not that it was mine to give or theirs to take, for that matter. What is Caesar's to Caesar and so on and so forth… but was it mine to give or divvy? No, no, it was not.'

Ronnie looked out the window, remembering half a world away, and he whispered as though to himself, then jumped when The Boy spoke.

'What arrangement did ye come to?'

'What?' Ronnie asked, half startled from his daydream.

'The arrangement? What was it?'

'Oh that, don't mind that shit. Good lord, forgive me, son. That's not why I asked you to come and see me, my friend. No, no, not at all. That business is for another time. I tell you that to impart to you, that I can accept and understand that things change and I'm very accepting of that. But this business with your brother and The Big Fella… that… I didn't see that coming. Carl and that other cunt, those fucking filibustering bastards. The fucking cheek, and for what?'

'Other?' The Boy asked, sitting forward, his heart pounding in his chest and echoing in his ears, Paddy at Ronnie's shoulder now, placing the two brandies on the table. The Boy took a deep breath, not sure if he was ready for what lay ahead.

'How much do I owe you, Paddy?'

'Four eighty Ron.'

'Keep the change,' handing him a five.

'Other? You said other,' The Boy asked again, more impatient now.

'I'll get to that, son. Don't worry, that's why you're here. Anyway, one day I was sat over there,' pointing to a stool at the end of the bar. 'About a month or two ago now. Maybe more, I can't remember. Anyway, I was sitting there reading the *Racing Post* one Saturday lunchtime, and I saw a bike pull up outside and there were two lads on this bike. And I thought to myself, *who's this pair of wankers now*, and I remembered what happened with your brother and The Big Fella and I thought, *fuck me*! so I jumped up from my chair and I made to put the bolt on the door. For fear they were planning on coming in here with bad intentions, like. It's one-way glass there so I could see them, but they couldn't see me. Are you following me?'

The Boy nodded, looking at the smoked glass window.

'Anyway, I jumped off the seat and made for the door but as I did… as I fuckin' did, didn't the passenger remove his helmet and I saw it was Carl. I know Carl – well, I used to know Carl, but we won't get into that, that too is a chat for another time. Anyway, I saw it was Carl, and I felt a bit stupid like for losing my shit, so I sat back down, but I'm not embarrassed to say my fifty pence piece was quaking. I'd gotten a fright like. Anyway, in walks Carl and he sees me, and he asks to have a chat with me. So I get him a drink and we are chatting and he's giving it the big *I am* and I'm thinking *no you're fuckin' not,* but I'm keeping it all friendly, and the whole time I'm watching his pal through the one-way glass and I'm thinking to myself all the while that I know this cunt, this pal of Carl's. And Carl is yammering on about things, that *the old arrangement still stands* and I turn to him and I say, "Carl what the fuck are you talking about?" He tells me in no uncertain terms that he's got a backer and he's gonna start bringing in gear wholesale and he knows I had an arrangement and that out of respect he wants to establish the same terms blah, blah, blah, and I'm thinking *Carl you're a cunt* but I'm humouring him like.'

'But the whole time he's here I've got one eye out the window and I'm watching matey boy and it's driving me fuckin' doolally cos I *know* I know him, but I don't know fuckin' how. And then Carl fucked off, and I thought no more about him until…' Ronnie waved his massive index finger in the air. 'Until last week when I heard about Carl's early demise and how he was linked to this business with your brother – Jaysus Christ it hit me like a bolt from above and it all fell into place and I realised who the cunt was and where the fuck I'd seen him.'

Ronnie picked up his pint, sank the second half, wiped his mouth dry and looked The Boy square in the eye. The Boy, on the edge of his seat now, willed Ronnie with his eyes to go on but Ronnie turned to the bar shaking his glass. Paddy nodded and

Ronnie turned back to The Boy and said, 'Will you have another Coke?'

'Coke? Coke? Are you having a fuckin' laugh?' The Boy spewed.

'Sorry, of course… Carl's friend… I've a cousin. Her name is Kathleen, a bit of a snobby bitch, but she's family. She works for this Englishy prick out Midleton way, real highflyer, owns half the county. Anyway, once a year he has a do at his house where he invites all his staff and stakeholders out to the estate and they do a barbecue and there's dancing and scutting, you know the scene. Anyway, one year out of the blue Kathleen rings me up and asks if I can get her any fresh salmon for this party. I do a bit of fishing, and I've got a few contacts, so I tell her I can get her a few salmon, and she asks me to deliver them out to this estate. So, I rock up with a dozen fresh salmon and when I get there, this cunt, the owner, comes over and he's all dressed in tweed, the real fuckin' deal. You couldn't make this cunt up, believe me. Anyway, he's showing me around and he's heard I'm into horses so he takes me around the stable and it's all over the top and he's all fuckin' this and fuckin' that and I can't wait to get away from this prick, but he keeps going on and on and eventually he shuts up and I fuck off and I thought that was the end of that, until…' He waved his index finger again.

'Until… I'm in here one evening, sitting over there,' pointing to the now vacant seat at the end of the bar. 'And I'm telling the lads about this prick and one of the young lads from Togher says "I know that cunt, Ron" and I'm like "Do you now?" and he tells me about this Englishy cunt and how he buys loads of yokes and gear and I'm thinking it can't be the same fella, it can't be Kathleen's Lord of the Manor, and so I do a bit of digging and fuck me sideways it turns out that it is the same fella and he is an animal for the gear. I thought *isn't that hilarious, Jaysus it takes all kinds* and I think no more about it until…' He waved the big finger again. 'Until he shows up here with Carl that Saturday lunchtime and I can see him through the one-way glass but he can't see me. But he's in there somewhere,' he continued, tapping the side of his head with the big old finger, 'and he stuck with me and although I didn't remember him at first I remember him now and I'll bet my fuckin' life that he was the second cunt on that bike the night they gunned your brother down, and I'll put double or nothin' on him being there when they gunned down The Big Fella, and fuckin' Dave and for what? Pair of useless wankers if ever there was a fuckin' pair.'

Ronnie's eyes glistened with rage. He picked up his brandy and sank it in one. The Boy did the same, and they shook 'em off then focused in on one another again.

'Where can I find him?' The Boy asked.

'I thought you might ask that,' Ronnie replied, and he turned to Paddy, motioning for a paper and pen. Ronnie wrote the address and accompanied it with a simple map.

'There's a black gate here that he closes in the evening,' pointing to the map. 'If you continue past that gate, you'll come to a dirt road on your right. Follow the dirt road on foot. It will take you to the rear of the house. There's loads of buildings scattered around the yard, but the farmhouse, you can't mistake it. It's a big white thing with a wonky roof. You can't miss it.'

'Have you got a photo?' The Boy asked, his affirmation rising in his mind.

'Of the house? What do you think I am, an estate agent?'

'Not the house, the bloke, Carl's friend.'

'You can't miss this cunt, either. He's about fifty with a big ould Englishy head on him. When you see him, you'll know him.'

'His name? What's his name?'

'Cromby, Cliff or Clifford Cromby.' Ronnie leant in conspiratorially. 'If you're paying him a visit, leave it until the nighttime. He's alone out there at night and when the sun goes down, it's as black as thunder round them parts.'

'Why are you telling me this?' The Boy asked, pocketing the map.

'I knew it was fuckin' dopes were behind these fuckin' antics. No cunt in his right mind would've dared to upset what we had going on. It was fucking Eden down here, boy, and them fuckin' snakes, them two fuck-apes thought they'd take it from our hands like we were a gang of sleeping babes. *Soft in the fuckin' head, soft in the fuckin' head*, I kept telling myself. These lads have to be soft in the *ceann* and wasn't I fuckin' right?' he said, squeezing The Boy's shoulder. 'Pair of fuckin' wankers. Anyway, it's up to you now, lad. Do with that information what you will. I'll say no more on the subject.'

The Boy stood from the table, a little unsure on his feet, the brandy taking hold. Ronnie took him by the elbow and walked him to the door.

'Will you be alright from here?' he asked. 'I won't walk you out. There's eyes abound and you don't wanna be seen with me, my friend. Come back again when it's all settled down. We can't put the apple back on the tree, but once you're done pruning, we might get a chance at a new crop.' And then he was gone.

Chapter Sixty

DIGGING 4

A TIDY JOB, CLIFF THOUGHT to himself as he eyed the row of neatly dug graves. He'd have some explaining to do if someone happened upon him now, he thought, chuckling.

He ran the checklist in his head for the hundredth time. The boat was ready, and he had gathered the cash. He would tell Kathleen he was going to England for a few weeks. She could keep things ticking over until he got back. The unfortunate consequence, however, was that he'd have to dispose of his guests before he departed, and so he found himself alone again in the woodland, digging. He could let the little bastards starve, but one might escape or worse and even if they didn't, he'd still have to get rid of the rotten corpses when he returned. On balance, he thought it would be best all round if he offed the lot then fucked off on the boat for a month or two until the dust settled, then he could return and start again.

They were getting a bit big and bold for his liking, anyway. Big and bold, all of them but one. Little Eoin, the poor wee crater. He remembered the first time he'd laid eyes on the poor devil. Standing by the kerb waiting to cross the road with his little bag of shopping and his lovely warm coat that screamed, 'somebody loves me'. He was the polar opposite of Cliff's normal type, but still and all he'd stopped the car, picked him up, put him in the backseat and drove. The poor little fucker hadn't said a word. He simply sat there looking at Cliff and then after a few minutes he worked out what was going on and he cried, and he cried, and he cried. Cliff remembered that drive home well. He'd worn a hole in the rear-view mirror that day. He couldn't believe what he'd done. Normally he'd research and scope a potential lad for months before he'd take them but this little fella he'd snatched from the street in his own car registered to his home address and Jaysus H Christ he didn't sleep for a month with the worry and the guilt.

It was all over the news. There were times when he thought about offing the little fucker, but he could never bring himself to do it. His little fat cheeks staring at him through the bars with his big blue eyes that asked, *Why, Why, Why*? And it made Cliff question himself for the first time.

'What kind of cunt are you?' he'd asked himself over and over, but he simply didn't know, and that was the truth of it. Anyway, his hand was being forced now, so the poor little fucker's days were numbered, regardless.

His new little fella, Gordon, was a right terror. In other circumstances, he'd probably like the little bollix, he thought to himself fondly. Loyal… he couldn't believe how loyal the little fucker was. He'd pulled out his teeth, broken his nose, slapped his balls repeatedly with a fish turner, a fish turner! Over and over, he'd smacked them until at last the sack ripped and still, he would not tell him where Dave and The Boy were holed up.

Unbe-fuckin'-lievable. The thought dawned on Cliff that maybe he didn't know… *ah well, too late for that now*, he told himself. He'd try one more time to make him talk, but either way, Gordon would meet the same fate as the rest of his guests, he decided as he dragged branches from the surrounding area and concealed the dig site.

Chapter Sixty-One

KILDUGGART

'Take me back to the pub,' The Boy asked, as he slumped into the passenger seat.

'Well?' Mucky enquired as he turned the car.

'I don't know. I need to process what he told me.'

'Are we in trouble?'

'No, no, nothing like that. What else do you know about the arrangement between Ronnie and The Big Fella?'

'Only what I told you earlier, but there was definitely something alright. Is that what he wanted?'

'No, I'll tell you later. I need to work out in my head what the fuck he said. It's been a long week.'

'Sound, sure I know well… you stink of booze.'

'I know yeah, I was drinking brandy.' They both laughed.

He let himself in the rear door at the St Leger, then slipped up the backstairs to the old family room where the green velvet sofa curved and called him to her comforts. Downstairs an old boy sang about all the stars that ever shone and daylight peeping through a curtain, and the words found their way up between the floorboards into The Boy's heart and carried him away to a day in springtime when snow melted and streams flowed, and there was peace in his heart and his mind, and he let the sleep take him.

When he woke, it was dark. Saturday night was everywhere. He could feel it in the air, charged, an electric potential like a storm-cloud before the discharge. Taxis and cars honked their horns on the street below as young girls in miniskirts took their chances among the traffic, then turned brazen with bold eyes blued in the headlamps howling, 'fuck off ya pervert' then cackling, click-clacking their way along Cork's cobbles as the night took them in its arms and carried them away.

He took from the fridge a bottle of Yop and a packet of ham, pushed an armchair to the window and sat there eating as he watched the night below unfold. The map, like a bleeding heart, burned, and he took it from his pocket, held it to the streetlight cast about the room and read. *Englishy-looking cunt*, he thought. He finished his meal of yoghurt and ham, took the keys from the mantelpiece, grabbed the helmet from the stand, then he slipped down the backstairs and into the night.

When he reached the graveyard, he parked the bike by the third lamppost, looked up and down the road, vaulted the high perimeter wall with ease, landed on the other side, then followed the wall along. When he reached the fourth pillar, he lay on the ground, rolled up his sleeve and slipped his hand inside through a gap in the blocks. It wasn't there; he rummaged a while, then stood back and counted the pillars again. Certain he was in the right place, he slipped his hand back inside the gap, up past his elbow this time, and there he felt it. He pulled the gun free, removed the cellophane wrapping, checked the magazine, secured it in his waistband, then he pulled himself up the wall to his chin. He checked the road for traffic, vaulted the wall again and ran to his motorbike, waiting. He kicked the bike into gear and headed for the Midleton road. *Englishy-looking cunt*, he thought as he rode.

When he rounded the hill, he could see the farmhouse in the distance. The moonlight pooled on its 'wonky roof', and he smiled as he remembered Ronnie's words. He pulled the bike from the road, concealed it in a ditch, then followed the ditch on foot until he hit the road at the bottom of the hill, where he followed it around until he came to the dirt road and he felt his way along in the darkness. *Black as thunder*, he thought, recalling Ronnie's words again, and he continued, feeling his way along in the night until the farmhouse came back into view and he used its lights to guide him on.

When he reached the house, he lay on a grass verge that surrounded the yard to the rear, and he watched. There was movement on the ground floor. The back door opened and an Englishy-looking cunt stepped into the yard. Ronnie had a way with words. A spot lamp above the backdoor burst into life and the yard came alive in the light. The Boy felt the beams on his face, and he ducked behind a ridge of grass and watched Clifford walk to an outhouse, then disappear inside. There was a mechanical rumbling of a roller door followed by the kick-start of an engine, then Cliff emerged on a quad bike and shot across the yard away from The Boy.

'Shit,' The Boy cursed as he watched Clifford disappear across the fields. He crawled the crest of the hill that bordered the farmhouse until he caught sight of the quad, idling by a ditch. He watched as Clifford climbed down, opened a gate, then climbed back on and drove through the opening, where he stopped, climbed off the quad, closed the gate behind him, then he climbed back on the quad and accelerated across the fields.

'Gates, fucking gates,' The Boy mouthed excitedly as he fixed the gun tight in his waistband and set off after the quad at a steady run. He lost sight of it a few more times, then he picked it up again, only to lose it moments later. Sometimes he thought he was gaining on it and other times he lost all hope and thought he might head back to the farmhouse and wait for Cliff's return, but he kept running, some drive in his core, deeper than bone, fuelled his pursuit and he ran like a man possessed. When the moon shone high and bright, he could see for miles, and then there was no moon at all and he had but the sound of the quad's revs to guide him on. He approached to his right a mountain of sorts, and as the quad veered left around the outcrop it came within shooting range. The Boy ran hard but the quad picked up a sound path and soon it was but taillights in the distance. Still The Boy ran.

When he rounded the outcrop, he could see Clifford's lights in the valley zigzagging in and out of rough terrain. He checked the gun once more and pressed on even harder. Cliff navigated his way through the brambled paddock as The Boy, running at full pace, advanced in the valley. The moon flashed another smile and the whole vale, livened in her glory, stretched out before The Boy. Moonbeams bounced from the wet roof-tiles of Kilduggart Hall and The Boy ducked behind a stone wall and watched the quad disappear behind a hedgerow as Clifford killed the engine. The moon decided she'd revealed enough and retreated behind the clouds, to wherever she goes. The Boy, still a mile in tow, stuck tight to the hedgerow and ran harder, picking up the pace some more, hoping to cut Clifford off should he decide to leave before he arrived.

When he reached the paddock wall, he leapt it with ease and ran headlong into a barbed maze of growth and confusion. He meandered in and out of the thornbushes towering high above his head, all the while sensing those night beasts, big and small, out there scuttling among the thicket, but he paid them no mind. He battled in the bush for some time, but he made no ground, and he realised he was no closer to the house than when he'd started. He got down on his hands and his knees, pulled his coat over his head and made a beeline crawl for the house. He could feel the barbs tearing at his head and back and he took it as a sign in the darkness that he was advancing in the brush, until he stopped by a clearing no wider than a yard and the moon shone a twinkle of consent that lit his way. He dropped again to his hands and knees and found Clifford's tracks in the darkness, and he clawed at the trail like a hound on the scent. It was all he could do not to crane at the moon and howl, until he came upon the quad by the hedgerow, hiding, and he looked up like a crazed lunatic to see the bright banner blazing by the light of the moon and read, DANGER. NO ACCESS ALLOWED.

He pulled himself up to his chin and peered over the perimeter wall. There was no sign of Cliff. He tried the door by the quad, but it was locked tight. He thought about forcing it, but thought again and decided instead to follow the fence around, hoping to find an opening, but the fence was sound. He dropped to his knees, looked along the fence, hoping, then sighed. A feeling of helplessness came over him. Out in the paddock's darkness, thick with thorns, he sensed once more all manner of beasts imaginable advancing upon him, hairy hands by the score poised for the pounce, and he turned to stand them down and then there were none.

He felt for the gun, secure in his waistband, walked back to the quad, stood on the seat, reached to the top of the fence, then he pulled himself up and lowered himself over into the courtyard to the rear of the house. A hinge, somewhere off in the yard, creaked in the wind and he followed the sound until he came to the kitchen door. Music echoed in the depths of the grand house. The Boy took the gun in his hand, checked once more the magazine, released the safety, then stepped cautiously inside. He followed the music, rock and roll of some sort, through a black corridor that led him to a majestic ballroom. The music, louder now, drew his attention to a far corner where a bookshelf sat oddly ajar. There was a faint light beyond, and he approached with care. He inched his way through the bookcase and found himself at the top of a steel staircase that led down to a dimly lit basement. A grunting of labour echoed from the depths, followed by a cry. Work afoot in the lair.

He thought about running. Whatever horrors awaited him below he could live without, but still he pushed on.

He passed through an opening at the top of the stairs, then took the steps one at a time, his gun trained toward the noise. With each step down, four cells slowly came into view and he squinted in the half-light then rubbed his eyes in disbelief as one by one, children emerged from the darkness and peered out from the cells, blue boys shining in the dark like fish at night drawn from the deep to the poacher's lamp and this one child, a fucking caged child with skin opaque and deathlike, no bigger than a sprat, placed his finger to his lips in warning, then pointed to the end cell where an Englishy-looking cunt, bent to the task, heaved and moaned in the shadows. The radio played 'Long Tall Sally' and The Boy felt the fear rise in his belly and it was all he could do not to turn on his heel and leave this fuckin' place and all its madness to fate. But it was beyond him now, and his foot took another step on the stairs, then another and soon he was stood by the cell door, held open by a table and on that table lay pain's paraphernalia, arrayed. In horror The Boy realised Clifford wasn't heaving some load as he'd previously imagined, but was bent over Gordon, who he'd tied to a chair with his jaw clamped open at some unholy angle. His mouth was ripped at the corners right back to his ears and Clifford, with pliers in his hand, worked free another of Gordon's teeth and sang:

'It's a very simple question: where is your mate? Hurry now and tell me lad or it will be too late, Oh Baby...' He asked in a singsong fashion, keeping time with the cassette.

The Boy held the gun straight in his outstretched hands, shaking. Clifford, sensing The Boy's presence, turned wild-eyed and startled like some night beast riled from the feed and he made for The Boy. He cleared the cell with a pounce. The Boy stepped to the side and squeezed off a nervous round, almost dropping the gun. The bullet hit Cliff in his left shoulder, blew him off course, and he landed to The Boy's right where he hit the ground, heaving. The Boy instinctively ran to Gordon, caged within the cell as a mighty cry of 'NO!' rang out in the basement.

He turned in despair as Clifford pulled the table towards him and the spring-loaded mechanism slammed the gate hard, caging The Boy within. Clifford rolled on his back and laughed out an agonising cry.

'You silly fucker,' Clifford laughed. 'You stupid fucking cunt,' he coughed and writhed in pain.

'Throw me the keys,' The Boy demanded, rattling the cell door. Then, remembering the gun, he trained it on Clifford's leg and let off another round, hitting Cliff above the knee. Cliff writhed in agony, took the keys from his belt and threw them up the stairs away from The Boy, then burst out laughing.

'You stupid fucking cunt,' Cliff wheezed, then laughed in agony.

The Boy aimed the gun again, this time at the hip. The boom filled the basement. Clifford spasmed on the floor, the pain unbearable, and still he laughed. The Boy rattled the gate in vain, then sat back on the bed as he realised for the first time that Cliff was beyond caring. He took his phone from his pocket, pressed the power button, and waited.

'Come on!' He willed it in desperation as it slowly cycled on. Clifford watched the comic scene unfold. He squeezed out a triumphant snigger as he watched The Boy dial frantically, then he laughed out loud at the horror spreading across The Boy's face as he looked at the screen of his phone.

'There's no signal down here, you dopey cunt… you're fucked,' roared Cliff, and he coughed out another laugh that turned into a cry, then back to a laugh again.

'I can't believe I've spent the entire week looking for you and, in the end, when I'd given up hope of ever catching you, you fucking come to me. What are the fuckin' chances? And not only did you deliver yourself to me on a plate, but you've only gone and locked yourself in the cunting cell!' He burst into another round of agonising laughs.

'Like your pathetic fucking brother and your old man. You are history, my friend. You know, your old man shat his pants and wriggled like a worm on a cunting hook when I pulled the chair from under him? I didn't mean to kill him, honestly. Well, not immediately anyway. I was going to let him choke for a bit, then get him to tell me where you were holed up, but the silly fucker only went and broke his cunting neck, didn't he?'

The Boy looked out from his phone in disbelief at Clifford rolling on the basement floor. He felt the rush of blood to his head, and he raised the gun.

'Oooh,' Clifford laughed. 'Hit a nerve, have I, darling?' The Boy pointed the gun at Cliff's chest and fired three more rounds.

Chapter Sixty-Two

GO TO PIECES

ANN LOOKED AT ALBIE ASLEEP in the bed beside her. He smelt like ten pints. He was too old to be drinking ten pints, she thought. She'd know when she came out of the ensuite how many pints he'd had. It was hard to gauge when she woke up in the thick of it. A break from it for a moment or two in the ensuite, amid the alpine Glade, would reset the senses like a nasal sorbet, and when she stepped back into it, she'd know.

She checked herself. What did she care how many pints he'd had? Hadn't he earned them with the last few months? Poor Albie, wasn't he suffering too in his own way? She placed her hand on his shoulder and kissed his cheek.

She stepped from the bed and headed down the stairs. She hit the switch on the kettle. She always filled it the night before. It saved her holding it under the tap with her wrist, in the morning. And anyway, didn't the water boil faster from room temperature? She was clever like that.

She walked from window to window, pulling up the blinds, then she went to the double doors that led onto the garden, pushed the curtain to the side and looked out. There was some hope of a summer out there, she thought. Maybe not summer yet, but it was definitely spring, strong spring, no trace of the winter for sure.

She walked to the fireplace, gave the grate a shake and watched the grey and white ash fall among the remnants of yesterday's blaze. A sadness came over her, and she gave a sniffle then felt the first tears roll down her face. She was used to them now, the tears. She could've cried all day long if she'd let herself. All day long she could've cried. She could've sat down here in front of the fire drinking tea til three or four in the afternoon, then wine thereafter, and cried into the fire.

She thought about The Boy, poor crater. She lived for the sight of his little face poking around the door. The smell of him, a waft of hope. She reckoned he was all she was living for right now. She loved Albie, with all her heart, she loved that man, but Albie needed nobody. Not even her. She was getting away with herself now, and she knew it.

She gave another sniffle. She took a tissue from her sleeve and blew. She wiped her eyes, shovelled the ash into the bucket, gave the grate another shake and shovelled some more.

She wondered where he was, her little man. She poked at the embers then placed a firelighter among the still-black, not-quite-spent-yet, coals. She picked a box of matches from the hearth, lit the firelighter, then placed some kindling over the flame. She lay two briquettes on the kindling, placed the spark guard in front and watched it take hold.

Her heart broke for him. He'd had a lousy run, her poor wee fella. And Daniel? Bloody coward… She didn't mean that. She did, and she didn't. He could've done more, for certain, but what, she didn't know. They'd had it all. Every-bloody-thing. She often tried to pinpoint where it had all gone wrong, started to unravel. She wondered if there was something she could've said or done. Some tiny intervention at the right time that might've steered them down a different path. And sure, what if she did, mightn't there be something twice as bad waiting down there for them?

'*Que sera*,' she said. '*Que se*-bloody-*ra*.'

The fire gave a roar. A briquette fell to the side and she looked at it, flame-side up. It looked so helpless. She moved the spark guard across, picked the tongs from the stand and placed the briquette back atop the flame.

'There ya go pet,' she said.

When her little man was near, all her worries and fears flew up the chimney. With him, she had a reason, a purpose. Without him, she was barely hanging on; down to the last finger, and she knew it. Not even the last finger, some fleeting tether, is all that remained; an act of sheer will on everyone else's behalf.

And fuckit she could've let go so easily. She could've closed her eyes and let it take her away. Secretly, she longed for it. The thought of it brought her great ease, and if it wasn't for her little man, she'd have been gone a long time ago. Death, madness – she didn't care. Anywhere but here. Anything but this, and she imagined herself going to pieces. A thousand million tiny pieces exploding, then exploding again, carried off on the wind, out over the river, up into the sky, an ever-decreasing series of miniature kabooms, tiny explosion after tiny explosion until at last she was gone, and she reckoned it'd be beautiful, out there, up past the clouds, away and away.

Chapter Sixty-Three

HEADS OR HARPS?

Banjo stood in the caravan door. A triangle of toast dangled from his mouth. The penned ponies, with their smoking backs, snorted, and he watched their nostrils' fleeting plumes float, then rise like dragons in the air and vanish.

'Close that door to fuck,' his uncle Christy growled from the bedroom of the four-berth.

'I'm going out,' Banjo answered. The ponies started and reared at this interruption and a young foal gave a short trot in the paddock with a soft lilting thrum that hung in the air, then faded.

'Well, fuck off out to fuck and close the hoorin' door behind ya,' Christy bellowed.

'I'm waitin'.'

'I'll put an end to your waitin',' Christy threatened, as he made from his bed.

Banjo stepped from the threshold and let the door swing closed behind him as his uncle eased back into the duvet, where a dream of dancing ponies pillowed him down.

Mossy's caravan, silent and still, told him that his partner had yet to rise. He strolled across the campsite swirling the keys of the HiAce van on his finger and he called out as he went.

'Are you up?'

When he got no response, he called again. Mossy's father stuck his head through the caravan door and scowled.

'Do you know what fuckin' time it is?'

'I do,' Banjo replied boldly. 'Is he up?'

'Of course he's not up, it's eight-o'fuckin'-clock of a Sunday morning.'

'We were supposed to meet at seven.'

'What... are ye runnin' away together? E-fuckin'-lopin?'

'We got a job on.'

'Job on me hole, hang on there. I'll give him a shout.'

Banjo walked to the campfire, picked a stick, blackened at the end from the previous night's poking, and gave the ashes a swirl. Embers glowed at its heart, and he took it as a good omen for the day ahead. He fetched some straw from the pony pen, stretched it out light as he walked, placed it to the embers and blew. Moments later it was ablaze, and he gathered some kindling scattered thereabouts and piled it on the flame. It's gonna be a great day, he thought as the flame took hold and soon he was stacking some logs, either side, and he stretched out easy and watched the fire grow.

Mossy's door opened with a creak, and he stepped out with an iced bun in one hand and a bottle of milk in the other.

'Have you eaten?' he asked Banjo.

'Yeah, I'm grand.'

'I've more buns there,' Mossy replied.

'I'd eat a bun,' Banjo said, and Mossy turned back to grab his partner a bite of food.

'What the fuck do you want now?' Mossy's old fella boomed from inside the caravan. Mossy closed the door swiftly, turned on his heel, waving his head from side to side.

'We'll get some food along the way,' Banjo said, and they burst into laughter.

'Grumpy old bollix,' Mossy sniggered as they climbed in the van and headed for Kilduggart Hall.

When they reached the Cromby estate, they parked the van in the layby. Mossy grabbed a flashlight and crowbar from the back, and they set off on foot for the stakeout.

'You're awful quiet,' Banjo said. 'Are you sure you wanna do this?'

'Yeah… I mean if *you* do.'

'I'm all in,' Banjo replied. 'Our bounty awaits.'

'Well, so am I then,' Mossy answered with some hesitation then continued. 'The place gives me the creeps, that's all.'

'How about this?' Banjo started. 'We go down, check the place out. If we see anything that's not right… we get to fuck outta there?'

'Okay,' Mossy agreed, before adding, 'It's the fence though, and we can't drive up to it, so if we need to leave, we are fucked. Ya know what I mean?'

'I do, I do, let's forget about it. We'll find another place with better access and no creepy cunt on a quad,' he jibed as he elbowed his pal, then ran on ahead.

In the basement, The Boy counted the remaining bullets in the magazine. There were eight. Enough… with some spares. They could work out the technicalities later, but it was possible. He looked at Gordon. He wasn't in good shape. *What have I done?* he thought, sitting there in the darkness. He couldn't have gone through all that shit to end up here in this cell. This couldn't be the end. He opened his eyes and looked about at the basement, swamped in hopelessness. He'd come so close, so close, and these poor bastards, these poor bastards down here… at least they had some chance at a life before he rode into fucking town. He jumped from the bed and rattled the cell door in a frenzied panic. He was fucked, and he knew it, and now all these young lads were fucked too, and they had him to thank for that.

The house looked quieter than usual, Banjo thought as they reached the stakeout. He rolled a sneaky number, withdrew in the bushes, sparked it up, took two long draws and handed it to Mossy.

'Well?' he asked, exhaling.

'I dunno,' Mossy replied, taking the joint. He pulled three long hard draws, then handed it back to Banjo.

'There's easier jobs,' he said as the smoke streamed from his mouth.

'There is,' Banjo agreed.

'Better access jobs.'

'Indeed.'

'Jobs that are dead certs.'

'There's no dead cert,' Banjo corrected.

'True.'

'Will we toss for it?'

'A coin it is,' Mossy agreed, and he took a fifty pence piece from his pocket and laid down the terms.

'Heads we go in, harps we go home.'

'Sounds good to me,' Banjo agreed, and he snatched the coin from Mossy's hand, placed it to his index finger's side and thumb's end, then flicked it high into the red morning sky. The coin danced and flashed a hundred times, maybe more, as the lads, faces heaven-bound, watched in fear and anticipation, its twinkle and spin of rippling vermilion hung in the morning sky glistening...

Acknowledgements

A huge thank you to James Gill, my agent, for finding *The Boy* and bringing him in. Thank you to Joanna Dingley for brushing *The Boy*'s hair, tucking in his shirt and warming his heart. And to Jamie Hodder-Williams and his team at Bedford Square Publishers, I extend eternal gratitude for giving *The Boy* a home.

To my wife, Suzanne, and my beautiful daughters, Lily and Ruby, thank you for your patience, love, and understanding.

Finally, I want to extend a warm thank you to my family and friends who have supported me throughout this journey.

About the Author

Mark Gyves is an Irish crime fiction writer. He has lived and worked in the UK and Ireland and now resides in his hometown on the outskirts of Cork.